Praise for *The Jou*

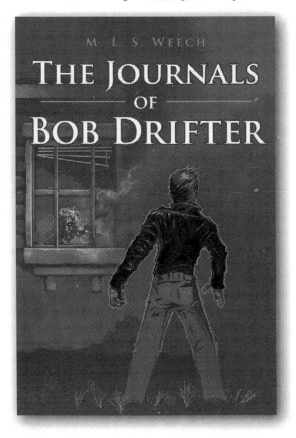

"I enjoyed the array of interesting characters, which I found well developed and credible."

-Stacie Theis
-Beach Bound Books

"What a thrilling, edge of your seat read. It's an amazing, fast-paced book that doesn't slow down until the end." "The world building was intriguing, and I enjoyed getting to explore this world."

-I Heart Reading

"Author M.L.S. Weech has definitely a unique and mesmerizing style of touching the most intense subject through his writing and keeps his readers on the edge of their seats and wanting for more, all satisfied in the end."

-Enas Reviews

"With equal parts humor and horror, Weech creates a world in The Journals of Bob Drifter that is populated by both a peculiarly intriguing mythos and masterfully drawn characters."

-Red City Review

"An often engaging supernatural thriller with an immortal protagonist with meritorious human traits."

-Kirkus Reviews

CAUGHT

CAUGHT

Book One of the Oneiros Log

To Ashley! Fight through fear to find Power!

M.J.S. Weech (signature)

M.L.S. WEECH

ISBN-13: 9781539663911
ISBN-10: 1539663914
Library of Congress Control Number: 2016918128
CreateSpace Independent Publishing Platform
North Charleston, South Carolina

DEDICATION

For my mother, who I believe is the standard by which all other mothers should be measured. Patient. Loving. Accepting. She told me about a nightmare she had once, and I decided to write a book based on it.

Chapter 1

MOTHER

Caden Carroll watched the blood seep through his fingers. He wanted to memorize every shade and hue of it and feel it cool as it oozed along his knuckles. He turned his hands to see how light and shadow affected the color. It fascinated him almost as much as how the blood got there.

The calico cat lay on the hardwood floor at the foot of his bed. It was a good animal, keeping quiet while Caden experimented.

He was alone, sitting quietly in his room. *No, that's not right.*

He hadn't lived in a room like that for a long time. Come to think of it, he hadn't thought of his mother in nearly as much time. How long had it been? Not long, or the blood would have dried and flaked away. So why was it so strange to be in his room?

He looked around. Everything seemed in order, except for the blood of course. His bed was neatly made. He could see his scrawny reflection in the polished dark walnut foot-board of his bed. There wasn't a speck of dust on his small wooden desk. His dresser, also a polished dark walnut, was organized, and the brass nobs of each drawer gleamed even in the soft yellow light of the tall floor lamp in the corner. Mother hated filth and punished it harshly, so Caden kept his room as immaculate as possible. It would take a ton of effort to clean the blood, but feeling it was worth it. He wanted to breathe in its coppery scent a few moments more.

A strange part of Caden remembered breaking free of his mother. The same part that told him there was something wrong with his hands. It wasn't the blood; it was the size of his hands that bothered Caden. They were a little small for a nine-year-old, but no one ever teased him for being small, not after the last boy had anyway.

He stared at his hands in wonder, watching the blood roll from his fingers, to his wrist and down his arms. *I'm not nine!*

The thought set off an alarm in his mind. He hadn't been nine for decades. This wasn't real. It couldn't be real. He couldn't be nine again. *I almost died the last time!*

The white door banged open. The brass door-stop buzzed for a few moments. The sound caused a chill to run up Caden's spine. His mother always expected him to be in some sort of trouble. Of course, he usually was. This time was no different. He spun, tucking his hands behind his back. The blood began to soak into the back of his blue pullover pajama top.

Even though she had the correct size and shape of a woman, his mother was a monster at her core. She was a demon wearing a Career Fair and Charmer dress. The black dress was covered in small white polka dots and came down to her tiny ankles, exposing bare feet and neatly manicured toenails polished a vibrant red.

"What have you done now?" she asked stalking up to him. Her jet-black hair bounced in its ponytail as she stomped across the blue throw rug. *How could such a small pair of feet sound so thunderous?*

Caden's shoulders were against the wall before he even realized he was backpedaling. "Nothing, I didn't do anything wrong. I didn't mean to get dirty!"

Her hands were cold iron vices that ripped his arms out from behind his back. She stared at his hands. Her nail polish and lipstick were the same loud red as that of her toenails. It always made her look wrong to Caden. A part of him knew this had already happened. *Does that mean I won't die this time?* His heart raced. In memory, or at that moment, Caden had only known fear when his mother's thin lips bent into a frown.

"You're a wasted birth!" she said in her sharp, nasally voice. "A child I should have known better than to bring into this world."

Her hand raised to his head, and a small whine escaped Caden's lips as she used bony fingers to yank him toward her by his mop of red hair. He fought for a moment, but at that time, his mother was much stronger than he was. Fighting only caused him to fall screaming. She simply dragged him by his hair through his door and then down the hall. He slid from the smooth, pine-scented floor onto the white carpet of the hallway. His pajama bottoms rolled down, allowing the carpet to burn into him as he slid along its rough surface. Streaks of blood stained the white fibrous floor.

"I'll clean you till the filth is gone, or you die from the cleansing."

"No!" Caden shouted. "No! Mother!" He'd called her Mommy once. She rubbed his mouth with a Brillo pad until his lips bled. She didn't like being called Mommy. "Mother, I'll be good. I'll be clean."

"If you'd stay clean, you little demon, I wouldn't have to do this," she said. Tears ran down her cheeks, but this time, the tears didn't streak her dark mascara the way they usually did. She wasn't crying for him. She cried because she had to deal with him.

Caden kicked. He cried out. He held on to everything he could as his mother dragged him, rolling and bumping down the hall. He managed to get a solid grip on a door jamb. She yanked until a handful of fiery hair ripped free. He ignored it. That would be the least of his worries. He had just managed to scramble to his feet when his mother grabbed him by his neck, her long fingernails digging into his flesh. That was far worse. She didn't concern herself with his choked pleas.

He tried to beg as she pulled him into the blindingly sterile, eggshell-white tiled bathroom. The red-enameled bathtub seemed all the brighter at the center of all that white. The tub's spotless exterior gleamed beneath the bathroom's bright lights. He tried to apologize. It never worked, but what could someone do when faced with something stronger than he was? He begged, but it never helped. The part of him who knew this was a memory hated himself for begging.

Just because you did it then doesn't mean you have to this time! His own voice was a sneer in his mind. However, the part of him that was nine took over as his mother pinned his bony shoulders onto the copper-lined tub. He felt the rubber plug dig into the back of his neck. The water was cool for a few moments. Then it got warm. Then it was hot, so very hot. He jolted up to escape it and smacked his forehead into the spout. A red haze clouded his view of her from the water. His mother turned on the cold water eventually, but not because of his crying. She didn't want to burn her hands. It was a good thing she didn't have her gloves handy.

"Mother!" he yelped, dizzy and choking. "Mother, I'm grown now. I'm not dirty."

She pressed him under the water. Bubbles of precious air floated to the surface. He fought. His lungs wanted to burst. He gripped the edge of the red, oval tub so tightly it felt like his knuckles would break, but she held him down. He gasped and got a lung full of water for his effort.

"Mo..." he gasped. He managed to poke his head above water for a moment. Talking was meaningless now. She meant to kill him. Getting as much air in his lungs as possible was all that mattered. Even knowing that, he couldn't get enough air.

He kicked and thrashed. He was very careful not to hit her. He'd done that once, and never thought to do it again. Mother liked getting hit less than she liked being called Mommy. He tried to knock the plug loose. He tried to slip away from her grip. He caught another gulp of air when he rolled to his side, but his mother's long nails left a nasty scratch on his neck. That was okay in his mind. He'd take a thousand scars for a single breath of air.

She gripped his face with the palm of her hand and plunged him down into the water. Panic surged as his lungs gave up. Black specks floated along his vision until his eyes rolled into the back of his head. He was going to die. *I didn't die! I didn't! This isn't right!*

"Mother!" Caden sat up screaming. A dim part of his mind wanted to look around, but he focused on taking deep, slow breaths. He felt like he had just been drowning. He was covered in sweat. His breathing slowed after a moment, but he couldn't make himself recall what he had just been dreaming about.

I must have gone away, he told himself. Sometimes, his mind left his body. He knew he'd gone away to someplace bad. He could hardly remember where. He hated the dreams. Dreams were where he was not himself, and nightmares wore his face. *I hate it when I go somewhere without telling myself to.*

He looked at his arms and hands. For some reason, he was afraid he'd turned back into a small child. But his wrinkled hands were as old and warped as they were supposed to be. His face felt as weathered as it had when he went to bed. Something tugged at his mind as his fingers grated along the rough stubble of hair atop his head. *Did I shave my head? When did I do that? Why did I do that?* Whatever the dream was, it must have been terrible, but it was over. Then he looked around.

His small cot was the only piece of actual furniture in the tiny room. A few machines made a cacophony. He followed a plastic tube from a bag of clear liquid to his arm. He felt his heart thunder in his chest. *There's a needle in me!*

"I don't belong here," he whispered, trying to remain calm. He was in the hospital. He was where they told him his thoughts were wrong and his eyes saw only lies. Just as he moved to get out, to run away, the white door banged open.

Three men in police or correctional officer uniforms entered on the heels of the door as it slammed against the wall. The light streaming in through the doorway behind them cast their faces in deep shadows, yet he could make out a bronze badge on the left breast of their dark-blue uniforms. Polished ebony shoes clicked on the black-and-white checkerboard tile floor as they swept toward him.

"I'm not supposed to be here," he told the officers. *I got out!*

The three men said nothing. He kicked one away, only to receive a punch in the face from one of the others. The third gripped his arm. His partners held him down as the cop with Caden's arm ripped off the paper-thin gray blanket and slapped cold handcuffs around Caden's wrist.

"You can't do this to me," Caden shouted. "They told me I wouldn't have to sleep if I didn't want to! They said I'd get better!"

Caden wasn't sure if they couldn't hear him or if they were simply ignoring him. With their faces masked in shadows, it was impossible to tell. As two of them continued to cuff Caden to the bed, the third pulled out a thin, rectangular, brown box.

"No!" Caden shouted. He pulled so hard at his bonds he felt the metal cuffs rip open flesh. He squirmed, careless about what parts of his naked old body may be revealed with him kicking about. "You can't do this. You can't kill me."

Reality was no friend to Caden. He lived most of his life trying to remake the world, but nothing about what happened to him made sense. He had to be dreaming. He'd never told anyone how terrified he was that men with needles would come to kill him.

As if reading his mind, the officer with the box opened it to reveal three long-needled syringes. "Please," Caden whimpered. He immediately hated himself. He hadn't begged since he was a child, back when his mother—he hadn't thought of his mother in more than half a century. The vague feeling of being held under water only stoked the flames of his fear. His whimpers turned into screams.

Slowly, the men passed syringes to each other. One needle grazed Caden's eyelashes as it passed from one officer's hand to the next. Caden pressed himself into the thin mattress to get some distance. Neither threats nor pleas for mercy had any affect on the attackers. They pushed the needles into his arms. Caden's heart raced so quickly his chest hurt. He hoped he would pass out before they injected him. The burn of the poison flowing into him seemed to mock even that silent prayer for mercy.

This can't be the real, real, Caden thought to himself. He wasn't supposed to be at the hospital anymore. He wasn't supposed to be dying. He faded, wondering if the dead had nightmares. He really hated going away.

Chapter 2

THE FACELESS BOY

The rough texture of the mud wall scratched Sal's hand as he unsuccessfully groped for a light switch. The feeling of the wall tickled a memory in the back of his mind, but an odd surge of fear caused Sal to push the recollection away.

As he ran his hand along the misshapen wall, the texture changed from rough and gritty, to cold and smooth. A tingling sensation flowed through him, as if the world had changed and not for the better. A door opened, revealing a flight of stairs and sending a shaft of light into the room.

Sal blinked until his eyes adjusted to the light and then looked down at the camouflage military uniform he wore. He didn't belong in a uniform. He knew that much, but that didn't remove his last name, Veltri, from above the right breast pocket. The sound of footsteps drew his eyes from his uniform to a small silhouette at the top of the stairs. Sal thought it might be a child. Before the kid could get too far away, Sal rushed up the stairs.

Sal was fit, but it felt as if he'd run halfway up a skyscraper instead of just one set of wooden stairs. Taking a deep breath, he finally reached the top and noticed a small boy with dark-brown skin and black hair approaching another door at the end of a narrow hallway. The boy opened the door, which led into another dark room. The hall seemed to stretch and shrink at the same time.

Sal called out to the child, but the boy entered the dark room without responding. Sal only had a moment to examine the kid before the door shut between them. Short and skinny, with a dirt covered t-shirt, a torn pair of shorts, and no shoes, the boy looked homeless.

"I won't hurt you!" Sal's boots clanged off the metal floor as he sprinted down the hall. He was relieved to reach the other side in only a few seconds. The impossibly long run up the stairs had frayed his nerves and drained his energy. He flung the door open. The hall seemed dim when Sal turned back, but it somehow managed to cast enough light to spill into the room, at least enough to reach the boy's bare legs.

Sal took a few steps into the room. The door slammed shut behind him. He spun around to open it, but his hand came up against a gritty mud wall. A terrifying memory clawed out at Sal. He stuffed it down.

Without thinking, as if he'd done it so often his muscles responded on impulse, Sal reached up and flicked on a small flashlight on his left shoulder. *It has to be on my left shoulder. I need to keep my right arm free to bring up my rifle.* The thought was almost as shocking to Sal as the light on his shoulder. *It wasn't there until I thought it was.*

"Hello?" Sal called out hoping to draw the boy's attention. A part of Sal thought he'd somehow, impossibly, ended up right back in the same room in which he'd started. *How'd I get there? How'd I get here?*

A shuffling sound drew Sal's attention. He glimpsed the boy walking away. The slapping of the boy's bare feet had a steady rhythm. Sal stepped up to him slowly.

"My name's Sal," he said. "I'm not going to hurt you."

Sal gently put a large, square hand on the boy's shoulder. Sal was always careful with his grip, and he was all the more careful with the boy. The child turned, and Sal backed away in shock. He nearly stumbled down a previously unnoticed flight of stairs. Sal looked down the stairs if only to avoid looking at the boy for a moment. Sal tried to tell himself he was imagining things. *Like flights of stairs appearing out of thin air.*

But when Sal turned back to look at the boy, nothing had changed. The kid had messy black hair that fell in locks around a face that wasn't a face at all. Where eyes, a nose and a mouth should have been was only smooth, dark-brown skin. His featureless face lacked any evidence that eyes, or anything else, even belonged on that rounded surface.

The boy, somehow moving at ease despite his lack of eyes, stepped past Sal and began descending the stairs at that same measured pace. His bare feet thumped against the wood, but each step also struck at Sal's heart. Whatever was down there, it wasn't safe. Face or no, it was only a boy.

"We should leave," Sal said. The boy didn't stop, and Sal felt a surge of panic. The kid was heading into danger, and Sal was the only person in this mad-house able to do anything about it.

He leapt down the stairs. As soon as his boots bounced off the first step, everything changed. Even as Sal descended from one step to another, the stairs faded, replaced by an uneven mud floor. Sal landed off balance and stumbled. He looked up from the ground just in time to see the boy walk to the corner of the room. The boy fit himself into the corner so tightly, if he had a nose, it would have touched the intersection of the walls.

Sal stood, desperate to reach the boy. He was only a step away when the back of the boy's head exploded, spraying blood and bits of bone onto Sal's face. Screaming, Sal lifted his hands to try and wipe the splatter off. He pulled his hands away to see the blood, but there was none. *What was I doing?* He dropped his hands and saw a slender boy with no face.

The sight of the boy startled him, sending him back a few steps. Sal nearly stumbled down a flight of stairs. He gazed down this newly-appeared stairwell, if only to again keep from looking at the egg-smooth surface where the boy's face should be. After a moment, Sal found the courage to look back at the boy, who walked past him and started down the stairs.

Sal scrambled down the stairs behind the boy. He felt certain he could catch the child, but just as he reached out, the youth seemed to shift away. The kid's shift took him to the corner of a room. Sal kept the narrow cone of his flashlight on the boy in the corner, making it hard to see much of anything else. He was desperate to get to the child, if he didn't get there in time. *What? What will happen?*

Sal was just a step away when he saw the back of the boy's head explode. Sal stopped and held his arm up in front of him to keep the gore from hitting his face, and then let his arm fall back to his side when he reappeared at the top of a flight of stairs. He quickly patted at himself. *How bad is the blood? Where's the blood? What blood? What?*

Sal wasn't sure why, or how, but he was sure he'd been in that exact same spot just a moment ago. Only before there was a— Before he could finish the thought, a small boy appeared in front of him. Despite the lack of a face or ears, Sal was more concerned for the child then the boy's impossible appearance. Something inside Sal screamed at him to wake up. *Am I dreaming? I suppose it'd have to be a dream.* The boy walked past him and started down the stairs, where Sal knew the kid would die.

Sal closed his eyes. "It's only a dream," he told himself. "It's only a dream." He repeated the phrase like a prayer to ward against evil. Sal heard the sound of marching and opened his eyes in confusion. Twelve faceless boys in two lines of six marched from the end of a long, narrow hallway.

"You can't go down there!" Sal shouted. He rushed up to stop the lines of marchers and stumbled as he shifted to the other end of the hall. He whipped his head around and saw the marchers descend the stairs. Sal dashed after them, hoping to chase the boys down. He didn't care if it was a dream or not. He didn't care what they looked like. He had to save those boys. If he could save just one of them, he knew he'd find something, some part of himself he'd lost.

Even as he focused on catching up to the children, his gut wrenched, and the world morphed around him. He had somehow entered the room before the boys. He didn't care how. He turned. The sound of bare feet slapping the ground seemed louder than possible. "Stop!" Sal shouted. The boys marched on obliviously. Sal knew they couldn't hear him; they had no ears.

Sal caught one boy, and he felt the splatter of blood and bone strike his army combat uniform. One by one, the boys lined up. Sal held one and tackled another. Screaming, he shoved a third out of the way only to end on his knees, covered in blood as nine more heads seemed to explode from within.

Sal wept.

"Please," he cried. "Just let me wake up. Someone help me!"

Something flickered at the top of the stairs. Sal looked up and noticed a man standing in the doorway. The man wore a flowing white robe and a pointed hat that reminded Sal of the Pope. The long, wooden staff in the man's hand made him an abbott, but if the man was a religious leader, he was unhappy. Sal could see the rage in the man's eyes.

The abbott raised his staff, thrusting it down in Sal's direction. He opened his mouth to speak, and Sal knew the abbott's words would break him somehow. Sal saw the abbott in two ways. In one, the abbott was at the top of the stairs, about to proclaim Sal's doom. In the other, Sal could see the man's face as large as if the abbott were right in front of him. The abbott started to speak, but Sal covered his ears and shut his eyes.

Sal jolted against a set of chains that held him to a bed. He flailed around wearing nothing but a paper-thin hospital gown with a set of IVs driven into each arm. He noticed a group of machines that made their own flurry of noises. Immediate panic set in, and Sal began shouting while yanking at his bonds. The bonds clanked each time he jerked at them. Pain shot down his arms, but he kept fighting to escape. His hysteria was so complete that he was barely aware of a group of men in lab coats just a few feet away, nor did he care that they were all looking at him in stunned silence.

"What the fuck is he doing awake!" one of the men shouted. Almost all of the other men appeared as shocked as the first, but none looked half as panicked as Sal felt.

"Let me out," Sal shouted at the cluster of men.

"Shut up!" someone said in a voice as sharp as a razor. Sal couldn't see the man. "Hold him down."

The group of men in lab coats seemed afraid of whoever had spoken, but they surged to obey the order. Sal struggled more desperately against his bonds, but he was already chained to the bed. He could do little to prevent the men from grabbing him with smooth hands that had clearly never seen a day of real, honest work in their lives. The bedsprings groaned in protest as Sal struggled. The mattress was so thin Sal could feel each part of the frame underneath. None of Sal's attackers weighed more than two-thirds as much as Sal, and they all looked more likely to win a debate match than a wrestling match, but they buckled thick leather straps across his body, and Sal was powerless to stop it.

"You're a monster," the unseen man said. "You're nothing like me. You'll never be good enough."

Sal felt something, maybe a needle, bite the side of his neck. One of the men picked something up that looked like some sort of small motorized saw. Everything seemed to get fuzzy, but Sal could see the tool with eerie clarity. It vibrated back and forth with blurring speed.

"What are you doing?" Sal shouted. "You can't do this to me!"

Sal tried to pull his hands free or force the hospital bed over. Neither attempt worked. Sal could do nothing as one of the men slowly brought the saw down. Just as it came inches away form Sal's inner elbow, he passed out. A single thought crept along his subconscious. *Could this be a dream, too? Can a man die in his dreams?*

Chapter 3

REALITY

hris Royd yanked at the leather straps that held him to a bed. For a few moments, he thought it was yet another nightmare. He didn't remember exactly when he fell asleep or how many nightmares he had had, but he wished he could forget what terrible dreams he could remember. He somehow knew the dreams he couldn't recall were worse.

His mind was foggy. Try as he might, he couldn't trace his memory back to any single point that didn't happen at least a week ago. *It was just after I saw the doc. Did something happen in the cab?*

"Help!" Chris called.

It wasn't likely that whoever left him out in the middle of some sterile steel room would leave him where anyone could hear, and that was assuming anyone could hear through the room's only door. Taking a deep breath, he found some sort of calm. The room was nothing more than an enormous steel safe. All Chris could see were stainless steel walls, but the straps that comprised his bonds were simple leather bands with two metal prongs that poked through matching holes in the cuffs. He could at least do something about those.

Methodically, he worked his wrists. If he could stretch the leather enough, he might be able to pull a hand free. Taut forearms and biceps flexed and coiled as he stretched his wrists back and forth while looking around for any evidence of where he might be. As far as Chris could tell, the room was completely empty. Some sharp fear in his mind wondered if there was a drain beneath him. Something that would let blood and other fluids drain from his body.

Come on Chris! You have enough nightmares when you're sleeping. There's no time to worry about what might be. Chris had a knack for keeping calm. One needed to keep his head while walking through a burning building or house. He was a firefighter, at least until he'd nearly died. He should have.

Don't even start thinking about that! Some memories brought the worst type of nightmare.

Suddenly, one of Chris's long, slender, arms slipped free. The leather portion of his bonds stretched just far enough to let a sweat-drenched hand slide away. Unsure how long he'd been working to escape, Chris used his free hand to remove the rest of his straps. He staggered to his feet and stepped away from the bed. Its white sheets were sweat-stained and rumpled. Chris himself wore a now-yellowed t-shirt and a pair of Bermuda shorts he'd never have chosen to wear himself.

There wasn't much to use as a weapon, and Chris wasn't sure what whoever kidnapped him might want. For that matter, Chris had no idea why anyone would want to kidnap some has-been firefighter who couldn't so much as look at a match anymore without breaking into a sweat. That only left escape as an option.

He'd just come to that decision when a S.W.A.T. team burst through the door. They filed into the room wearing sleek black outfits with bulges that indicated thick, bullet-proof plates. Each pointed his rifle in a different direction. They wore dome-shaped helmets with black visors that hid their faces. Chris had worked with police, even S.W.A.T. a time or two. He got down on his stomach to let them do their work. He was about to thank them for saving him when one of them kicked him in the side.

Boots thumped into his stomach and back, creating a morbid rhythm as blow after blow found a mark. It was already hard to keep his breath. Each stomp or kick just made the next breath harder to take.

Chris reacted on impulse and covered himself up. Three men, all taller and more stout than he, assaulted him without any hint of remorse, much less any intention to stop. He pulled his arms away from his head for an instant to surrender or ask what he'd done. Instead, one of the S.W.A.T. members clubbed him over the head with the butt of a rifle.

He opened his eyes. He didn't feel like a man who'd just been beaten to death, but dreams were funny things. Chris wasn't sure the beating he'd just taken was a real or not, but he recognized the nightmare world he'd just entered. He never remembered the details. Only the two most important aspects lasted more than a few minutes after his eyes opened.

The dunes of ash were the first detail he could always recall. It was so much more than a desert. It was an entire world of ash. At the end of the white hills, he could see vacant charcoal skyscrapers that stood against gusts of wind causing waves of soot to fall.

The wind and the soft whisper of falling ash were the only sounds in the dream. He stood, watching the embers drift from the skyscrapers above to the white, dusty dunes below.

It'll happen soon, Chris thought. Standing on a powder-white hill, wearing a firefighting ensemble, he could feel the temperature rise from an unseasonable heat to an uncomfortable blaze. He tried to ignore the pain. He had to. Nothing he ever tried since the first time he dreamt of the ash world ever worked. Now, all he tried to do was accept the pain when it came. *It's the least I can do.*

Chris had never actually seen a man spontaneously combust, but if what he felt was any indication, he should have burned like the sun. He opened his mouth to scream in agony, only to find out his tongue had exploded, which allowed a pitiful moan to escape lips that had already burnt away. He wondered if he even had a right to shout. After all, he knew what was coming for him. That was the second thing he always remembered, burning alive. He'd almost died that way in the real world, only to be saved.

If he had a choice between actually burning to death once, or burning to death a dozen times a month in dreams, he'd burn the one time. Not because of the pain of burning again and again, but because the price he paid for surviving the first death, the one that should have happened in real life. A flame erupted from his chest. It grew and spread, burning him as he watched the fire grow. All the while, he tried in horrible, unmitigated failure to accept the pain. *I deserve this,* he thought to himself, one of the last coherent thoughts he had before he was engulfed completely. *I deserve this and so much worse.*

Chapter 4

TERMINUS

Sal smiled as he exited out the glass door of Dale's Tavern, wrapping his pea coat around himself against the cold. He hadn't been there in years. He hadn't been to Jenkintown, Pennsylvania, in nearly as much time. Even without the snow of winter, his hometown could be frigid in spring.

He reveled in the crisp air as he strode down Greenwood Avenue in a good pair of boots and jeans. He loved small towns because they always reminded him of home. Being home made him all the happier. He paused on the corner where Greenwood intersected Walnut Street. *Why'd I leave?* He pondered the question for a moment, but his train of thought was derailed when someone bumped into him.

"Sorry," Sal said, moving aside as an old man shambled past. The bald man wore a tan trench coat and brown slacks. The outfit was wearing the spindly elder more than the other way around.

The sky grew dark. Sal looked up to see a blanket of thunderclouds had formed over the small shops along the street and covered the once bright sun. A loud roar ripped through the air, but it wasn't thunder.

"You should get inside," Sal told the man.

The frail old guy raised a gnarled index finger. Sal couldn't tell if it shook from age or if the gesture was more of a failed attempt at a wave. Another rumble drew Sal's attention down Walnut Street.

A mud-covered military Humvee rounded a turn and charged down the street. *There's hardly ever traffic, so what's that doing here?* Sal wondered to himself.

"Hurry across, sir," Sal said. He glanced to the old man and back. In that moment, the military vehicle seemed to blink from the far stop light to a few dozen feet away. The old man had hardly made it half-way across the street.

"No!" Sal screamed as he rushed toward the poor elder. His shout only caused the bald man to stop and get plowed over by the Humvee. It didn't so much as slow down. The vehicle bounced as a tire crushed the old man's skull. His body twisted and skid along the pavement.

Sal fell to his knees. He closed his eyes and turned away. In that moment, he remembered the other dreams. He had had dozens. The faceless boys were the worst. He had had that dream so many times. He had failed them and so many others in every single possible way.

Sal looked at the man's crumpled body and the blood-stained tire tracks that led down the street. The clouds vanished, mocking the tragedy with bright sunshine. Nothing made sense. *Is this a dream? Does it matter?*

"How many?" he wondered aloud. He turned his head to the sky. "How many!" he demanded.

A chill ran down his spine. He lifted his head to see a small boy. The dirt-covered, brown-skinned kid looked out of place walking around barefoot. His lack of a face was terrifying to Sal.

"Stop," Sal said, slowly rising to his feet. "I tried to save you. I swear. What do you want?"

The boy turned away from Sal, bare feet slapping against blood-stained pavement.

"Wait," Sal called. "I…I can't let you die! Don't go!"

Sal meant to follow the boy, but something held him back. Images flashed through Sal's mind. Blood mixed with dirt. A head exploding. He saw himself crying while surrounded by small bodies.

"Oh, God…" Sal whispered. "Please God no."

Sal stopped, afraid to chase the kid. He watched the scrawny boy walk down the street.

"Where are you going?" he called.

The boy stopped. Sal couldn't remember the kid ever stopping before. The youth raised a slender arm and pointed to a white, three-story, single-family home. The child blinked out of the air only to reappear at the doorstep to the house.

The clouds returned, darker than before. The air roared again, this time with thunder.

"Momma," Sal whispered. He charged down the street as rain began to fall.

Sal managed to shuck off his coat just as he skidded to a halt at the blue steps that led to the front door of the house in which he grew up. Sal slammed his shoulder into the blue, framed-and-paneled door, easily bursting it open.

He heard something squish under his boots and looked down to see he'd trampled a tarantula. He leapt back in disgust. He only had an instant to realize his living room was covered by the hairy creatures. They scurried toward him on eight legs over the hardwood floor, across the oak dining-room table. They drifted from the ceiling on webs. *Do they even make webs?* They skittered along the white walls.

"Mom!" Sal shouted. "Momma, are you here?"

One of the arachnids landed on Sal's shoulder. A pair of the disgusting creatures seemed to jump from the wall onto him. *Do they even jump like that?* It shouldn't have been possible through his thick, button-up shirt, but he felt every single hairy leg as each arachnid made its way to his neck. Their black fangs spread wide, glistened and dripped with venom. Dozens of malevolent inky black eyes shimmered up at him.

Fear took over, and Sal ran out of the house flinging the spiders off in revulsion. Those that were on him fell off, but the rest chased him out. Wave after wave of tarantulas flooded out of the house after Sal, who leapt off the stained-cedar deck and landed on slick mud.

He steadied himself and spun around, expecting the chasing spiders to pile onto him, but they were gone. The house was still there, but everything else had changed. They weren't in Pennsylvania any longer. They were in a strange valley. Mountains surrounded a patch of land mixed with weeds and mud that was somehow both slick and sticky. The cloudy sky Sal had seen before entering his house had been replaced by a night sky bright with a full moon. The house seemed ripped from its original location and plopped down in the middle of the valley. One light shined from the window nearest Sal.

"Momma!" Sal shouted. With no spiders to worry about, he rushed back into the house.

He couldn't help but glance around, certain the next turn of his head would reveal some eight-legged monster just before it jumped at his face. No spiders drifted down the brown, wooden beams. The hardwood floor was clean. The brown couch and black coffee table were just as he remembered them even after two years.

He saw his mother's profile and her curls of shimmering blond hair just on the other side of the chocolate-colored love seat. His heart burst with relief as he rushed over to her.

"Momma, we have to go," he could smell her lily-sweet perfume as he reached for her shoulder. She turned, and her form changed.

Her curly, blond hair turned straight and black. It lifted into a ponytail. Her face shifted from round and soft to sleek and hard. By the time she faced Sal, she was a different woman. Whoever she was wore just a touch too much makeup. Her lipstick was a shade too bright, and her eyeliner was a shade too dark. The hardness in the woman's eyes belied her tiny frame.

"You're a wasted birth!" the woman said. "You never should have been born!" Sal hardly had a chance to blink as a full-armed slap slammed into his face.

Sal tried to jerk up only to realize he was tied down. There was some sort of mask over his nose and mouth. He tried to shout, but the mask muffled his attempts. He couldn't see in the black room. He felt like he was on a bed of some kind. Each time he flung himself up he heard the distinctive clink of metal slamming against metal. He struggled to turn or slide around, but there wasn't enough room to move.

His mind grew more clouded. The air of that mask had a strange, medicinal taste. It stank. He tried to slow his breathing. He tried to remember what had happened, but he couldn't even recall what was happening in whatever dream he'd just woken up from. *Had I been dreaming?* It was his last thought before darkness consumed him again.

Sal stumbled back feeling his shoulder blades press against the mud wall of the hut. Now dressed in an Army combat uniform, Sal tried to keep his distance from the figure before him. The faceless boy, even without eyes, somehow stared at him for a moment.

"No," Sal said. "I can't. I can't do this anymore!"

Half-formed memories of dozens of failures sped through his mind. "I'm sorry," Sal whispered. "I tried. I swear I tried, but nothing worked! Everything I did just made you die faster. Please don't make me watch."

The boy's head exploded in answer. Sal slid down the wall, using his fingernails to scrape away blood and bone from his face and buzz-cut hair.

Marching brought his attention upward. What seemed like a hundred faceless boys began to march down a flight of steps that probably appeared at the same time the barefoot children had begun their procession. It was torment. It was punishment. Sal had no idea how many he had seen die. When he didn't fail the malnourished kids dressed in torn shorts and dirt-covered shirts, he failed others. He failed them all.

You're nothing like me. The memory bubbled to the surface of Sal's mind. He'd never heard his father's voice, but who else would have said those words? Sal's pop had died before Sal was born. He was raised on stories of a hero who died fighting for his country. So naturally, whoever Sal's father was would be disappointed to see what a failure he'd grown up to be.

You could never be me.

"I'm not a hero," Sal admitted to himself, letting his chin fall to his chest. "I can't save anyone."

The boys marched on. Sal looked up. They'd all die once they finished their walk down the rickety wooden steps. He felt crushed under a wave of shame.

"I can't save you," he said again, "and I just can't watch you die."

He scrambled to his feet and ran up the steps, past the boys. He bowled a few over, surprised none of their heads exploded. He didn't turn or check to see what had happened. All he wanted to do was get away. He rushed through a door that led into the living room of his childhood home. He didn't look for his mom. If she were there, she'd be ashamed to see her boy flee when others were in danger.

He sprinted through the door, somehow unsurprised to feel his boots slide along the mud of a valley. Even as he flailed onto the ground, he rolled into the fall, mixing brown earth with the red blood on his camouflage uniform. He knew he'd seen the valley before. Even in the moonlight, he recognized the shape of the mountains. He just couldn't understand why he recognized the location. He lumbered to his feet, and kept running.

His lungs burned with effort. His heart filled with regret. But he ran. He didn't stop until he felt certain he had run for a mile. He bent over, weeping in shame and sorrow, gulping down air.

He looked up to see the house he had grown up in just a few dozen yards in front of him. He spun the other way, and found the same scene. Wherever he turned, he saw the three-story, white home.

The door opened, revealing a small, silhouetted form. The faceless boy stepped out into the moonlight, and Sal stepped away.

"Please!" Sal begged. "Don't die." His last words came out in a whisper.

The boy took another step toward Sal, who stepped back again. The kid's featureless head tilted for a moment as if, even without ears, he had heard and considered the request. The child turned around and walked back into the house. Despite the still, dry air, the door shut on its own.

The house didn't explode. Spiders didn't rain down from the sky. No one got maimed, and, most importantly, the boy didn't die.

Chapter 5

EGGS

D r. Graham Strickland, lead scientist in a variety of fields, watched as a crash team worked to pull Subject 126's heart out of ventricular fibrillation. The ECG next to the rickety cot skipped faster and faster. The normal steady beep from the machine shifted to an off tempo staccato. A medical doctor tried to revive the patient, but a person's heart could only race so fast for so long, and Graham needed a subject whose heart could take more. He needed a lot of subjects who could take more.

Even amid the beeps and medical technicians working to keep Subject 126's heart working, Graham heard a familiar shamble. Dr. Donald Parker had a lazy habit of sliding his fat feet along the concrete floor.

"How many are still alive?" Graham asked as a spindly doctor who looked moments away from passing out himself prepped the paddles to counter the fibrillation.

"Fifty eight," Parker said. "Only twenty two of those are in stable condition." The pudgy little man gulped down air as if the 50-meter walk across the warehouse was some Olympic event. He was fat, but he was also a genius when it came to Anesthesiology and Neurology. Graham had recruited him out of medical school.

Under one of the halogen lights that hung from the ceiling, the attending doctor for the crash team shocked his patient, causing the dying man's body to spasm. The ECG flattened as electrolytes of the subject's heart were forced out. Everyone waited for a moment in hope that 126's normal heart rate would return, but nothing happened. The attending doctor prepared to begin CPR.

"Stop," Graham said.

"But…" the medical doctor argued. His hair was frazzled, and he hadn't shaved in at least a week. Graham didn't have time to learn all of their names, and in truth, some of them wouldn't be allowed to live after the program ended.

"He's dead," Graham said. "Even if you could bring him back, he wouldn't survive another treatment. Would you really save his life to torture him one more time? We knew most of our original 182 patients wouldn't survive. I don't see a reason to force a person to live when he's already been through more than he can handle." *Not to mention the fact that he's proven he won't succeed in the program.*

The rest of the crash team stepped back. The doctor looked down at the patient, and then back to Graham. Graham held his blue eyes for a few moments. The doctor's head sunk to his chest, and he let out a sigh before turning the monitor off.

Graham looked down a row of dilapidated beds.

"I don't want any of them to die," he said quietly. "I wish they'd all shown signs of success, but the trait we're looking for is rare. How do you imagine we'll find any likely candidates without sacrifice?"

"We're still well below the projected mortality rate among the patients," Parker said, the fat on his neck waggled as he spoke.

He seemed to be trying to justify his own guilt. Maybe he was trying to convince himself most of the subjects wouldn't die. He may as well try to convince his thinning hair to grow back.

"I know," Graham replied gesturing at the section of the warehouse designated Field Test Station Two. "We expected to lose about 75 percent of our patients by now."

That was the main function of Phase One. Graham and his team of 15 doctors used all the stolen or repaired medical equipment they could get their hands on in an effort to keep the subjects alive until they advanced to Phase Two or died. Most of the raggedy beds were empty already; their former occupants did not advance to Phase Two.

Graham walked up to Subject 126 and pulled the thin sheet over the deceased's head.

"Humanity hasn't taken a significant evolutionary step in centuries," he said. "We have stronger viruses and more diseases, and all of that is on top of limited resources and an expanding population."

He walked down rows of beds until he came to Subject 144. He instinctively used his free hand to tuck his security badge back into his pocket. The entry card had an annoying tendency to clatter against things from its lanyard, and tucking the clear plastic case into his pocket kept that from happening, at least until it slipped back out and started swinging around again. The doctors followed him, unsure what else to do. Graham gazed along the wires leading from the patient's shaved head to the monitor. He was stable and maintaining a Delta Wave Emission rate of 3.7 cycles per second.

"It's time we evolve," he said. "He's ready to be moved."

The crash team loaded the lanky black man onto a rolling gurney, and a few technicians started to transport him to a new facility. The sleekly muscular subject had already proven unusually difficult. He'd required an entire team to obtain, and that same team had to re-insert him into the program after a single D-W-E spike event. It was definitely time to move him.

"Put the subject on the third floor when you get to the Phase Two compound," Graham said before they could roll the gurney away.

"Dr. Strickland, are you sure?" Parker asked.

"This subject seems to have a particular knack for causing problems," Graham said. *This one isn't even the subject I'm worried about.* "I've worked out a scenario that should help the subject integrate into the program more easily."

Troublesome or not, Subject 144 was the third Phase Two subject. *Three! If my idea works, he may even become a valuable resource during Phase Two.*

"I was actually coming over to let you know," Parker said. He paused before he started his usual rambling. "I didn't know you were observing another patient."

"What is it?" Strickland asked. *Does the man have to have an entire preamble before he makes a point?*

"You wanted me to inform you when Subject 182 stabilized at 2.5 cycles per second."

"It can't be happening this soon," Graham said. He immediately wanted the words back. It was unprofessional to make guesses or assumptions. He knew better. But for the last subject to already be further along than the rest of the group was something truly unexpected. Less expected than the small number of fatalities, statistically speaking.

"Doctor, she's..."

"The subject," Graham cut in. "If we give the subjects a gender, we begin to see them as more than test subjects. If we do that, it'll only make it harder if we lose them."

"I understand," the doctor said. The little man looked as if he didn't, but Graham didn't have time to explain how to be a professional. "The subject," Parker emphasized the word with only a little less frustration than callousness, "has maintained a D-W-E of 2.5 cycles through four attempts."

"Four?" Graham asked. His brown eyes must have frosted over when he asked the question because the chubby assistant waddled back a few paces, bumping Subject 144's former steel bed frame. *I have to be more careful how I react.*

"Yes, we ran a fourth attempt because her...er....the subject's vitals were well below the danger line."

Graham focused on the information. He slowly ran a hand through one of the gray streaks in his brown hair. He considered walking down the long line of empty beds to check on those vitals himself, but if he couldn't trust his staff to follow well established guidelines, then he had a much larger problem. He looked across the warehouse. He knew exactly where she was. *And if I go to check on her, the rest of the staff will want to know why.*

"What explanations have you considered for the anomaly?" Graham asked.

"Age is the only factor that's vastly different than the other subjects."

"Are you talking about biological factors or the changes we made to the dosages to account for the subject's age and weight?"

"For now Doctor, both. We didn't think it wise to try and alter the dosages just to find out why the subject was performing so well."

"Have you considered using those dosages on an older subject?"

"No Doctor, again, we didn't want to risk losing one of them."

"Find a subject who's shown the least promise but is in the most stable condition. Alter that subject's dosages to match 182."

"Doctor, isn't that a bigger risk to the subject?"

Graham took his square, clubmaster glasses off long enough to rub the bridge of his angular nose. Breathing deeply, he tried to explain. "Any other subject has already shown a reaction to the injections. We need the most stable subject to give the most accurate results of how a viable subject would react to the altered dose."

"And if the subject dies?"

"We have to pursue every possible way of reaching our standard. If this subject dies, we learn that altering the dosage could kill the others. But if the subject lives, we could save the rest and increase our success. One for many."

"One for many, Doctor." Parker's reply was flat, but well meant. It was the mantra of the experiment. Though, in truth, they had a very specific number in mind. That's how they determined the initial 182 subjects. The future was what mattered. There wasn't a cost too high to reach his goals. If everything worked out, one more little egg would hatch, and the world would change. It had to change.

Chapter 6

INTEL

"Team Two in position."

Steve Delmas listened to the rest of his team report. He and Brandon were at the front entrance. The clear night sky was bright with a full moon. Steve took a few breaths of muggy air, lamenting the humidity as he depressed his headset's talk button, "Overwatch, report."

"No sign of anyone, Sir," she said. Kira Rusche, call sign: Overwatch, seemed a bit confused.

"Copy." Steve let out a breath of frustration. If Kira said no one was around, there wasn't anyone for at least five miles. Her confusion was probably related to whatever reason explained why the area was clear.

He took position next to the low-roofed building. A path barely wide enough for a mid-sized truck to drive around separated the dense woods from the target. There were a few trails that wove around the trees, but none of routes looked to have been in use for months.

"Oneiros, prepare for a soft breach on my command. Standby.... standby...Go!"

On his command, Hardwire, Brandon Karst, pulled open the steel door, which screeched on rusty hinges. Steve brought up his M-4, lightly squeezing his pressurized light switch, and entered the abandoned warehouse. He stepped in smoothly and chose a side knowing Brandon was right behind him.

Steve swept the area with his rifle, casting a cone of light wherever he aimed. The large bay was empty. He knew that of course, but just because Kira said there wasn't anyone around didn't mean there wasn't any danger.

"Clear!" Steve shouted.

A moment passed before he heard Brandon repeat the call. Brandon turned the lights on. Steve lowered his rifle and took a look around. Empty. The whole damn building was nothing but rusted metal walls and stained concrete.

"There aren't any traps here, Sir," Brandon reported. That was his job. From the moment they reached position until they actually breached, the gangly, string-of-a-man who still looked ten years younger than anyone half his age, made sure that any electrically powered equipment was harmless. With Brandon's report supporting Kira's, there was only one thing Steve knew. He'd just wasted a whole month.

"Breach!" Steve shouted using Dom Moretti's call sign while communicating with his headset. "Tell me why we're here!" Steve wasn't normally quick to anger, but he had it on good authority that hitting this warehouse would bring him one step closer to completing his mission.

"We're still searching our sector, Top," Dom reported. His use of Steve's call sign was a way to deflect.

"Don't stall!" Steve said, making his way through the windowless building to where Dom and Kira had entered.

"Sir, we've found what's left of a command center," Dom replied. Steve's path to Team Two shifted from a brisk walk to a light jog. His leather boots clomped through small pools of water that had collected among the mid-sized pocks in the concrete floor. He could hear Brandon's footsteps behind him.

A few turns brought Kira into view. She stood outside a small partitioned area in the back of the warehouse. Her long, wavy black hair looked a little matted down by the moisture in the air. A wry grin seemed to light up her narrow face as he walked past.

Dom stood in the partitioned room, which looked like it had been burned out days ago. A pile of melted metal and plastic sat in the middle of the floor. It looked like every monitor, keyboard, and CPU tower was piled up and burned. The congealed mess felt like an insult to Steve.

Dom, a reed-thin man, stood a bit straighter just a few steps from the pile. He always did that. They were opposite in every way. The most obvious was in their body-types. Steve was square and stout. Dom was sleek and tone. They were both as fit as any man could be, but whenever Dom felt threatened, he stood straighter as if it made a whit of difference in comparison.

"This is the third dead end, Breach!" Steve said.

The blond-haired man, who looked like someone out of a lifeguard commercial, opened his mouth, probably to remind Steve that Kira was responsible for intel. Steve cut him off.

"You're in charge of OPS! You take the information and develop plans. You, Breach." A few deep breaths reminded Steve that he was in command. He took those plans that Dom made and approved them.

The first time they hit a dead end, Steve took it in stride. It happened sometimes. Steve was disappointed when they hit the second target, an abandoned farm in Virginia. Now facing his third operation without anything to show for it, Steve was running out of flexibility. He'd left his patience in Virginia.

Steve turned to find Brandon standing beside Kira. They were probably talking about what an asshole he'd been for the last week. "Hardwire!"

"Sir," Brandon said turning from his conversation and heading into the room. Steve couldn't help but notice Kira wink a blue eye at Brandon. The brown-eyed man gave his usual 'awe-shucks' Texas shrug in return. Steve would have jumped down both their throats if it didn't give him a kick to see the steam coming out of Dom's ears. Kira was a flirt, and Dom didn't like that.

"Make magic happen," Steve said. If this room had been fragged, then it would take a miracle to get any information from the melted metal that used to be computers and servers. Luckily for Steve, Brandon had a way with computers. They all had special talents, whether they wanted them or not.

"I need ten," Brandon said.

Steve nodded and left with Kira and Dom behind him. "I should have called the OP off as soon as you told me no one was around."

"Just because the place is empty doesn't mean it doesn't have any information, Sir," Kira said, spinning around to face him so quickly her hair flowed over a shoulder. Her tone told him she wasn't at all pleased at the indication that she might have led him on a goose chase. Those blue eyes that were so bright for Brandon or Dom were suddenly ice daggers.

"No," Steve said, clenching his fists. "I suppose not."

"And I suppose you've forgotten why I selected this location?" she asked. Oh yes, she certainly didn't like any suggestion that she might have slacked in her duties. "I suppose you think I just jump at the first shadow I see under my bed. I suppose you think I don't want to find him as badly as you."

Truth be told, she probably wanted to find the general more than any other member of Oneiros.

"You're right," Steve said, letting out an exasperated sigh and unclenching his hands. "I'm sorry."

Neither admitting he was wrong nor apologizing would soothe her temper, but it would keep her from pulling a knife on him. She spun back around and stalked off.

"Hardwire will find something," Dom said. He'd lain on the floor with his back carelessly against a brown-stained steel wall. He already had his body kit off. The bulky, plated vest sat next to him. Steve took a moment to look at the patch Velcroed onto Dom's kit. It was a graphic design of a statue of Hypnos, the Greek personification of sleep. They all had that same patch somewhere on their body armor. It served as their unit patch, the symbol of their team. Steve shifted his gaze from Dom's unit patch to his own, which he had on his left breast. Without any reason for physical protection Steve started to strip his own vest off as well.

"Are you still blocking for us, Overwatch?" One look at her told him he'd just made matters with her worse. Why would she be blocking for them if there wasn't anyone around? A picture may be worth a thousand words, but one look and a turn of Kira's thin lips were an entire novel. Right now the book on Steve was titled, "Obvious Statements from Complete Assholes." *Yep, she's pissed.*

Steve sat down and kept his mouth shut as Dom dozed off and Kira made it a point to stay on the other side of the partitioned area, sit down, and glare like a cat who'd had her tail stepped on. There just wasn't any point in apologizing. Most importantly because, as far as his friends were concerned, accidents and bad days happen. Just fix the problem.

Brandon stepped out of the ruined command center, hardly making it two steps out before Steve popped up from the ground. "The general has three more warehouses across the U.S.," Brandon said. He looked like he'd just run ten miles. His brown hair was matted in sweat, but it was the sadness in those brown eyes that caught Steve's attention.

"He used the locator program," Brandon said. Dom and Kira suddenly found any location other than Brandon's infinitely more interesting than looking at their teammate stand there ashamed of himself. "I gave him that program, and he's using it to find more people."

Brandon was gifted with communications long before Steve had met him. He'd only gotten better, but it took effort to pull information out of machines most thought were destroyed.

"Do you have the locations?" Steve asked. He tried to keep the hope out of his voice. He placed a hand on the boy's shoulder to try and show a little sympathy for a kid who just learned he was used yet again.

"Someone very good wiped the drive before they fragged the room," Brandon said. "I found one file that referenced the warehouses, but the folder wasn't about the locations. It was labeled "Naturals," with a question mark."

"Looks like he's still trying to replace you, Captain," Kira said, a heavy emphasis on Steve's former rank.

A brief rage flickered in him, and Steve fought the urge to tell her not to call him that. After all, it was exactly why she said it. "Do you have any idea where the warehouses are?" he asked Brandon.

"I know what states they're in," Brandon said with a tired smile. Whatever effort he used to pull that information out of the computers had cost him.

"We'll hit all three. We leave first thing tomorrow. I don't want the general to ruin any more lives than he already has."

Brandon stared at him. It was frustrating to Steve. Brandon wasn't a telepath, but he could look right through a man. "You want me to go back in there don't you?" he asked.

Steve nodded. "I need you to see if you can get any of the names in that folder. They're all in danger."

"He can't be selecting subjects already," Dom said as if the current conversation was little more than an interruption of a great nap.

"Best case, he has his list," Kira said. "It lines up with what intel I've managed to gather." She emphasized the word "I've," and those icicle eyeballs stabbed in Steve's direction again. Steve didn't take the bait and left his attention on Brandon.

"Is he really going to do it again?" Brandon asked. He was 19 when he and the rest of Oneiros had accepted "special training." That 19-year-old was put through hell just to see what would happen. They were all at least ten years older than Brandon, and that nightmare was almost seven years ago.

His team was the result. Brandon, Dom, Kira, and Steve met at the training, and their lives were changed forever. Not for the first time, Steve thought of where his life would have gone if he hadn't accepted the training. The general probably didn't have any military to pull from, at least none that were viable candidates for the program. That meant that only innocent people, people who didn't have any business being treated like lab rats, would be plucked out of their lives. All so the general can run a sick science experiment.

Chapter 7

ORDERS

Graham gazed through his square-framed glasses at the printed readings for Subject 4. The chart and monitor printouts showed more progress than Graham could have hoped. He'd already reorganized the subjects' designations based on potential and elevation to Phase Two.

He stood in the upgrade cell looking at the heavily sedated subject on a rolling hospital bed. They'd taken whatever monitors they needed from the subjects who didn't show any promise and would therefore be handled shortly. The small cell was more hospital room than prison, but the steel, windowless door made it clear whoever was in the room wouldn't be allowed out. Graham compared the heart rate and brain activity. The results were promising. Subject 4 had the third-highest D-W-E spikes in the history of the program, discounting the odd spikes Subject 1 displayed on very rare occasions.

The door opened, and Brigadier General Leeroy Pederson entered the already cramped room. The large, square man was an imposing enough specimen. The ironed and spotless dress uniform only made him look more intimidating.

"I thought I'd find you in here," Pederson said. His deep, baritone voice made Graham want to stand a little straighter.

"I've already checked on the other subjects," Graham said. "This one was just next in the rotation."

"Of course," Pederson said, standing with his hands clasped behind his Army combat uniform. "I'd expect nothing less from you. What are the reports?"

"Most of the subjects have arrived," Graham answered, using a nimble index finger to push his pesky glasses back up his nose. "Subject 3 should arrive shortly, but Subject 2 regressed for some reason just after we brought him here."

The general's gray eyes turned cold. He knit his thin eyebrows together and set his jaw. "What do you mean?"

"I had thought that subject would have Broken by now, but just when his D-W-E patterns seemed to be near their breaking point, they normalized," Graham explained.

"What's being done about it?" the general asked.

"I'm monitoring his progress," Graham replied. "Sooner or later his psyche will force him to confront whatever it is he's used to repress his memories. If he doesn't make progress, I may begin joint subject situation treatment."

"Is that why you instructed my men to take the fireman to the third floor?"

"Yes," Graham answered. "It's hard to predict when and how things may progress, but I thought it wise to have someone serve as a control model. Subject 3 is the only one who didn't have to undergo memory alteration treatment."

The general looked down at Subject 4 and smiled. "She's small for her age," he said.

"Yes," Graham admitted, "but I'm excited to see what skills the subject develops upon Breaking."

"Still no luck accurately predicting those variables?" Pederson asked.

"With such a small sample to study, I can't accurately determine much more than viability for the program," Graham said.

"Prime Unit's betrayal was unfortunate for a great number of reasons," Pederson said.

"I believe the intelligence reports indicate they call themselves Oneiros now," Graham said.

The general's dark-skinned head jerked in Graham's direction, and Graham couldn't help but back against the white wall. Pederson let out a sigh.

"They can call themselves whatever they want," he said after a moment. "That doesn't change their intended mission, nor does it give back the amount of effort we put into creating them."

Graham said, "We couldn't have revamped the project any sooner, Sir. What funds you were able to liquidate combined with whatever you embezzled from military accounts or sold from federal evidence rooms after your...dismissal...could only do so much."

"I'm well aware of our financial limitations, Dr. Strickland," he said, his voice lowering to a growl. "I gave them exactly what I promised."

"And it was unfair of them to have such criticism for so many unforeseen issues," Graham added, trying to keep the fear out of his voice. "Sir, I wasn't trying to imply any fault. In fact, I was trying to point out how well we've progressed given our circumstances."

The general looked back down at Subject 4. The subject was tossing around under a sweat-drenched white sheet. The sedatives must have been wearing down.

"It'll be time for another scenario soon," he said, looking at the small subject. He paused once he noticed Pederson's smile. "What is it you're thinking, General?"

"She's perfect," he replied. "That face already looks like something out of a cereal commercial, and once her hair grows back, she's going to look even more innocent."

"I'm more interested in the subject's progress in the program," Graham said. "Whatever skill develops, it'll be a great asset. This one will be an example to follow in future iterations."

"Whatever she becomes, that kid will be a perfect spy," Pederson said. "Reminds me of Brandon."

"Perhaps if Subject 4 develops Subject 02's same skills, we can consider remote measurement updates? At least a central computer that isn't connected to any network?"

The general shook is square head. "Still too risky," he said. "I had three men wipe every drive at our recruiting base before I personally fragged the room. I'm still concerned it was a liability. It was necessary. We needed to run Brandon's program through the database to look for other likcly candidates."

"Even if they find the recruiting base, they wouldn't know exactly where to strike next," Graham said.

The general shook his head again. "There's no sense in worrying over what could happen. I've established protocols for any attacks on the remaining compounds. With things going so well here, I'd be surprised if something didn't go wrong. We have all four subjects in Phase Two in three-fourths the time you quoted me, Doctor. I'd think that's cause for optimism."

Graham forced his lips tight to keep from revealing a smile. It was hard not to show happiness when a project was going well, but it was premature. He glanced at Subject 4. *You are even more promising than I could have hoped.*

"As I predicted, Subject 4 has advanced to Phase Two," Graham said.

"Gloating?" Pederson asked flashing a rare, but still brilliant, white smile. It was half challenge and half gentle teasing.

"Each time you can readily predict an outcome proves the theory," Graham explained. "I may be able to improve on Subject 02's formula."

The general looked from Graham to Subject 4 and back. "I'm sure that's the only reason."

Graham wasn't foolish enough to dignify the implied accusation with a response. He tightened his large lab coat around himself and tucked his badge back in its pocket.

"What?" the general asked.

"I didn't say anything, Sir."

"You're about to," he replied, "so stop fidgeting around and speak your mind."

"It's…" Graham took a moment to consider how to best approach the issue. "I'm still concerned about Subject 1."

"What is there to be concerned about?"

"General, he's unpredictable. He was unstable before we began treatment, and there's no telling what the project will do."

"Could it possibly be worse than what happened last time?" Pederson asked.

"I'm not going to try and make assumptions based on so little data," Graham replied.

"Isn't that exactly what you're doing?" the general countered. "You claim you don't have enough data to accurately predict how he'll react, so how can you possibly assess the risk?"

"I'm assessing the risk because of the subject's background and mental state," Graham said. Pederson glared at him, and Graham reflexively pressed himself back against the wall. The general had never hit one of his own men, but that didn't stop whomever he was angry at from establishing a safe distance.

"Let's assume you knew the Veltri boy and this one would advance," Pederson said, pointing at Subject 4. "You knew that based on your data in combination with Brandon's search program."

"Yes," Graham admitted.

"Has anyone else even shown promise?"

"No," Graham admitted again.

"We don't have the luxury of being able to pick and choose our subjects," Pederson said. "Even if we had ten subjects advance to Phase Two, I wouldn't let go of a single prospect. That's why I had you develop the new security measure."

The general glanced back at the sleeping subject. "You have made sure the security measures are in place?" He put an ounce of frustration in his voice. The general wasn't above using his deep voice and size to cause a bit of intimidation when necessary. Graham felt no shame at how effective that tactic was.

"Of course, General. All the subjects have been secured."

"Then there should be no fear of Subject 1, regardless of the risks. If he proves unsuitable, we'll make due with what we have."

"Which is further evidence that we should neutralize him now."

"I won't throw anything away until it loses value," Pederson said. "Remember why we are here, Dr. Strickland."

"To discover the limits of humanity," Graham said. "Sir, you know I'm loyal to the cause and the program."

"Then focus on my orders," Pederson said. "Why fight me on this one issue? You've trusted me on every other point. Trust me on this one. With our security protocol in place, we've ensured we can correct any problems with the push of a button."

"I understand, General," Graham said. "I'm sorry to bother you with it. I promise I won't bring it up again."

That was the end of it. A promise from Graham was as good as a written contract, and the general knew it. For Graham's part, Pederson was notified of a risk, and would take it into consideration. It was all anyone could hope for from the man.

Pederson was absolutely resolute. It's one of the things that made him so charismatic. Men of real conviction were rare, and who wouldn't want to follow such a person? Most times, that certainty was quality to imitate; not a problem. In this case, pushing the issue would only make matters worse.

Subject 4 let out a yelp, whimpered, and rolled around. Graham checked the monitors. The subject's heart rate was up. It was time. Subject 1 might have been a concern, but Subject 4 more than made up for it. *You are going to be inspiring.*

Chapter 8

SILLY DREAMS

S al couldn't do anything but feel his heart race. He begged his body to move. It was an effort just to breathe. He felt a malevolent presence loom over him. Without understanding why, Sal knew the being was responsible for his paralysis. Whoever it was, whatever it was, it was stronger than Sal.

A steady roar, the sound of a crashing wave, rose in Sal's mind. It was coming. It was coming for him, and he was helpless to do anything about it. He would have laughed if he could. He wondered if he was losing his mind. Running made it so he never had to watch someone die, but it didn't stop the nightmares. He remembered being hunted like an animal. He'd held a live grenade with the pin pulled.

He'd been locked in a dungeon where he was forced to listen to a baby crying for hours. In that dream, someone had set a meal in the room. Sal ignored it for what seemed like hours. Eventually, hunger drove him to eat his fill even as he listened to the crying. He had to; he was so hungry.

In all of those nightmares, he'd been able run or hold his ears. Every impossible situation he faced, he took solace in the knowledge that he could at least avoid taking action that would get anybody hurt.

Now, lying naked on a cold, concrete floor, Sal could do nothing at all. He was smack dab in the middle of lunacy and sanity, and the difference depended on his ability to move. Even if he could just turn his head or shout, he'd find the ledge of sanity and cling to it.

His eyes could move, which allowed him to look at the horrors that surrounded him. Chains, glistening black with blood, hung from the pitch black ceiling. Even if Sal could rise, he'd have to find a way to navigate around those chains. Something told Sal that if one so much as grazed him, he'd break. He couldn't begin to understand where his certainty came from, but he knew in his core that it was true. More so, the word "break" was the most accurate term.

It seemed as if darkness followed his gaze, preventing him from seeing anything more than the blood-drenched chains. If he focused on the rusted, oval links, he could sense an open pathway out of the room. It felt like the room was bare except for the chains and concrete walls, but each time he looked for the source of whatever light let him see the chains, everything grew dark.

Drips of blood slipped down the chains closest to Sal. He could hear the droplets slap the ground so close to his ear they rivaled the noise of the thick, heavy chains as they swayed in the air and clinked against one another. Each drop that fell urged him to move. Drop.

Please, just an inch. Just a small movement. Drop.

Dear God, if you're real, please just let me move!

Drop after drop fell. Sal imagined a pool forming. Inevitably, that pool would flow and seep onto him...into him. He may lie there forever only to end up eventually drowning in blood, and he couldn't even scream.

Move!

For an instant, Sal thought he imagined the sound of dripping blood get louder. As each drop fell, a new sound emerged. Clop, clop, clop. The sound grew closer. Sal could only strain his eyes to find the source of the noise. A shadow swelled on the dark, rough block wall. It should have been impossible, but the same ethereal light that illuminated the chains also cast the shadow, which was taller than a man, wider. The shadow was all wrong. It seemed more appropriate for a devil, for The

Devil, than a man. Sal thought the next step would reveal the monster's form. A loud moan echoed from somewhere. Sal thought it was from a young girl. The shadow's horrible form froze. He could see the silhouette raise its head as if sniffing the air.

Still paralyzed, Sal foolishly tried to shout, to draw the creature's attention. *Not another child. Please, not another child. I'm trying to run away. I don't want any more people to die!* The figure turned and faded in the direction of the girl's voice. Rage filled Sal. Focusing his thoughts, Sal concentrated on his arms and legs. *I'm going to get up. I'm going to save whoever that is.*

The girl yelped again, and Sal was running after her, no longer afraid of touching the chains. He didn't even stop look at the Army combat uniform that appeared out of nowhere on his body. He turned a corner in the stone corridor and skidded to a halt. *Everyone I try to help dies.*

He heard another roar, which was followed by another moan.

"I'm sorry," he whispered. "I'm so sorry."

He turned the opposite direction, and ran away in shame.

Kaitlyn Olhouser forced herself to keep running, but she wouldn't hold out much longer. Her lungs refused to fill with air as she ran through the alleys of a city she wasn't sure she'd ever been to before, and she didn't have her inhaler. It was simple though, if the beast caught her, it would kill her. She ducked into a tall, narrow alley and behind a green garbage dumpster. Her lungs couldn't take any more. Gasping for breath next to a slick pile of sludge, she simply tried to beg air to fill her lungs. She focused. *Just a small breath...a little one. Good...another. A bigger one.*

A goat's hoof slammed down in front of her from around the dumpster. She glimpsed a bull's horned head just as she turned to scurry away. The dumpster flew in front of her, landing on the black pavement just in the direction she meant to run. The creature screamed, and it was all the more terrible because it was a man's scream coming from that monster.

She tried to run in another direction. A bolt of lightning streamed across the cloudless sky and lit up the night. In that instant, she saw it. It was huge, bigger than any man she'd ever seen. It had bowed goat legs and black hooves. Its bull's head had horns as long as her arms. Between the impossible combination of animals were the chest and arms of a large, muscular man. The lighting faded just as the creature turned black eyes at her. Rain plummeted from the sky.

Kaitlyn turned to run and slammed right into the man-shaped chest of the creature. She moaned. For some reason, she'd never been able to scream. Some part of her prevented her from producing anything more than the occasional shout. She heard herself whimper and knew it would be a wail of terror from any other girl her age. She turned away even as the creature snatched her by an ankle.

She fell hard on her stomach, grunting as she flopped onto the rain-soaked pavement, which stained her gray t-shirt black. Her bluejeans soaked up the wet, freezing water and held it to her legs. Her asthma struck again. She gasped for breath through wet strands of black hair that stuck to her face. She tried to breathe even as she tried to shout for help.

Sal spun around the grasp of what he could only describe as a demon. He wove around it even as it attacked one of several children. Each was a boy of 9 or 10. Each was being attacked by some form of monster. The fiends were small and red with long tails or huge and black with curling horns like that of a ram. No matter the shape and size of the evil spirits, every single one of them had Sal's face.

Sal occasionally had to resort to shimmying along the narrow, red-walled hallway to maintain his distance. He made every effort to avoid the creatures. After a moment, they started to ignore him. Sal hoped they'd simply leave, or the children would vanish. Neither happened.

A boy cried out in pain as a cherub looking demon with yellow eyes shoved a knife through the kid's chest. Sal dove at the cruel wraith. He wrestled the blade away from the monster and shoved the knife through one of the demon's yellow eyes. He unleashed a howl of rage. *How many? How many must I watch die?*

Kaitlyn struggled to breathe even as she used her white, rain-soaked sneakers to kick at the minotaur-like beast and keep it from wrapping chains around her arms and legs. It had dragged her into one of the buildings of the alley. The structure seemed to shape itself as the beast brought her in. The structure seemed to melt from an empty building, maybe an old department store, into a dungeon. She had more success getting her breathing under control than keeping the monster from using chains to tie her up like a knot.

"Help!" She wanted it to be a shout, but she hadn't done that for years now. She could talk loudly, if she tried, but any extreme sounds from her were next to impossible.

The creature brought its grotesque face down to hers. It was so close she could only see the top of its snout and those black, lifeless eyes. She could feel its hot breath against her cheeks. That stare was more effective than a gag.

It let out a human grunt of approval before it rose, towering above her. Shaking, Kaitlyn stared at it. "Please..." she whispered. "Please don't hurt me."

The creature let loose a deep chuckle. It wanted her to be terrified. It wanted her to die from fear more than anything else. She clenched her eyes shut, not wanting to see it kill her. She heard three loud clops before she opened her eyes to see the creature walking through a door out of the dungeon. The room was still large, but instead of being empty, it began filling with stone slabs and metal cages. The white-stone walls became gray. Moldy beams formed above her, and black chains hung loosely around the beams. She saw someone hanging by his neck from one of the chains. The wood creaked as the body swung from a metal noose. The beam held if only to provide Kaitlyn a horrific pendulum to keep the time.

A surge of fear gave her the strength to pull at her bonds. She focused her attention on escaping, knowing she only had moments. Struggle as she might, it actually seemed as if the chains grew tighter as she fought to be free.

As if to mock her efforts, a roar echoed throughout the room. She lifted her gaze expecting to see the monster return, and was shocked to see a golden-maned lion stalk into the room. It was him. She'd had a thousand nightmares, maybe a million. She'd never counted. But recently, for some reason, the lion had started appearing just when she thought she'd die. She saw the lion, and understood she knew him. She knew it was a him, and she knew he wasn't really a lion. He was more than that.

A part of her, the part that knew lions weren't particularly picky eaters, was still afraid. But, for the most part, Kaitlyn thought the golden lion would die before it hurt her, or allowed her to come to harm. It looked at her. It's huge dark eyes held so much compassion Kaitlyn thought it was about to weep.

"Help me," Kaitlyn whispered. "Don't let it get me."

The lion drew itself up and let out a sigh. Kaitlyn thought it looked like a person who was about to do something that would hurt. It turned and stalked out of the room.

"No!" Kaitlyn said. It was a shout to her, a wail of betrayal and sadness, but it only came out a flat request.

A wet, ripping sound drew her attention back to the warped beams above her. The chain noose still swung from side to side. Something seemed tangled in the links. It was narrow and tattered; it might have been a wet sheet. A dark liquid dripped from the cloth's tattered edges.

Slap. Slide. The sounds came from the concrete floor ahead of her. Slap. Slide. Kaitlyn craned her neck and strained her eyes, but her sight was blocked by a wooden crate. A red hand slapped down onto the floor just beyond the crate. Slide.

The beast that brought her here was scary. It was large and wanted to kill her. It had horns and sharp teeth. It was strong. It didn't scare her half as much as the creature that dragged itself toward her now.

"Red man," she said, wasting the last ounce of air she had. She froze in fear as he rolled toward his outstretched arm. He flung his hand out again. It splattered onto the floor, flinging droplets of blood into the air as he reached out. He used that arm to drag himself another foot closer. Kaitlyn sucked in pitifully small bits of air and tried to roll away. The chains held her tightly, but they weren't attached to anything.

The mutilated man let out a deep, mournful moan. White eyes peered from a red, skeletal face. Kaitlyn couldn't turn away from his gaze.

"Get...you..." he whispered.

Something grabbed her ankle and yanked her away. Kaitlyn rolled painfully a few times. She groaned in agony. In a daze she looked up and saw the beast had returned. It let out a guttural howl at the red man before turning and stomping toward Kaitlyn. She didn't even hear it enter. *Did it just appear when the red man got too close?* Both haunted her nightmares equally. Both seemed to want her. Neither seemed to like the other at all.

She jerked in her chains, realizing they'd loosened when the beast pulled her away from the red man. She struggled harder with each booming step the beast took. She slipped out just as a massive hand snatched the chains she'd just escaped. She didn't bother looking back as she rushed out of the door and into a narrow, red-brick hall.

The hall, barely wide enough for her to fit, seemed to close behind her. She could hear the beast howl in rage at her disappearance, but she still ran. She snaked around corner after corner until she stumbled over something. She tumbled to the ground unable to find the air to breath or the energy to keep running.

"You can't be here," someone said.

It was hard to hear over her own short gasps of air, but someone had spoken. Kaitlyn looked up to see a man she thought she recognized. He was a soldier, or Marine, or some type of military person. She'd seen movies, and the uniform the man wore looked like the military men from the films. He was square and strong, with short, black hair. He sat against the wall with his knees huddled against his chest.

"You're going to save me." The words left Kaitlyn's mouth on their own, but they were true. She knew it when she saw him, even before she saw the strange patch on his right shoulder. There, Velcroed onto the man's uniform, was an embroidered golden lion. He'd been watching over her for a while now. He just looked a little different. For starters, he was a man. He sat there, hunched over despite a back that looked like it could carry a mountain if it had to. His dark eyes made it seem as if he'd already carried a heavy burden.

"No," he said. "You don't understand. You have to run! Everyone I try to help dies."

Someone grabbed her around her waste from behind. She looked over to see a red-scaled creature with small, pointed horns and the same face as the man she'd just met. Another creature, an exact duplicate of the thing that held her, appeared with a knife.

"Stop!" the man begged, closing his eyes as the creature with a knife charged at her.

She slipped free and tripped into the man in the military uniform.

He opened his eyes. "You're alive," he whispered in wonder. More demons appeared. They were each armed with a knife, sword, or axe. They all had his face, but their maliciously gleeful smiles looked so out of place below eyes that gentle.

She turned and looked at him. "Please," she said. "Don't leave me this time."

"You'll die if I try to save you," he said as the creatures approached.

"Please!" she whimpered, looking into his deep, dark eyes.

"God, help me," he whispered.

She expected him to fight. Some part of her knew it's what he wanted. Some part of her knew how ashamed he felt at avoiding the fight.

"I'm not a hero," he said. She wasn't sure if he was talking to her or himself.

Instead of fighting, he grabbed her hand and ran. "Stay with me," he said, dragging her down the corridor.

They shifted from one brick path to another until they rounded a corner that led to the exact same dungeon she'd just escaped. The red man was nowhere to be found. The beast was out of sight too.

"I know this place," he whispered.

"You left me here," she said.

He turned and knelt in front of her, brown eyes full of sorrow. "I know," he said. "I'm sorry, but I had to. I *can't* try to help you."

A beastial roar cut the explanation off. They both turned just in time to see the beast charge toward her. Kaitlyn clenched her eyes shut, waiting to feel the monster crash into her. She felt a gust of wind and heard a collision of bodies. She opened her eyes to see the monster lift the man, her golden lion, with one hand. The monster sneered at the man, tossing him aside like a bag of garbage.

Kaitlyn gasped as the man fell in a heap. The monster turned to her. It stalked toward her, and nearly tripped as the man dove at one of its goat legs. He held onto it so tightly his knuckles turned white. "You can't have her!" he said. He sounded every bit the lion he appeared to be minutes ago. "Not this one. Damn you, just take me!"

The monster let out another howl. It bucked its goat leg and the man rolled more times than Kaitlyn could count into a heap of tools and chains. She thought his head hit something. "Don't hurt him," she said. She wanted to shout at it. She wanted to unleash every ounce of bottled up anger she'd ever had, but she didn't know how.

The monster turned its black, hate-filled, eyes at her. A few quick strides brought it to her. Just before the beast could grab her, the man shot past, faster than a man as square as he was should be, and scooped her up. He charged out of the dungeon and set her down.

They stood in a rain-soaked alley next to a green dumpster. Small, squat, square buildings lined each side of the black pavement.

"I'm trying," he whispered. "Dear God, I'm trying." He looked down at her with deep, brown eyes. "Run."

"What?"

"I can't help you, but maybe he'll settle for me."

"Are you real?" she asked. She could feel her asthma trying to take her breath from her. She focused on breathing. She reveled in every one of the minuscule breaths she could wheeze into her lungs.

"I was about to ask you the same thing," he said. He sounded tired, but there was an edge to his voice, like he was scared.

"I'm real," Kaitlyn said. Her breathing became more normal.

"That's what scares me," the man said, "but real or not, I don't want to watch you die."

"But I'm real," she said.

He clenched his eyes and his fists shut. She reached out to him.

"Please, don't leave me."

Her fingers approached his hand.

Startled, Kaitlyn's eyes blinked open, and she wondered where she'd been. She wondered where she was. Wherever it was, it was a small room with some medical equipment. *Am I at a hospital? Is this another dream? Was that only a dream?* It was the worst of any of the dreams she'd had. To be saved, and it only be a dream. For the first time in her life, Kaitlyn was glad she couldn't cry. If she could, she'd never stop. Someone had found her. She *knew* he wanted to save her. He was *going* to save her. But it was only a stupid little girl's dream.

Chapter 9

TWO TO GO

"You heard right," Steve whispered over his secure radio. "No Delta Techniques. I want the general to think it was the government. Any extra information might lead him to us."

Dawn was still an hour away. The night-vision goggles gave everything a green and grainy cast. It made it more difficult, but approaching in broad daylight left too many concerns. For starters, there wasn't any way to hide their approach in the middle of a desert.

It was hard enough using stolen credit cards to buy a set of all terrain vehicles just so they could get themselves and their gear close enough to walk the rest of the way without being heard or seen. Sure, Brandon could always use his skills to get money in a pinch, but Steve generally avoided using any of his team's more unique skills as much as possible. Hence the reason for his current order to Dom.

"Yes, Sir," Dom replied. He and Kira should be at the south end of the compound. Steve waited for Kira to argue, but no more sound came over the radio as Steve assessed the area.

The chain-link fence and barbed wire enclosed compound was active. At least one company occupied the large warehouse in the desert between California and Arizona. They had mobility in the form of about ten Humvees parked just a few hundred yards from the compound. No

one saw any helicopters though, and that was good. It simplified most
of the contingencies when you weren't worried someone was going to
launch rockets at you. Fighting positions, Hesco barriers, and simple
30-gallon barrels filled with rocks, pocked the area of the compound.
That was also good. If this place was built to defend, it meant they
wanted to protect what was inside, and they were more willing to fight
than run. *This could be it!* Steve tamped down his excitement and focused
on the plan.

The plan was about as easy as Steve and Dom could make it. The first
priority was to knock out communications.

Steve looked down at Brandon, who tinkered with an EMP bomb for
longer than most would deem necessary. Brandon would tinker with a
brand new piece of equipment, and Steve would be damned if the kid
didn't end up making it better. He quietly shifted from the tan ruck sack
at his side to the bomb. God only knew what the kid had in that bag.
Whatever was in there always seemed helpful though.

"Times up, Hardwire," Steve said.

The scrawny man turned his camouflaged cranial toward Steve.
The night-vision ocular was almost comically large on his face and cast
a perfect circle of green light on his normally tan skin. "I need thirty
seconds."

"You said that thirty seconds ago."

"You want this to knock out the outer perimeter or the whole
installation?"

"You know the answer to that."

"Then give me thirty seconds." With that, he swung his head and
attention back to his gadget. He shifted from that canvas sack and back
to the EMP.

The kid is taking after Kira far too much. Steve activated his squawk box.
"We go in thirty."

The second step was more difficult. Kira would have to take care
of the towers. If the company guarding this facility reacted before they
could get into the inner perimeter, the whole operation was pointless.

Brandon's long, nimble fingers danced along a spherical steel ball filled with stuff Steve couldn't begin to identify.

"Go dark in five," Brandon said.

Steve shut down all of his electrical equipment including his night vision. He could vaguely make out Brandon's shadow set the bomb down.

"Don't look right at it," Brandon said.

Steve covered his eyes an instant before he heard a strange vibration followed by an electrical surge. A blue haze of light forced Steve to close his eyes even more tightly. The light and sound faded after a few moments.

"Good to go back on, Top," Brandon said.

"Start the next countdown," Steve said. He flicked on his night vision, optic holographic sight, and night-vision laser. With all the tech Dom packed onto the rifles, the things practically thought for the shooters.

Kira had one minute to take down two targets. It was an ambitious goal, even by her standards, but she seemed certain she could do it.

Dozens of soldiers surged everywhere all at once. As the compound's security detail scurried around, Steve sucked in a slow breath of warm desert air and released it. No alarms meant no communications. Brandon's gadget worked.

The security detail started taking positions. Steve saw a few groups head toward the Humvees.

"Hardwire, did you take care of those?" Steve asked looking at his partner.

In reply, Brandon gave a lopsided grin and opened his tan bag all the way revealing ten hand-sized remote control helicopters. Brandon held up a remote and pressed a button.

Steve watched the toys buzz to life and take off faster than anything he had ever played with could go. The mini-choppers' buzzing lasted a few instants until they reached their targets. Buzzing became booming and any Humvees in sight started smoking. The men who were headed toward the vehicles fell back and took cover.

Steve wasn't surprised by the reaction of the compound's security. At least everything was going according to plan. Steve and Brandon took position behind the outer most barrier and began their assault. The security detail was moving quickly. Unfortunately for them, they all decided to use the main door, and Steve's team knew it. Steve and Brandon unleashed lead fire on the door, and no fewer than six members of the enemy company died before they changed their tactics. Without checking to see if Brandon remembered his mark, Steve began to monitor his sector of fire. On occasion, some poor bastard would make the mistake to try the main door again, where Steve and Brandon's sectors of fire overlapped. It wasn't that they weren't well trained, but who could expect to do well against anyone who had the opponent's playbook.

"Towers," Steve said. He stood, watching bullets riddle anyone who even brought a rifle to his shoulder. Steve rushed to a stone large enough to lie behind. He put down cover fire while Brandon ran past. It was a dance they'd done a hundred times in combat and a million times in training. Brandon set up behind the tower and gave his own cover fire. Steve surged to his feet and ran to his partner. Sweat started to form on Steve's brow and under his body-armor kit.

"Ten seconds," Steve shouted.

"Copy," Brandon replied throwing a grenade.

Steve hardly heard the explosion or subsequent semi-automatic fire. Focused on his task, he trusted Brandon to keep him alive long enough to set up the grappling hook and fire it at the base of the guard tower.

Another grenade went off as Steve reached the window of the guard tower. Steve looked inside. His heart froze for an instant as a guard pointed a rifle at his face. A spray of blood erupted from the guard's head. Kira had her part well in hand.

Steve pulled his rifle to his shoulder and started covering Brandon's climb to the tower. Step two was complete. Draw the company to the main entrance and gain the high ground. Steve couldn't see Dom or Kira on the east side of the compound, but he could tell they were there. The enemy forces were too thin.

"Top," Brandon said after firing a few rounds from his M-4. "Something doesn't add up."

"It's too easy," Steve said in agreement, taking a knee for the few moments it took to reload. "Breach and Overwatch are doing their job. We just have to keep them covered."

Steve looked toward the large metal swinging gate that marked the compound's entrance. He saw a trio of security men take up position. Steve brought up his rifle and sent a flurry of 5.56 rounds into them before they could cause Dom or Kira any trouble.

The ground started to rumble. The largest building in the compound shook and then roared to life.

"Is that building big enough to hide a transport?" Steve asked Brandon.

"It's long enough, but it's too low for anything like a C-130," Brandon answered.

The building burst into flame. Steve shut his eyes and turned away from the explosion. Seeing it through his night vision could have burnt out a retina. Steve flipped the ocular up and checked on Brandon.

He was already providing cover fire.

"I'm good, Top," he said. His jaw opened and closed a few times before he gently placed his index finger on the trigger of his M-4. "They...they set off the explosives without even bothering to get out."

"We're out of time!" Steve shouted over the din as he hustled down the ladder. They moved past one another trying to make it to the main building.

They'd managed to get a hundred yards closer before a large secondary explosion sent them down to the ground. On a good note, the explosion took out the last remnants of the enemy company. However, that was meaningless because that same explosion destroyed most of whatever was in there. Unfortunately, Steve was already painfully aware of what was in the building. People. *No time to be angry. There might be some survivors.*

Dom and Kira approached, ready to respond to enemies, though none seemed to be around.

"The crazy assholes killed themselves!" Dom shouted.

"Let's just make sure they did it in vain," Steve replied. He was the strongest on the team, but even he wasn't so good with fire. "Hardwire and Overwatch are security. Breach with me."

Steve removed his pouches, belt, and any excess magazines. He heard Dom do the same. They were in the building in seconds.

Heat and smoke hammered at him. He heard Dom coughing. They knew not to say too much. They'd need the air, and trying to talk only meant inhaling more smoke. It was nearly more impossible to see than it was to breathe. Whatever devices had gone off were in the center of the building. As soon as he was able to glimpse the area, his brown eyes hurt more from the view than the heat.

Perhaps fifty beds lined the longer walls of the building. Nearly all of them were already enflamed. Fifty people lie helplessly dying. At least most of them wouldn't be lucid enough to realize what they were going through. A sickly sweet smell, almost like prime cut beef on the grill, hit Steve's nose. He resisted the urge to vomit.

Save who you can. Even if it's just one. Save at least one! Steve moved to the nearest bed, pulling the sheets off. He managed to smother the few flames that had started to burn into a young woman. She looked perhaps twenty four, maybe closer to thirty if she was older than she looked. She had been pretty before the general entered her life. Now she had a horribly scarred bald head, a burned face, and her arm was next to useless given how damaged it was. *Am I really saving her if I pull her out?*

His body answered the mental question by pulling the woman into his arms. Moving slowly, deliberately, Steve carried the woman out. He made it out of the building, and looked behind himself to see Dom carrying a bald, middle-aged man over a shoulder. Instead of setting them down and rushing back, Brandon waited for Dom to get clear before whirling into the building. Kira kept a watch on the area.

Brandon rushed out of the building, carrying another victim and shouting for the team to move. Steve didn't have time to pick the woman up. It was drag her or leave her there. He grabbed an arm and hauled the woman behind him. They ran and turned behind a Humvee just in time for a third explosion.

Steve allowed himself an instant to watch and mourn. They came to stop the general. They had a chance to save fifty lives. Instead, they caused the enemy to panic. Even the three that survived would never be the same. That would be due to more than just burned flesh. Steve wanted more than anything to punish anyone who would do something like burn a woman to death just to cover his ass.

He took another deep breath and pulled off his cranial, letting it fall to the ground. Then he ran rough, square hands over his shortly cropped black hair.

"Overwatch, Hardwire, first aid," Steve said in a cold whisper. He moved aside to let the two work. They had the most medical training. Steve had the least. He'd been trained to kill, even in some ways most would believe impossible. He had just killed some eighty enemies, but he was also responsible for forty seven other deaths. *Can killers ever save a life?* He didn't know the answer.

"Top," Kira said. "They need more help than I can give them."

Steve didn't say anything, but he noticed Kira check the woman's abdomen, probably to check for a scar below the belly button. Kira had a scar like that after the general finished with her.

The general didn't just steal Kira's life; he stole every life she could ever create as well. It made sense that Kira would want to know if the burn victim under her care suffered the same tragedy. Kira didn't mention anything, and Steve didn't ask.

"Someone's sure to see this disaster. Just stabilize them. If no one shows in five, we'll make an anonymous call."

"Understood. Top?" Kira stood, pulling off a pair of blood-soaked surgical gloves.

"What?"

"The woman doesn't know much. She just remembers being taken from her home."

Steve glared at her. She knew what that glare meant. She gave him a flat, blue-eyed stare that told him exactly how much his frustration meant to her. The woman was infuriating!

"There wasn't anything else to do, Captain," she said. Her normal melodious voice frosted over. A shake in that voice betrayed even more rage. Everyone who wasn't injured was dead, and no enemy troops were around.

Once the woman was stabilized, what else was there to do but see what she remembered? *We're all on the edge of our limits.*

"Sir," Brandon said. That was his usual habit, jumping in to keep Steve from raging at one of the other members of the team, usually Kira. "We couldn't have seen that coming without—"

"I know," Steve interrupted. He was surprised at how calm his voice was. "If we'd have done anything differently, the general would have known it was us. Which is exactly why he put the protocol in place. For the next two compounds, I'm taking the gloves off."

"That'll make it a little easier," Dom said.

"No," Steve whispered. "No, it'll make it harder, and each compound will be more alert than the last. That's if we're lucky, and the general isn't burning the other locations down right this moment."

Can a killer ever save a life? I'm trying. God help me I'm trying.

Chapter 10

MAKE BELIEVE

Caden sat in the comfortable brown leather chair of his home watching his favorite show. A lamp with a yellow-and-white patterned lampshade sat on a square, black coffee table beside him. The lampshade gave the small room a strange yellow overcast. A small part of him wondered why the room didn't have any windows or blinds. He didn't remember replacing them. The other oddity was that the sound to his show wasn't on, but that wasn't so bad. He simply liked to watch. TV was second only to books, but he loved stories in any format. There were so many wonderful varieties of people. They all seemed so odd to Caden. It fascinated him to see what made one man laugh or cry. He considered TV to be his escape. It certainly kept him from his mother. *Musn't think of those days!*

His favorite TV show was about a man who hid from the bad guys in plain sight. The bad guys would search for him, and no matter what they did, the hero, calm and collected, always got away. Everything worked exactly the way he planned, and his mother never....*Mustn't think about it!*

"They're on to you!" Caden shouted through a mouthful of popcorn. He replaced the buttery bites with a fresh handful from the glass bowl in his lap. The snack was fresh and left a pleasant warmth in his hands from the butter that stuck to his fingers. "Finish the job and run!"

The hero on the television always had to fight one particular man. Caden couldn't remember the man's name, but he was very clearly a villain. He stalked the hero endlessly, threatening to take the hero, or even kill him.

The villain pounded on the door. Caden's hero was stuck. Caden launched to his feet, spilling popcorn everywhere. The glass bowl cracked. He didn't care. Bowls were things, and things could be replaced. "You can't catch him!"

Just as Caden moved to kick the TV, he truly hated the TV when it showed him things he didn't like, something caught his leg. Whatever it was caused him to fall back into the chair. Abruptly leather straps exploded from behind the chair. Suddenly alive, it used pieces of itself as tethers, which grabbed Caden and held him down. They bound his chest, arms, legs and even his neck. The straps gripped him so tightly, it was hard to breathe.

Caden struggled. He wanted to think of something clever to do, but he wasn't a hero. The bad guys got him. They caught him and put mud in his brain. It was all the more frustrating because Caden couldn't remember what it was they took from him, except that it was very important to him.

"Lemme go!" he shouted.

The glass bowl at his feet came alive. Hundreds of tiny legs, like a centipede, popped out from the rim of the bowl. Caden watched as the bowl climbed up the chair toward him. The glass frosted over and hardened turning into steel. Caden jerked as the hairy little legs skittered along his arm and onto his head.

He fought desperately stretching his head away from his shoulder. Another brown strip of leather ripped itself off the upholstery of the chair and tied his head down, allowing the bowl access to Caden's skull.

Even as the bowl lowered onto his head, his wiry white hair fell off in clumps, making a strange pattern with the buttered popcorn still laying on the floor. Something that felt like a wet rag grew from the inside of the bowl. A splash of warm water flowed over his head and eyes, forcing Caden to spit out a mouthful of the salty liquid.

The lamp and yellow-patterned lampshade mutated into a square, gray electrical box on the wall.

"What's this? I'm not playing anymore. I don't like this game. I don't like—"

Electricity pulsed through him. Every thin, ropy muscle in his body flexed. His dentures clamped so tightly together that he feared he would shatter them. The pulse increased and Caden felt his hands flapping.

The pulse was gone, and Caden took a few deep gulps of air. The room had changed. He was still strapped down, but he wasn't in just any chair; he was in the chair. The Bad Chair. The room was hardly big enough for him and the wooden monstrosity. It was too tight.

It wasn't right. None of it was right. He found a way to hide from the bad people. He thought he remembered remembering a plan. Two nice men came and promised him his own fairy tale. They said he could have a hundred wonderful dreams where fairies would fly into his ears and make his brain shine like the sun. They said he could make believe. In the end, it's all he'd wanted to do since the bad men came. They captured him and took away his TV and fairies. Every dream he'd had since then was one of theirs, not his. Now he had dreams he remembered, but he didn't like them either.

"I'll show you!" Caden cried out. Electricity coursed through him again, but, this time, Caden was ready for it. He focused his thoughts. He was stronger than this chair. No bit of wood told him what to do. He could make believe the chair wasn't there. "I don't feel anything!" he lied. The power increased.

He clenched his eyes shut as energy coursed through his body. He felt simultaneously alive and in agony. The power faded, and he opened his eyes, revealing his living room. The popcorn was still on the floor. The clumps of his white hair had dried. Caden smelled something burning and was horrified when he realized it was his own scalp. The TV, still playing his favorite show, flickered as another wave of electricity forced every muscle in his body to clench.

The TV stopped flickering. The channel had changed. Caden saw himself on the screen. The reflection wasn't perfect. Both chairs were brown, but one was wood where the other was leather. One was in his home while the other was in a red-brick cell.

"I'm getting stronger!" Caden shouted. "I'll beat you soon!" He wasn't sure to whom he was talking.

"Was she real?" a voice asked. It was like the question cut off whatever power made the chair work. Caden looked around. He couldn't see the man, but maybe it was just because he was tied to a chair. Caden remembered seeing a lot of "shes."

"They're all real," Caden answered struggling to get free and testing each strap of leather to see which one might be weakest. "Let me out, and I'll take you to them."

"Who are they?" the voice asked. It was a confused voice. Confused people were stupid.

"The girls," Caden replied. He hated talking to stupid people. The bowl slid off his head, clanking onto the brown-carpeted floor, and he let out a sigh of relief. He might still be trapped, but at least that metal bowl couldn't shock him again.

"There was only the one girl."

That was wrong. Actually, Caden thought it was all wrong. The voice wasn't behind him, or even in the room. *There's a voice in my head!*

"Who are you?" Caden asked, still flexing his arms, hoping to stretch the leather enough to escape.

"Who are you?"

"You're in my head, so I get to ask the questions! How did you get in there! If you don't get out right now you'll be sorry!"

Could someone threaten a voice in his head? Caden wasn't sure, but that didn't mean the voice needed to know. "I said get out!" Caden shouted. "Get me out of this chair and get out!"

He didn't recognize the voice, and he didn't like it. There were voices other than his, and sometimes they said things, but that was only when he wanted them to, when he made believe. This voice wasn't one of his. That made it worse.

"Are you there?" Caden shouted. "Get out if you are," he finished before giving the intruder a chance to reply. He hated voices in his head, especially unfamiliar ones. Worse, sometimes they tried to trick him into thinking things he didn't think.

Now, what was I thinking? Caden wondered to himself, confident whoever had invaded his mind had run off. *Right. Make....Believe.* He could change everything as soon as he remembered how to make believe.

Chapter 11

WORSE THAN FAILURE

There was more detail to this particular nightmare than the others. At least it felt more real to Sal as he rested a hand against the rough texture of the red brick wall and the mortar that held each brick in place. Dragging his hands along the path left a gritty powder on them.

He could only remember a few terrifying fragments of the dozen or so nightmares he'd had. One thing had become consistent during the last few dreams: the young girl.

Walking along the wall of a tightly cramped maze, determined not to pull his hand away no matter what appeared, Sal focused on the idea of avoiding the small, thin girl who knew him even though they'd never met. She had night-black hair that fell down just past her shoulders and a pale face composed of sharp lines. He didn't want to see her because he didn't want to cause her death. If she was going to die, he couldn't stand the idea of having to watch. It was more disturbing because some part of Sal knew she was real. Even that odd voice in his mind verified that.

I'm hearing voices. Does that mean I've gone crazy? Are you there? He called out softly to that other voice. Someone, or something, had spoken to him, no matter how briefly. Sal gave a wry chuckle. It was much more likely he'd gone out of his freaking mind. After all, he didn't know how he got there. Hell, he didn't even know what happened to his hair. Someone had shaved it all off. Only a bit of stubble remained or had grown back since it was cut. His clothes were different. He wore a blue t-shirt, a pair of jeans, and thick, leather boots. If he wasn't crazy, he was in a deep pit of shit.

Sal followed the wall turn for inexplicable turn. Each corridor of the maze was about two arm-lengths apart. The tight corners and small path made every alley look like a dead end. Just as he started to wonder if the labyrinth was changing shape as he walked, he noticed a rifle on the ground. He looked from his hand on the wall to the rifle. He'd have to pull his hand away from the wall and use it to carry the weapon properly. Some instinct told him no rifle should be carried in one hand. Sure, some people did it, mostly because they saw one too many action movies, but some part of Sal rejected the idea. He'd held a gun before in more than just half-remembered dreams, but each time he looked at a weapon, he felt more and more fear.

To Sal, the weapon seemed like a choice. He could pick the weapon up and fight, or he could continue to try and run. His hand trembled as he considered picking up the weapon. He wanted to find her. He wanted to save her, but every effort he made to save anyone ended in that exact person dying. He couldn't protect anyone.

He simply had to escape the maze and hope that staying away did more to save her than fighting appeared to. He passed the gun as if it were an angry rattlesnake, suppressing the urge to use his black boot to kick it away.

He'd managed to avoid the teenage girl at least twice. The weight of the shame was only surpassed by the mountain of guilt he carried after failing so many others. Dreams or not, he failed them. He couldn't bear another failure.

He turned a corner to find a corridor so narrow he had to turn side-ways. He held his breath as he squeezed through. One of the bricks was broken, and its jagged edge cut into his side. Shifting between walls, Sal felt blood seeping into his blue t-shirt.

Sal stumbled out from between the walls into a room within the maze. Though more spacious, the room had only the narrow exit behind Sal and a wider passage on the opposite side. Three apparitions stalked toward him from the wider corridor. Shaped like men, they wore straightjackets and odd black nylon masks that covered their faces. Chains were wrapped around each figure. The chains themselves were covered in barbed wire.

Sal backed away, already knowing he couldn't possibly slip through the same path he'd just come from before they reached him. When his back came against the wall, he considered simply letting them kill him.

What good am I?

One of the twisted nightmares charged. Sal instinctively used his free hand to slam a fist into the thing's face. Sal looked at his trembling hand. *I don't want to die.*

The other two creatures seemed content to howl at him for now, but that wouldn't last. They were working themselves into a frenzy.

Sal focused his thoughts, preparing to fight. It came to him like the answer to a riddle he'd been pondering for some time. It felt like he'd just remembered the name of a song he'd been humming. The girl was just that direction, past the other two goons and down another hall. Sal *knew* where she was. He could follow his thoughts to her blindfolded.

But I can't!

Sal again reconsidered his options. He wanted to retreat through the narrow passage, but the straight-jacketed monsters probably wouldn't just let him run off. Whatever else he would do, he'd have to take care of his other two opponents first. Then he could backtrack away from the girl. The clarity of her position vanished from his mind. He remembered where she was, but he could no longer feel her presence.

Sal pulled his hand away from the wall and charged the two straight-jacketed monsters. One yelped as Sal slammed an open palm thrust into its face. Sal felt cartilage give and knew that cartilage would stab into his opponent's brain. In one fluid motion, Sal turned his body and rotated his wrist turning his hand into a single edge that crushed the Adam's apple and windpipe of the last figure. It coughed and gurgled as it fell to its knees.

The girl came back into Sal's mind. She was perhaps a few dozen yards away. Sal looked down at his opponents. Whatever they were, they died if you knew where to hit.

But how do I know where to hit? Sal felt his mind try to flee the question. With those thoughts, the idea of the little girl's location faded. Sal focused, pushing the fear and questions of how he knew how to fight away. It was connected somehow, the training of how to use weapons and his odd connection to the kid.

Sal shimmied back through the narrow alley, making sure to head away from the girl. The process cost him a few more cuts and bruises, but he knew he was moving in the right direction. When he made it through the narrow stone path again, he realized the surroundings had changed. It couldn't have been five minutes from the last time he'd been through the path, but the corridors on the original side now led in different directions. The path seemed shorter. *It doesn't matter as long as I'm going away from her.*

Sal rushed through the hall. He ran about a dozen yards before a panel in the floor broke away. He only just managed to grab the edge of the cement floor. Sal took a panicked glance down. The ground at the end of a long fall seemed to move. A light pulsed in the room, and Sal realized that on the floor writhed every type of spider he had ever had a nightmare about. There had to be hundreds, maybe even thousands.

Fear gave his arms a strength he didn't know he had, which helped him pull himself onto the floor and sprawl out to catch his breath. He would face a hundred goons in straightjackets. He'd willingly leap into a fire before he ever came anywhere near a spider. The image of a half-foot long, brown arachnid with hairy legs popped into his mind. The mental image was almost as shocking as the realization that he'd actually seen that creature. It wasn't just some half-terrified creation of his mind, it was a memory of his own past.

Was that my first day in Afghanistan? No, my third. Wait, I remember! I was a soldier! How could I have forgotten that?

The flood of recollections seemed to revolve around the arachnid. The memory was nearly more terrifying than the hoard of eight-legged monsters that crawled beneath him.

Another shout from the girl pulled him out of his thoughts. "I'm coming!" Sal shouted. He scrambled to his feet and froze. She sounded scared. She probably thought he was going to save her. She needed someone.

Sal's head hung in shame. He took a deep breath. No matter how much he wanted to help, even if he was willing to try, he couldn't turn back with a section of the floor missing. He had to get away. He had to be as far from that girl as possible. As he realized the thought, his picture of where she was vanished again.

A handful of the straightjacketed assholes came down the hall. Two charged him. Sal ducked under them and barbed chains raked along his back. It hurt, but it allowed him to jerk up and pitch them over. The pain was worth it to hear the bastards scream as they tumbled down the trap. They screamed even louder when they realized what they'd fallen into. Three remained.

He really wasn't as good at fighting as he was at grappling, but fighting any opponent that couldn't use his arms was fairly simple as long as Sal avoided punching chain or barbed wire. Sal struck one where a human's nose would be. Something nose like shattered as Sal's fist made contact.

The remaining two charged into him. Sal braced to fight, and then he heard the girl yelp again. The instant was enough to distract him. The two barbed-wire freaks tackled him. Several new gashes joined a handful of old ones. Without arms to strike with, they simply slammed their heads into his chest and stomach.

Sal grit his teeth. He looped his left arm around the back of one monster's head, using a choke hold. It felt like hugging a cheese grater. He rolled the creep around, forcing his partner to shift position. Using the asshole as a shield, Sal tightened the choke hold until he felt the bastard go limp. It wasn't like in the movies. True, in a matter of moments, the monster was out, but once Sal let up the pressure, the blood would flow again.

The thing's remaining partner lumbered to its feet. Sal rose as it charged. Sal meant to use the freak's momentum to throw it against the wall, but as soon as he thought of the maneuver, the man flew backward. *Did he slip?*

Sal diverted his attention to the bastard he'd choked out and stomped the black mask where its face should be until he was sure it wouldn't wake no matter how much blood managed to pump into its brain.

Sal heard the girl shout again. He stopped, afraid that his fight somehow put her in more danger. The last apparition must have sensed the opportunity. He came at Sal, letting loose an strangely human yell.

"Get away!" Sal shouted, shoving his attacker backward. Oddly, the man seemed to float upward, over Sal's head. It floated an instant before plummeting into the pit of spiders behind Sal. *What just happened? Am I dreaming? This feels too real to be a dream.*

He gulped down air and grimaced in pain. "I won't be the cause of her death. I won't be responsible."

Turning, Sal ordered his feet to keep the promise. He ran away from the pleading voice and stumbled down the hall. The path seemed to circle around. He turned again and again, certain he was lost. He ran until he reached what must have been the center of the maze. It was built like a nightmare version of a medieval blacksmith's forge. He stopped inches away from a table littered with various tools and half-made objects that could only have been designed to maim or kill.

Sal stared in shock. He'd been trying to get away and failed. The girl sat in what seemed like a large, custom-made gilded birdcage. She wore a hospital gown. Shockingly, her hair was gone. It looked as if it had been shaved a while back leaving only a patch of black hair.

A man shoved the cage, laughing. Each time the man pushed the cage, it swung on the chain that kept it attached to the ceiling. The goon rattling the cage was only a few inches short of impossibly large. If one of the men on any of the muscle magazine covers doubled his steroid intake and grew six inches, he'd look like the man in front of the cage. He wore a long sledgehammer at his belt. Sal wasn't sure he could lift that hammer, much less walk around with it tucked in his pants.

The man turned, looking through long, greasy strands of black hair, and Sal ducked back behind the wall. Aside from the hammer, the man looked nothing like a blacksmith. He wore dirty blue jeans under a threadbare, black duster. The asshole's bare chest muscles were bigger than Sal's entire midsection.

Sal waited until the man turned back before taking a few cautious steps inside the dungeon. He looked at the man and the girl in the cage. Neither noticed his presence yet. He wanted nothing more than to kill that son of a bitch and take that girl somewhere safe. His father would have done that. Any of the soldiers he fought with would have. He should have. He stared at them, wanting to do something. Instead, he turned to sneak away, gritting his teeth in self hatred.

Something seemed to pull at him, like a rope tied to his waist. He jerked his hip and heard the table behind him skid along the rough, pocked concrete floor. The noise was just enough to announce his presence.

"You," the man said. His deep resonant voice sounded amused. He pulled that hammer from its leather loop at his waist. "You look half dead already."

Sal stood dumbfounded. He still couldn't figure out what had caught his waist. Now, with both the rhinoceros of a man and the too-thin teenage girl staring at him, he scrambled for what to do. If he fought, she died. What if he tried to run?

"Then catching me should be simple," Sal said. He turned to run, but the giant didn't follow. Instead, he turned to the cage, causing Sal to stop.

"Run if you want," the goliath said. A chuckle rumbled from his chest. "I'll kill her. You won't be hard to find after I'm done."

He reared back his hammer. The teenager in the cage gave a quiet yelp. "No!" Sal shouted.

One of the links holding the cage up burst, causing the enclosure to drop and break open. Maybe it simply crumbled under the idea of that mammoth hitting it with a hammer. Whatever happened, the cage tumbled to the ground, creating a barrier between the man with the hammer and the girl, who tumbled out of the cage.

"Run!" Sal ordered her.

The girl grunted. It seemed like she might be hyperventilating, but she still managed to find her feet and take off. The behemoth ripped the cage away. It had to be a hundred pounds, and it slid to the side like an empty cardboard box.

Sal turned sideways to let the girl pass. The giant stomped in their direction. Sal smiled, hearing the prisoner's feet as she scampered away. The demented blacksmith roared as he swung his hammer. Sal ducked out of the way. The pull of the air as the weapon missed Sal's skull by inches told him what would happen if he didn't dodge away in time. The hammer came down on the wooden table that had somehow revealed Sal's presence, and the wood splintered loudly enough to pop Sal's ears.

"She's gone asshole!" Sal said, ducking another swing. He noticed a half made machete amid the pile of toothpicks that used to be the table. The knife didn't have a handle, only a long, mangled bar of steel.

Sal dodged another swing. The hammer had to be at least fifty pounds, but the bastard waved it around like a kid's toy. He sidestepped a swing that would have crushed his skull. The cement floor crumbled and cracked as the head of the hammer crashed down. Sal rolled to the ground and grabbed the misshaped handle of the machete, holding it so the blunt end rode along his forearm. The behemoth swung his hammer again. Sal ducked under it and slid the blade along the titan's side.

Sal didn't need the howl of pain to verify the giant was mortal, if not human. Dark-red blood oozed from the wound. The man growled. In a sudden move, he brought the long handle of the hammer down against an enormous thigh, splitting the handle in half.

With the handle shortened, the colossus swung the hammer even faster. Sal ducked, dodged and spun, letting his smaller blade slice wherever it landed. Sal worked to wear the giant down, all the while knowing that if the towering dreadnought hit him even one time, the blow would crush bone.

The man feigned an attack that caught Sal off guard. Inches before the hammer could shatter bone, Sal lunged into the attack. The hammer didn't connect, but the wrist-thick handle slammed onto Sal's shoulder. Something popped and pain exploded from where the blow landed. A shockwave of pain traveled down Sal's arm to his very fingertips, numbing them instantly. Sal felt the blade leave his hand. It felt like some force ripped it from his grip.

The anvil-sized hammer fell to the ground as the leviathan took two deep gasps of breath. Sal looked up to see the knife was now buried to the hilt in the giant's heart. Sal slammed the palm of his left hand into the base of the steel bar and drove the blade all the way into the giant's massive chest. The move cut off the man's breathing, and he fell to his knees.

Sal shook in pain. Black flecks crossed his vision as he swayed on his feet. He dropped to all four limbs, fighting to stay conscious. A small pair of hands touched his back.

"You're okay now," a soft voice said.

Sal turned to see the girl. Not a hint of emotion showed on her sharp face. Her hazel eyes didn't betray any fear either, but Sal knew she was terrified. She was afraid, but she wanted him to feel safe.

"What the hell are you doing here?" Sal asked.

She jerked away. "I was worried," she whispered.

"You were supposed to run! You can't be around me!"

The image of a boy's head exploding. Blood spraying everywhere. A rifle in his hand.

"You're okay," she said again. "Don't be scared."

"I'm not afraid for myself; I'm afraid for you."

He stood, meaning to run. A small hand clamped onto his. The girl looked at him. A wave of emotions flooded into him. He couldn't tell what he was feeling or why. His shame, concern, and fear seemed to amplify for a moment before they were replaced by determination. He was determined to help her. It was buried under everything else, but it was all he'd ever wanted to do.

Sal grunted in pain as he took a knee. "I'm going to to lead the others away," he said. "If they're chasing me, they can't be hurting you. Do you…"

He paused, realizing he didn't even know what to call her. "What's your name?"

"Kaitlyn," she said.

"Okay Kaitlyn, I have to lead them away from you."

"What makes you think someone else won't find me?"

The comment stoked the fire of rage in Sal's stomach. A little girl, maybe 12, or 13, had just escaped one monster, and she expected another to come after her no matter what Sal did.

"I don't think they'll hurt you if I run away," he said.

"You shouldn't lie." Each word was delivered slowly, quietly. There was no inflection or emphasis on any particular word.

"I'm not lying," Sal replied, wincing in pain.

"Yes, you are," she said. "They want to kill me, and they want you to watch me die."

Sal's mouth hung open as she spoke. *She can't possibly know that!*

"Don't let them hurt me," she said. She melted into his arms. "Please." She was breathing hard and fast, like any scared child would be, but not a whimper escaped her.

"I know you're scared," Sal whispered, "but I can't protect you."

"I know you want to." Her thin lips trembled. It was like she knew what he was going to say next. Either that, or she knew how awful he felt about having to say it.

"That doesn't mean I can."

Something bit the back of Sal's neck. He remembered holding the girl tightly and trying to make sure she fell on, not under, him. He landed groggily, noticing her unconscious in his arms before darkness took him.

Chapter 12

ESCAPE

Chris woke in more pain than he imagined possible. Vague thoughts formed through the clouds. The first thing he considered was that he was truly awake. The second was that he was in some sort of ambulance. Had he been in an accident? Had that been why he'd had so many odd dreams in addition to his normal terror-filled nightmares? He thought he remembered being kidnapped, but his mind was only half out of its fog.

The smallest amount of light trickled into the back of the ambulance. He was lying on a gurney. *Maybe I'm just being taken to a hospital, but if I haven't been to the hospital yet, why am I wearing a hospital gown?*

"…said he's the last one," Chris heard from somewhere. He craned his neck to get a better view of the front of the vehicle. He was surprised to see two soldiers, at least they wore fatigues instead of EMT outfits.

Chris strained to hear over the sound of the engine and the rattling of the equipment in the back. The gurney he was on had a squeaky wheel, and one of the metal cabinets clanked whenever the vehicle hit a pothole or dip in the road.

"So these four are supposed to become what? Superheroes?" the driver asked.

"Shut the fuck up!" the passenger said. "Our job is transport. What you need to know is this guy is the last. Anything else isn't to be discussed."

Last what? Chris wondered.

"Relax," the driver said. "It's not as if the guy's awake. Hell, it's still likely the poor bastard will die rather than, well…whatever he's supposed to do. One of us will kill him, or his body will just give up."

Why would they kill me? What the hell is going on?

"You just focus on the road," the passenger snapped.

Chris looked around, trying to gain his bearings. The most important thing was that he wasn't strapped down. Wherever they were taking him, they expected him to be asleep for the whole ride. Everything seemed to be in order, at least from what Chris could remember about what he'd seen on the rare occasions he'd helped load people into an ambulance.

"Do you have to smoke that?" the driver asked.

They were both silhouetted by the ambulance's headlights, but Chris could see the passenger slip a cigarette into his mouth.

"Yeah," the passenger replied as the cancer stick waggled in his lips.

Chris shut his eyes. He could swear he felt the heat of the flame. It didn't matter how tiny it was. It didn't matter that the small, silver butane lighter was at least five feet away. Chris felt like he could reach out and touch it.

He opened his eyes. Moving as slowly as he could force himself, Chris tried to sit up. He fought the fear in his heart and the strange feeling of the lighter's flame. The passenger had clicked the damn thing shut and put it away, but Chris still felt as if he could sense it just in front of his body. He listened carefully, hoping to hear any indication that those up front had noticed he was awake. Whatever happened though, he was going to have to try something.

The vehicle must have turned because he felt the gurney he was on roll slightly, sending that loose wheel into another fit of screeching. Certain that he was out of time, Chris allowed himself to lean out of the gurney. He was terrified that flame was going to burn him alive. *It's just a damn lighter you coward!*

The driver cursed. The passenger pulled something from his hip. Chris didn't wait to verify if the passenger was armed; he simply hurled himself at the side of the ambulance. Something in the front of the vehicle flashed, like a sudden gout of fire. Chris panicked for a moment, afraid the flames might reach him, but they never did. They faded before they could do any real damage to anything. In fact, whatever erupted into flame was hardly enough to cause a scare, at least to anyone but him. It felt like someone lit a barbecue with too much fluid. *Did the passenger shoot?*

The driver managed to pull the ambulance over. The lurch of the vehicle forced everybody inside to brace a hand against whatever was closest. For Chris, the closest option was the rear door. The driver and passenger both turned toward Chris, who yanked on the metal door handle. Thankfully, it opened, and Chris ran from the ambulance and its operators as quickly as he could, bare feet slapping against cold pavement. The full moon above seemed to cast a spotlight on him, but it also let him see where he was going.

He wasn't sure where he was. He was on a long stretch of black top road. The silhouettes of pine trees, dark against a star-studded sky, encroached upon him, blacking out most everything else except for a brick warehouse surrounded by a high fence topped with barbed wire. White lights bled out of most of the warehouse windows. Without any other options to try, Chris ran for the structure. Gunshots sounded as sparks flew inches from Chris's feet. He didn't know the first thing about avoiding gunfire, especially while wearing nothing but a paper-thin, flower-patterned hospital gown.

He veered into the woods hoping the trees would protect him from his attackers. However they got him in the ambulance, they kept him alive thus far for some reason, but the driver had said they might kill him. Pine needles and foliage stabbed at his feet as he shambled from tree to tree, feeling like every step was an audible signal flare indicating his location. He kept the road in sight to keep from getting lost. He heard the men chasing him, shouting orders at one another. Maybe he had an advantage in the trees aside from not getting shot.

He stumbled around until he found a bush large enough to hide him and slid under branches covered in pine needles. They ripped at the flimsy hospital outfit and stabbed his skin. He shimmied in and tried to position himself in a way that didn't make him feel too much like a human pretzel. Not for the first time, Chris found himself frustrated by his stature. He was as fit as any firefighter, but he was all arms and legs. Strong as every part of him was, hiding those too-long limbs was more an effort in contortion than his body wanted to provide. He ended up sitting with one knee against his chest, and the other bent awkwardly around a large root. He didn't have any way of knowing if his foot was visible or not. He simply had to hope.

He felt a branch scrape the top of his head. He reached up to scratch at the spot and stifled a gasp. He normally kept his hair cut short, but his hand felt only a hint of stubble. More alarming was the feel of a scar where the base of his skull met the top of his neck. It was as long as his finger. *What have they done to me?*

The shouts grew louder. Chris heard twigs snapping and leaves crunching. He stamped down the fear that he'd made a poor decision. There was no way he could have made it one or two hundred yards barefoot with armed men chasing him. The only option was to hide.

With nothing to do but see if someone decided a bush in the middle of the woods needed to be shot, Chris tried to think. They wanted him alive. They kidnapped him, and they had medical gear. Perhaps they were hired guns harvesting organs? That was ridiculous. People didn't just walk around capturing other people and harvesting organs, *did they?*

What else would they want? He didn't have any money. His mother would worry, but she was just as broke as he was. So why would a pair of men, or even just one man, want to kidnap him?

He remembered getting in a cab after seeing the shrink. Two men pinned him into the vehicle. They held him down and injected him with something. He was as certain that memory wasn't a dream as he could be about anything, but that day he saw the doctor was supposed to be followed by a crescent-mooned night. Chris looked up, trying to see the full moon he knew to be in the sky. *I've been captured for at least two weeks.*

He didn't know much about the phases of the moon, but he understood that a change in how the moon appeared meant a long time had passed.

The beam of a flashlight blasted into his eyes. He worked to adjust his vision as a man walked only a few feet in front of his hiding place. Chris tried to control his breathing and remain as still as possible.

"Mattox," someone called out in a harsh whisper. The light swiveled around to reveal the passenger from the ambulance. The man, wide-eyed with an equally wide, square face, squinted and waved the light away.

"I thought I heard something," said the man with the light, Mattox. Chris figured it was the ambulance driver.

"It doesn't matter," the passenger said. "I've already called for backup.

"You did what?" The flashlight jerked up, washing the man's face in light again. Chris squinted to see, but all he could make out was the cone of the hand-held light.

"We're going to sweep the area."

"We're dead if the general finds out."

"We're dead if we lose the subject."

Chris frowned in thought, futilely straining to see anything but multicolored after-images of light. What would the military want with him? He'd never done anything even remotely interesting in his life except fight fires, but there must be a million firefighters in the world.

"I'm not taking the blame for this," Mattox said. "It was you and your damned cigarette."

"You're worried about blame?" the passenger asked. "Don't be an idiot. A team is on the way. We'll find this shit-head and get him back to the site."

"You'd best be willing to bet your life it blows over the way you say it will," Mattox said.

Chris watched the pair walk away, using the fading light of the flashlight to judge their distance. Then he gave a slow count of 50. He wasn't sure where their back up was coming from, but he didn't plan on waiting long enough to find out.

He shuffled around and slid back out of the bush. He paid a high price in terms of scrapes and scratches, but he started rushing through the woods as soon as he unfolded himself from his hiding place. He counted a hundred trees before he shifted his path to take him back to the road to his left and toward the warehouse he'd seen before hiding. The road was empty, so if he noticed a set of headlights, he'd have time to hide in the woods.

Luckily, no cars came as he began to cautiously approach the warehouse. From a distance, he could see barred windows through which shadows passed by, indicating someone was inside. Not sure of where he was, Chris didn't want to call out for help. The structure was nearly three times as long as it was wide. Chris counted three floors. Oddly enough, the gray-brick building only had a few doors. He didn't see any signs, but a high fence made the building feel unwelcoming. Chris didn't exactly have a list of better options.

The fence had an open gate, which allowed Chris to sneak next to and around the building, hoping that he'd run into someone who could help. He feared running into more people who probably wanted to dissect him. The long side closest to Chris had a single open metal door with a small, square window. Chris noticed an electronic key lock, like that of a hotel room, beside the door. He couldn't see very far into the room. He took a deep breath and stepped inside.

He followed the wall until he found a light switch. As the lights blinked on, Chris stared in horror. It was a slaughter house. Slender chains covered in thick, red liquid dangled down from a ceiling about twenty feet high. Chris turned to run, only to see the door slam shut. He only caught a glimpse of the man at the door, but Chris was certain it was Mattox.

Chris felt his feet fly out from under him. For an instant, he feared the chains had come alive. Small, sharp points bit all over his body. Doubled over, he realized he was in some sort of a net made of thin wire, perhaps barbed wire judging from the amount of pain he felt.

"Subject secured," a reedy voice said over a loud speaker. *Doc?*

Chris heard a whooshing sound before he saw a white gas fill the room. A part of his mind knew not to struggle, but as the gas rose to fill his lungs, he couldn't help but fight to find some way out. Chris felt as if he were being skinned alive as he tried to grab the net and pull himself up.

The white gas filled his lungs when he opened his mouth to scream, in pain, in terror. It didn't matter. The sound never formed as darkness took him.

"Chris!"

He jolted awake at the sound of his name. He was still kicking and thrashing, trying to fight out of the net he could have sworn held him. Instead of hard steel and sharp, metal barbs, he was on a comfortable, black, faux-leather-upholstered futon.

Chris screamed as he leapt off the couch and spun around. The memories were already fading. Dr. Strickland gripped his shoulders.

"Chris," he said. "You're okay. You're safe. I need you to calm yourself."

Chris's eyes darted around. He was clearly in the shrink's office. The diplomas and degrees hung just where Chris remembered them, behind the cedar desk, just above where the doc's head would be if he were sitting down in his brown, leather office chair.

Chris turned to look out the window, but it was boarded up. His limbs stung as he shifted around. He inspected his arms and saw bandages everywhere. He must have looked like some kind of B-rate mummy.

He felt his head. His hair was still too short. That damn finger-length scar was still just at the back of his skull.

"Chris," Dr. Strickland said again, his voice calm and soothing. "You need to calm down."

The comment was pointless. Chris was already regulating his breathing. So long as there wasn't any fire around, he could handle just about any other situation.

"Good," the doctor said. "What do you remember?"

Chris didn't answer right away. He took a moment to look around some more and sat on the futon.

"The worst thing about these damn night terrors is how real they always feel," Chris said. "I can't tell you what I remember because I don't trust my own memories. Is this real? Are you here?"

"Do you remember the procedure?" Strickland asked, taking a moment to hitch his oversized white lab coat around himself more properly and press his glasses back up his nose.

"Procedure?"

Bright lights over his head. Someone injecting him with a needle. A scream. Someone attacking him in a cab.

Chris shook the flashes out of his mind. "Everything's fuzzy."

"You've been in treatment for three days, Chris," the doctor explained. He moved around his desk and sat down in the chair. "You volunteered for an experimental, outpatient surgery that's designed to reduce the output of your brain patterns and your night terrors."

Chris let out a burst of air. "Well that plan sucked."

The doc held up a hand. "We expected there to be a spike in activity. We can't eliminate the dreams entirely until you address the core problems in your psyche. That means facing your nightmares."

A world of ash. A man on fire. An ambulance in the middle of the night.

"I heard you," Chris said, feeling uncertain. "I could have sworn you were in…" he paused. "Was it a dream?"

"All of your dreams are simply reflections of yourself, Chris," the doc said, flashing a gentle smile. The gray streak in his brown hair made him seem more fatherly in Chris's opinion. "I expect you to recognize me and my staff. Your psyche will produce several avatars of yourself with which to interact. Tell me. Have you seen anyone else?"

Chris closed his eyes. "A pair of soldiers."

"What about a young girl? A teenager? She may look like a child to you."

Chris's eyes popped open. "A kid?" he asked. "Why would I see a kid?"

The doctor looked away suddenly. "Like I said, you're mind is going to create different representatives of your own emotions and thoughts. A little girl would be just as likely as an old man. Race and color have no meaning either."

He stood up and walked around his desk. He leaned on the front edge of it. As he moved, an ID card fell out of his pocket and dangled on a lanyard from his neck. The doc tisked and shoved the card back in his coat pocket.

"Everyone you encounter is simply a reflection of you. Sometimes, your subconscious mind uses faces of people you've recently seen. You've seen me at least twice a day for the past three days, so I'll naturally be given a role in your mind's depiction of reality. You have to remember it's not real."

"It always feels real, Doc," Chris said.

"I know," Strickland said smiling again. "It's not my goal to punish you or cause you pain, but if you want to end these dreams, you must face them. If you do, you'll find out more about yourself than you could imagine."

"I just want the damn dreams to stop. I just want to sleep without waking up somewhere I don't recognize."

Chris looked down at his arms again. The bandages were damp and spotted with blood.

Strickland grimaced. "Yes," he said, pointing at the plywood-sealed window. "It seems you felt as if you'd caught fire. You tried to leap out of my office. My staff orderlies managed to stop you before you jumped. We're on the third floor."

Chris looked at the window as the doctor explained. "While they were able to stop you, you still managed to roll around in some glass. We had to put you under to remove a few of the more embedded bits of debris. You're going to be very sore for a while."

"How long until the procedure takes effect?" Chris asked.

The doc gave a noncommittal shrug. "That depends entirely on you," he explained, "but nothing will stop until you find the other parts of your psyche. You're not looking for brief appearances, but rather, people whom you see more and more with each dream. If you see someone like that, if someone approaches you and tries to help, that'll be an avatar. You'll have to help the individual. Try to remember everything you can when you wake. Do you have your journal?"

"My journal?" he asked.

Dr. Strickland pointed under the futon. Chris gingerly got down and looked under the sofa. A small, brown-leather book lie flopped open near the wall. Chris reached out a long arm and snatched the book. He noticed a few scribbled notes in his own handwriting. Reading the entries brought a precious few memories back.

"My dream journal," Chris said, flipping through the few pages on which he'd written.

"If you keep that, it'll help with our sessions, and I can advise you on what to do next," Strickland said. He looked excited for some reason. His arms were folded, but his index finger tapped his elbow. Chris wasn't sure the doc was even aware of his own movements.

The door to the office banged open, and an orderly brought in a tray of food. It smelled of steak and mashed potatoes. He saw a mountain of fruit, and a metal pitcher beaded with sweat. His stomach growled.

He looked up at the orderly, jumped to his feet, and backed away. *It's him!*

"Mattox!" Chris shouted as he prepared to dart out of the office.

"Chris, what's wrong?" Strickland asked.

"That's the guy who chased me in the woods!" Chris said, pointing at the man with a narrow, sharp face and a hooked nose. It was dark, and the flashlight played hell with his eyes, but Chris knew what he saw.

"Chris," the doctor said. "Mr. Mattox is just an orderly. He's interning here at the institute for the summer. He's watched over you for a few sleep cycles now. I promise you, he wouldn't know a soldier from a mall cop."

Chris might have imagined it, but it looked like Mattox glared at the doctor as he made his joke. *Solider or not, he didn't like hearing that.*

"It's alright," Mattox said in that same nasally voice. "I had a bout with night terrors myself when I was a kid. I won't take it personal. I'm just here to take care of you. Doc here said you'd be hungry."

Chris's stomach gave another demanding growl. He felt like he hadn't eaten for months.

"That's some awfully nice food for a hospital," Chris said.

"It's mine," the doctor explained. "At least, it's from my personal kitchen. Considering the amount of work your doing to get through this issue, I don't mind sharing. Unless, of course, you'd prefer your regular hospital meal?

"No," Chris said, wanting to leap at the steel tray. "No, I could use a good meal." *Did I really just dream it all? Has it only been a few days?*

He simply couldn't get his mind to form any memories.

"If you're calm, I can leave you alone to eat, then return to take you back to your room," the doctor said.

"You're just gonna leave me here?"

"You're wearing a hospital gown," Strickland replied. "You're not a prisoner here, Chris. The procedure really had that much of an effect on your memory?"

Chris looked down at the flower-patterned outfit. *It's the same as the dream. Was it really a dream?*

"Did you want to eat?" the doc asked.

Chris nodded his head, and Strickland nodded back. The gesture caused those square-framed glasses of his to slide back down his sharp nose.

"So I'll leave you to eat," he said. "Mr. Mattox, we have other patients to see to." The orderly stepped out of the room. "I'll return to take you back to your room when you're finished. Take your time. You've earned a good meal."

"Thanks, Doc," Chis said already digging in. The food was amazing.

"I'm only too happy to help," the doctor replied as he shut the door.

Chapter 13

TOGETHER

Sal bolted to his feet. He jerked his head around until he saw the girl looking out of the mud hut they were in through a roughly door-shaped hole in the wall. She looked like she did the first time he saw her. She wore a nondescript t-shirt with some faded jeans and a pair of sneakers.

Most importantly, she was alive. Sal snatched his arm away before he could reach out to her. He looked at the dirt-covered fatigues he wore and let out a sigh of relief when he failed to see a weapon. He didn't belong in a uniform, and the last time he had a weapon...

A boy's head exploding. Bodies all around. Blood everywhere.

I did something terrible, Sal thought. *I left. I wanted to get kicked out.* The thought didn't change what he wore, and his mind couldn't seem to pull up the memory of what he did and why it hurt him so much.

The door let in a rectangle of white light, as did a miss-formed square to Sal's right. A few rolled-up blankets sat between a set of bright, color-ful pillows. A red curtain separated the room he was in from whatever was beyond. It felt familiar to Sal, but his mind resisted any attempts to understand why. None of that mattered.

How is she still alive? Everyone else died.

He felt as if there was some sort of timer ticking away in his mind. *The longer she's with me, the more danger she's in.*

"Hi," she said, without turning to look at him. Her long, raven black hair shone in the soft light from the door.

"Kaitlyn," Sal said, walking to the door. He meant to leave, but his feet froze when he reached the exit. Staring out at the whiteness gave him a sense of dread. Something horrible was out there.

"I have to get out of here," Sal said.

"You don't like it in here," Kaitlyn said.

"That's putting it mildly," he said. He moved to the window and experienced the same surge of fear. He looked back at her. *Better I die than she does.*

He made his way toward the door, but the mud wall sealed itself in front of him.

"No..." he whispered. He turned and dashed toward the square window. He saw it start to change shape even as he leapt toward it. He slammed into solid, dry mud and dropped onto the floor.

Ignoring protesting bones and sore muscles, he scrambled to his feet.

"What's wrong?" Kaitlyn asked. Her dark hair flipped over her shoulders as she spun her head to find an exit.

"We're trapped," he said, moving to the red curtain. He yanked it away only to find a solid mud wall. Whatever was beyond the curtain had been sealed away.

She moved toward a corner of the room, and Sal surprised himself by rushing between her and her destination, horrified at the idea of her going near that spot.

"I won't move if you don't want me to," she said. "You don't have to worry about me so much. I'm safe with you."

It was the worst thing she could have said.

"No one is safe around me," he said. "Just stay in the middle of the room."

Her breathing started to quicken, and her eyes darted around. "What's wrong?" she asked again.

"I told you; we're trapped," he said.

"Where did it go?" she asked pointing to where the door used to be.

The walls started to close in. The once hard sand seemed to flake and pour in on itself. The wave of dirt grew larger and faster. Sal shimmied toward the center of the room. The room wasn't going to let him run. He was going to have to watch another person, another child, die.

As the room shrank, Kaitlyn's breathing grew more rapid. She was hyperventilating. Sal took a knee in front of her.

"I'm sorry," he said.

"I...don't...understand..." she managed to say. "Why?"

"It's my fault," he said. "Everyone around me dies."

She couldn't force enough air in her lungs to speak. Sal felt the sand fall around his boot. He looked to see how much space there was and found a gun strapped to his right leg.

I know what I have to do.

"Kaitlyn," he whispered. "Kaitlyn, you're going to be okay."

She gasped several times. He smiled at her. "Breathe.....calm down. You're going to be safe. Try," he said. "Deep breath....good."

He watched her take a few more slow breaths as the sand started to pile around his legs. Sal unholstered the gun. The teen's hazel eyes widened at the sight of the pistol.

"What are you going to do?" she asked.

"Don't worry," he said. "You'll be safe once I'm gone."

He took a breath, closed his eyes, and pressed the barrel to his temple. He started to pull the trigger.

"Please don't."

It was only a whisper, but Sal felt a wave of fear and sadness wash over him as a small hand grabbed his. He instinctively moved his finger off the trigger as Kaitlyn lifted his hand and the gun toward the ceiling. He opened his eyes.

The room was back to normal. The door was open. Everything had reset for some reason.

Their gazes met, and Sal realized what he thought was a stoic expression was little more than a mask. Her face and eyes didn't betray any emotion, but she was devastated. She was lonely and scared, and if she let out a single tear, she might never stop crying.

"Please," she said.

"I don't want you to die," Sal replied.

"Then protect me."

The gun disappeared from his hand, and he used the phenomena as an excuse to turn from those multi-hued eyes that seemed to know much more than a girl her age should.

"I can't."

Her silence forced him to look back at her. That still, porcelain face didn't show any emotion, but he could swear he felt her fear. More surprisingly, he felt her faith in him. *How am I doing this?*

"I don't want to be alone," she said.

"Is being near me worth your life?" he asked.

"Yes," she replied without hesitation.

He stared at her dumbly. He couldn't form any sort of response.

"Why?" he finally asked.

"Because you'd rather die than see me hurt," she answered.

Why did the gun vanish? Why did the room stop shrinking?

"I can't," he said, remembering failure after failure.

"Maybe not," she said, "but can you please just try?"

I want to!

"I'm dangerous. This place is dangerous."

"I don't think this place is real," Kaitlyn said, her brow furrowing in thought.

"What makes you say that?" Sal asked. His eyes drifted to the brightness beyond the rectangular entry to the hut. Again, he felt something tell him they were both far safer inside.

She was about to answer when they heard a scream. They both looked in the direction of the doorway. Sal felt the urge go see who had cried out, but he froze when he noticed Kaitlin staring at the door. *I can't leave her.*

"Someone's out there," she said.

Sal glanced from her back to the door. Then the room around them started to fade.

"Kaitlyn!" he shouted, reaching out to her.

His hand grabbed hers, and he pulled her to him just as a stream of blades zipped into the spot in which she had previously stood. The chamber was a mad house. Everywhere he looked was a different tableau of grim mutilation. Over it all, an old man hung by his wrists from a beam. He let out a high-pitched squeal.

Sal held Kaitlyn's face to his shoulder as he scurried away, unsure of where those blades had come from. He hid her face because no human being, let alone a teenage girl, should see the nightmare unfolding in the chamber.

The room was too big to be real. He couldn't even see walls, just darkness and shadows surrounding them. The man hanging above the scene screamed again. Below was a human butcher shop. Skinned corpses hung from enormous hooks. Their blood dripped into tin gutters that ran like rivers into an ocean of gore just under the spindly prisoner. Men of all descriptions murdered row upon row of women. Each man looked distinctly different, but the women all had straight black hair and sharp faces. They weren't the same woman, but they could all be sisters if it was possible to have that many siblings. A memory scratched at Sal's mind, but the scene in front of him was too powerful to put aside.

One man scalped his victim. Another drowned a woman in a tub that appeared just as the man grabbed her. Another man was skinning...

...Sal turned away. He brought his eyes back to the older man hanging above it all. The man was at least 60, if not 70 years old. He looked so frail. A frame that was just short of emaciated was visible under the shreds of what looked like something that used to be an orange prison jump suite. The outfit was so tattered, it was just one thread away from being immodest. Curls of white hair fell over the man's eyes, but Sal had no doubt the old man could see everything that went on below.

"He must be horrified," Sal whispered.

"I'm not sure," Kaitlyn replied. She'd pulled herself away from Sal and diverted her eyes to the man, but Sal could only describe the look she gave the old man as confused.

"How could you be sure what he feels?"

Kaitlyn looked away again.

Soldiers, all dressed in combat uniforms and body kits, appeared like ghosts from everywhere. The women being slaughtered all disappeared, as did their murderers. Sal swallowed a surge of fear. He braced himself to run, but discovered he'd somehow moved to the center of the room, or maybe the room had shifted around him. Whatever happened, he moved, but Kaitlyn didn't.

The soldiers weren't attacking. They were cutting him off. The old man vanished from his bonds above, then reappeared in a guillotine. Sal noticed the pitch of the old man's scream shift. It sounded like a man living his worst fear.

Instinct forced Sal to search out Kaitlyn. He saw her running from the very same minotaur he'd originally found her with. It was attacking her, and Sal was too far away to do anything, and even if he rushed to help either person, the soldiers were standing guard between him and the people he wanted to protect. *They're both going to die. She saved me, and now she'll die for it.*

Kaitlyn rushed away from the minotaur only to skid to a halt as what appeared to be a skinned human being burst from the floor and reached out to her. Her eyes widened in horror, but no sound escaped her.

I'm tired of people dying around me.

He remembered first meeting Kaitlyn. *"You're going to save me,"* she had said.

I'm tired of failing.

The old prisoner continued to fight to escape the guillotine as a group of women, all looking just like those who only moments ago were being murdered, appeared in chairs as if to watch the event.

You're not a hero, a voice, probably that of the father he never met, had said. *You'll never be like me.*

Maybe I'm not a hero, Sal thought, *but as God is my witness, I'll never just run or watch someone die again!*

The guillotine started its descent. The old man strained to push himself away. The bull mutant somehow snatched Kaitlyn. Sal wanted to save them. Dear God, he just wanted to save people!

"No!" His voice was impossibly loud. It rang through the endless room as if it were as small as a closet. At his word, everything froze. Something inside him shattered. It felt as if he'd been living behind a barrier his whole life, and he'd just burst through it. He wanted everything to stop, and it did. He felt his face grow harder. Nothing was ever going to hurt anyone again. Not as long as he was there to stop it, and he could stop it. He knew it with a certainty that defied reason.

The push he sent from his mind felt like a gentle exhalation to him. He felt as if he were stretching from a long night's sleep. He saw the grotesque bull hybrid in his mind flying helplessly from Kaitlyn. He formed the thought, and the creature flew away as if pulled by an unseen rope. Kaitlyn hung in the air and gently drifted to the ground. Sal was about to get rid of the skinned man at her feet, but the wretch faded just as Kaitlyn's shoes touched the ground.

The soldiers surrounding Sal rushed him. "This is over," Sal whispered. He stood. His mind had somehow connected to everything. He could see Kaitlyn, hear her thoughts, and feel her feelings. The soldiers were there, but not real. Each aspect around him was from some nightmare, probably his own. The old man was real, but he wasn't as vibrant in Sal's mind as Kaitlyn—he was there, but clouded.

It didn't matter. Sal's mind was the center of an elaborate spiderweb, and all he needed to do to make something happen was to pull on the right thread. Sal focused on the guillotine. The blade pulled itself from the mechanism.

The rest of the guillotine exploded away from the old man. It was reduced to splinters, but the would-be-victim didn't have so much as a scratch. It happened that way because Sal's mind saw it happen that way. The women seated in front of the old man all ran in terror. Sal didn't blame them, he must look horrifying. The guillotine zipped off as if it wanted to be certain it didn't harm the old man. Every event happened faster than a blink.

Stay down! Sal sent the thought to Kaitlyn and the old man. They both lay down. Speaking to the others with his mind was different from moving things, but, somehow, Sal knew the skills were related. He wondered for a moment if there was anything he couldn't do.

To start, Sal pictured the large guillotine blade spinning, and it spun. He looked from the blade to the soldiers surrounding him. Where Sal looked, the blade zipped through flesh, muscle, and bone.

Sal didn't see two soldiers behind him come closer. He simply knew where they were. He could understand Kaitlyn's surge of fear and hear her mental shout that the soldiers meant to attack. Sal didn't bother to look behind himself. He saw through her eyes, and mentally ordered the blade to decapitate one soldier as Sal used his newfound power to toss the second up and onto one of the large hooks that seemed to magically hang in the air.

Sal couldn't read the soldiers or see them with his mind. He understood why as well. The soldiers were a dream. They weren't real. Sal could have simply ordered them to cease to exist, but that wouldn't be nearly as satisfying.

Part of what he did resulted from the certainty that he was in a dream. He had read once that when a man knew he was dreaming, if he was strong enough, he controlled that dream. Sal just wished he could remember where the hell he'd read that book. He wished he could remember the name of the book. *Why can't I remember anything clearly?*

The telekinesis was only a portion of what Sal did. He opened his mind and stretched. The rifle in one soldier's hand suddenly veered away to point at the rest of the soldiers. The rifle's selector lever toggled from semi, to fully automatic at Sal's mental order.

The soldier let the rifle go, but it didn't fall. Sal didn't want it to. He wanted it to fire, and it did. Every single bullet plowed through a soldier. Sal reached out, using that mental spiderweb connecting him to everything around him. He meant to pull the bullets back, to call them to zip around again and again, but he felt himself drop to a knee. Ordering that much with his mind felt like trying to lift a car with his bare hands. A part of Sal realized that he *could* order everything. He could control a million different things a million different ways...in time, but he wasn't strong enough yet. Strong wasn't the right word. The part of Sal's mind that said what he was doing should be impossible created some sort of block.

The rifle fell to the ground, and the last soldier standing pulled out a pistol and fired at him. Sal forced himself to focus. He felt the web in his mind flicker, then solidify. That web extending from his mind reached out to the bullet as it approached from the soldier's pistol. Sal opened his eyes, and the bullet stopped inches from his face.

Sal shouted in rage, and the bullet obeyed his command, zipping away from him and through the throat of the soldier who had originally fired it. The soldier fell to his knees gurgling. Blood spurted from his throat as he tried to shout. Sal looked at the dying bastard. The walking nightmare that had tried to hurt those he had decided to protect. Sal thought, and the man was ripped apart by an unseen force. What remained of the soldier fell to the ground in a spray of blood.

Sal stood at the center of the room. *Did I really just do all this with my mind? It had to be because I was dreaming.*

A dream that's real isn't less real because it's a dream, someone said in Sal's mind.

"That voice!" Sal said. It was the same voice that had spoken in his mind earlier. It was the voice that told him Kaitlyn was real.

Kaitlyn!

"I'm in here!"

Sal turned to the sound of her voice. She was in some sort of dome. It was pitch black, but he could hear her through it. Somewhere in the back of Sal's mind, he knew what he did would be horrific, so he'd unconsciously shielded her, and, however he made the dome, he shaded it so she wouldn't see the gruesome event.

Again Sal pushed with his mind. The gore, blood, bones and bodies slid around the nightmare setting of hooks and tables, and faded away. Sal let the shield go, trying to work out how he'd made the dome in the first place.

"He wants me."

Sal spun to look at the old man, who huddled on the ground hugging his knees.

"Did you? Were you the one who spoke to me in my mind?" Sal asked. "Are you real?"

Sal knew the answer. Something was odd about the man, but he was real.

"I'm a dream in the real world," the old man said. "I'm real if you dream of me, but I see you, and the little one. What I see as real is, so I must be real."

Sal's mind spun trying to understand the old man. Sal walked over to him.

"We're as real as we think we are," the geezer said. "I'm more real though because this is my thought and not yours. I'm real, but He wants me. He wants to think my thoughts and make me do what I want, but only when He wants me to."

"Who? Who's He?" Sal asked. Whatever the hell the old man was ranting about, Sal could make out that someone was after the loon. He knew that much based on what the geezer said and thought. Those thoughts were in far shorter supply than the words.

The man gave a green-eyed glare that was so harsh Sal nearly moved back a pace. The look hardened, then faded back to a wandering gaze.

"Oh, He wants me and my thoughts," the man said. *I'm Caden,* his thoughts said. *I'm Caden, and I see you.* The mental projection of Caden's voice had an eerie sing-song pattern.

Sal could only stare. His hand froze outstretched, and the old man took it. Sal grimaced at the power of the old coot's grip as Sal helped him up.

You're Caden? Sal directed the thought at Caden, and the man nodded.

"He wants me and my thoughts," Caden said again, "but you, you He wants to own most of all."

Chapter 14

A FRIGHTENING POWER

Sal stood beside the rambling Caden, who was sitting on a blood-stained table that was covered in knives. He huddled against himself in that tattered prison outfit. The man seemed careless about getting cut. His disheveled white hair only added to his wild appearance.

Kaitlyn looked around. She had to have some idea of what Sal had just done. He'd moved all the blood and gore. He even moved the bodies that had previously decorated the large hooks above them, but they were still in a human butcher farm. The hooks swung in a wind Sal couldn't feel, and the chains for those hooks clinked together. Whatever objects of torture and murder Sal hadn't used in his onslaught, still laid on their respective tables or slabs.

Some of the details of the room seemed to fade in and out like bad reception on a television set. One of the tables covered with knives seemed to disappear if Sal didn't look at it, but as soon as he tried to forget it entirely, it reappeared.

Just as he began to feel the full weight of the past few minutes, *had it only been a few minutes,* Kaitlyn rushed to his side. A part of his mind sensed her emotions. They seemed to be rolled tightly into a ball, but he knew she worried for him.

He was still fighting the impulse to run. He looked down and realized he was holding her head against him more than simply holding her close. *I'm still waiting for her head to explode.*

Sal quickly pushed the thought away, briefly worried that imagining the event would cause it.

"I don't think I've actually introduced myself," he said, forcing his hand to hang loosely at his side. "Name's Sal."

"Hey," she said.

"That's Caden," Sal said, pointing at the older man.

Caden raised a few fingers in the air. It might have been a wave. He might have been shooing an imaginary fly away. His fidgeting caused the table he was on to wobble. He kept muttering under his breath. Sal couldn't understand half of what he managed to hear.

"Caden," Sal said. "This is…"

"Kaitlyn," the man said pointing a gnarled finger. "Her name is the mother's, mother's name."

Sal frowned.

"I was named after my grandmother," Kaitlyn explained. *Right,* Sal thought. *He reads minds.*

"Too loud," Caden muttered, covering his ears. "You don't have to shout to hear yourself."

"Do you and your grandmother have a lot in common?" Sal asked Kaitlyn. He looked at one of the other tables, and mentally flipped the knives out of sight before taking a seat. He made sure his spot at least looked more sturdy than Caden's.

Kaitlyn opted to stand next to him. "I never met her." The girl had an odd monotone to her voice. Everything about her seemed too even. "It's just me and my stepdad now."

"It's not fair to dream happy dreams only to wake in sad realities," Caden said, looking at Kaitlyn. "Some of us remember angels who sing songs and protect us. Others remember demons who didn't like unclean things. Dreams are great for those who live in them. They're all the more terrible for those who wake to nightmares."

Sal looked around at the scene. Wherever they were, it was still too large and ominous. Everything seemed to spring from or hang in darkness. Even the beam Caden hung on when Sal first saw him didn't seem to suspended from anything. It simply floated in the air. Caden was forced to watch such horrible things. *What could be worse than this?* Sal wondered.

"Phthonos can want all he wants, but he'll never find trust," Caden said, shaking a finger at Sal. The table groaned in protest against Caden's constant fidgeting. "Stop looking for your lover's lovers in my bed!"

The whisper-quiet thoughts that were drifting from Caden's mind cut off completely.

"It's a collection of nightmares and broken toys," Caden said pointing at his temple, "but it's my collection."

"You're right," Sal said. "I'm sorry. I'll try not to do it."

He looked down at Kaitlyn and smiled. He was afraid he had become a monster. He feared that what he'd done would make her sick or a hate him. Somehow, he could sense that all she felt for him was concern and appreciation.

"You've been able to do it this whole time?" he asked. Her hazel eyes drifted away from his, but her shrug answered the question.

"Not until the first time I saw you," she said. Sal remembered turning his back on her.

"It's okay," she said. "I get it now. You were always afraid for me. You were always trying to help."

"I was trying to avoid feeling responsible," Sal said.

She looked up at him through locks of black hair. "You're trying now," she said. "You stopped..." She trailed off. Her eyes lowered. The silence didn't stop her memories from drifting into Sal's mind. She didn't see anything, but she'd heard it.

Sal stood. He'd done horrible things. He may have kept her from seeing it, but he'd still done it all.

"They weren't real. I can—" she paused. Her multi-hued eyes squinted as she thought about the word she wanted. "I can see you. I can sort of see Caden."

"Sometimes we know things are there because of what happens around them," Caden said. The table shook again and Caden nearly fell. He managed to stumble off the table and onto his feet. He glared at the table as if it had intentionally tried to shove him off.

"I don't like you anymore," he told the table. It vanished, and he sat down and crossed his legs.

"How'd you do that?" Sal asked.

"The dreams obey if we remember we're the masters," Caden said.

"Is that why we can do these things?" Sal asked.

Caden shook his head far more quickly than necessary. "Dreams are silly, but they let reality in." His lips pouted out in thought. Sal noticed the older man's mouth was covered in odd circular scars. "Or maybe the dreams leak out? Whether reality slips or dreams escape, what we can be is always related to what we think we can be. The table isn't real. I just remembered."

Sal looked from Caden to Kaitlyn, who shrugged. *She doesn't know what he means any more than I do.*

"I don't think the people here are real because I couldn't sense them," she said. "Could you?"

Sal shook his head. *What if I wake up and none of this is real? What if I wake up and I can't find her? Will she think I've left her again? What if...*

"You don't have to be afraid," she said. "I know you won't abandon me."

He smiled at her and cleared his throat to give his best Yoda impression. "And scared, you must not be! Brave are you."

"Star Wars was stupid," she said, rolling her eyes. Her expressionless face made the gesture feel even more drastic.

"Did you watch all six movies?" He cleared his throat when he realized he'd asked that question in his Yoda voice.

"Why should I? The first three sucked."

"One is four, and four is one, but no one likes the four that's one," Caden said, rolling back and forth on his butt. He gave a chuckle. "They don't like four as one because it's dumb. Dumb. Dumb. Dumb. Dumb.

Dumb-dumb." His ramblings matched the ever-popular them to the saga's villain.

"See," Kaitlyn said, "even he agrees."

Sal switched to his Mickey Mouse. "But you still won't be scared will ya?"

She stared at him for quite a while. "I'm 13...not 3."

"Tough room," Sal muttered running a hand through his dark hair. He only wanted to make her laugh.

"Don't be disappointed," she said. "I don't laugh."

"I'm not."

She stared at him again. "I can sense emotions."

"Okay," Sal admitted, switching to his Goofy. Everyone said Goofy was his best. "We'll just have to find something funny."

Caden cackled. The laughter shifted from mirth to hysteria. "I like when people pretend," he said.

Sal glanced at him and smiled. "At least I can make him laugh."

"That was actually funny," she said as if reading instructions on nuclear fission. "I didn't say I don't think things are funny. I just don't laugh."

"That's as obvious as a muddy elephant in a snow storm," Sal said.

"How many voices do you have?" she asked. He didn't realize he'd used his Barney Fife until she asked her question.

"I don't know," Sal said trying to remember. "I just sort of pick them up as I go. My friends would ask me to do another, and I'd figure it out. What about you? What do you and your stepdad do for fun? Where are you even from?"

"Me and my stepdad live in New York, but we travel a lot. He's a psychiatrist. He's an expert in a lot of things. Mostly, he just tries to help me."

"With what?" he asked.

"Dangerous," Caden muttered. "Most demons only come when called. Talk about them long enough, and they'll think you're calling."

"Demons?" Sal asked.

"Demons," Caden said, peeking through curly strands of bleach-white hair. "They come when you close your eyes."

"You mean nightmares?" Sal asked.

"They're actually called Night Terrors," Kaitlyn said. "They're like dreams that force you to act out things. Scary things."

"And who made you the expert?" Sal said. He used his Abbott voice and waggled a finger.

"My stepdad," she replied. "He's sort of a genius, I guess. He's actually the expert, but because I have them, he lets me read about them."

"What ever happened to Repunzel or Rumpelstiltskin?"

"One traded her hair for love," Caden said. "The other lost everything because they learned his name. Names are power. Don't take my power. I worked hard to be me. Please don't make me not me."

Sal walked over to him. "No one is going to hurt you, Caden," Sal said, taking a knee in front of him.

As slowly as Sal moved, Caden still scooted back from him like a scared animal. "They always say it won't hurt," he said. "It always does."

"Whatever this was, it's over now," Sal told Caden. He waved a hand around the scene. The hooks still clanked along their large chains that seemed to hang from mid air. The tables and slabs still faded and popped back into existence without any observable cause.

"We're dreaming now, I think," Kaitlyn said.

"Why don't we wake up?" Sal asked.

"People who have night terrors stay asleep through a lot," she said. "We can sit up, walk and even act things out."

Sal nodded. His memories still seemed full of holes, but he could remember waking up in a corner, screaming. He couldn't remember where he was when it happened. He couldn't remember any details about the dream either, but he remembered the fear. He remembered crying out for help. It was like only fragments of the memory would come to him.

"I think you're at least right about us all having night terrors. You learned all that from your stepdad?" he asked.

She nodded her head.

"What's his name?"

"False!" Caden shouted. It sounded even louder because of how quiet he had been. "False! They lie to find the truth. It shouldn't work but it does. They lied!"

He vanished and reappeared back on the beam on which Sal had first found him. Sal mentally tore the ropes away from Caden's wrists and pulled him free. The bone-thin, old man wailed and kicked the whole way down.

"Caden!" Sal shouted. "What's wrong?"

"Their lies hurt me," Caden answered, slinking down to his knees in front of Sal. "They hurt me."

It was nearly impossible to sense anything from Caden. If Sal relied only on his new power, he'd say Caden felt cool. The man wept, but Sal couldn't feel his sadness.

Sal slowly raised a hand toward Caden and set it on the man's shoulder. The old coot looked as frail as a twig. Kaitlyn moved over to stand beside them. "Who hurt you? The ones you hear in your mind?" Sal asked.

"They're not my thoughts! I hear them and think them, but they're not mine, and I don't want them!" Caden used gnarled fingers to thump his temples. It looked like he was trying to jar something loose. If the daft old man hit himself any harder, something might actually fall out.

"I know," Sal said. He gently grabbed Caden's hands. A glare from the man caused Sal to let go, but he still offered a smile. "I won't let anything happen to you."

"You say you'll punch a mountain and make it break," Caden said. "You say you're strong, but strength is a relative measurement. What happens when a man who can break mountains faces the world?"

Trying to talk to the man was like learning rocket science through humorous riddles. *What did the plane say to the air resistance? Man, you're a real drag. Hardy-har-har.* "I don't know anything about mountains or the world. I have no clue how strong I am."

"You can do more," Kaitlyn broke in. "I can sense your feelings. I can sort of sense his," she pointed at Caden, still wary of what he might do. Sal couldn't blame her. Whatever had been done, whoever had done it, drove Caden insane.

"You already know he can read minds. He can also talk with his mind." Was telepath the right word? It was the only one Sal could think to describe it. *What the hell does that make me?*

"You're at a movie, and you've just realized you can do all the things the actors can, only it's real." Caden rocked on his knees some more. Those green eyes focused again, only for a second, but their sharpness cut at him. "You're at a dance and realize you can step however they step, but that doesn't make you graceful." He finished that last comment looking at Sal.

"Maybe I just...I don't know...learned faster," Sal said. "Besides, I'll wake up, and it won't matter. We all will."

"Dreams when his eyes are open and thinks the world is different just because his eyes are closed," Caden said. Whatever the man meant, he said it the way someone would talk about a child who refused to learn not to touch a hot stove.

"I don't think either of us can do more," Kaitlyn said. "At least, I don't know how you do what you do. I've been able to..." she glanced at the floor. "I've been able to do this for a while. Like I said, since I first saw you. I can do it here, and I know we're all dreaming, but I can always do it. Sleeping or awake."

She ran a hand down her long, black hair. She touched her t-shirt and jeans. Maybe she was checking to be sure it was there. She seemed to notice her appearance changed sometimes, especially her hair. In this dream it was long, but Sal had seen both his own and Kaitlyn's hair shaved away. Sal reached to the back of his head. He thought he remembered feeling a scar there once, but it had faded. Maybe it was never there.

"Sleeping or awake, we dream," Caden sang. "You, her, me, and the Arsonophobe."

"What did he say?" Kaitlyn asked.

"Something about arson," Sal replied. He smiled gently at Caden, helping the man to his feet.

"There were lots. Now, there's just us," the old man said looking at Sal with a vague expression. "From many, to few, to four we dwindle, but one hasn't learn he's special. Maybe he's not. Lights shouldn't stand next to stars just to seem brighter."

Sal thought for a moment. From many, to few, to four. "Can you sense any other feelings?" he asked Kaitlyn.

She shook her head.

Sal closed his eyes. He wasn't sure what was real or a dream anymore. In this dream, real or not, he had these powers, and he'd be damned before he refused to use them. He didn't so much think about what part of his mind did what. He knew each of his newfound abilities were different the way people know their pinky from their ring finger, and he used those parts of his mind the same way those people used their fingers.

He stretched out. There were other figures out there. Forms of energy that had no feelings. Those had to be figments from a dream or nightmare. He stretched further. He began to feel tired, like he'd just gone on a nice long run.

He nearly gave up when he found something. It was a form of energy, but that form felt panic. It felt a fear that Sal thought would give him a heart attack. *We're coming!* Sal sent with his mind. *Don't be afraid. You're not alone. We're coming to help you.*

He opened his eyes. Damn he felt tired. He took a few breaths.

"Just learned to crawl and he wants to fly," Caden muttered. He had silliest grin Sal had ever seen.

Sal looked at Kaitlyn and gave his best Sherlock Holmes impression. "Eureka!"

"You found someone?" Kaitlyn asked. He could feel her shock and amazement. It was hard not to just respond before she even spoke.

"That I did, Watson," Sal replied in his same accent. "The game is afoot!" He knew it was pointless trying to hide his fear from her. He knew she could sense how much what he did scared him. *Scared? It fucking terrifies me!* He could do impossible things, and the first way he used those abilities was to slaughter more than a dozen people.

He felt Kaitlyn's small, nimble hand grab his own only an instant before he felt her affection. Why did she care for him so much? Sure, he'd saved her, but why wasn't she the least bit afraid of him, of what he could do? She was right about her limits. While Sal was sure he could have an entire conversation with his mind, she couldn't even understand his thoughts. She couldn't tell him why she wasn't afraid, and he didn't want to ask.

For whatever reason, she wasn't afraid. In fact, she felt safe with him. So he made himself swear he'd never let her down. Not her, or anyone else who'd been pulled into this nightmare. "Let's go see if we can help someone else."

Kaitlyn didn't smile up at him. Her face was the same blank slate it had been since he meet her, but he felt her smile. A tiny thread in the tightly bound emotions in her mind slipped, showing him how happy she was. "Okay," she said.

Chapter 15

PROGRESS

Graham stared at the bank of four monitors in front of him. Each monitor showed a different room, but each room looked identical save for the individual sleeping in it. Sitting in his large, white lab coat, Strickland leaned over, using a long, nimble finger to clack the toggle button for the main monitor to cycle through each subject. He tucked his badge back into his pocket before it could slip all the way out.

The subjects were properly secured and strapped down, so not to thrash about and accidentally pull out the IVs or monitoring equipment. They'd come too far to lose any valuable data because one of the subjects rolled the wrong way.

His finger stalled, seemingly of its own accord. He used the delay as an excuse to adjust his glasses. He used the adjustment as an excuse to look at the monitor. The subject there slept soundly. Truth be told, the small female subject was progressing farther than Graham thought possible, and that was saying something. The second highest Delta Wave Emissions in the group, and third highest all time. Thinking about how much Delta Wave Emissions each subject offered, Strickland clicked the display over to a less impressive subject.

Subject 1 was a disappointment in almost every way. A portion of Graham was happy; though there was little likelihood that the general would see the information and demand the subject's elimination. Still, there were odd spikes in the old man's Delta Wave numbers. Graham wanted to study those. Perhaps the subject simply hadn't reached its potential.

The door opened, and Graham turned to nod at the general, who walked in, instinctively smoothing out nonexistent wrinkles from his olive-green dress uniform jacket. Broad and solid, he looked every bit the authoritarian he presented himself as.

Only Strickland, the general, and the general's two personal guards knew the small room near the center of the building even existed. The general didn't have his guards with him at the moment. They were likely standing watch outside the general's quarters to make it appear is if he was in his room.

Most people assumed the larger control room near the rear exit was the actual control room. The general had made certain to ensure everyone realized how important that room was. That way, if anyone attacked, they'd have time to move to the real control room, where Strickland stood with the general now.

This room only had the most essential equipment. Even if someone managed to peek inside, they'd only see a set of monitors, each one measuring 42 inches, and one control panel with a variety of switches, buttons, and toggles that would look like a back-up to the dozens in the false control room. The general was brilliant. A mind in pursuit of not just a secure nation, but a nation comprised of only the strongest citizens, the most advanced population in every way imaginable. Brilliant didn't begin to describe him.

"It seems the government is on to our experiment," the general said in his gruff whisper of a voice. Only the narrowing of his gray eyes betrayed any hint of emotion. Not that Strickland could identify what emotion it was. The general never shouted or grimaced. The man even had the most eerie way of hanging his enormous arms limply at his sides at all times. The only thing he ever did to display any hint of emotion was narrow those eyes.

"I heard about Warehouse One," Strickland said. "Whatever danger we may have risked from that was negated by your evacuation plan, General."

In truth, it was a security measure designed to eliminate leaks. Burning the evidence is very effective, especially when you have men willing to burn with it to make sure it's gone.

"Our other locations are cleared and sanitized except, of course, for this one."

The general nodded. His lips thinned, which was the biggest smile Strickland had ever seen his leader offer.

"It was only a matter of time before they noticed our activity," the general said. "They have too many resources for us to keep them away. I actually expected them to react faster.

"It's hard to react to shadows, General," Strickland said. He tried to limit the amount of awe in his voice at the general's genius.

"So I understand all units from those facilities were sanitized as well?"

"Yes, General. The only people alive who know about the program are in this building." No loose ends. No potential leaks."

"That's good."

Strickland felt his back straighten proudly, though his narrow frame was comically less impressive than his supervisor's. He served the general with pride and efficiency. His reward for that service would be the opportunity to push mankind to its highest possible level. The general would lead a nation stronger than any in history, and that was only as it should be, but Strickland would be the man history remembered as the father of a mankind reborn.

"What's your progress here?" the general asked almost as an afterthought.

"Subject 2 shows the most promise," Graham reported in his dry, nasally voice.

He watched his leader's eyes narrow again as he looked toward the monitor showing Subject 2. Oh yes, the general never forgot a wrong, and he never forgave it. Strickland didn't insult the general by speaking about previous miscalculations. Besides, he was equally responsible for those errors.

"Subject 2's Delta Wave Emissions are the highest we've ever encountered. Whatever terror his mind produced, it Broke him, and the results are very encouraging." Graham couldn't keep a degree of eager delight out of his voice.

"The highest ever," the general said as if that was all he heard.

"Yes, General, by perhaps 25 percent."

"And Subject 1?"

That was a test. Strickland took a frustrated breath. The general knew him better than that. "That subject seems to be stuck at a D-W-E of 2.6...the lowest average of the group. There are spikes of up to 3.8, and we'll investigate to determine if those spikes are anomalies or signs of ultimate potential."

"Very good," the general said. He was complimenting the doctor's honesty, not the statistics.

"Subject 3 hasn't Broken yet, but that subject's Delta Wave Emissions are steady. It's only a matter of time. We're about to move the subject to a scenario room for another push."

"Do what you can to see it happens quickly," the general said. "We're running short on time."

"Yes, General," Strickland said, smiling. Time was short, but when it came, Strickland would record it down to the millisecond. It would be the exact moment in time the future began.

Chapter 16

WHAT CAN AND CAN'T BE

C hris jerked up with a shout. He ran his hands along his body, check-ing to see if he was still burning. He wasn't, but he could still feel the heat from the fire. He could still hear the man screaming.

A part of him realized he was in his room at the hospital. He sat up in his hospital gown and winced. His bandages were itchy as hell, and if he moved the wrong way, he irritated one or more of the cuts. None of them needed much in the way of stitches, but a night of tossing around made the bandages a bigger inconvenience. The digital alarm clock on the stainless steel table in his room read 3:24 a.m.

He slid his feet off the twin-sized bed. The sheets were clean before Chris had a chance to sweat buckets into them, and the springs screeched at his every move. *It's a wonder I got any sleep at all.* His muscles were tense, but it was otherwise quiet in the room. The night was dark judging by the narrow window high above the left side of his bed.

He reached for the bin under the metal surface of his small table and pulled out his dream journal. He'd done what the doc asked, but he wasn't sure what good it was doing.

It's foggy even now, he wrote. *What I remember is ash. It was everywhere. Sometimes I see someone; sometimes I don't. I think it's worse when I see him. He was my best friend. He saved my life. Am I horrible because seeing him makes me happy even if I know I'm going to die right afterward?*

It was just a dream. Even if it really had happened, this time, it was only a dream. He was crying before he realized it.

"I'm sorry," he said trying to pull himself together. No wonder he was offered "early" retirement. He was a wreck.

He got out of bed and stretched to try and loosen stiff muscles. Doc said the bandages were more about keeping the cuts clean and dry. *Pretty pointless,* Chris thought pulling the sweat-stained bandages off. *They're more of a bother than anything else.* The cuts traced his rope-like muscles.

Chris wasn't a doctor. Sure, he could perform CPR and check a pulse, but he left the medical work to doctors and EMTs. Regardless, the length of the scrapes bothered him. He searched his memory. He could remember being caught in a barbed-wire net. *Why can I remember some dreams so clearly and not others? Was I dreaming or not? Why does it all feel so real when it's happening?*

He turned around, inspecting his room. He'd woken up from the ash world he'd dreamed of most consistently. That was definitely a dream, so this had to be real. Another memory popped out of whatever cell locked the night terrors away in his mind. He scribbled the thought down in his journal.

*Could have sworn someone called out, h*e wrote. *I heard a man's voice saying, "We're coming."*

Given what he experienced, it was possible he was losing his mind. Just a night ago he would have sworn he was kidnapped. He clearly remembered Mattox chasing him through the woods.

Where's he been all day? Chris wondered. *Maybe Doc realized the guy creeped me out and assigned him to some other poor nutjob.*

He looked at the hospital room's only door. He had a guard. It made sense given what the doc told him about the last time they let him sleep unobserved. They probably didn't want him to impersonate an eagle again. *Did I really try to jump out a window?*

"Can I get some water?" he called out to whoever might be there to watch him.

No one answered. Odd. Normally someone swooped in right after he woke up.

"Hey," he tried again. "I'm thirsty, and I have to piss. I'm coming out, so don't tackle me unless you want to clean up the mess it makes."

He crossed the room, bare feet slapping on the checkerboard tile floor. He opened the door and stared in terrified awe. A charred, two-story house was where the hallway should have been. A lawn, wet from hundreds of gallons of water, looked black from smoke. It was surrounded by a pristine white-picket fence. The flames had died, but there was still a faint heat in the air. And smoke...so much smoke. In front of it all stood...*it can't be.*

"Pete?" Chris whispered. Whoever it was, he was horribly burned. Every ounce of flesh had burned black and was cracking. Some bits of flesh flaked off and tumbled to the ground like a falling withered leaf as the figure walked toward him.

"Why?" the man asked. "Why didn't you help me?" Oddly, his teeth and mouth seemed perfectly fine.

Chris turned to look behind him. He wasn't sure what he expected, but his hospital room was still there. The normalcy of the room made the nightmare in front of him seem more terrible. He couldn't run back in there. He had to face his friend. He had to explain.

"Pete I—" Chris turned to talk to his friend.

The man rushed toward Chris, stabbing him in the arm with a needle.

"Why did you let this happen to me?" the man asked. He didn't sound like Pete, but who could sound like himself after burning to death?

Chris opened his mouth to say something, maybe apologize, but he felt the energy leave his body. His vision blurred and blackness took him.

A fit of coughing forced Chris awake, and the chains that bound him clanked together as he fought unsuccessfully to both slip free and catch his breath at the same time. He recognized the interior of the house. It was the house he was supposed to die in—the house he'd died in dozens of times before.

Everything felt more intense. The smoke made seeing every bit as impossible as getting a solid breath of air. He rolled on the ground until he slammed into a wall. The impact of the wall combined with the thick, heavy chain caused his bones to rattle. The details of the room seemed to shift if he tried to focus on a particular area.

The firefighting ensemble he'd entered the dream in only added to the heat and discomfort. He was wearing his protective gear that night, when Pete died, but he hadn't fought a fire since. *Not again! Please not again!*

Footsteps announced someone's approach, but Chris didn't need to look up to see the man wrapped in flames again. The burning man stepped into the room.

"No!" Chris shouted. "Pete, no!"

The flaming man stopped in the doorway. He took another step forward. Chris could see still burning footprints stretching down the hallway behind the flame engulfed man.

"Pete, I'm sorry! It shouldn't have happened!"

The flaming man stopped again. As he stood there, the floor and wall nearest the man came back to life. The fire grew faster than it should have. Chris could have sworn the man stared at him before turning and walking away. He didn't make it out of the room before he faded away, or maybe he transformed into the raging inferno that was about to burn Chris alive.

The fire grew far too hot, too quickly and black smoke started to thicken. He coughed out a cry for help. "Someone!"

He would have laughed if he could. Who was going to save him? He was chained up on the floor with a roaring blaze growing ever hotter and closer.

Three people popped into existence in front of Chris. The first was a dark-haired man wearing some kind of military uniform. Beside him was a petite girl, maybe a teenager, with long night-black hair. The last person was a much older, emaciated looking man. He looked like he'd been slapped in an orange jumper and thrown in a blender. Chris looked at them dumbfounded. They hadn't walked into the room; they had just materialized. They looked around for a few seconds, as if they themselves were unsure how they got there.

The younger man with dark hair and hard, dark eyes was the first to recover himself. He rushed to Chris and started looking for a weak link in the chains. The man actually thought he was going to pull the chains apart. Chris's sharp eyes noticed the name "Veltri" on the pocket above the man's shirt.

"Hurry," the girl said. Her small, flat voice somehow sounded urgent, even though she didn't shout. Her t-shirt and jeans had started to blacken from the smoke. The old man stepped back. The wrinkled husk of a man had a wild look in his green eyes, but he was the only one smart enough to step out of the burning room. But, of course, it didn't matter because none of them were real. He was losing his mind and life at the same time.

An impossible gust of wind gave new life to the fire. It was well out of control. Any responders outside would have no choice but to let the flames burn themselves out.

"I can't be saved," he told the stout man trying to free him. "You won't be able to save me. I deserve this." These people were likely representatives of his psyche or something. Maybe they were the avatars the doc mentioned. *What good are they now? I'm going to die, and these figments of my imagination choose now to show up?*

Odd that he'd think up such a trio as this, or was it? Some memory tried to form in Chris's mind, but as he focused on the thought, pain, like being jabbed in the skull with a railroad spike, stopped him. Whatever it was that made the trio feel familiar to Chris was pointless. *It doesn't matter,* Chris thought. *Avatars or not, I'm still here, and I'm still going to die.*

"Bullshit," the man said. He stood and glared at the chains. Somehow, they snapped and flew away as if pulled by an invisible wire.

Chris looked at the room. It was hopeless. *Great, now I'll be able to run around all I want as I burn to death.*

"I said bullshit!" the man said.

Well, I made him up, seems right that he knows what I'm thinking.

"You didn't make me up, and you're not going to burn to death." The man found his feet. Dusty brown boots stomped shoulder-width apart as if gearing up for a fight. He glared at the wall behind them, and it exploded. That was a huge problem.

The sudden rush of air hit the flames and caused a backdraft. Chris clamped his eyes shut, waiting for the oven that falling wall had turned on to cook him like a turkey. He heard the roar of the fire. He waited, and waited. He opened a dark-lidded eye. The younger man looked as if he'd just been pounded on by an entire football team. The young lady, yes, definitely a teenager, looked at the man like some hero from a movie. The old man just clapped like some kid who'd just seen a magic trick. Obviously his mind was substituting this reality for the one where he was currently burning to death.

Some invisible force yanked Chris out of the room. He cried out as he hung in the air and looked down at the ground. He wasn't afraid of heights, but if whatever held him up gave way, he might break a leg, or worse. The man picked the girl up, his muscular frame made her appear smaller and younger than she had a moment before. The uniformed man, *is that a Marine uniform? No, Army,* grabbed the girl and glared at the older man. That glare was predatory—like the lion embroidered on the patch Velcroed to his left shoulder.

I'm not all that bad. By the way, my name's Sal. Chris felt his jaw drop. It was the same voice he'd heard in his head during that other dream.

I really can't tell one from the other anymore! Chris thought. Trying to keep his mind in reality was impossible.

Chris drifted to the ground as the man, Sal, jumped. They landed on some sort of invisible cushion. As they did, Chris heard Sal grunt in pain. Chris rolled instinctively.

Chris stood and looked up in time to see the old man fly out of the window. The old bastard actually shouted, "Weeeee," like someone on a ride at a fair. The shreds of that orange outfit, *is that a prison outfit?* fluttered in the wind like the tail of a kite.

The old man landed softly, and again Chris noticed Sal grunt as if he caught the older man himself. Though as thin as the old bastard was, it was a wonder the wind didn't just blow him into the next county.

"Hi," Sal said breathing hard, giving the firefighter a small smile. "Nice to meet you, Chris."

Chris stared at the man. Sal was an inch or two shorter, but much thicker than Chris was even in his firefighting ensemble. The soldier helped the girl dust herself off as she wheezed. Sal knelt beside her.

"It's okay," he said softly. *Is that his daughter?*

Sal whispered to her as she got her breathing under control.

"She's not my daughter," Sal said. "I'm sorry, but it's hard to think with three people's thoughts floating around my mind. He shook his head as if he were dizzy. "Kaitlyn's thinking her asthma is acting up. Do you have any medical issues I should know about, Chris?"

Chris shook his head. "Wait…" Chris said as realization struck him. "How do you know my name?"

"Jedi mind trick," he said using a ridiculous Yoda impersonation. He gave another smile and pointed behind himself at the old man who watched the fire. "That's Caden."

He pointed to the girl. Just as he was about to introduce her, she simply vanished. Chris was still too stunned to react, but Sal looked horrified.

"Kaitlyn!" he yelled. "Kaitlyn!" He closed his eyes, maybe to collect himself. "Caden can you hear her?"

The old man turned to look over his shoulder. "She's where we're not." He didn't seem concerned at all.

"No....God no. Not now."

Chris worked his eyes open and closed. No matter what he did to wake himself, he was still by the smoked out house with the two strangers. He wasn't sure what was real anymore. Was he burning right now? Was he dead? Was all of this really happening?

Sal moved up to him, those black, lion eyes were back. "I don't have time to explain everything to you right now, Chris, but I will if you come with us." His voice was gruff and impatient. Chris couldn't help but glance at the rank insignia on the center of the man's uniform. Three pointed chevrons were connected by a loop underneath. "That girl, Kaitlyn, she came here to save you, and now she needs us."

Chris took a step back, but Sal put a surprisingly gentle hand on his shoulder.

"Stay here if you want. I won't force you, but I don't recommend it." He paused, looking beyond Chris. "But someone I promised to keep safe is missing, and I mean to find her. Are you coming?"

Avatars! Chris said, remembering what he was supposed to do when he found them. There was more, but each time he tried to focus on the thought, that blinding pain came back. *These are avatars, and helping them will help me.*

Chapter 17

ESCAPE TO REALITY

While walking along the smoke-stained sidewalk, Sal swallowed another surge of panic. His mind couldn't touch Kaitlyn's. What did that mean? *She's gone, not dead!* he reminded himself. He couldn't find a way to prove it to himself. All he knew was he'd watched too many people die. Ironically, the fact that he didn't see her die was the only thing that let him believe she was still alive. While taking quick breaths of air, he tried to keep his pace controlled. Rushing wouldn't help, but the man named Chris seemed to want to stop every moment and ask questions for which Sal didn't have any answers.

He made another effort to hear Kaitlyn's thoughts. He could hear Chris's thoughts as clearly as if the former firefighter were speaking. Caden's thoughts sounded like someone singing through a pillow. Sal wasn't sure what those muffled sounds meant, but he *could* hear them.

"I don't know how else to convince you," Sal said with just a hint of exasperation as he led the group down an abandoned street that would have seemed normal had there been any houses other than the charred husk he'd pulled Chris out of. "I am not a figment of your imagination, but yes, this is a dream."

More like a nightmare, Sal heard Chris think to himself. The black man's dark eyes scanned the empty dirt plots of land surrounding the smoking house and burnt grass.

"Well, yes...more like a nightmare." Sal looked back to Chris. He offered a half hearted grin in an effort to hide his impatience. "May want to work on masking your thoughts."

"He thinks he's emperor of the world," Caden muttered, waggling his head about. "But the emperor has no more clothes than the last time everyone laughed at him."

"If that's a joke, Caden, it's not the time, and it's not funny," Sal said, stopping. It was either a joke, or the old man had called him a fool.

"I did both," Caden said. "You're running on a treadmill, and you need to catch a bus."

"Does that guy always talk like a fortune cookie?" Chris asked. His narrow face had a perpetually wry look. The quarter-smile he offered was more from disbelief than humor.

"There's more truth to my future than a cookie," Caden said. His pale green eyes hardened for a moment. Sal didn't know the older man very well, but the look was almost a glare. "But if you don't like cookies, you don't have to eat."

Sal stepped in front of Caden, who jerked back a few steps. "I'm sorry!" he shouted. He fell to the sidewalk and held his hands in front of himself like a child who expected Sal to loom over and slap him.

Sal took a deep breath and backed away. He didn't mean to scare Caden. He knew better than to make sudden moves around the skittish old man. Sal wouldn't harm him, but Caden's frail, scarred body was clear evidence that he was used to being beaten. *I shouldn't be scaring him just because I'm worried about Kaitlyn.* "I'm not going to hurt you."

"Usually just what they say before they put you in a chair and turn on the power." Caden made the sound of a buzzer, and shook as if being shocked at that moment. Wild locks of white hair flopped about as the old man thrashed. "Should have known better than to put my hand in His."

"Who is He?" Sal asked. There was certainly someone behind all this, and Caden seemed to at least know whoever was behind it was male.

"Your fault," Caden said. He stood, leaving a few more tattered remnants of his orange jump suite on the smoke-stained sidewalk. "Zeus is all grown up, and He thinks to do to him what He couldn't do to Cronus." He looked at Sal. "To call you Zeus is to place you on Olympus. Wrong. Very wrong. You're Icarus, and Daedalus isn't here to tell you where the sun is. I'll not stand near you to burn."

"Now he's quoting Greek myths?" Chris asked aloud.

Sal heard Chris think, *Makes sense. I do love Greek mythology.*

"You actually understand what he's saying?" Sal replied.

"I heard Zeus and Cronus," Chris said shrugging. His firefighting outfit bulged in response to the gesture. He chose to take a seat on the sidewalk. They'd been walking for a while, but no matter how far they walked, they were always just a few dozen feet away from the burnt house. "That's about all I understood. Took a semester of it in college. Look at me; I'm fucking talking to myself again!"

"For Christ's sake, we're not figments of your imagination," Sal said after another exasperated breath and a shake of his head. They weren't getting anything done. He looked over to Chris. "Have you noticed that injuries you've taken in some dreams last longer? Or maybe they come back?"

The man pulled off the bulky jacket of his firefighting outfit and set it behind himself on the sidewalk. He had a plain, blue t-shirt on underneath, and a pair of suspenders held the large trousers up. Chris looked at his dark, muscular arms closely, as if to find something. He wasn't as thick as Sal, but every muscle was more sculpted, sharper. Sal could hear him still trying to fit the information into some community college psyche course explanation and spoke before Chris could.

"That's odd," Sal said.

"What's odd?" Chris asked.

"You remember being captured," Sal explained, pointing to Chris's arms. "Are you blocking me?"

"Blocking you?" Chris asked.

"I can't see some of your memories," Sal said. Sal had never really tried to see someone's thoughts. He usually only saw bits of memory or heard random musings. As Chris remembered being kidnapped, there was no memory of what happened after. Sal closed his eyes and focused on Chris. From Sal's point of view in Chris's mind, there were black domes around his memories. Some of the domes pulsed with electricity as Chris tried to recall the events.

Maybe I don't remember, so this aspect of my imagination can't see the memory either. Sal heard Chris's mental assessment of the situation.

"Why are you so determined to make us into some figments of your imagination?" Sal asked.

"Because this kind of shit just isn't real! People don't move things with their minds. They don't talk with them either. Teenage girls don't disappear into thin air."

"They do if they aren't watched closely," Caden said.

"Not like a ghost," Chris argued, shaking his head.

"Bottom line," Sal said taking a seat beside Chris so they could talk at eye level. "You want to wake up."

"Yes!" Chris shouted. That quarter-smile came back. Apparently that was the look he gave when he thought the person he was speaking to was a moron. "I want to wake up! I want to be back…" he froze in mid sentence. "I don't remember where I was."

Chris grabbed his forehead with the palm of his hand. Sal could feel the man's sudden headache. He watched Chris slide nimble fingers over the top of his head to the base of his skull.

"You had a scar there, too?" Sal asked.

"A scar?" Chris asked. *Didn't I? Yeah, it's cause I had that—* "Aah!" Sal felt the man's headache surge, like one of those electronic pulses only Sal could see had burned through Chris's skull the closer he got to whatever memory he was trying to recall.

"It was just here wasn't it?" Sal asked turning and pointing to where the base of his skull met the top of his neck. "It's maybe four inches long."

Sal stopped, feeling Chris's headache grow even more painful as he tried to access his memory. It was still weird for Sal to look at a person's mind, and if trying to help Chris remember events only hurt, Sal didn't want to put him through any more pain.

"I can't remember," Chris said, "but I know I want to wake up now."

"Well then," Sal said. "Let's go. If we can find out how to get out of here, we can work on waking up next."

"Columbus swears the world is round, but why should I be one of the fools he convinces to sail right off the edge of the Earth?"

"We help each other," Sal said before Caden could get too far into another rant. "Call it your way of helping yourself wake. Call it karma. Hell, call it luck. Fact is, we're trapped in a nightmare, and we're trapped together."

"Treadmills!" Caden shouted. "The bus is driving away, and we don't know we're not catching up."

Treadmills? "Caden, are you saying Kaitlyn is already awake?" Sal asked.

Caden giggled. He was a old man, but there was no other way to describe the sound. "Look at Archimedes," he said laughing. "He's so happy he's learned something, but he's running around naked."

"I know that one," Chris said. "Um...Archimedes discovered displacement in the bath. He ran around naked yelling..."

"I found it!" Caden shouted in a burst of laughter. "Must have been a relief. Who knew it was missing?"

"Actually," Chris said. "He yelled 'eureka,' but it means the same thing."

Sal tried to follow the conversation. The biggest book he'd ever read that wasn't a manual had pictures in it. Kaitlyn was awake. She was out of the nightmare. Did that make it better or worse? She was in the waking world, where the one Caden only referred to as 'He,' could hurt her. No, Kaitlyn being awake was actually much worse.

Chapter 18

MISSION PREP

Steve stood at a window that faced a blank brick wall. The view was soothing to him. It was just the back of another building. The neon lights of Vegas were flickering as quickly as he'd seen them in any movie or TV show. He had never been to Vegas, or Nevada for that matter. It was a city that offered rooms for rent by the hour. More importantly, it was about a half-tank of gas from the team's next target.

He stood, watching the wall seemingly change color from lime green to vomit yellow and so on to colors that were too loud and obnoxious for words. He listened to the loud music, horns honking, people shouting, laughing. None of it could drown out the noise in his head. He took deep, regular breaths. Hopefully, the team would think he just wanted to be alone. That only worked if Kira kept her damn nose out of his business. She must have been because she wasn't lecturing him.

Dom, Kira, and Brandon were circled around the room's only bed, gearing up and prepping their weapons. Steve hadn't worried about his weapons for years, neither had the rest of the team. Dom acted like nothing ever mattered, but he could calibrate, zero, clean, and prep anything ever designed to kill long before he ever became a weapon himself. They didn't need to check the gear or even select what they wanted. It was more than likely that the team was searching for a bit of camaraderie from one another.

I should be there with them, he thought to himself. *I should be with her.* He closed his eyes, and focused his attention on some argument happening in the room next door. The paper-thin, horribly-stained walls did little to provide any real privacy, but no one in this sort of hotel ever really paid much attention to anyone else. The argument was a distraction for Steve. It gave him something to think about, which kept him from thinking about the one he lost eleven years before the general showed his true colors. Steve heard another round of shouts. Someone, it sounded like a woman, threw something and stormed out. Whatever it was hit the wall. Steve didn't so much as flinch even though whatever the woman threw caused a bit of something to flake down from the ceiling.

Steve took a few more breaths. He was dressed in some sturdy cargo pants and brown, steel-toed boots. His body kit, a metal-plate-filled protective vest, was propped up beside the room's only exit. The damn thing was hot and heavy, and dry as the air may be, the damn place was too hot to add another layer just yet.

Steve turned away from his view of another building's wall to look at his team. They were all similarly dressed, leaving their kits off for likely the same reason as Steve.

"I'm gonna go home," Brandon said, looking at the assortment of weapons on the bed like a salad bar in a restaurant. It did sort of look like a shopping display. The weapons were arranged by size and sub-organized by maximum effective range. "When this is over, if it's okay with Steve, I'm gonna go back to Texas and start up my own business."

"Let me know where you set up shop," Dom replied. He picked up an M-9, took it apart, and reassembled it as easily as a child might tie his shoe. "I'll need you to set me up with free internet and satellite."

"I'm not gonna break the law no more," Brandon said in his southern twang. "Not after we're done." Brandon was how they funded their operation. He was a good young man doing bad things for the right reason.

Steve heard his knuckles popping before he realized how tightly he held his fists.

"I'm gonna find a good woman," Dom said, clearly ignoring the way everyone's eyes shifted to Steve. The comment caused Kira to look Dom's way. Dom gave her a wry smile. "I mean to find a woman who's nice."

Kira turned her attention to an M-4. She snapped on a sling and needlessly checked the sight. "Good luck with that," she said.

Steve let out a chuckle. That brought a scowl to Dom's face. Those blue eyes of his hid behind a furrowed brow that promised honest brooding in the future. "I suppose you and Steve will just find a new war."

"Whatever I do is my choice," Kira said. The M-4 was suddenly the most interesting thing in the room to Kira. Brandon seemed to think his boots were in need of scrutiny.

"I'm retiring," Steve said.

"Men like you don't retire," Dom said in that overly causal way he always did. "They find causes to fight for until they're out of fight."

"I've been out of fight for years now," Steve said. He walked over to the bed, ignoring the crunching sounds of whatever insect he stepped on along the way. The room was small. It only took a few steps to reach the twin bed. Another two would take him to the door. Someone thought it'd be funny to cram a large dresser and vanity mirror in the room, so if Steve really wanted to reach the door, he'd have to turn sideways to get between the bed and the dresser.

"You don't mean that," Brandon said. He raised a hand to scratch a patch of brown fuzz under his chin. He hadn't shaved in two weeks. Steve would have that much facial hair and more if he failed to shave the next morning, but the man wanted to look his age, and Steve wasn't about to tell him how ridiculous the beard looked. "Hell, I'm half afraid you won't let me go back home."

Steve put a large hand on the man's scrawny shoulder. Brandon's eyes met his. "You can go home whenever you want. You hear me?"

Brandon gave one of his patented ah-shucks shrugs. The gesture was a noun, verb, adjective, and adverb all rolled into one. "I want to finish this."

"He's been wiping his own ass since before he met us," Kira said. "He wants out, he'll tell us."

Steve must have looked ready to bark at her because Brandon cut him off.

"I don't want out," he said in that panicked, "Don't fight over me" tone he had whenever Steve and Kira were about to fight over him. "I will go home, when this is over."

"No you won't," Dom cut in. "None of us will."

Everybody stopped to look at him. "Oh, we'll talk about all the things we mean to do, but at the end of the day we're all just like Steve."

"Seem to remember having breasts," Kira mumbled.

"And a sight they are, I'm sure," Dom replied. "But we're fighters. We're weapons. So we either decide our own targets, or someone will come point one out to us."

"Seems..." Brandon paused. He did that when he was about to say something he thought anyone in the history of ever might not like to hear. He didn't finish the comment, but he did quiet the rest of the team.

"I said I'm out," Steve said, cutting the conversation short. "When this is over, I'm done."

"Only over your dead body," Kira and Dom said together. They looked at each other like a pair of strange cats.

Good Lord those too need to just get it over with, Steve thought before saying, "Mission brief."

The team instinctively formed a circle, trying with limited success not to bump into each other in the crowded space. Brandon's hand brushed Kira's arm. He jerked away like the touch burned. He was the shyest man Steve had ever seen. Kira gave one of those winks of hers and wrapped an arm around Brandon. It was her way of making him comfortable, but it didn't stop steam from shooting out of Dom's ears. Dom shook it off and stepped in the center of the ill-formed circle.

"As we know from Kira's work, we're about to hit one of two remaining hiding spots for the general," Dom said fishing out a map from one of the pouches in his cargo pants. He opened it, and gently placed it on the bed over the remaining weapons from the small arsenal they'd picked for the mission.

"The warehouse is here," Dom said stabbing a spot on the topographic map. "The grid is reliable as far as Kira and Brandon can tell. We'll take a single jeep. I'll drive, and Brandon's on shotgun so he can use his who-dads and what-nots to scan for mines."

"Who-dads?" Brandon asked.

Dom smiled. "You keep changing the names of your inventions. What are you calling it this week?"

"Um…a mine-scanner? Cause, you know, it scans for mines."

"Last week it was a counter-mine locator."

"Right," Brandon said. "Because last time it didn't just scan for mines it…"

"Off topic, Brandon," Steve cut in. He forced a smile to take the edge off.

Dom gave a more genuine smile and continued. "Steve will carry all the big guns and Kira's the medic and anti-personnel detector during transit. We'll approach from the east and make a hard entrance."

Dom stepped out and Kira filled his place. "We just don't know if this is the right place or not. It's either exactly what we're looking for, or exactly what we're afraid we're gonna find."

"Why'd you select this location first?" Steve asked.

"Honestly," she said, a wide smile making her blue eyes sparkle. "It was just closer. If we passed it to go to the more distant location, and we're wrong, it's all the more time lost."

Steve nodded, understanding her explanation was more about keeping him from having another meltdown if they find nothing, than justifying her decisions. Kira stepped aside. Something screeched and skittered off. Steve was just glad whatever it was didn't decide to make a fight of it. It sounded like a rat, and he hated those.

Brandon stepped into the center of the circle. "The *mine-scanner* is all ready," he said, emphasizing his beloved name for his newest tech and glaring at Dom as if expecting a challenge. Dom only smiled. "Per your orders, Steve, I won't be using any EMPs."

Dom looked at Steve, and Brandon cut in before Dom could ask anything. "If I fire off an EMP, the people who are relying on machines to stay alive will die. So instead, I'll approach the system directly. If the site is active, I can hack in and use what I want the way we feel is best. If the site is sanitized, there's not much for me to do but try to scrape intel out of whatever they left in the place."

Brandon stepped away and let Steve take the floor. "We have two remaining locations to search. We're going to secure this site, rescue any civilian assets we may find and neutralize any enemy forces. Our priority targets remain. We want to capture and kill the general and that doctor as quickly as possible."

Steve took a breath, thinking about that particular issue gave him a headache. "That doctor" was the only name they had for him. Steve could describe him right down to his oversized lab coat and square glasses, but not even Brandon could pull up a lick of information on him, and without a source image to work from, facial recognition wasn't an option. It would have been nice if anyone on the team could draw much more than a straight line.

Steve pointed at Kira. "You will be our primary link for communications. I have operational control followed by Dom."

"You sure you want me handling all coms?" Kira asked. *She has to question every damn decision I make.*

"Yes," he said flatly.

"And you'll be in that comm link?"

"Yes."

She looked at him.

"That's the call."

She shrugged. Steve took another breath. He'd been taking a lot of deep breaths lately.

"We're wheels up in two hours," Steve said. "Kira will make sure no one sees us leave the hotel. Brandon, the room's handled?"

"Yeah," Brandon answered. "As far as this place knows, we were never here." He paused for a minute, those brown eyes sinking back to his boots. "Do you really think we'll find him?" he asked.

"Either here or in the last location," Steve said. "Either way, it's only a matter of time."

Chapter 19

COMBAT

No amount of knowing he should wake was helping Sal accomplish the task. There was little worry that Chris was trying as hard as possible to wake up. However, Sal couldn't so much as guess what Caden was up to. The old man said he was trying to wake. At least that's what Sal thought Caden meant.

They'd all taken a seat on the curb of the road. They'd alternated from walking to running for what seemed like a half-hour, but each time they stopped for a rest, they didn't appear to be so much as a step farther from the charred remnants of the house than they had started. In fact, the muted full moon still hung in its same position in the west.

"Why don't you just do whatever you did to appear where you want like you did when I first saw you?" Chris asked. His toned arms rested on his knees while he looked down at the asphalt between his legs.

"I found you here in the dream," Sal explained. "Not honestly sure how I did that yet, but even if I work out the how, I can't do that in the real world." He tilted himself back on his hands and leaned his head back to the sky. The smoke did little to hide the moon's light, but the stars couldn't penetrate the blanket of smoke.

"Twisted lands of make believe," Caden said. "The Sandman's dust keeps us where we don't want to be, and the only way to leave here is to stay." He found a charred stick and was doodling on the sidewalk next to him.

"I'm gonna be as nutty as he is if I don't get out of here soon," Chris said, looking over to watch Caden scratch at the concrete. Sal's ability to sense emotions told him a part of Chris wondered if he wasn't already as nutty as Caden.

"Rapunzel doesn't like her tower, but she moved in," Caden replied. "She moved in and then used a siren's song to bring us to her. She doesn't want us here, but she won't let us leave."

Neither Chris nor Sal understood the comment, so they chose to ignore it. It must have been the wrong choice because Caden stood, tossing down his stick, and started pouting like a child who'd just lost his favorite toy.

"Dr. Jekyll has to choose to become Mr. Hyde," he said. "The Sandman's dust keeps us here, but we choose what here is. One fears to leave too much, and one fears to go anywhere else. Your thoughts are strings tying me to a place I don't want to be, and it's mean. It's mean to keep me here when there's more to do in the different here."

Sal worked desperately to combine Caden's words with the random, muffled sounds he could hear in the madman's mind. Chris stood and approached Caden. Sal could feel Chris's frustration. He could hear his thoughts screaming at the old man, but all Chris did was smile.

"You're being as blunt as you can," Chris said. He had a soft, fatherly tone that belied the anger Sal knew he felt. For some reason, the effort to be kind when Chris was so frustrated seemed so genuine to Sal.

I do that some times, Sal heard Chris think to himself. *I talk in circles. Why should I be mad if I do it to myself?*

Sal chuckled. "Does it seem odd that we're figments of your imagination and we're both white?"

"No," Chris said without hesitation, turning to look at Sal. "I've never identified myself by the color of my skin. I'm actually more surprised you thought of it." And that did cause Chris to hesitate as he furrowed his brow in thought.

But that's not the only reason. Someone said something. Chris's thoughts started to drift. For a moment, Sal heard a different voice, a memory in Chris's mind. *"A little girl would be just as likely as an old man."* The instant Chris focused on the memory, a surge of pain hit him like a bolt of lightning.

Regardless of whatever pain he felt, Chris shook his head as if it were nothing.

"You okay?" Sal asked.

"Yeah," Chris answered. Sal knew it was a lie. "Every now and then I get a bit of my memory back, but none of it makes any sense."

He was trying to cram the unexpected thought into some nonsense about challenging one's own perception. Chris dismissed the thought and turned his attention back to Caden.

"Where are we?" he asked, gesturing to the entirety of the landscape.

"Here," Caden said in a way that made it sound like he was answering the dumbest question ever.

"And if we leave here?" Chris's tone was still patient and soothing.

"Can't," Caden said quickly. "Can't. Can't. Can't. We're under a spell and no princesses are coming to kiss us."

"OK. OK," Chris said, making calming motions with large, slender hands. "So we can't leave, but why haven't we gotten anywhere new after all this walking?"

"All the world is a stage," Caden mumbled. "This is a stage. It's vast and small, but we don't leave the stage, just change the props and tragedy." He looked at Chris, those green eyes flashing so quickly Sal wasn't sure he didn't imagine it. "We've seen this part of your tragedy, but no one else seems to want to share, and you don't seem to want to go to the next scene."

"Um..." Sal said. "The dream doesn't change unless we think of a new nightmare?"

He uttered the words, and the world flickered. It bounced from a child's bedroom, to a world of ash, to a village in Afghanistan. It flickered so quickly between the three that some parts seemed to lie over others until everything blinked back to the way it had started.

"First no one wants to go, and now everyone wants to go to different places," Caden muttered. "Back seat drivers all grabbing at the wheel."

Sal's mind was still stuck on that village. It blinked so quickly in and out of existence, but he couldn't press the memory back. Where Chris's mind instinctively recoiled away from his thoughts, Sal's mind froze, and the world faded into something new.

His memory was still like a puzzle that was missing a good number of pieces, but he recognized the village. The fact that night had changed to day in an instant wasn't nearly the most alarming thought in Sal's mind. The memory of what happened in that village was infinitely more disturbing than the sudden arrival of the sun and the crisp winter air that seemed to pass right through his uniform. This village was where his life changed. It was comprised mud huts, which lined a few sparse stretches of dirt road tucked in a valley, surrounded by patches of high grass.

"What the?" Chris said. Sal looked over to him and noticed both Chris and Caden were wearing Army combat uniforms. The digital patterned outfits looked out of place on them.

"War movies are scary," Caden said, looking as if he wanted to shrug his way out of the uniform. At least the outfit finally covered him up. "There's more bad guys than good, and this isn't the sort of place where good guys win."

Sal worked to control his breathing, as plumes of breath misted into the cold air, but his heart rate was a whole other monster. The stench of stale water and garbage was hard enough to deal with, let alone his treacherous body. In real life, his unit had approached this village from the south mountains. They made it through the grass and started to patrol one of the streets. It was odd to his unit because...

"Is this place abandoned?" Chris asked from just behind and to the right of Sal.

"No," Sal whispered. "They're all inside somewhere."

They vanished from the tall grass and reappeared at the edge of one of the two dirt roads. Maybe Caden was right. Maybe what really happened was the world shifted around them. However they got there, they were at the edge of a bazaar. The mud huts were surrounded with bright colored carpets. Tables filled with wares lined the front of each building.

"It's creepy," Chris said. Rifles appeared in their hands. Chris looked at his like a rocket in need of nuclear fuel. Caden set his down on the ground, but it kept reappearing in his hands.

"Stupid gun," Caden said. "Guns are useless tools. They only do one thing, and I'm not a fan of the tedium."

Sal wanted desperately to put the rifle down, but his hands wouldn't obey. All he could think about was the same thing that bothered him in real life, the memory that was born here in blood.

Sal noticed something move from the corner of his eye. He brought up his rifle on instinct, but kept his finger straight and off the trigger. A little boy darted out from behind some sort of vending table. Sal quickly lowered his gun.

"Hey," he said softly. "You shouldn't hide around here. It's dangerous."

The boy didn't look like he understood, but he took the chance to rush into a different mud hut.

The building from which the boy ran exploded. Sal rose, wondering how he ended up on the ground a few feet from where he was. His ears were ringing, and his head spun. The building he'd just been looking at had slumped over and crumbled. The building next to it had a portion of the wall missing. The surrounding area was blackened.

Sal looked for his friends. Caden was hiding behind one of the mud houses, weeping and ranting. All hell had broken loose, except for around Chris. Ohh, he looked bewildered and stunned, but the explosion seemed to simply skirt around him. The blackness of it left a perfect "V" on the ground around Chris as if the fire refused to touch him.

The fact didn't register in the firefighter's mind. Instead, he rushed toward Caden. Sal followed the man's movements. A short, incredibly skinny Afghan man had appeared out of nowhere just behind Caden. The man brought up an AK-47, which was covered in a variety of ridiculously colored stickers.

Sal wanted to focus his mind, but he was simply too afraid. He watched as Chris furiously pumped his legs and dove, knocking over Caden just before the man with the AK-47 fired a round. The bullet tore through the building, but Caden was fine. Sal brought up his own rifle and quickly fired three rounds into the attacker's chest.

Bullets started flying everywhere. It was as if the entire bazaar had decided to attack him. He ran as quickly as he could into a hut. He couldn't see his friends, but he heard their thoughts. Chris was baffled about something.

What's wrong? Sal asked.

He heard Chris shouting. His ears didn't pick up the sounds over the gunfire and the ringing of the explosion, but Chris's thoughts were loud and clear. *We're in some sort of dome. Are you doing this?*

Just stay there! He sent the message, but they appeared out of thin air just next to him.

"You tell us to stay, and then call us to you," Caden said. "It's not nice to move people without asking."

Something clicked behind them. Sal brought up his weapon, spun around and fired. Chris shouted, shoving the rifle upward just as Sal pulled the trigger.

A little boy cowered in front of Sal. The thin, dirt-stained boy had his hands in front of him as if they could have stopped the bullet.

"What are you doing?" Chris asked, sweat beading his forehead. He was horrified, but his tone was calm.

"I was alone," Sal whispered. "I'd taken cover just like now. I was laying down cover fire. A few of my battle buddies came inside when we heard that same clicking noise."

Eerily, the boy seemed frozen. The sounds of gunfire and shouting were still filling the air, but none of it seemed to penetrate the building in which the group stood.

Sal dropped the rifle. He was half afraid the damn thing would reappear in his hands, but it remained on the ground.

"It was so loud, and the fighting was so chaotic," Sal said. *Is that me whimpering?*

The boy faded, leaving Sal alone with his two companions. Caden moved over to where the boy had just been. He looked around as if trying to decide which of the carpets he wanted to buy.

"I shot him," Sal said, his voice cracking a bit. "We were supposed to talk about plans for a well. We got ambushed, and I shot a…I shot a kid." It grew more difficult to breathe. Sal couldn't tell if it was because of the bile climbing up his throat or the sob threatening to surge out of his chest.

Chris didn't know what to say. Sal's abilities told him that much. But the taller man didn't feel rage or disgust. He felt incredible sorrow.

"What about the other soldiers?" he finally asked.

"They had just gotten inside," Sal said. "One of them had a gunshot wound. They were just trying to do some first aid. We all heard the sound."

"But they'd put down their weapons to help their friend. You were armed."

"It doesn't make it right!" Sal shouted.

Chris didn't have any real answer, but again, his emotions didn't betray any sense of disgust.

"I was discharged," Sal said. "I just can't remember the circumstances. Every time I try to pull up some memory it fades away, but I know I got out of the Army, and I know I've never been the same since."

"Who would be?" Chris asked. Sal saw Chris's thoughts. His memory of being trapped in a burning building. A man, covered in flame rushed at him. For a moment, the world flickered, but it didn't change.

This is the part of my mind that feels responsible, Sal heard Chris think to himself. *It's the part of me that hates myself for letting Pete die.*

"This isn't your damn issue," Sal said. "Whatever happened to you was real, but so was what happened to me! Only I pulled the trigger." He quickly jabbed himself in the chest several times with his thumb.

Another explosion, large and powerful, rocked the building they were in. They all fell. Caden screamed in terror. "Watch Caden!" Sal shouted over the din. Sal focused his thoughts. All he had that day in real life was a rifle. He had so much more now.

Everything went still when he stepped out of the building. It was as if everyone that had been shooting had vanished. It was harder to trust his ability to read minds in the dreams. None of the dream figures would have real thoughts or feelings. Chris came out of the building, gently guiding Caden by an arm.

"All the men with guns are gone," the madman said quietly.

Chris gently handed Caden to Sal. "I still don't *believe* you're real," he said. Sal heard the doubts in Chris's mind. "But if you were, whatever happened..." He paused, thinking that he couldn't honestly say it wasn't Sal's fault. The firefighter understood no man could take away what another man chose to accept as his responsibility. The only way Sal managed to beat down the animalistic rage at the lanky man's words was by listening to Chris question himself even as he spoke. Amid Chris's thoughts was the image of where the boy ran from and where the explosion came from.

Sal maneuvered around rubble. He glanced again a the strange scorch mark on the ground where Chris had somehow avoided getting hurt when the first explosion happened. The other nearby buildings weren't as lucky as the former firefighter. One hut that sold cookware had slumped over. The other nearby buildings, a bootleg DVD shop and an electronics store were singed. The merchandise was broken and scattered around. He did his best to steer clear of the collapsed tobacco shop next to where the explosion occurred. He stepped over the remnants of a wall and into the remains of the building the boy had originally come from.

He didn't know what he was looking for. Then again, he did. He realized he was checking the burn patterns without actually knowing what a burn pattern was. Then he suddenly knew what a burn pattern was.

"How much do you know about investigating fires?" he asked Chris.

"About as much as anyone does fighting fires for ten years."

"I'm sorry," Sal said.

"For what?"

What could Sal apologize for? He had just been pulling Chris's experience to look for the source of the fire. He didn't mean to do it, and Chris didn't seem to notice, but it felt impolite. Chris's thoughts reflected the man's expectation that Sal would know how to investigate a fire in some way because Chris had that same experience. The guilt was a moot issue as Sal noticed something on the ground.

It was just a scrap of black cloth with a few colorful threads, but Sal had enough experience in Afghanistan to recognize the remnants of a brightly-colored backpack.

"That would be my guess," Chris started, pausing to point at the ruined backpack, "for where the explosion started. I'm not an expert, but it's as straight forward as I've ever seen."

"Sometimes terrorists give a kid a backpack and tell them to set it somewhere," Sal said quietly. "The kid doesn't know anything. He was just doing what he was told by an elder. He probably set the bag there and ran."

"But why did the kid run to that building?" Chris asked, pointing at the building they'd just come from. "I believe that he probably didn't know, but why not just run off."

"The queen sends the drones to do her bidding," Caden said. "She says, 'Fight my battles then return to the nest.' "

Sal looked at Caden and then jogged back over to the where they'd just walked from. Chris quickly caught up, but Caden seemed disinterested.

I don't like it here, Sal heard the man's thoughts and recognized them as Caden's own brand of speaking to someone's mind. *I don't like running, and I don't like explosions. I don't like guns, and I don't like war movies, so impersonal.*

Sal only half-listened to the comments, as he rushed to the mud house and stepped over to where the boy had been. The hut was little more than a dirt floor with some blankets thrown around it. It was a bedding shop. Stacks of foam cushions with colored fabric sewn around them lined all of the walls. A small, battery-operated radio sat on the ledge of a window that cut a rough square out of the wall. Sal looked at a few of the colored carpets, kicking at a one. He turned to walk away when he heard a hollow thud. He reached down and pulled up the carpet, finding a trap door.

Did you know this was here? Sal asked Caden. Sending thoughts to the man always felt like trying to be heard in a crowded room.

Jack popped out of his little box and didn't expect men with guns to be surprised.

Why didn't you show it to me.

Because you knew it was there.

No I didn't.

Your mind is a book, Caden said. *Apparently, I read it better than you.*

Sal thought for a moment. *What made you look for it?*

I like to know where people hide. It makes me better at finding them.

He always thought like a child. He always thought in terms of games, books, and movies. How was he supposed to know what memories Sal could access? At least Sal knew his memories were in there somewhere, just nowhere that he could find.

Maybe it was the same with Chris. Maybe Sal just had to figure out how to access the man's memories. Hopefully, they wouldn't be as painful as Sal's past was to him.

"It doesn't make it right," Sal heard. Chris was standing at the entrance, looking at Sal.

"You think I don't know that!" Sal replied.

"I think that you think that," Chris said. "You're the mind reader, but I know guilt when I see it."

"Me too."

"That's my point," Chris said. "You could open that and find the devil himself, and you'd still feel the responsibility because you've chosen to be responsible."

"I pulled the trigger."

"And no one was there to stop you or look around, not like I was this time," Chris said. "You were in a fight, surrounded and probably ready to shit yourself. But none of that matters or will matter in your eyes because you did it. You pulled the trigger. Maybe he was just doing what someone told him to. I saw on TV these kids get trained from a young age. Maybe the kid was just trying to earn respect in someone's eyes, but it still doesn't matter."

"So what's your point?" Sal asked. He stomped over to Chris, but the man's own sorrow and commiseration was nearly enough to overwhelm Sal.

"My point is that the kid is dead," Chris said. "And I think I get it now. I think you're trying to help me, Caden, and that girl because you couldn't be there for that kid."

"Shouldn't I try to save someone?"

Chris shrugged. "I would."

And there it was, the man's asinine theory that everyone else was just some part of his own psyche.

Sal took a breath to say as much, but Chris held a hand up to calm him. "Yeah, I still don't think you're real, but let's say for a second you are real. You didn't join the Army out of guilt."

"My dad was in the Army," Sal explained. "He died before I was born. My mom never talked about him much, but she always said he lived to protect others. I wanted to be that way, too."

"So protect," Chris said. "Let this go."

"Can't let it go," Sal said.

"Fair enough. So focus on getting me out of this dream so I can tell my shrink all about it."

Yeah, Chris realized. *My shrink said I should help anyone who tries to help me in the dream. He said it after*—another surge of pain cut his idle thought away.

"Why does it hurt you?" Sal asked.

"Why does what hurt?" Chris responded, massaging his temples with the tips of his fingers.

"My memory is shot to hell, but it doesn't hurt when I try to remember," Sal explained. "It's just not there."

"I don't know," Chris said. "It's all coming back though. Maybe it hurts if I try to remember too quickly. Maybe it hurts because I'm trying to jam dreams where reality goes. Maybe I just have the worst hangover ever, and I'll wake up next to a beautiful woman and ugly headache."

"Waking up next to a woman is a headache," Caden said. "They're never pleasant the next day."

The comment was shockingly relevant and simple to understand. Neither Chris nor Sal could stop from laughing regardless of how crude the joke was. The laughter was short lived, but needed in the moment. *Did Caden know that?*

I always know when to speak and when to stay quiet. Caden said in his own telepathic way.

"I'll help you wake up," Sal told Chris, "but I don't know that you'll thank me when we do."

Images flashed through Chris's mind. Men chasing him. Someone attacking him in a cab. Kaitlyn vanishing after they rescued Chris. There was a blank spot in the sequence. Sal didn't understand how he knew, but he knew something critical was missing from that string of memories. He didn't ask Chris about it though because the mental images were already enough to cause another headache.

"We're getting distracted," Sal said. "Kaitlyn is awake, and we need to get her back before we can deal with whoever's doing this to us."

Kaitlyn's eyes fluttered open. Her head felt groggy, and everything seemed to be more or less a blur. She was in, well it could have been a hospital, only she doubted it. White sheets and a soft bed meant nothing to her. The pale green hospital gown wasn't enough to convince her she was in a hospital either. The setting was something she'd become accustomed to since she was younger.

Her mother and step-father met while seeking help for her night terrors, which were a result of her real father's death. It wasn't her dad's death that caused the dreams; it was her role in the event. She wasn't at fault. She was just a little girl trapped in a car that had skidded into a highway divider. She'd been a girl trapped in her own body ever since.

Hospitals had a feel to her. Even before her ability surfaced, hospitals felt too clean. The room she was in was meticulously sterile, but it didn't feel clean. She stood, her bare feet slapping down on the cold, black-and-white-tiled floor. She wobbled slightly from the effort and used the stainless steel medical cart next to her bed to hold herself up for a moment. She stumbled to the door. It was locked. She glanced around, noticing a camera in the top-corner of the room.

She took a step toward it, wondering what the camera was doing there and started, catching her own reflection in a small, rectangular mirror above a tiny sink. Her hair was almost entirely gone. She rushed to the mirror. Her long black hair had either just started to grow back or was recently shaved down to a few inches. As she felt her scalp, she noticed a vertical scar where the base of her skull met the top of her spine.

She nearly fainted before she realized her breathing was erratic. She'd been so engrossed in the horror of her scarred head that she didn't even feel the burning of her lungs until it was enough to make it seem like she was suffocating. She backpedalled to her bed and opened one of the medical carts, hoping her inhaler would be there. Strangely enough, the only object in the drawer was an L-shaped, gray inhaler. She picked it up and sucked in a bit of medication. Her breath came more and more regularly. Once she realized she wasn't going to pass out, she examined the inhaler. Her name and prescription were printed on a sticker that resided on the back of the inhaler. She reveled in a few luxurious breaths. She couldn't remember much more than what she'd recently gone through with Sal, Caden, and Chris. She couldn't remember how she got to where she was. She couldn't trace any memories back very far, so something strange was definitely happening.

She focused her mind. To her, feeling other's emotions was odd. Firstly, she could only reliably sense Sal's emotions. For whatever reason, she connected with him. Something about his desire to see her safe resonated in her. For anyone else, sensing their feelings was like trying to listen to a radio that was constantly cutting out and buzzing static. Her mom used to take her on long drives. Kaitlyn remembered her mother constantly playing with the radio.

She reached into her mind, crying out her thoughts. She couldn't tell if Sal heard her or not. Her ability didn't seem to work that way. After sending out her frantic message, she stretched out with her mind. As off-and-on as her strange talent was, she had come to identify Sal by his emotions. He was a combination of determination and concern. Fear or shame would seep into him from time to time, but Sal's sense of focus was how she came to recognize him.

She stretched out as far as she thought she could. Nothing. She felt a rush of anger, her own anger. When she was younger, she had to work to hide her emotions. After a while, they just sort of stopped showing. She told one of the doctors that her mom had taken her to that she'd simply forgotten how to show emotions. That's when her mother took her to a different sort of doctor. Her mom married her stepdad, and things seemed to be okay until her mom died. *It feels like it's been more than a year,* she thought to herself.

Without some sort of horrible creature chasing her, or Sal using those stupid voices to cheer her up, she felt incredibly alone. Maybe Chris was right. Maybe the whole thing was a figment of her imagination.

Fear, shame, frustration, guilt. The emotions hit her hard. It seemed odd for her to be able to know what others felt, considering she'd spent so long keeping people from seeing her emotions. She was young, but the idea of irony wasn't hard to grasp. She accepted the feelings. It was either that or cry out, and for her, that wasn't really an option.

Boredom. Another set of emotions, dominated by the urge to sleep or walk away, came to her. They both vanished, flickered, then came back. She hated how hard it was to focus. With nothing better to do, she stood, inhaler clinched firmly in hand, and moved over to the door and pulled at the handle as hard as she could.

Curiosity. Kaitlyn turned. At first, she thought the small camera in the top-corner of the rectangular room had felt curious. Then she concentrated on the emotion. Whoever it was, watched her from that camera. *Pride.* The emotion surprised her. Why would anyone feel pride while watching someone trapped like a rat? *Annoyance.* She wasn't sure why, but she easily identified each emotion as coming from one person. One person, who watched her through the camera in her room.

Her eyes got heavy. She didn't hear or smell anything. She just suddenly felt tired. Her own panic was enough to keep her on her feet, at least until she could stumble back to her bed. Once she got close enough, she felt her legs give way. She landed on the small bed an instant after her eyes shut. *I'm coming back!* She was sure he'd hear her. A part of her thought she felt that core of Sal just as she lost consciousness.

Chapter 20

PATIENCE

Graham had to turn sideways in order to fit through the door to the general's office. He shimmied in and shut the door behind himself before turning to face Gen. Leeroy Pederson. Pederson was shaking his head as his eyes raked along a progress report. More reports formed a small stack behind the saber on the general's large, oak desk. It was the only furnished room in the compound outside of Graham's office. Graham needed his office to look a certain way to maintain his progress with Subject 3. The only possible reason the general had for keeping such a large desk was to make others feel small. It certainly made Graham feel tiny.

Pederson set down one report and began scanning another. Graham recognized his progress reports for each subject. *So that's why he sent for me.* He stood in front of the general because he hadn't been told to sit. He focused his attention on the American flag, which hung on the wall just behind the general.

"They haven't Broken yet," Pederson said. "Why?"

"With respect sir, two of our subjects have Broken in less than half the time we expected them to," Graham replied, tapping the small, leather book he held against his leg. He brought it intending to share what he'd found in Subject 3's dream journal.

Pederson's calm stare was unnerving under any circumstances. He looked down at the report again for a moment before speaking. "I expected Subject 1 to be more than a communications and reconnaissance tool. It seems to me no D-W-E spikes are going to make him any more than that. Do you agree?"

Is this another test? Graham wondered. "Yes." The best practice when speaking with the general was to answer the exact questions he asked. Graham had seen many a soldier end up confessing to mistakes the general never new about until the unsuspecting grunt insisted on flapping his gums.

"Very well," Pederson said. "I'll work with what I have. It seems Subject 4 is nearly ready to Break as well."

"I'm confident Subject 4 will Break very soon," Strickland said in agreement. He couldn't keep his chin from rising.

"I'm thinking she'll make an excellent personal protector," Pederson said. "Since we already know what skill she has, I think that's where she'll be most useful. That is, of course, once she Breaks."

"Truth be told," Graham replied, taking a moment to run a hand through his gray-streaked, brown hair, "Subject 4 could function even at this point. It stands to reason the subject will surpass the previous," Strickland coughed into a boney hand before he could talk himself into real trouble. *Bringing them up would be foolish.*

"I mean to say, Subject 4 will be second only to Subject 2."

The general didn't move a muscle on his face.

How many years of training must he have had to keep his expression that calm? Graham wondered. It would be unnerving if Graham hand't already had so much experience with people who hid their emotions.

The general leaned back in his chair and let out a long breath. His head came only inches away from one of the dull gray metal file cabinets that lined the walls. Those were a necessity so long as Subject 02 remained a threat. With that former asset on the loose, computers weren't an option, which meant any records would have to be kept the old fashioned way.

"At least Subject 2 has proven historically successful. I should congratulate you on that much progress."

Graham wasn't asked a question, so he didn't respond. He stood listening to the hum of the air conditioning as it pumped into the room.

Another moment passed before Pederson leaned forward and offered a smile that stretched across his face. It looked primal under a set of eyes that betrayed no emotion at all. Graham fought the urge to ask what was going on. He kept his head straight. He refused to wipe away the sweat that formed on his brow no matter how much cold air the vents above his head provided.

"Sit down, Doctor. Relax," Pederson said in his gruff baritone voice.

The sudden change in the general's demeanor threw Graham off guard. It was easy enough to discern what Pederson wanted — results. The question was how quickly he wanted them.

He thinks the program should continue at the incredible pace in which it started, Graham thought to himself as he sat in one of the small wooden chairs in the cramped office.

Pederson smiled again, and this time, Graham noticed the general's gray eyes reflected at least a little happiness. "So it should be soon for the last, correct?"

Graham lifted the dream journal he'd brought in. The moved caused his badge to slip out of his lab coat, and his glasses slipped down a bit. Graham adjusted the glasses and shoved the badge back in its pocket before speaking.

"Just before we put Subject 3 under, he'd made another entry," Strickland explained, opening the journal to reveal the scratchy handwriting inside. "They may be linking already."

Pederson steepled his thick fingers together and nodded his head. "So what do we do to push Subject 3 into line?"

"Well considering this entire experiment is advancing faster than any estimation we had, regardless of previous data. I really think patience is the thing. Perhaps you demand faster results than are altogether realistic? I presume this is because Subject 1 broke faster than anyone could have dreamed, General."

It wasn't the most tactful way to explain his point, but Graham hoped it worked.

"No one could have imagined Subject 1 breaking that quickly," Graham continued. "Even with less than impressive abilities and power, it set a tone that I don't think either of us initially anticipated."

How could something be so impressive and disappointing at the same time? It didn't make Graham wrong though.

"That might be, but I'd like to move on before we're interrupted," Pederson said. "Our funds are nearly gone, and unless this last subject develops Brandon's particular skill, we can't count on another influx of money."

"Are we in that much danger?" Graham asked, trying to ignore the desk in front of him.

"I put Brandon's last act of loyalty to good use," Pederson replied. "But no amount of embezzlement or proper investment of our initial surge of funds can last forever. This is our last stand, Doctor, and this is our last fighting position."

"Does this have something to do with the reports of the loss of the Warehouse One?" Graham asked.

Pederson nodded again. "It may be my own prodigal children have come back," he said. "Which would be good so long as these new recruits get the training they need."

"Do you really think it's the original group of test subjects?" Graham asked.

"No," Pederson answered. "If it was them, they'd be here already. I think it's more likely the government found the warehouse. They might have even found this location when they shut down the hatchery."

Graham let out a frustrated breath. The hatchery would have been the best, most cost-effective option. He barely got out of the building undetected before soldiers swept in and destroyed three years of work.

That setback forced Pederson and Graham to start over from a test subject standpoint.

Pederson reached over the reports and picked up the ceremonial saber. Graham knew it was the very same saber the general received upon his commissioning. The man's face may never betray emotion, but he demonstrated his ability to hold a grudge in other ways.

"So what can we do if not push the other subjects to Break?" Pederson finally asked. He slid an inch of blade out of its scabbard. He stared at the reflection of his gray eyes in the polished steel, which gleamed in the florescent light of the room.

"The best option is to wait, Sir," Graham said.

"Doctor, the world is on the brink of advancing. Had we waited for the world, for nature, to move forward, no one would know what humanity could do. Worse, some other world power, or God forbid, terrorist group, would have blundered into the next age of warfare."

"You know I agree with you in that, Sir," Graham said. "But we're doing all we can."

"It isn't enough," Pederson said, slamming the saber back into its scabbard. "The U.S. gained its status because it ushered in the nuclear era. Should it fail to usher in the next era, whoever does will dominate, and that domination would be born by my country's fall. That's the price we pay if we choose to wait while others choose to do."

Graham took a deep breath. "I'd like to see what Subject 3 has learned since we put him under," he said. "He can verify my theory that they're finally linking. If that's the case, the most prudent thing would be to put Subject 3 back under and keep the test subjects sedated until they Break, then we can plan for what they'll do when they wake."

"Which would mean they'll want to lash out?" Pederson asked as he sat back down. Graham heard the leather in the man's chair stretching as he sat.

"Using their new power," Graham said.

"The back-up measures will keep things from getting out of hand."

"All the more reason to establish a test of their skills," Graham said, smiling proudly and shoving his glasses back up his nose. "The scenario I have in mind will do that, General. But we'll need the time to prepare, so while we wait for Subject 3 to get in line, we'll prepare for when all four subjects are active. It'll be a preview of their capabilities."

Leeroy smiled. "That would be excellent."

Chapter 21

REFLECTIONS OF THE PAST

K aitlyn's thoughts and feelings abruptly flowed into Sal's mind like a tidal wave, causing him to stumble mid-stride as he walked along the pot-hole riddled mud road in his dream version of Afghanistan. Panic, fear, and desperation pounded into Sal over and over again. He, Chris, and Caden hadn't managed to wake, so it was reasonable to assume that she'd fallen back asleep or had been put to sleep.

"The glass doll has fallen back with the rest of the toys, but she might shatter soon," Caden said. He sounded disappointed, perhaps even sad. Sal could only rely on Caden's tone. The old man's thoughts were as cloudy and tightly bound as always.

Not wanting to waste an instant, Sal reached out to her through her storm of emotions. *Where are you?* Sal asked telepathically.

No! her thoughts said. *The beast and the red man.*

I'm coming! Sal sent.

"But will you get there in time?" Caden asked in his crackly voice. He brought his gnarled hands in front of his mouth in what might have been an attempted prayer. It also might have just been a way to hide his face. The man's emotions were a mystery to Sal, but his expressions still betrayed a thought or two. "It's her fears she's trapped by. Can you out-run your fears?"

"What's going on?" Chris asked, completely oblivious to all the mental and emotional communication. He looked around the ruined Afghan village they'd been in since Sal's mind brought up the memory.

"Kaitlyn is back in the dream," Sal said. Though he found himself less relieved by that prospect than he'd initially assumed.

"We walk in dreams. We walk in minds," Caden said. "You and I can walk from mind to mind the way others visit people across the street."

"What's he talking about?" Chris asked.

Sal didn't wait for Chris to say more. Back when Sal had first found Chris, Sal managed to shift and appear where Chris was as soon as he found Chris's thoughts. It was a matter of connecting his mind to another's, then seeing himself there. If Sal understood what Caden said correctly, he could move to Kaitlyn the same way they'd found Chris.

Sal grabbed the taller man's shoulder. Caden touched Sal's arm as if it might shock him. Chris opened his mouth to demand what was going on again. Sal didn't wait to listen or explain. He touched Kaitlyn's mind.

He felt himself drift. It was the most accurate word he could think of to describe the experience. He drifted into his own mind. In the blackness of his thoughts, he could somehow see Chris and, to a lesser extent, Caden. Simultaneously farther away and no farther away at all, Sal found Kaitlyn. He focused on her, saw her thoughts and became a part of them.

Sal opened his eyes.

"What the hell are you..." Chris's words fell away as he realized they had moved. He now wore a pair of faded blue jeans and a blue sweater over a white t-shirt. His change of clothes had nothing on the change in scenery. "Fuck." The word seemed a fine summary for the litany of thoughts crossing his mind.

At the moment, Sal, now wearing a pair of cargo pants and a gray, button-up shirt, had to admit his own thoughts mirrored Chris's. They were on a highway. *Or did the world just change around us?* Sal pushed the thought away. Trying to understand what they were going through was a mental track he couldn't run around at the moment.

It was dark. The moon was a sliver of light in a partly cloudy sky. A cobalt blue, mid-sized car lay on its side. Moonlight gleamed off the metal divider that separated one direction of the highway from another. The divider coiled in a ribbon from the car to a devastating mass of dirt, wood, and metal where the vehicle must have veered off the road.

Sal followed the twisted and contorted divider back to the car. The steel looked like a boa trying to eat an alligator the way it wrapped around the '67 Mustang, though Sal, who didn't know much about cars, wasn't sure how he knew the make, model, and year of the vehicle. Kaitlyn was inside of it. A few feet down the road from the Mustang stood the odd half-man, half-bull hybrid of a monster Kaitlyn called the beast. It towered over the car, even at a distance, letting out a huge, guttural roar that was more a human scream than animal. Perhaps equally as far away, on the opposite side of the Ford, was a man without skin. He crawled toward the car, dragging his own legs behind himself.

Sal tensed to charge in to save Kaitlyn.

Wait!

The mental shout froze him in his tracks. Chris, unable to hear Kaitlyn's thoughts, started to run toward her. Sal grabbed Chris before he could get too far.

"What the hell are you waiting for?" he asked. His feet scrunched the dry bushes that lined the otherwise empty terrain surrounding the highway.

"Just wait. Kaitlyn doesn't want us to move yet," Sal said, knowing he didn't sound confident with this course of action.

"I like this movie," Caden said. He was in a dark-gray suite. A white shirt with blue pinstripes looked dated. Seeing Caden reminded Sal of an old black-and-white movie of some kind. "I haven't seen the ending yet." He sat down on the hard dirt as if honestly watching a major motion picture in a theater.

Chris moved to pull away. Sal gripped the man harder. Chris spun swinging a fist at him, trying to push Sal away. Sal ducked under the attack and held the taller man as tightly as possible. "You don't know what's going on. I don't think this is a dream."

Trying to fight Chris and listen to Kaitlyn was like trying to juggle while balancing on a unicycle. "Just wait," Sal said, gritting his teeth in a struggle to keep Chris confined. He hoped he didn't sound as doubtful as he felt. "We have to trust her."

Chris stopped struggling. Sal could feel the man's uncertainty.

"I'll never let her come to harm," Sal said in response to Chris's thoughts. As if to prove him a liar, the beast stomped toward the car, hooved feet leaving cracks in the black road with each step.

Fear. Concern. Anger. Frustration. Fear.

Someone's emotions flooded through Kaitlyn faster than she could process. She'd decided she would not break when her mom died in yet another car crash. She would *not* break, though life seemed to want her to.

Fear. Rage. Anger. Concern. Fear.

There was something else in the jumble of emotions, but it felt weird. She thought the feelings her abilities sensed might be Caden's. His emotions were always muted, but this set of emotions didn't feel muted exactly. She struggled, trying to figure the emotion out. Then she noticed her reflection in the cracked rearview mirror of the overturned, cobalt-blue Mustang. It was her face, but not. The eyes were the same hazel; the hair was the same shade of black, but her face seemed more vibrant. She had seen pictures of her younger self. She smiled before her father died. She had even been quick to laugh.

Something about that reflection, the one of her as a little girl, bothered her. In those dreams, the red man always tried to grab her. "Sal," she said.

If this dream remained the same as it usually did, the car would burst into flames just as the red man grabbed her. Maybe the red man wanted to hold her in the car to keep her from escaping.

Fear, and...something else. Her asthma threatened to kick up again as she sensed the emotions. She realized they belonged to the red man. She forced herself to take deep breaths. She looked behind her at the beast as it took a step closer. Puff's of hot air steamed from its mouth and snout.

It didn't feel anything. It was a dream. Whatever link her dream had to her memory, the beast was only connected because she was afraid of it. She'd read about dreams and night terrors, fascinated that so many people could break down what she feared into just so many symbols. Most considered those things in her dreams to be bits of herself.

The beast roared a deep, guttural bellow that shook her to her core. She looked away from it, if only to avoid seeing that creature. Only, by turning away, she looked at the red man. Skinless, the wretch looked toward her with a skeletal smile. She continued to watch it. Then she looked at the reflection of her younger self. Something inside her, something that had fractured earlier in this string of nightmares, Broke.

Concern. Fear. Pain.

Love.

She shuttered. Her breath came in quick fits.

"Kaitlyn!" Sal shouted. He must have felt her emotions. She hoped Sal could read her thoughts, because she could hardly put them in order.

Concern. Fear. Pain. Love. Unconditional, unfettered love. The emotions surged through her like electricity.

She thought they were Sal's emotions. In dreams, nothing from the dream had feelings, but this wasn't exactly a dream. It was her memory. The reason she hid her emotions all the time, the cause of her night terrors, was this accident. The night her father died. Her father, who loved her more than life itself, who only ever wanted to see her laugh, died in this car crash. But not before he saved her.

I understand, Sal's thoughts helped her focus. Her breathing eased, and she knew Sal would stop the beast. The beast was a guardian, something her mind had made up to protect her from the memory. She couldn't hide from it any more. The beast was the threat. *He's keeping my father from me,* she thought.

She turned her head. Through the fractured rear window, she saw the beast float into the air. She could feel Sal's emotions. *Focus. Determination. Concern. Hatred.* The beast didn't stand a chance.

She turned away, hearing the beast cry out for an instant in rage or pain. The sound cut off quickly in a sort of yelp that reminded Kaitlyn of a dog that had had its tail stepped on. She looked at her reflection. She saw tears on her face, the last tears she'd shed from what doctors had told her. She was only a toddler then, but inside that toddler's body, the older version of herself watched. Her eyes looked from the mirror to the windshield. The hole was laced with blood, and something that looked like a jumble of wet rags.

Suddenly, her father, the red man, vanished only to reappear at the opening of the windshield. Her father, Donald Olhouser, was ordinary in her memory. Before the glass of the car had mutilated him, he was a skinny man, who passed his sharp features onto her, right down to the straight, black hair he kept combed to one side. He was just a man, but his resolve was anything but normal.

Pain. He was in so much pain, but even as he suffered, his love for her overwhelmed his agony. No one, except maybe Sal she supposed, would ever believe that the pain her father felt could be controlled by anything, but her dad's love and unrelenting resolve to see her safe, kept the pain at bay.

Her father flickered again, from the windshield to the front seats of the car. He reached at her and let out a wail.

Agony. Fear. Pain. Above all the other emotions her father felt was love.

"Kaitie," it was a quite whisper. She barely heard it escape her father's throat after his shout. He reached and pressed the buckle that kept her in the car seat. She fell on top of him. *Pain. Such blinding pain.* She felt his emotions so strongly she cried out. *Joy.*

In her nightmare, she thought the red man's skeletal smile was one of triumph. In truth, it was. Her father smiled at her. He had saved her. He let out another roar. In that roar Kaitlyn felt every ounce of strength, love, pain, fear, concern, and determination her father could muster. He pushed himself. For the third time, he drove himself through the glass of the windshield. He used his own body to keep her from getting cut too badly.

The part of him that held her fell outside of the car, away from the flames. He didn't make it the rest of the way out when the flames surrounding the car found their full strength. He died before the fire took him. He died before the flames burned him away while Kaitlyn's younger self lie crying on the road.

She remembered the whole thing. The memory faded away into a full-fledged dream. It was just her on the road with her father lying in front of her. He was no longer the red man. He was Donald Olhouser, a skinny man with sharp features who picked his little girl up first thing every day after work to tickle her.

"Is my little girl still able to laugh?" he'd ask. He'd tickle her until he felt certain she was capable of feeling joy.

The last thing he felt when he died was happiness. No, combining that with joy and glee would still not be a good enough word. He saved her. Her father had saved her. Now she remembered.

"Daddy!" she shouted. She scrambled to hold him in her lap. His green shirt was freshly ironed. His black slacks and shoes remained spotless despite the gas, oil, and dirt on the road. She noticed her hands had changed. She was her right age again. "Daddy no! Please don't die! Don't leave me!"

It was no use. The body in her lap was only a reflection of how she thought she remembered her father. It wasn't enough for her, but it was all she had. She tilted her head back and screamed. Every emotion she'd held back for ten years escaped. She let them out. She let them all out. Someone embraced her.

Concern. Sadness. Love. Focus. Determination. Sal. He held her as she held her father and let the pain pass through her.

"I'm so sorry," he whispered.

She tried to collect her thoughts to speak.

"I'll be quiet," he said. He must have heard her thoughts, felt her desire to just have him there, but not speak.

He was a kind man. Sal cared for her. He'd protect her. Her stepfather was a nice enough man, too. He kept her when her mother died. He taught Kaitlyn a lot about her problem. He let her study and made sure she had all she needed, but her stepfather's kindness was nothing compared to her real father's love. She hated knowing it almost as much as she truly loved feeling it. Only she would know, truly know, how much her father loved her. She couldn't even tell him how much she loved him back.

"Daddy," she cried. "Oh, Daddy." She let her head rest against Sal's chest, but she had eyes only for her dad. They blurred with tears. She'd never hold back her emotions again. Her father gave his life just to know she'd smile and laugh again. So she'd let herself feel, even this sadness that was almost more than she could take. She'd feel it because that's what her dad wanted.

Chapter 22

RAGE

Steve Delmas barely waited for Kira to pull the matte-black Jeep Wrangler to a stop before he leapt out, his booted feet sending up puffs of dust as they landed in soft sand. They came in the dark, night-vision goggles helping them see, though the sliver of moonlight tested even Brandon's modifications as so little ambient light made for piss-poor vision. They formed up at the location where the compound was supposed to be fortified, but there wasn't a hint of activity anywhere.

Steve looked through the green-cast display of his goggles even as he activated his powers. He reached out with his mind, probing the area to feel if anyone was around, if anyone was even alive. His mind confirmed what his eyes saw. The compound was completely charred and devoid of any life. Out in the middle of a Nevada desert, it seemed even the wildlife was giving this place a wide berth.

Dom and Brandon appeared beside him, their M-4 rifles raised. Steve could sense their Delta Wave patterns. He didn't know what made him unique. He could use any mental power that he'd ever heard of, and, using his mind to read the Delta Wave Emissions of others, he could sense another's power and abilities.

"There's not a single active electronic device," Brandon reported in his southern drawl. "The area feels muted, so I imagine they used an EMP. Then they fragged the place."

"Door," Steve said in his gruff voice, allowing his frustration to bubble to the surface.

Dom focused on the closest wall, and it imploded, creating a point of entry for the team. Steve used the same telekinesis to clear the dust from the air.

Link complete, Kira's thoughts flowed through the group. She always could use her innate telepathy to degrees Steve just couldn't manage. Maybe it was because Steve blocked a part of his mind away. For whatever reason though, Kira was stronger than he was in her own way.

Their boots crunched on charred wood and soot-stained stone. Steve let Dom take point. They moved in a standard wedge formation, with Steve behind Dom at the apex of the wedge.

They flowed into the building as a single unit and shifted into paired columns. Dom and Kira moved side-by-side. With Kira's telepathic link, Steve and Brandon kept their eyes shut, seeing through her eyes and sensing the area with Steve's telepathy. They moved as one because they were one.

There were advantages to the technique. They would move flawlessly. They would react instantly to a threat. What Dom or Kira saw, heard, or felt would transmit itself along the link to the others in the blink of an eye. The disadvantage was why they only used this technique when they were certain there wasn't anyone in the immediate area. If anyone ever shot Kira while they were linked, they'd all die.

The reason for the link was to gather and pass along information at the same time as they moved through the building. Steve had to mute his emotions and kept those of his friends to a dull ache. They all hated what they saw.

Ten bodies.

Four here.

Fifteen.

Ten bodies over here.

Small rooms sat between steel-paneled walls. Each room had a handful of beds, now charred husks that only seemed to make the burnt bodies in them more obvious. The night vision should have made it easier, but instead of muting the blackened skin, it intensified the contrast, making each body look more menacing. Dom actually reacted more strongly to the blackened remains than Kira, but that might only be because Kira had to learn how to shut herself away from others when she Broke. For some reason, Steve and Dom broke with complete control of their powers. Brandon didn't Break so much as fall apart with what the Pederson did to him.

Five bodies.

Nine Bodies.

Six Bodies.

Though most of the building was burnt or charred in some way, the group noticed thick black lines, which traced the burn pattern from room to room, indicating that the people who set fire to the building took the time to pour accelerant along every room and onto every bed. Steve wondered if they at least sedated the patients before lighting them on fire.

Seems compartmentalized, Steve thought, which meant the rest of the team had the same thought at only a fraction-of-a-second later. They'd passed the smaller rooms and entered a larger area. What was a series of small sleeping chambers became warehouse-sized areas. Each warehouse seemed decorated like a scene from some horror movie. A reason came from Dom's mind before Steve's original thought made it through the rest of the group.

They were in a scenario compound. No one could sleep forever, but sleep was the key. So the assholes who did this had a batch of lackeys create various nightmare scenarios, a combination of b-horror movie sets with mercenaries to play roles. Steve still remembered the first scenario he had faced. *Alexia...*

Knock it off! the group of minds shouted at Steve. Suddenly, Steve was alone in his thoughts. Kira severed the link.

"Of all people!" she shouted at him. Her voice trembled with sadness. She let out a sniff. She might have been crying. She literally felt Steve's agony.

"I'm sorry," Steve grunted.

Dom just walked away.

"It's okay," Brandon said. Always the mediator. "Hang on. I think I can get some lights going."

Steve switched off his goggles and locked them in the up position on his cranial, closing his eyes. After a few moments, he felt the lights come on. He slowly allowed his eyes to flutter open. The room was bathed in a red glow. Brandon found some way to convince the emergency lights they were operational.

"Why?" Kira asked, the red glow reflecting off the tears she'd shed in sadness before she could cut Steve out of the link. That same red glow seemed to amplify the rage that was boiling to the surface of her emotions.

"We're close," Steve said. "I'm sorry. I've been an ass for the past two weeks."

"More like since ever," Dom muttered. His half-smile, and the fact that he was right, took the sting off the comment. He pulled off his cranial. The clunky goggles always weighed them down, and any chance to take even a small amount of weight off was one Dom was going to take.

"You're stronger than us," Kira said. "It's why I don't like having you in the link. It takes everything we have just to process each other's thoughts and put them in order. You have time to think, and for you that's dangerous."

The tears were gone and the shake in her voice faded away, replaced by that stern, almost insulting tone she loved so much when talking to Steve right after being proven right. She didn't want him in the link in the first place, and his mental lapse was proof she was right.

"I know," Steve said. He finally admits he'd been hard on them, and she takes that as permission to rub his nose in it.

"I'm not saying this to hurt you," she said. She was reading his damn mind! She raised an eyebrow at him as if to ask, "Why wouldn't I be?"

"I'm saying this because you need to hear it," she said. "I'm saying this because you don't know how close you are to the edge."

Suddenly, he could see inside himself. Kira linked with him, showing him what she saw. It was one thing for a man to admit he was on edge. Most men worth half their ass knew enough of themselves to admit they were stressed. It was another thing entirely to see how close to the edge he was. Steve saw his thoughts through Kira's mind. It looked like some incredibly complex system of wires. Each of them seemed ready to short out. *If* he'd lost control of himself for an instant, he'd have killed his own team.

"What are you hiding in there?" Kira asked unkindly. With her life at stake, Steve understood why.

"You're going to pick that fight now?" Dom asked. He took a step back as if to stay clear of the blast radius.

"I damn sure will if there's a chance his memory might be the last thing I see before I become a vegetable."

Steve's empathy allowed him to feel her rage.

"I think it's his right," Brandon said. "We can do what we do so naturally now. It doesn't give us the right."

"Enough!" Steve shouted. "Obviously, linking is a bad idea. At least with me in the link."

"Also kind of limits our best gun in a way," Dom added.

Steve looked at him. Dom was usually the first in line to claim he shouldn't be in charge. Come to think of it, Dom only admitted Steve's value as a weapon, not a leader.

"You've led us this far," Kira said.

"That's the last time you invite yourself into my head, Kira," Steve said, allowing his own fury to show.

"No," she spat. "I need to know if you're going to go over edge before you kill any of us. So if you want me out of your thoughts, keep me out. It's the only way I can know you're not a danger to us."

She stalked up to him, the fury in her eyes a stark contrast to the soft curves of her face. "In one instant you forced us to feel how much this means to you. You get that right?" Each word was a knife in his gut.

They couldn't help but know now. They'd all had one reason or another. They all had their time in the scenario compound. They all woke up from nightmares only to find themselves attacked by men in straitjackets or psychos with knives. It brought them together, but that didn't make the nightmares stop.

"Are you back, sir?" Brandon asked. *Damn! Brandon?*

"Yeah kid," Steve said. "I've got it locked down."

He felt a tremor in his mind. It felt the same as the moment before a fall. He glared at Kira and slammed a mental shield around his thoughts. She smiled at him.

"He's back," she said, a little of the hostility leaving her voice.

Steve gave her a chagrinned smile. She'd been digging in his head just to prove he wasn't focused enough to keep her out. The whole thing was a test to help him get his shit together.

"I'm not gonna hug you," Dom said. "You slip, and I get to be in charge. I'd just prefer to prove I'm more capable than you."

"You'd die for him," Kira said. "Hell, you're more loyal to him than Brandon."

Brandon let out a guffaw. Steve stared at Dom. He'd never thought Dom did more than put up with him. Of course, Steve refused to root around his team's minds. Was that out of chivalry, or because he feared what he might let out while he was in there. *Alexia...*

Steve opened his mind, sending out the image of the building they'd generated using their link. The image of more than 50 dead bodies, burned beyond recognition, brought a solemnness to the husk of the room in which they now stood.

"There's only one place left for that asshole," Steve said.

Dom's eyes burned with a rage that equaled Steve's. Kira started checking her weapons. With nothing to shoot, there wasn't anything else to do with her anger. Brandon turned away.

Steve walked over and spun the youngest member of the team around. "No more shame," he told Brandon. "No more regret. No more fear."

"I am *not* afraid of that man," Brandon said. His voice could have slit steel.

"Damn right you're not," Steve said.

"You haven't mentioned what this means," Dom said. "If this was the large scenario compound, then he has his new team."

"Or there's a handful of people out there somewhere about to realize the nightmares they've been having are about to get worse," Steve said.

"I don't know about that," Brandon said. "That first compound wasn't shut down yet. The information I was able to pull from their system says the project had just started. There hasn't been enough time for more than one, maybe two of them to Break."

Break was the term that Pederson's lab rat used to describe the moment a person's ability surfaced. It stung to use that asshole's word for it, but there didn't seem to be a better one for the experience.

"We either get there in time, or we don't," Steve said. "It doesn't change the mission."

"It does if whoever managed to advance to Phase Three is on the general's side," Kira said.

Dom shook his head. "I don't care if they Broke the second they got there." He waved off Brandon before he could argue if anyone could Break that fast. "I said I don't care. We've had years to work together. If they're on his side, they go down with him."

"They can't have all Broken this quickly," Brandon muttered. He would know. He Broke well before the rest of the team.

"Dom's right," Steve said. "We either save those last few people and kill Pederson, or we kill him and anyone trying to help him. Either way, he's a dead man."

Chapter 23

LET IT BURN

Chris watched Kaitlyn cry. Standing dumbfounded on the side of an unfamiliar highway, he didn't have the first clue as to what to do in the situation. It just wasn't possible. Every ounce of him held onto the idea that life had a set of rational explanations. Otherwise, what control did he have? If recent events were any indication, he had less than he thought. Unless it was all just some horribly realistic dream. If it was a dream, it was the worst he'd ever had.

He wanted to rush to help Kaitlyn when they had first arrived, and he had to force himself to trust Sal. He hadn't felt the drive to rush into danger like that in a long time. Ever since he met Sal, Chris started feeling more and more like the firefighter he once was, so he had trusted Sal, and it all worked out. Once it was over, Chris couldn't do anything but stare. How could Sal have known the girl would be fine?

He wasn't sure how long they'd been there. The body of Kaitlyn's father faded away just as Chris thought of the question. The car faded next, but the coiled highway divider and black-top road remained. She looked up at Sal and stood. Even with her back turned, Chris knew she was wiping tears from her eyes.

He closed his eyes. No one needed to watch that sort of thing. He took a few deep breaths. A small hand grabbed his. He opened his eyes to see her small, nimble fingers wrapped around his own, her creamy skin appearing all the lighter against his deep black skin.

"Thank you," Kaitlyn said, her face splitting into a smile that, surprisingly, forced Chris to smile, too. "You don't have to be sorry for me though."

"How did?" Chris stopped. If he accepted this dream as real, what would he do? No, she'd know how he felt because she was some part of his own subconscious.

"I think you haven't gained any powers because you refuse to believe it's possible," she said. She was in a simple pair of jeans and a purple t-shirt. Her black sneakers looked completely clean despite the dry air and dusty road.

"The wisdom of babes," Caden said. The old man's voice startled Chris. He'd forgotten the crazy bastard was there. He seemed all the more startling because of that ridiculous suit of his. Some 1980's high school kid must have wanted his prom suit back.

"I've told Sal about my stepdad." Kaitlyn began to explain at length about night terrors. Everything she said sounded familiar in some way to Chris. He couldn't remember where he'd heard about type A or B night terrors, but Kaitlyn seemed to represent whatever part of his mind heard the terms.

"You wake up screaming at night don't you?" Kaitlyn asked, her hazel eyes gleaming, digging into him.

"Yeah," he said.

"But you don't remember the dream, at least not most of them."

Chris certainly remembered one vividly, but not the rest. "I'm seeing a doctor." He admitted. "In fact, I'm…" he paused.

"Are you okay?" Sal asked.

"I can't remember," Chris said. A sharp pain stabbed his mind.

"Pandora shouldn't go opening boxes," Caden said. "What's inside isn't going to be pleasant."

"What do you remember?" Sal asked. He had this way of squaring his shoulders. Chris started to recognize it as some sort of stance, like Sal was getting ready for a fight. When Sal stood like that, even a few inches shorter, he was imposing.

"I'm supposed to help you," Chris said. The pain in his skull surged into a blinding headache. Chris clenched his eyes shut and massaged his temples. Even then, a high-pitched tone rang in his left ear.

"Why are you the only one who feels pain whenever you try to remember something?" Sal asked.

Chris was more worried about keeping his head from exploding than answering the question, but he couldn't help but think the reason was because he was the only real person in the dream.

"You're right," Sal told Kaitlyn, "at least as far as his refusal to believe we're real."

Kaitlyn looked from Sal back to Chris and said, "Sal got his powers when he felt like he couldn't protect me or Caden. It's all he cares about."

Chris looked at the man, who turned away.

"I had my ability when Sal came and saved me. My stepdad says that we," she paused as if trying to remember the right words, "self-actualize. We can only achieve our highest state of being by facing what caused our trauma to begin with. I think he works so hard to help me because he promised my mom he'd make sure I got better before she died."

The term "self-actualize" caused the siren blaring between his ears to pick it up another decibel. He covered his ear until the sound dwindled to a low hum.

"What do you mean by trauma?" Chris asked. He tried to bite off the question. She was maybe 13 years old. That's how he knew she couldn't be real. No kid could know that much. Even if she was Freud's kid, she shouldn't know that much.

She might be my mind's representation of the doc, all the parts of my subconscious that remembers what he said. Why can't I remember his name? Why can't I remember what he looks like? The memory seemed to pop into his mind, and that headache flared up in response. *Is it because I'm starting to wish everyone here were real? Is that why my head is screaming?*

"Don't do that!" she said. That was new. Since he'd met her, Kaitlyn was usually as quiet and meek as a mouse. Then again, there were differences. Her face seemed relaxed. Her eyes seemed more alert. It still didn't make her an expert in anything.

"Some girls play with dolls or talk about boys," she rolled her eyes as if that last part was the dumbest thing a girl could do. "I wake up screaming. Sometimes I woke up in different rooms. Once, I tried to crawl out the bathroom window. It's on the second floor of my house. People like us do that. We don't just have nightmares we wake up from and realize were simple bad dreams. We relive and reenact whatever crap we're trying to deal with."

Chris felt his jaw sag as she spoke. It was terrible to hear, even if she said it without any real venom. She spoke simply, if a bit pointedly. It was the most inflection he'd heard her use since he met her. Worse, her information was far too close to how he spent his evenings.

"So instead of getting to talk about dances or homework," she said, her voice picking up speed as she tried to control herself. "I tied myself to my bed just so I didn't try to fly while sleeping. So yeah, I asked my stepdad every question I could think of. I visited his office whenever he let me, and I read every book I could find about it."

Suddenly her breath caught. She stammered a few times. Was she asthmatic? He and Sal got to her at nearly the same time, each taking a knee at her side. Caden seemed content to watch. His green eyes were locked on her, but he didn't so much as budge. He tilted his head, as if unsure what to do. Maybe that's why he stayed where he was.

Sal whispered encouragement to her, and her breath started to come more regularly.

"I didn't mean," Chris said. Sal stood, but Kaitlyn didn't give Chris a chance to say anything.

"Well you did!" she said. Chris wanted to take it back, but he couldn't find the words even if she let him speak. "And it sucks because you're scared half to death right now. You're scared because everything I've said made you think about your own crap."

He didn't have a response to that. From the moment she'd started talking, Chris focused on his own nightmare. Could he really remember the dream, or was it just the heat? He could almost feel the searing flames he'd nearly been consumed by in real life once, before everything got fucked up. He remembered vague fragments like a man burning and screaming.

Something touched his head. Chris looked up to see a fleck of ash drift down and land on his forehead to join the one that had first gained his attention. He looked around, and the world had changed. They were back in the same cul-de-sac they'd originally found him in. All that walking, all of that fighting, only to wind up right back where they started. Chris would have laughed if it wasn't so terrifying.

"We've just changed dreams," Sal said. His posture stiffened. His fingers clenched into fists.

"Snow!" Caden shouted. He was more of a child than Kaitlyn. He ran in circles trying to catch the ash as it fell. The looney was uninterested in the burning house just a few hundred feet away.

"We're back in your dream," Sal said to Chris.

"Chris?" Kaitly asked. "Chris calm down."

Calm? He was as still as a post. Then he realized why. If he so much as blinked, he'd run screaming.

"Chris," Kaitlyn said. "Chris you have to breathe."

Was that why he was light headed? Was that why everything seemed to be going black? He wanted to breathe, but he couldn't. He could see the house. It was part of a cul-de-sac that had gone up like the Fourth of July. It was all just how he dreamed it was, and his dreams were a perfect reflection of the real-life event.

"Chris!" Sal shouted. It took Chris a second to realize the man was shaking him. "For God's sake man, we're real, and we can help, but you have to tell us what to expect."

"I'm going to die," Chris whispered, and Sal stopped shaking him. "I deserve to. I know what's about to happen and who's going to do it to me."

"You remember?" Kaitlyn asked. She seemed somewhere between curiosity and shock.

"Yeah, it's not a repressed memory, just an awful one," Chris said.

"Then you can fight it, or—"

"No," Chris interrupted. "He's come to punish me, and I'm tired of it. I'm done being ashamed of it."

He looked at the house. *Damn, were the flames that bad when it really happened?* It was like the whole block was burning. "Pete! I'm here man! It's okay!"

Pete died during the fire. He had pulled a beam off Chris. They nearly made it out of the house when the weight of that beam caused the floor to collapse. Chris wanted to save him. He *tried* to save him, but the damn fire was out of control. They never should have gone in. Someone said something about a person being trapped. Turned out, the person everyone thought was trapped in the building had gone out the back door.

Chris was a damn fool and charged in without thinking. It was his fault they were in the house. It was his fault he'd gotten stuck. It was his fault his best friend died. "Come on, Pete. I won't run!"

He expected Pete to come out of the building. Instead his dead friend appeared behind him. The sound Pete let out had to be one of rage. It had to be one of hatred.

"I can't feel its emotions," Sal said.

"Can't feel air either," Caden muttered. He was the only one who didn't seem to have to step away from the sheer heat. "Still there."

"It's not our memory," Kaitlyn told Sal. "You couldn't feel my dad's emotions either because you weren't there. It's just a dream for us."

"He wants to kill me," Chris broke in. He stood in front of Pete's burning body. "What are you waiting for?!"

"I don't think he wants to kill you," Sal said.

"What the fuck do you know?"

"I know the same way you helped me when my thoughts took us to Afghanistan." The world flickered for a moment, from a night lit by a fire too strong to control, to an afternoon in Afghanistan. "I know guilt when I hear it, too, Chris," Sal said. "I don't need my powers for it. I'd know it from a mile away blindfolded."

"I guess I was a bit of a hypocrite, huh?" Chris said. It was easy to tell a man to let go. It was another thing entirely to do it.

"I shot a kid," Sal said. The world flickered again. Chris remembered the bazaar. He remembered helping Sal. Could Sal really help him?

Pete was still right in front of Chris, but the cul-de-sac flickered as Sal spoke.

"You helped me," Sal said slowly. "I've shot that kid a hundred more times in nightmares. All I've ever wanted to do was help people, and I can't wash away that guilt, but maybe we can. You've already helped me. I *swear* I'll try to help you."

The world finally stopped shifting. They were back in front of the burning building. Bits of soot and ash fell, dotting the sidewalk. Kaitlyn walked over to wrap her arms around Sal's waist. His own attire shifted back into a military outfit. He sounded so earnest. He even sounded desperate. It was like helping Chris was just like Kaitlyn said it was, the most important thing in Sal's world.

"Okay," Chris found himself saying. That was it. He couldn't find any way to convince himself he'd ever make up something as terrible as what Sal went through, nor could he ever imagine anything like what he'd just witnessed with Kaitlyn. Pete made sense. It happened. Chris realized he didn't have any control over anything. There wasn't a rational explanation for the world. As he accepted the idea, his clothes shifted from the blue jeans and sweater he'd been wearing, to a firefighting ensemble.

"I don't know what that kid would do if he saw me again," Sal said. "But if that man saved your life, I don't think he'd kill you for it now. It's not punishment Chris. It's need. You're the one punishing yourself. You're the one making his memory into some twisted nightmare. You're making him into a monster he never was."

I'm making him a monster? Chris thought. Pete was a hero, and the reason he kept torturing Chris was because Chris couldn't let it go?

"Pete," Chris said. "Pete, I'm sorry."

Pete let out another scream. It didn't sound human, but Chris *knew* it came from his friend. He was only a few feet away, and Chris felt the heat of the flames that covered the other man.

Chris fell to his knees. "I'm so sorry," he said. "I didn't want you to get hurt. Every second of every day, I know it should have been me. I'm sorry. I never wanted you to die, but I'll always be thankful to you for saving me." He hung his head, closing his eyes against tears.

A furnace of warmth flooded through him, and though it should have turned him to ash, Chris felt no pain. He opened his eyes to find the man of fire had embraced him. Without knowing why, Chris hugged him back.

"I'm sorry," he said. How long had he spent running from his best friend? How long had he kept pushing the man's memory away? Two years? Maybe three? The fire surrounding his friend started to creep along Chris's arms. Every instinct Chris had told him to pull back, but he wouldn't have let go of his friend for anything. Besides, the fire didn't burn. It hardly felt warmer than a good bath.

Chris started to laugh. The very idea that the fire was shifting from Pete to himself was impossible. It was the most irrational thought he'd ever had in his life. The thought that the fire was Pete's way of protecting Chris was even more ridiculous. But Chris believed it. That fire was his now, and it always would be.

He knew fire was alive in a lot of ways. It ate and breathed. He looked at it as it wrapped around him, and he told it to sleep. The flames faded like a candle out of wax, but they didn't die. The fire went inside Chris, where he knew it would wait until he called it again. White smoke drifted off of his arms and fogged the air for a few moments. When it cleared, Chris saw his friend.

Pete didn't have a mark on him. The stocky bastard just stood there with that smile of his, like he'd just sawed the leg of a chair and wanted you to sit down. His blue eyes twinkled with mirth. Pete was fond of jokes. *I don't want this to be a dream anymore,* Chris thought to himself. *But if it is, it's the greatest I've ever had.*

Chris couldn't begin to understand how he'd fit this into his thoughts. There had to be a reason, some cause to make it make sense. Whatever made this real, Chris would figure it out. For the moment, he just watched his friend.

Pete brought his large, rough hands up to the brim of an old Niner's hat he always insisted on wearing. A few strands of jet black hair managed to jut out from under the hat. As he adjusted his cap, his pale fingers began to turn black. Pete turned away. His square frame was large enough to block Chris's view of the house. He lifted the same hand in the air, extending two fingers. "Peace out." It was Pete's way of saying goodbye after work. His blackened fingers turned to white ash. Then his arm started to change as well. A gentle breeze lifted the ash skyward. It flowed across Pete's body, lifting the ash higher and higher. It sounded like a great sigh of relief. Maybe it was. His memory wouldn't ever be a source of anguish to Chris again. Instead, it would be a source of joy and, amazingly, a source of power.

Chris's eyes popped open, and a quick glance told him he was back on the leather futon in Doctor Strickland's office. *Strickland!*

"I remember!" he shouted as he sat up and pointed at the doctor, who sat at his desk.

"Remember what?" the doc asked as he began writing. "What exactly do you remember."

"I remember your name," Chris said. "Every time I tried to remember who you were, I got this incredible headache."

The doctor said nothing as he scratched at a legal pad on his desk. He pursed his lips. "Selective memory loss? That…" he paused. "I'll have to investigate possible causes."

"I can control fire," Chris said. He wasn't sure what part of the dreams he'd had he was going to start with. He wanted to talk about his dream avatars and how he'd finally let go of his guilt. He wanted to start with Pete, but the memory of his best friend caused the fire sleeping within him to stir.

The sudden absence of the scratching pencil seemed ominous to Chris. The doctor looked up at him. "What do you mean?"

"It's weird," Chris said. "I don't feel any different. I remember the dreams. I remember finding my avatars."

"Why don't I start by getting you something to drink?" Strickland said. "I'll be right back."

"Doc, didn't you hear me? Isn't that what you wanted?" Chris asked. The doctor didn't respond. Instead, he slammed the door shut behind himself. *What's that all about?*

"Doc? Doc where are you going?" he called out, walking to the door. He peeked out of the small, rectangular window in the door.

Chris took a few steps back. Something wasn't right. Doctor Strickland was panicked. Chris thought the man would be excited. He didn't ask about anything. *He rushed out as soon as I said I could control fire.*

Chris looked down at his hands. They were no warmer than usual, but he felt the same pulsing heat in the pit of his belly as he did during the dream. He took a deep breath. As he exhaled, he focused his thoughts on that imaginary spot.

Flames sprang to life on his hands. Chris scrambled backward, cursing. "Doc!" he shouted. "Someone, get in here quick!"

He rolled around. Wherever he placed his hands, more flames came to life. He nearly worked himself into a panic before he realized the fire didn't hurt him. *Am I still dreaming?*

Chris stood, looking at the trail of flames that began to grow along the floor. He focused his mind, and the flames died.

He shook his head. "Just another dream."

"Confirmed, Subject 4 has Broken," the doc's voice cut in through the a speaker in the ceiling.

"Doc?" Chris whispered while looking at the speaker.

"Neutralize with extreme caution," Strickland said. "Subject has pyrokinesis."

"Neutralize?" Chris asked. The steel door burst open to reveal four armed men dressed in body armor over black outfits.

"This has to be a dream," he said.

One of the men raised a rifle. Chris reflexively lifted his arms. Flames shot out from his hands and covered the attacking individual. The armored man screamed even as the flames consumed him.

"Put him down!" one of the others shouted. *Mattox?* Chris recognized the man's voice.

Chris turned, screaming in confusion. More gouts of flame burst around the room. The three remaining people raised their weapons.

"What's going on?" Chris asked. They fired, and Chis saw long darts bloom in his chest. *I'm already dreaming,* he thought to himself. *Can a person fall asleep in a dream?*

Chapter 24

THE COST OF FORGETTING

A strange feeling, like waking from a dream, washed over Sal. He rubbed at his eyes. When he opened them, he was standing in a '50s-style diner, complete with checkerboard tile, links of red and blue neon tubing acting as a boarder running along the top of the walls, and chrome accents everywhere. The place looked like it might once have been a train car. Whatever Sal focused on appeared clear, but everything in his peripheral vision seemed hazy, ephemeral. No matter how he turned his head, the phenomena continued.

Memories slowly trickled into Sal's mind. He recalled meeting Kaitlyn in a nightmare dungeon. He remembered poor Caden hanging above a massacre. He remembered—An oldie suddenly started playing on a neon infused Wurlitzer jukebox at the end of the diner. The song was familiar, but Sal couldn't think of the name.

Caden, still wearing his dated suit, stepped up to the center of a stainless steel bar that ran the entire length of the restaurant and plopped himself down on one of the red, vinyl bar stools. A chocolate shake in a thick soda-fountain glass appeared in front of him. The shake was topped with a few inches of fluffy whipped cream and an incredibly red cherry. Standing just behind Sal, Kaitlyn giggled at the old man about to enjoy a child's treat. Sal was only mildly surprised to see that she was now wearing a pink poodle skirt, the black leash of the poodle design trailing up the skirt to blend with her tucked-in, black polo shirt. Her dark locks, held in place with a pink ribbon, were now trussed up into a high ponytail. A pink scarf was tied around her thin neck, and black-and-white saddle shoes peeked out from under the hem of her skirt.

Sal's eyes strained as he shifted his gaze. He turned to look at Caden, but as he did so, Kaitlyn became foggy in appearance. He jerked his head back to her, only to notice Caden become indistinct. It took a few passes to reassure himself one wouldn't disappear if he focused on the other. Sal felt a memory try to resurface. A strange numbness followed. Sal shook away the sensation and focused on the wiry man sitting at the bar.

"I like intermission," Caden said, a straw popping into existence in his hand. "It gives me a chance to use the bathroom and grab a snack before the next big scene."

Sal, now dressed in a white t-shirt and a pair of jeans, the bottoms rolled up in true '50s fashion to reveal a pair of black motorcycle boots, suddenly placed the music, "All I Have to Do is Dream" by the Everly Brothers. In spite of their situation, Sal had to smile at Caden's sense of humor as he continued to study the boxcar diner. Miniature, chrome-plated jukeboxes dotted the booths. The windows of each booth, and even the double doors of the entrance, were covered in tight blinds.

Oddly out of place, each booth was separated by stained glass partitioning. He had just turned away from the booths to look at the long counter that dominated one whole side of the diner when something about the partitioning finally registered, and he spun back around. The smile faded from his face as he realized each piece of stained glass art depicted one of the more recent events he or one of his new companions had experienced. *Just when I think things are calming down, I notice something incredibly creepy.*

He jerked his head again, looking to be sure Kaitlyn hadn't vanished. She hadn't. *So why do I keep thinking someone is missing?* The thought flittered away. Sal resumed his study of the partitions again.

"You did this," Sal said, turning to Caden. Caden nodded his head without pulling the straw out of his mouth. He used the toes of his black leather shoes to swing the bar stool back and forth.

"And the 'art?'" Sal asked with a raised eyebrow as he pointed to the closest partition. It depicted Sal fighting the behemoth that had kept Kaitlyn in a cage.

Caden swung a few more times before stopping. He plopped his glass down. Sweat beaded the cup, and there was less than half of the shake left. Curiously enough, while he had materialized the shake, including the cherry on top, that glistening red fruit now sat ignored on a white napkin draped over the stainless-steel counter top.

"You're loud," Caden grumbled in his wheezy, whiney way. "I wanted a turn to visit past memories, and your thoughts all kept trying to force their way in, so I put them somewhere they wouldn't bother me."

Sal looked around again. He'd certainly never been in this restaurant. His glance caught another stained glass partition. That one depicted a man on fire. Something tugged at Sal's mind. He almost asked Caden about the image when it suddenly changed to an image of Sal holding Kaitlyn right after she'd lost her father.

"We've all learned that we're special," Caden said, drawing Sal's attention away from the panel, "but you don't seem to understand what that means yet. I'm waiting for you to do what you don't yet know that you're going to do. Then the movie will start up again. It'll be time to take my seat and enjoy the show." He said the last part with a wide grin, the scars on his mouth became more visible when he did that.

Sal walked up and took a seat next to Caden, who instinctively shrunk away.

"It's all right," Sal said, trying to sooth the man.

"Everyone says they won't hurt me, but that doesn't stop them. Words are useless. Plea for help or promise mercy, it doesn't matter. I still end up in trouble."

A flicker happened. It was so fast Sal wasn't sure he didn't imagine it. The world shifted from the diner to a bathroom and back. A woman stood there, one who seemed familiar to Sal even though he didn't get a good look at her.

"I know people have hurt you," Sal said, "but I won't let that happen anymore."

"So sure you can protect them," Caden said. "Don Quixote's hacking at the windmill, and he doesn't know there's a dragon creeping up behind him."

Kaitlyn, who'd been quietly studying the diner herself, sat down next to Sal. Sal chuckled a bit looking at her in the outfit in which Caden had imagined her. She looked down at her pink poodle skirt and shrugged, seeming only mildly annoyed at the forced change of attire, but not the clothing itself. Sal's ability picked up an odd sense of unease. She was trying to remember something. Her unease faded when she looked at him.

"I think it's cute, but you should see your hair," she said with a half-hidden smile.

Wrinkling his brow in confusion, Sal picked up the nearest chrome-plated napkin holder to see his reflection. He peered into it and had to grin at the long, pompadour hairstyle that now adorned his head.

"Yeah," Sal said. "This isn't really going to work for me as far as hairstyles go. What do you think Chris? Chris?"

Memories flooded Sal's mind as if the name burst a dam. Sal jerked his eyes back to the partitions. He remembered. One partition showed Chris tied up with a room burning around him. Another showed Chris saving Caden during one of Sal's nightmares. Sal had forgotten it all, and in an instant, he remembered it all vividly. *What the hell happened?* Sal frantically looked around for Chris.

"Whose idea is this!?" Sal heard Chris bellow from behind a set of double doors, on the other side of the counter, which separated the grill from the dining area of the restaurant. Chris burst through the doors. He was wearing a bus boy's outfit. He held his arms in front of himself helplessly. His brilliant white outfit was covered by a water-dampened apron. The paper hat was so ridiculous. The comedic appearance was overpowered by Sal's own concern, and the fear flowing out of his friend.

"I'd like a cheeseburger please," Caden said, as if Chris were there to take his order.

"I was stuck in the dish area," Chris said, panic clear in his mind. "I was just back there washing dishes." He sounded baffled, wrinkling his brow in thought. "For a minute, I actually thought I was a dishwasher."

"Actors get lost in their roles if they're not careful," Caden said. "They might even play an entire act believing they're the heroes of the story. People who don't keep their attention on their own existence can find themselves characters in their own dreams."

Chris's thoughts sent images of a different life into Sal's mind. A life where Chris was just a young man working for tips. Chris was terrified.

"You didn't look for me?" Chris asked. A wave of shame washed over Sal. He was Chris's friend. He was supposed to protect all of his friends.

"When the dreamers forget themselves, the other dreamers forget, too," Caden said. "If you can't be bothered to remember yourself, how can we hold on to your memories?"

"What does that mean?" Chris asked. He looked from Caden to Sal. "Sal, did you forget me?"

Sal's own horrific sorrow kept words from escaping his lips. Kaitlyn surged to her feet, flipped up a hinged section of the counter top, and nearly tackled Chris in a hug.

"He forgets himself and is mad at us for forgetting," Caden grumbled. "You must be you. We can't remember you if you forget yourself. You're in a mine field, and you've decided to dance around just because you think yourself a ballerina."

Cupping her shoulders, Chris gently pushed Kaitlyn to an arms' length away from him to look her in the eyes. "I'm sorry I forgot myself," he said softly. He glanced at Sal for a moment, nodding at him. Chris's eyes widened. A tear fell down his cheek. He pulled Kaitlyn back into a tight hug again.

"I know," he whispered. "It's okay."

Sal could feel what she'd done. Kaitlyn had taken her feelings of friendship and sorrow and given them to Chris. No words could express her sadness, so she simply let him experience it.

"Did you at least clean everything up while you were back there?" Caden asked. "If you aren't done, I'll have to let you go."

Chris stared at Caden for a long moment. Sal felt Chris's fear fade away. A smile came to his lips.

"Now that you can cook," Caden said, pausing for another sip of his bottomless shake, "it's only right you do the dishes, too."

Sal could only gawk at Caden. Chris seemed at a loss. Then Kaitlyn, her arms still firmly around Chris, burst out laughing. She felt better, but she probably didn't want to let him go. She probably wanted to keep him where she could reach him because things had that odd habit of fading away when someone wasn't looking right at them.

"I think I get it!" she said.

"I'm not amused," Chris said. His tone was serious, but the smile on his face only got bigger.

"The comic relief in movies never likes his job," Caden said. "Everyone laughs at him like they're supposed to, but he doesn't want to be funny. He just is. But if you don't like the job, fine. You're fired."

Another round of laughter escaped Kaitlyn. "Fired," she said between fits of giggles. She grabbed Chris's hand and practically dragged him back through the flip-top section of the counter. She sat next to Sal, pulling Chris to sit next her.

A strawberry shake appeared in front of her. She looked at the shake and then at Caden. "Thanks!" she said.

"Chris," Sal said. It was the only word he could bring himself to say.

"You gonna do that thing where you act like you're responsible for everything?" Chris asked. "Kaitlyn let me feel."

"But," Sal said.

"No," Chris interrupted. "It wasn't just how she felt. It was how you felt, too. So if you're going to tell me how sorry you are, don't. I already know. I've already felt it. I get it."

"Sal's got more powers, but I'm waaaaaay better with emotions," Kaitlyn said.

Sal felt a surge of relief. It wasn't his own. It was Chris's. Kaitlyn was sending Chris's relief and forgiveness to him. And, according to Sal's own abilities, doing so a bit smugly. Sal used his telekinesis to slide Kaitlyn's shake away from her. She reached for it, and he slid it back.

"Yeah," he said, playfully mocking her tone. "You're waaaaay better with emotions."

"Leave my shake alone before I make you feel how childish you're acting," she said smiling.

"Children shouldn't have too many treats," Caden said. "But you've done all your homework, so a small treat is okay. Just don't tell anyone." He whispered the last part, and the room flickered again from the diner to the small bathroom, back to the diner. Again Sal caught the slightest glimpse of a thin woman. Something was familiar. Though, Sal could only focus on the woman's insanely bright-red lipstick, the same shade of red as Caden's discarded cherry.

Caden covered his ears as if he were trying to hold something in, or keep something out.

"I'm trying to be nice!" he whined. "Don't make me look! Don't kill me again. I like this place and this is where we'll stay!"

"It's okay," Sal said. An idea occurred to him. He looked at the diner and focused on it. This is where they were. This is where they belonged, and they didn't want to go anywhere else.

Something like a warm breeze plumed outward. Sal felt the energy of his mind flow through the diner. The energy rippled away from him, causing the air to shimmer. Once the ripple faded, the diner seemed more real. The haze faded away, and the details solidified.

"Damn," Chris said. "What did you do?"

Kaitlyn gawked from her seat at the counter. The straw she'd been using hung from her open mouth.

"I'm not sure," Sal replied, getting up off his stool and walking toward a window. Inside, the diner was vibrant. The colors seemed so vivid. The air felt so clean. But as Sal used his thumb and index finger to open up the blinds of the window, the world outside was pitch black. Not a single star shined in the sky. No lights shined from any cars, street lamps, or other buildings. It was as if the diner were the only thing that existed in the universe. Even the bright, florescent light that slipped out from between the blinds died in the inky blackness. A shudder ran through Sal's body as he thought about what would happen to them if the darkness got into the diner.

"Thank you," Caden said. It was such a small whisper, Sal almost didn't hear it.

"Any time," Sal said, taking the opportunity to turn away from the darkness and back to the man. He seemed much calmer. Whatever Sal did, stopped the world from flickering. And whatever Caden had buried in his mind, was terrifying to him. It wasn't anything Sal could sense. Caden's thoughts and emotions were as muted as ever. Instead, it was the mundane body language Sal noticed.

Caden slouched over, taking a deep breath before gulping down a few inches of shake from his glass.

"The players are on the stage," Caden mumbled to himself, pulling his mouth away from his straw. "They have their costumes, but they still don't understand their roles."

Chris looked at his long, slender arms. The man still expected to wake up, which was exactly what they all needed to do. Something else occurred to Sal. With all of their minds in control, the dreams weren't nightmares. That left them an opportunity if he could use it properly. He couldn't fail them, not now that they'd come so far together. Not ever. He needed everyone to get through this.

"Why?" Kaitlyn asked. He understood her question. Reading minds was helpful. She wanted to know why he cared about the group so much.

"It's my nature," he said. "To put people at ease, to help them...to protect them."

She smiled at him. Her affection reverberated with his. She'd come to see him like an older brother or a kindly uncle. She trusted him utterly to protect her. *No pressure,* he thought.

"Diamonds are pretty things," Caden said. "But without the right pressure, they fracture."

Sal glanced at the old man, his shake had refilled, and he was more interested in sucking it down than saying much more. He'd have to remember Caden could read minds as well.

"Whoever took us knew this would happen," Sal said.

"Who could possibly expect something like this to hap—AHH!" Chris slumped over the counter, causing that idiotic paper hat to fall off his head.

Sal rushed over to Chris. "What's wrong?" A stream of images flowed from Chris's mind, but the mental pictures were distorted.

"Chris!" Sal shouted.

Kaitlyn, still seated next to Chris, reached over and placed a hand on his back and whispered to him. She hadn't done anything with her powers. She was just trying to comfort him as the pain faded.

Chris's breathing slowed. He still gripped his head as if trying to literally hold it together, but the agony he felt had dwindled. He lifted his head off the counter, but he braced his hands on the surface to keep himself upright.

"I remembered," Chris said.

"Remembered what?" Sal asked.

"I—" Chris stopped and grimaced in pain. Sal felt the man's suffering surge. Sal was about to tell him to stop before Chris raised a hand. "Let me fight through this."

Sal resisted the urge to argue. He watched the taller man grimace. Sal felt his friend's pain ebb and flow. A few thoughts would surface. Sal saw them as images that turned white with pain as they came into focus.

"Every time I remember, this blinding pain hits me," Chris explained. "It feels like someone has a cattle prod in my skull and fires it off whenever I get too close to remembering.

Sal looked around the room. Kaitlyn hovered next to Chris. Caden sat quietly drinking his shake. "I think you're close to something. The pieces to what's happening to all of us are in our minds."

"Mine!" Caden yelped. He put his hands against his ears like he'd just heard a loud noise. His shake spilled off the counter as he jumped off his seat and backed away. "It's mine, and you can't play there."

"I'm not going to hurt you, Caden," Sal said.

"Mine!" Caden shook his head, backing away until his back hit the glass door entrance of the diner, disturbing the blinds hanging there, allowing hints of the blackness outside to peak through. Did he really think he could avoid Sal's mind by moving his head? "Get out! Get out!"

"It's okay!" Sal said. "I won't look in your mind if you don't want me to."

"The walls of my fortress are high," Caden said. "And you lack the ladders and men to climb over." He looked so scared and helpless.

The truth was, Sal wasn't sure he could get anything out of Caden's thoughts, even if he could somehow learn to push through whatever that opaque layer around Caden's mind was. Just seeing if he could get inside Caden's mind would have been interesting. Maybe Sal could help him with his madness.

"You can read my mind," Kaitlyn said, pulling Sal's attention away. She jumped off her seat, causing the pink frills of her dress to bounce, and she stepped around Chris's stool to stand next to Sal. "I'm not scared."

She was, but Sal didn't throw it in her face. He looked at Chris.

He shrugged. "I might as well go first since my memories seem to be clawing their way out of my skull anyway. I don't know what else to do, so, is this like some Vulcan mind meld?"

"Your mind, to my mind," Sal said in his best Leonard Nimoy. Kaitlyn let out a burst of laughter. Lord, the sound of it made him want to laugh.

Sal closed his eyes and let the webs in his mind form. Each mind was a web, and all he needed to connect to Chris was to stretch out another silvery thread. Sal reached out from his own web to Chris's. The moment he touched Chris's mind, Sal was overwhelmed by memories and images. None of it came in order, and none of it made sense.

Chris was trapped in a burning building. He was an infant in a tub. He was kissing a woman named Cassandra for the first time. He was hitting his first baseball, tossed to him by his father, Curtis. The thought's bombarded Sal. Chris's mind was an ocean, and Sal was a dingy caught in a typhoon. Sal pulled himself away. It felt like trying to stop himself from falling after he'd already jumped off a ledge.

Sal hovered between his own mind and Chris's. The web looked too large for him to travel. It was one thing to hear random thoughts a person wasn't closely guarding or feel strong emotions a person was keeping just under the surface, but diving into a person's mind without knowing what he was looking for just couldn't be done.

Sal opened his eyes. He gasped for breath, reaching for the counter to stand up. He was covered in sweat. When had he fallen to his knees? Kaitlyn was at his side. Worry and concern flowed out of her.

"I'm okay," he said still trying to slow his breathing.

Chris held his head as if someone had just hit him with a frying pan. "Fuck man! What are you doing?"

"I'm sorry," Sal said.

Caden leaned down to his ear. "Charlotte didn't spin the words around the webs silly pig." Sal jerked at the comment. He hadn't seen Caden move from the door of the diner.

Sal stared at the man. Just once he'd like to understand what Caden said. Just once he'd like plain English.

Caden shook his head. "He opens a fire hose and expects a sip of water!"

"You're damn right it's too much," Sal said. And if he sounded a bit embarrassed, it was because he was.

"I know how the spider thinks," Caden said, his voice a somewhat creepy sing-song. "It waits in the web for someone to fall in. That's why I smack the web. Smack the web, kill the spider. Pluck a strand, and the spider comes looking to see what it's caught."

Sal thought about it. He had tried to look at all the thoughts at once. He thought reading a mind would be like looking through a toolbox for a wrench. Only there had to be an infinite number of memories to sift through. What if he only focused on one part of Chris's mind at a time?

"Wait!" Chris said in a panic, holding up one hand as a ward while the other rubbed at his temple.

"For Christ's sake, Chris, it's not like I mean to stomp around in there."

"You still managed to do a fine fucking job of it!" He sounded more wounded than angry. Sal couldn't really blame him. His own head wanted to split open.

"If I start to feel overwhelmed, I'll stop."

"Are you serious? You don't know what you're doing. And what if I start to feel overwhelmed?"

"Please?" Sal all but begged. He knew they were close to understanding what was happening, if only he could learn what everyone else knew and compare information.

"Just read my mind," Kaitlyn said. She was twice as scared as before. *I can't let her down.*

"No!" Chris and Sal shouted together. Chris was the first to speak in the few seconds of silence between them. "No, if you insist on driving someone insane…"

Sal's glare must have been enough to shut him up. "I won't hurt anyone!" Sal said, his voice gruff and intense.

"Fine, then I'm ready, but you owe me one now." Chris had a forced but not unkind smile on his face. *Let's not fight in front of the kid, right? You don't really want to try this on her first do you?*

You can talk to me! Sal sent.

You heard that? Chris sent. *Huh, guess if I think about what I'm trying to say, you hear hear it.*

You sure you haven't just found a new ability? Try talking to Kaitlyn.

Chris shrugged. Sal heard his thoughts. *Kaitlyn,* Chris said. *Kaitlyn, can you hear me!* His eyes bulged and the veins in his neck looked ready to burst.

"Kaitlyn, can you hear Chris's thoughts?"

"You and I have satellite," Caden said. He had a flat look on his face that made Sal feel particularly stupid. "We can see all the channels, but they haven't paid their bills." Caden pointed at Chris and Kaitlyn. "They can use public access, but only on local airwaves."

"So I can hear them, and they can talk to me?" Sal asked.

"You can watch whatever you want, but I'm bored already," Caden answered.

Sal looked at Chris for a moment. Chris was right. If Sal messed up while searching Kaitlyn's mind, she might get hurt. He didn't like the implication that he'd hurt her, but it was possible however unintentional it may be.

"Ready to try again?" Sal asked.

"Yeah," Chris answered. *No,* his thoughts sent.

"I'll be careful," Sal promised.

With that, Sal closed his eyes again. This time, he looked at the web of Chris's mind. The interconnecting, shimmering gossamer threads seemed more numerous and beautiful than any spiderweb he'd seen in real life. He could see the strands, but there was something behind the weave. His instincts told him the surging circle of light was a source of some kind. Ignoring the brilliant pulsing light, Sal instead focused on a particular strand.

Images flowed into Sal's mind, but not so quickly he couldn't make them out. Chris was in college, a dorm room with a USC pennant tacked on the wall above the bed. He studied chemistry while an attractive young lady, Indian, Sal thought, lay in his lap. Her name was Pari. Focusing on the name brought on a sort of tension, as if something were trying to pull Sal away from the memory.

I can't focus on her, or I'll go to where the majority of his memories of her are. The thought of it made for some fairly uncomfortable mental pictures. Sal pulled back long enough to see the web of Chris's mind and selected one of the outer threads.

Men were chasing him down a road. There was an ambulance in the background. Sal followed that thread of memory. There were large black breaks in the strand. He touched one, and only felt a sense of uneasy rest. Were the black breaks parts of his dreams? No, they were nightmares.

Sal thought to pull back into his own mind, then reconsidered. *I can see it!* The sense of surprise he felt told him the trick worked. He could use his mind to talk to everyone while moving through Chris's thoughts.

Their thoughts flooded toward him. It sounded like standing in a closet full of people who were all screaming. *Calm down!* Of course that shout only added to the noise, and a torrent of apologies and questions as to how the hell they were supposed to calm their thoughts.

Instead of trying to listen to them all, Sal focused on Chris's individual thoughts. Kaitlyn's thoughts became a muted buzz that eventually faded into curiosity about what he saw. He could sense Caden's presence, but couldn't identify any of the man's thoughts or feelings. A number of Chris's recent memories were similar to experiences Sal suffered. Sal traced back to the memory of men chasing Chris down a road.

What happened here? he sent the thought to Chris.

I thought that was a dream, Chris said, the memory still playing in his mind. *I don't understand. I couldn't remember, not until just now.*

What do you mean? Sal asked.

Someone—

A sudden spark forced Sal's consciousness from Chris's mind.

You okay? Sal asked, feeling Chris's pain.

I'll be fine, just keep going! Sal listened to the man's thoughts as he revisited the memory. *Yeah,* Chris said. *I've been having so many nightmares. It got to the point I couldn't tell what was what. But in this dream, I thought I escaped. In a way, I guess I did. Those men chasing me were moving me somewhere.*

Sal watched the memory. Chris ran off a road into a batch of woods to hide in a bush. He stood there as people hunted him. Someone approached, and the man's face caused Chris's mind to surge in pain again, but the man remembered a name.

Mattox! Chris said.

A series of images flowed through his mind. They caused another jolt of pain to assault Chris, but Sal stayed with the chain of memories. He saw a warehouse. He saw Chris get captured. Chris woke up and faced a man who wore glasses and an oversized lab coat. The white-coated man had brown hair streaked with gray.

Sal pulled himself away from the memories to look at the web of Chris's mind. The memories went black. The thought Sal had already seen pulsed with a strange energy.

I think I can tell the dreams from reality in your mind, Sal told Chris. *That office. Where was it?*

I'm not sure, Chris answered. *I went in that warehouse. You saw what happened. I woke up in the doc's office.*

The memory brought back the face of the same man in the lab coat. It also caused another painful bolt of electricity to course through Chris's mind. Sal saw the wave of arching blue light surge its way through Chris's thoughts.

Sal reacted. He didn't actually step in front of the blast. He didn't actually have a form in Chris's mind, but he forced his presence to block the energy. It plunged into Sal.

Sal opened his eyes feeling as if he'd be burned alive. "What the hell happened?" he asked, looking up at his friends.

"You tell us," Chris said. "One moment, I'm remembering that office. I start to feel another migraine coming on, and then you drop right in front of us."

"Something was hurting you," Sal explained. Chris stepped off his stool and helped Sal to his feet.

"You stopped it?" Chris asked, he sat back down once he was sure Sal wouldn't just fall right back down again.

"I sort of jumped into it," Sal said.

"It's all well and good for Sydney to fool Mr. Darnay, but better thing or not, the guillotine still falls," Caden said.

Sal was still catching his breath as Caden spoke. He couldn't help but smile at the scrawny, old man. "One day, Caden," Sal said, "you'll make sense."

"I'm a dictionary," Caden said. "It's no fault of my own if you don't know the meaning of words."

Sal didn't push the conversation. It wouldn't help anyway. Instead, he turned to Chris. "Someone, or something, is causing that pain," Sal explained. "It flairs up when you remember a face."

Chris grimaced again as he tried to recall the man with glasses.

"Does anyone else remember a warehouse?" Sal asked. "Maybe a scrawny guy in a white lab coat."

A bolt of shock came from Kaitlyn.

"What?" Sal asked.

"Nothing," she said quickly. Sal felt her trying to convince herself she was wrong.

"You remember something," Sal said.

"It's just," she paused. She was growing more uneasy by the second.

"Can I see?" he asked.

Kaitlyn looked at him for a moment. She was scared and sad, but she nodded her head.

Sal took a deep breath before he closed his eyes and used his thoughts to see the minds of his friends. They looked like ghosts, white blobs of energy floating in nothing. He wondered if the strange sensation of floating he felt was what other people claimed they felt during a supposed out-of-body experience.

Focus your thoughts, Sal said.

He pushed toward her. That was the only way he could think to describe it. He didn't get any closer physically, but he sent his thoughts in her direction. He entered the white, nebulous cloud of energy he recognized as her and found the web of her mind. Just as with Chris, Kaitlyn also had a pulsing circle of energy behind the web of her mind. Her circle pulsed faster, more brightly. He focused on it a moment longer, drawn to the energy, feeling as if that pulse was connected to something even deeper. *Could that be where our powers come from?*

He discarded the thought, hovering over the web of Kaitlyn's mind for a moment, hoping that something would happen as Kaitlyn focused on the memory. A flash, like a mirror that had caught the sun, drew Sal's attention. He turned to see a single thread, a single memory, flashing. Sal pushed in. He saw the same reedy man with brown hair streaked with gray lead Kaitlyn by the hand into a warehouse. The memory was a pleasant one.

What am I seeing? Sal asked, trying not to betray his concern.

That's my stepdad, she said. *He's taking me to where he does his private research. There's nothing there but old equipment and books. I must have read half of them. What's wrong?*

She must have sensed his unease despite his efforts. Sal couldn't be sure. They looked the same, but Sal wanted to be certain. He couldn't just accuse someone. He couldn't go off half-cocked.

He pulled away from her memories. He looked at Chris and Kaitlyn's mind-webs together and had an idea. He pushed back to Chris's memory. If they were really anything like a web, then maybe all he had to do was tie one memory to the other.

Sal tied a bit of his own energy to Chris's memory. He let that energy trail as he left. He felt himself grow tired as he brought that string of conscious thought into Kaitlyn's mind. He looped the energy around her memory and pulled it tight.

Shock. Rage. Denial. Sadness. The emotions slammed into Sal. Then something pushed Sal away. For an instant, it looked like an opaque dome, similar to the way Caden always looked from Sal's mind. It faded away, but the string of emotions drove him back even more effectively.

Sal retreated into his own mind. The diner came into view. He was on the floor yet again. Chris sat dumbfounded on one of the diner's red-cushioned stools. Caden stood back. Sal followed the old man's eyes to Kaitlyn, who was shouting and pacing back toward the jukebox still playing at the rear end of the dining area.

"It can't be!" she shouted. "He wouldn't do this. He wouldn't have lied to me all this..." Her breathing came in fits and gulps of air. "This whole time?" She started to wheeze and cough.

Sal struggled to find his feet. He was still trying to collect his thoughts along with those he'd observed in his friends' minds. He and Chris approached her, but she backed away, pointing at Chris.

"Don't..." she gasped. "Don't...come...near...me..."

Sal took another step forward.

"I said don't!" she screamed.

Chris placed a hand on Sal's shoulder, gently pulling him back. Sal looked at the man and felt his confusion and frustration. Sal had somehow unlocked all his friend's memories. That doctor had used Chris as a sort of spy, and Chris felt horrible about it. He felt furious. As Chris looked at Kaitlyn, Sal felt something else from the man: remorse. Sal stepped back.

"You didn't do this to us," Chris said. He raised his arms and stepped toward her. "You've never done anything but try to help us."

"He's...my...step...dad," she managed to say between fitful gulps of air.

"And he did this to us," Chris said. "He used me. He used Caden. He used Sal."

He took another step toward Kaitlyn. "I'm not even sure this is real. I'm not even sure what is real anymore."

"I'm...so...sorry..." Kaitlyn's shoulders heaved with each breath. Tears streamed down her face. Chris took another step forward, finally within an arm's reach, and he took a knee before her.

"He did this," Chris said. "Not you."

How is he doing this? Sal wondered. He could feel Chris's rage. If Sal felt half the hatred Chris felt for this doctor, Sal would lash out. He'd kill the doctor and anyone in his way. It's all Sal wanted to do at the moment. He looked into Chris's feelings to learn, to understand, how Chris could sound so gentle when he felt such anger. He saw Chris's compassion for Kaitlyn, which Chris used to mask his other emotions.

"You didn't do a damn thing to me, Kaitlyn," Chris said, "except save my life." He put a hand on her shoulder. Her breaths came in longer and longer intervals. "Thank you," Chris said. "Thank you for helping me. Thank you for caring about me."

She flung her arms around Chris and wept. "You didn't do anything wrong," he whispered.

Sal looked over at Chris and sent a single thought over. *You're amazing.*

"What do you mean?" Chris asked, turning to look at Sal, which was awkward because Kaitlyn refused to loosen her grip on Chris.

"You just let it go," Sal said. "You let that anger go to help her."

Chris shook his head and smiled. "I didn't let it go."

Sal's abilities confirmed the fact. Rage simmered alongside the fire sleeping in the slender man.

"He used me," Kaitlyn said, still keeping her arms wrapped around Chris. "He might have used me as a test for what he did to all of us."

"You know none of us blame you," Sal said. She had to know. Her abilities would sense their compassion and affection just as easily as Sal's.

"Why?" she asked. "I still don't understand why?"

A thought occurred to Sal. Kaitlyn had told Chris and him that her stepdad wanted her to "reach the peak of their potential." He kept that thought to himself.

"It'll be okay," he said, "because we're going to show him that he's made a very big mistake."

Chapter 25

A STRANGE SMELL

Graham Strickland plopped down on his leather chair. He stared at the black streaks on the floor and wall of his office. He pulled out his notebook and scribbled observations as they occurred to him.

Pyrokinetic abilities do not require normal accelerants or sources, he wrote. *I suspect the subject's mind is able to provide localized combustion.*

He found himself smiling. *I'd have been burned to a crisp if I hadn't left as soon as he told me about his ability.*

He was just glad to be alive. That thought caused Graham's eyes to drift to the largest scorch mark near the entrance to the office. A review of the security footage gave an accurate timeline. Subject 3 had reduced a man to ash in 11.323 seconds. The soldier was neutralized in less than a second.

Graham would have resorted to the biometric security measure had the security team failed to sedate Subject 3. The soldier's death was unfortunate. He was one of the general's loyalists, a good man with a common vision, not one of the thugs for hire. The general was probably trying to find some way to notify the man's next of kin without compromising the operation.

The loss of life was unfortunate, but the discoveries and information were undeniably invaluable. Death or not, he couldn't wipe the smile off his face no matter how objectively he tried to look at the project. It was more than anyone could hope for. A perfect success projection with only one trial as a control. Exactly four made it to Phase Three, and all four developed complete cognitive function.

Subject 4 was particularly rewarding. That subject had managed to produce the third-highest delta wave emissions ever. The subject wasn't a true tactical asset as far as Graham could tell, but the general said he had a plan.

Graham saw her potential years ago when her mother brought her in for treatment. He kept his word and helped her reach a level of existence few even knew were possible. She was the next stage in evolution, and he had helped her reach it. It was very difficult for him to detach from her. Keeping the proper label helped. When it was over, he'd be able to respond emotionally, but, until then, utter professional detachment was necessary.

It seemed a little cliche for Subject 3 to develop pyrokinesis, but it was wonderful when one considered the subject was the first to do so. Graham looked at his notepad. He'd need another one soon. Just annotating the temperature readings from each of the burn marks in the office took three pages.

A strange smell hit Graham. It was awful. He stood, making sure he didn't knock any of the reports off his desk. He nudged a pile of books with his shoe so he could close his door. The smell faded. He thought, for a moment, that it was odd. Smells normally linger. A part of him considered investigating, but he simply decided not to. He had more important work to do.

He thought he caught a whiff of the smell again, but it passed just as quickly. He'd been pushing himself too hard, and he could have been burned alive. Maybe that was the cause of the smell. Graham glanced at the burned leather futon. There were very clear, hand-shaped holes melted into the furniture.

While it would have been nice to receive more information, Subject 3 still confirmed a few things. The subjects were linking. They'd all Broken, and Phase Three could begin.

Graham moved back over to his desk. The office was usually more organized, but Subject 3's outburst caused one sort of mess while the amount of data pouring through his office made another. He hardly had time to find a place to put the research, much less organize and catalogue it properly.

He scribbled a line, more a reminder to himself. *Investigate correlation between traditional and non-traditional abilities.* The first experiment yielded very similar results. True, Subject Four may have skewed the results, but it was worth investigating.

He let out a yawn. He took a few moments to drag his nimble fingers through the gray streak in his brown hair. His badge popped out of his pocket, and rather than tuck it back inside, he pulled it off and set it on the desk. He was tired of trying to keep it put away. Another yawn escaped him. Hadn't he just napped after re-sedating the subjects? He pulled off his square, clubmaster glasses and rubbed the bridge of his sharp nose. He jabbed the call button of his phone. "Someone bring me some coffee."

There should have been an assistant nearby. It was possible that Subject 3's Break had people scurrying to collect more information.

Subject 4 was a success, a gold mine for the value of the dosage issue alone. He was right to choose that long term project, and the dues were paid in knowledge if not capability.

That smell hit him again. Had someone left something rotten in the trash? Where was his coffee? Another yawn cracked his jaw. He had to focus. Looking at the note he'd written himself, he grimaced in frustration. He wasn't some grad student trying to study for a final. He had just proven a theory that would change the world.

If he repeated the experiment, and there was no doubt the general would want another group as quickly as possible, would the results be the same? It was likely the ratio of subjects to successes would match, but would there be one unique ability per four subjects? Would there be one Full Talent as well?

He wrote the term "Full Talent" down. It was short and accurate. Full Talent worked for Subject 2 and the program's original candidate.

Now that was a real problem. Graham was certain the D-W-E breaking gene was hereditary, but would that produce the same ability? If he bred Subject 4 and a later candidate of appropriate age, would the resulting offspring carry the maternal or paternal trait? Was one trait dominant?

The loss of the hatchery burned even deeper. All that data, all that potential was just callously destroyed by a government too blind to understand what they were doing. That was okay. Subject 4 was almost fertile, and once Graham could explain how important follow on projects were, they wouldn't have to use such invasive methods like they had to use the first time.

He smiled again. Oh yes, he'd only scratched the surface. He yawned. That was odd. Hadn't he napped when they re-sedated the subjects? He'd have to call someone for coffee. Didn't he already? He chuckled. There was too much to do. He'd been pressing himself hard since Subject 3 Broke. He'd get some rest after he finished his report. *What was that smell?*

Chapter 26

INFILTRATION

From his vantage point in the woods across the road, Steve used his own ability to scan the lower level of the three-floor warehouse. That would be a scenario level. The fact that no one was on that level didn't surprise him. Although, something didn't feel right about that.

"What can you sense?" he asked Kira. He kept his voice at a volume that wouldn't carry easily.

"Same as you," she replied, blue eyes squinting in confusion. "Weird."

Neither could understand why the facility felt off to them. Perhaps one of the general's new recruits Broke, and that ability could fog their own. *But why isn't there any external security?* All Steve could see were cameras and some barbed wire. *It's like they're daring us to come in.*

"Hardwire," Steve asked. "How do the systems look?"

Brandon turned to look at Steve. Only the whites of his eyes were visible. "Everything is online." He paused briefly, and when he spoke again, a hint of anxiety edged his voice. "Top, all four have Broken. The last just a few hours ago."

"Stack on me," Steve said.

They used their standard formation. They crept from the tree-line, staying low as they crossed the road. The half-moon was hidden behind the trees, making it less likely anyone would see their silhouettes on the road.

The gate opened, seemingly on its own. In truth, Dom used his telekinesis to pop the lock and slide the chain-link fence open. Their feet moved silently over the sidewalk of the warehouse as they approached a single door.

Steve took position at the entrance. Kira was behind him. Dom took the rear after Brandon. They always kept Brandon near the back. He was the most vulnerable, not just because he didn't have any offensive psychic abilities, but because he was only half in his body when he linked his mind with any systems.

"Let us know when you have security," Steve told Brandon, never taking his eyes off the door in front of him.

"That's already done," Brandon said hesitantly in a low drawl. He had news he knew Steve wouldn't like to hear.

"So what's wrong?" Steve asked in a hushed tone.

"There's a system I can't access."

"Could be someone like Top," Dom said, using Steve's callsign. His voice was its ever casual, "I don't care about anything," tone, but he kept flicking the selector level of his rifle up and down. Even he was nervous. "Maybe this guy is trying to keep us out."

"We can walk in right now, and security wouldn't even see us," Brandon said. "That's not the system I can't access."

"Does it hinder the mission?" Steve asked, impatiently.

"No," Brandon said. "We're good to go." Steve heard the unsaid "but" in the comment. He even heard Brandon's thoughts. The young man was worried, but he didn't really feel this system was a concern. Whatever it was, Steve didn't give a damn. He was inches away from the general. If the system didn't matter, it didn't matter.

"Then let's go," Steve said.

Dom came to the front, M-4 held low. His jaw set as he used his telekinesis to push the latch of the door back. The instant Dom pulled the door open, Steve was in the room. The rest flowed in behind him, clearing the doorway and scanning the room in less than a few seconds. Each shouted that his or her area was clear.

The front room was a dressed nightmare set. Chains hung everywhere. A trap net was suspended in the air. One of the subjects apparently stumbled into it at some point. Steve focused his thoughts. There were five psychic prints. Each was a sort of echo of the thoughts and emotions that were most powerful in the room recently. Most of the prints seemed focused on the subject. Steve couldn't read an imprint's thoughts. He could only gain a sense of the strongest emotions in the room. Panic, frustration and an intense desire to get away lingered in the room like a bad smell.

"At least one of the subjects is here against his will," Steve said.

"Then this won't be a complete waste of time," Dom said. The steady clicking of his selector level finally stopped. Dom liked having targets, a sense of purpose.

"There aren't any names in the system," Brandon said, sounding a bit awed. His head turned side to side. He wasn't looking around the room. The lack of pupils told Steve that much. He was looking at radio waves or fiber optic networks, or some other high-tech part of the electro-magnetic spectrum no one else could see. Steve wasn't exactly sure. "Smart, I can't see what isn't entered into the files."

"If they're not using a system," Kira speculated, "it might mean the general knows we're after him."

"More likely he's just being cautions," Dom said. "If he thought we were onto him, there'd have been a full company out waiting for us."

"I think Breach is right," Steve said, "but to be safe, we assume the general has planned for us."

"Top," Brandon broke in excitedly. "The power levels for these people are ridiculous. One of them is higher than all of us, another is only slightly less powerful than you, and only one of them is weaker than any of us. A lot weaker, even if I factor in his D-W-E spikes!"

"So we go on?" Dom asked. His voice dripped with anticipation.

It was either that or stand in the first room and talk all night. They had the advantage of time and planning thanks to Brandon and Kira, but they'd reached the point of no return. Their target was in this building.

"Overwatch," Steve said, addressing Kira by her callsign. "You're with Hardwire. You stay in your pairs. Overwatch and I will report to each other."

The short, raven-haired woman's oddly advanced telepathic ability may give them an advantage. She could link and block others. It was sort of like psychic cryptology. They stacked on a set of double doors under a large observation window. She nodded, signifying she'd not only understood him, but she'd also scanned the next room for other minds. Her eyes were colder than he'd ever seen, and Steve silently thanked God that her rage wasn't directed at him. Both Steve and Kira's abilities told them no one would be there, but with other psychics in the area, it was best to check and double check. It was also best to follow standard military tactics.

Steve's team had a huge advantage for more than a decade. With the general and the possibility of an enemy team, the odds were even at best on a psychic level.

"It's too big," Dom said, grunting. "Top, help me out on the left side."

Steve focused his mind. He imagined lines extending from himself to everything in the room. He targeted the line stretching from his mind to the left side of the door. Sending his energy at it, he pushed. These lines weren't visible to others, of course. All anyone else would see were the doors sliding open. Looking at the other door, even though they were using the same ability, Steve still couldn't see the telekinetic energy that Dom was using on his door. *I wonder if he even envisions lines? Maybe he imagines a large hand, pushing.* It was all about psychic energy and how each member of the team channeled that energy.

The doors opened, and a noxious odor assaulted Steve's nose. He momentarily clenched his eyes shut and shook away the smell.

"What was that?" Dom asked rubbing at his nose.

"Could be a few victims weren't collected before they decomposed," Kira said. "Opening this door probably let some much needed fresh air in."

"Sir?" Brandon asked.

Steve jerked his head one more time to erase the memory of the smell. "We're not stopping."

His three teammates nodded their heads.

Kira and Brandon flowed through the large bay doors. Steve went in next with Dom. It was finally time. He was going to kill the general.

Chapter 27

WAITING

Caden lie strapped to his hospital bed wishing he had a book or a TV. He was back in the other world where things were supposed to make sense. Brown leather straps held him down when he should be free. He was where doctors and mothers did bad things to little boys who never listened. He was in a room where white sheets and machines that beeped made people feel worse when they should feel better. The straps weren't frightening anymore, not since he'd learned how to make believe.

His three friends had told him to wait. He didn't like being told what to do. People who did what they were told were controlled. No one deserved to control him.

The Hero was the worst. He spoke as if the world should spin at his direction, all for the sake of what he thought was best. The little girl might think the Hero was a knight in armor, but it didn't mean he was. At the end, he was just another pawn in the game. They were all pawns, so why act the player?

With nothing better to do at the moment, listening to the Hero was at least something to occupy time. But when he told Caden to wait until he could hear everyone, it was enough to make Caden go mad. *I can always hear everyone!* There were so many people in so many places. In fact, four new pieces just landed on the board, and not even He knew about that yet.

A pair of white-clad doctors walked in. What was the point in wearing white? Doctors wore white. Nurses, psychiatrists, and even dentists wore white. If everyone wore white, what significance did white have?

They approached Caden as if they thought they had control. Caden laughed. They stopped and stepped back.

"What's so funny?" one asked. He had a narrow face and hair that was too red. Caden hated red.

"You think you're the puppeteer," Caden said. "But do you see any strings on me?"

These people in white coats and their leader in green and gold had scared him. They hurt him and showed him terrible things. They made him remember nightmares that came whether he was sleeping or not. Now they'd pay.

Caden formed a hand in his mind. It reached out and grabbed the men by their heads. "Time to let me out," he said.

They looked at each other, walked over, and began to unstrap his hands. That made things interesting. A new handful of people burst in. Two had guns and black body armor. The other three were more stupid men in white coats. They all seemed shocked. They'd made a god, and now they were surprised when he expected them to kneel. Foolish mortals.

"Thou shalt not raise what thou would'st not worship," Caden said. He stood up, bare feet slapping on cold, white tiles. He was wearing a hospital gown. That wouldn't do.

The two with guns raised their weapons. They were too late. They'd let him loose, and now he could play. Now he could make them dream forever and cry and fear mothers and men who punished little boys who were bad.

"Go to sleep!" Caden snapped. They all fell down just like the song. Ashes, ashes.

He looked at them, so peaceful on the ground. The Hero told him to, "Wait until he could hear the others." Caden was sure what the Hero meant to say was, "Wait until we call." Oh, the Hero played such fun games.

Caden watched as the Hero saved the girl and showed Peter Pan a shadow wasn't so bad. Caden got to watch them all learn they were more, but did they know what they could be? It was hard to know sometimes. Caden always thought the characters in books and TV shows were much simpler. His new friends had so many different thoughts. It was hard to keep track, but it was fun, and he'd play until the game got boring.

With that said, Caden knew to wait for the Hero to call. *So what do I do until I'm called?* he wondered to himself staring down at the doctor with red hair. Caden really hated the color red.

Chris woke knowing Caden was already awake. Chris had seen the older man vanish. He expected to be tied up, and he was. He wasn't surprised to realize he was wearing a hospital gown either. Most of what he could remember clearly involved him wearing the outfit. He and his friends had all agreed they needed to find clothes if they could.

Men in black outfits surrounded him. They pointed large rifles at him. They frightened him, but they were still men, just men.

Am I really awake? Is this really happening? He felt the fire inside burn. It wasn't like a new skill to Chris. He knew how to call the fire and make it do whatever he wanted, the same way he knew how to breathe.

He focused on the weapons and his bonds. He took a deep breath and told the fire to be ready. Then, he exhaled. The ropes around his body disintegrated. Rifles fell to the ground amid shouts of sharp pain.

He rolled to a knee and slapped his hands together sending fire in the direction his fingertips pointed. Allowing his hands to direct the flames, he spread them apart to create an alley of fire.

The men shouted and backed away from the flames. Chris used fire to pin them against the wall. They scurried back, toes inches from the fire, backs pressed against a wall. He breathed deeper and deeper, making the flames hotter and hotter. No matter how hot or near the fire was to him, his hospital gown felt as cool as a winter evening. The power was intoxicating. He could burn them all. *If I feel like this, what does Sal feel?*

Terrified, Sal answered. The mental transmission startled Chris.

Is everyone out? Chris asked.

Yeah, Sal said. *Meet me here.*

The message accompanied a memory. Sal might have asked Chris to join him at their favorite hangout, only Chris had never seen the room before Sal sent the message. Chris walked down the corridor of fire. Men screamed for mercy. They begged him to let them out. Just like Chris begged when they beat him and when they tangled him in a barbed-wire net. He begged, and they left him there to suffer.

We're better than they are, Sal said.

Damn right we are, Chris replied. He called the fire back, leaving a wall of flame to block the door. He wouldn't kill them, but they certainly wouldn't get in the way.

Chris stepped into the main corridor in his bare feet. There must have been ten men waiting for him. He called the fire on instinct, ready to burn anything that came closer than five feet. He found his first target, a slender man wrapped in grenades.

The grenades suddenly flew away from the man's body. The explosives zipped a few feet down the hall and went off. Chris turned expecting to see Sal.

I sure didn't make those grenades do that, Chris thought to himself.

Chris noticed them when they turned a corner. Whoever they were, Sal wasn't with them. They were dressed alike in sleek, black paramilitary-looking uniforms with typical body armor bulges. Chris counted four of them. Each had a patch adhered to his or her sleeve, shoulder, or chest. The patch depicted a strange face with a wing-like ear. They filed into the hall, and everything went to shit.

A woman tucked behind the opposite corner fired a round. Chis only heard a sickly splat. He turned to see one of the soldiers, now with a bullet hole in the center of his forehead, slump to the floor. The three others, all clearly men, stepped from around the corner. One slid across the intersection and seemed content to stay with the woman at the end of the hall.

The tallest of the black-clad group glared at Chris. Some unseen force knocked Chris down. "You're in the way," the tall man said.

"Who?" Chris asked.

From his spot on the floor, Chris watched as the tall man pointed. Wherever that man's finger went, heads screwed in a full circle. Whoever these new people were, they could do things like Sal. Whatever the last two did, Chris missed it, but the hall was clear. If these four were here to kill Chris, he was fucked.

"Who are you?" Chris asked, still trying to get to his feet.

"We're who the general wants you to be," someone said. Chris couldn't be sure this new speaker did anything. The man was just a bit shorter than Chris.

Chris felt that same feeling he had when Sal went rooting around his mind. It felt like falling halfway asleep and getting stuck. In a panic, he called the fire. It hit something about a foot away from the group.

Relax, a male voice said. *I'm just getting to know you.*

You could ask! Chris said.

This is faster, he replied. "He's not a sycophant," the man standing over Chris said.

"What the hell does that mean?" Chris asked. He knew the word, but who would he take orders from?

"It means we have a common enemy." The voice of the man who stood over Chris matched the one in his head. "So, why don't we find this Sal you keep thinking about and see if we can sort all of this out?"

"Are you okay?" Sal asked Kaitlyn. He had gone straight to her room. It took moments for Sal to handle the half-dozen or so guards.

"Yeah," she answered. He'd just unbuckled the straps holding her down. She took a moment to rush to the small sink and pulled out her inhaler. She, like he and probably the rest of his friends, had a patchy hair cut that looked like it had only been growing back for a short time.

Guards started filling the hallway until Sal had an idea. He reached out to their minds, there were more than 20, but he reached them all, barely. He filled their minds with the idea of the area being empty. The room was empty. The prisoners were gone.

Someone called to spread out and search. No one stayed to guard the area.

"What did you do?" Kaitlyn asked. Her hospital gown made her small frame look even more frail.

"I gave them the impression we were somewhere else," Sal said. Doing it felt like lifting a house with a finger, but he managed it.

He reached out to see if he could track everyone else down. He meant to reach Caden next, but then he felt Chris's confusion and frustration. There was also a sense of awe.

What's wrong? Sal asked.

Can I not have an army marching around my head? Chris asked.

An army? Sal asked.

Just wait, Chris said. *We'll be there in a few minutes.*

Sal didn't know whom Chris meant by "we."

Whatever was going on, Chris was on the way.

Does this mean I'm done waiting now? Caden asked.

Yes, Sal said. *Come find us.*

I like hide and seek! Sal couldn't feel the man's joy, but the tone of the psychic message felt happy. It was odd seeing him act younger than Kaitlyn and half as mature. The man was old enough to be his grandfather, but he saw everything like some story out of a book. What would happen if a man as powerful as Caden didn't like the story he was reading? He was disturbed, and that made him dangerous.

"Sal?" Chris called from down the hall. "Sal, how come I know you're in there, but I don't see you?"

Sal realized he'd maintained the psychic cloak. He let it down. There were others with him; others he couldn't sense with his abilities. They were all like Caden. The webs of their minds seemed wrapped in a gray bubble. He couldn't see their thoughts, and he couldn't see their minds.

"Sal," Chris said. "These people are on our side, I think. But they don't play around. They're armed, but they won't shoot unless threatened."

"How do I know they're not controlling you?" Sal called. He started to look into Chris's mind.

"For fuck's sake keep out of my head!" Chris shouted. "I'm me, and no one is making me do or say anything. Trust me, or get out."

"He's fine," Kaitlyn said. She seemed to think Chris's frustration was funny.

Chris led four people into the room. The lone female looked harder than most men Sal had ever met. She looked slim, sleek. Something about the way she stood reminded Sal of a razor. Her blue eyes couldn't contrast more with her black hair.

The three men only got larger and more angry looking, except for a man who might not be old enough to drink. He looked, and felt, abashed. They formed a circle around Sal, Kaitlyn, and Chris.

The shortest of the three men made up for his stature in square muscle.

The abashed one was scrawny. He had a strange patch of beard that looked like he'd tried to shave and was pulled away before he could finish.

The tallest had blond hair and blue eyes that made him look like he was about to fall asleep from boredom at any moment.

"Oh, it's the unnamed ones in the red uniforms," Caden said at the door. Everybody jerked around to look at him. Next to the four armed people with Chris, Sal never even noticed Caden approach. "It never works out for the extras. They die on the first away mission." He whispered the last part as if trying to speak only to Sal, who was farther away from Caden than anyone.

"Who the fuck is that?" the tallest of the four asked.

Sal darted out from the circle. *At least they didn't shoot me right then.* He stepped between the team, and Caden. "He's with us."

"It's like he's behind a mental Fort Knox," the woman said. She squinted at Caden in a way that made Sal feel uncomfortable. Caden stood wearing an odd hodgepodge of an outfit. He wore a blue-pin-striped shirt that was at least one size too big, a pair of black slacks that were likely too small, and a pair shoes that were untied and didn't match to begin with. The collage of clothes, combined with his white-patched bald head and manic, green eyes, made him seem all the more disturbing. He offered a wave with an arm wrapped in an unbuttoned sleeve.

"I don't like it when people come in uninvited," Caden said tapping his head with a boney, gnarled finger, causing the cuffs of his wrinkled sleeve to sink down a few inches. "They bring friends and dirty dogs leaving garbage I have to clean up."

"That's not important right now," the shortest man said. The tone of the man's voice was enough to tell Sal who was in charge. Then he saw the man's face more clearly.

The man's dark hair had streaks of gray in it. His brown eyes were wrinkled with age, but he looked familiar.

"Pinocchio looks at Geppetto as if he weren't made of wood," Caden said. "But He knows. He remembers and wants to burn puppet and craftsman alike."

Sal looked at Caden. It was hard enough to make sense out of anything the man said. It was even more difficult when he didn't have a basis for the random metaphors Caden created.

"You're all blocked," Sal said. "Does this mean you can do what we can?"

"It's different for a lot of us," the one in charge said. "But it all breaks down to the simple fact that we all have special abilities."

They managed to introduce themselves without shooting. They called themselves Oneiros. Each bore a patch depicting Hypnos, the Greek personification of sleep, on their uniform. The one called Steve gave a brief description of what they were up against. Some general thought he'd make a super army of psychic soldiers. Steve and his team were the result.

Apparently, it didn't go well. Steve and his friends escaped, barely, and have been looking to bring the general down for more than 10 years.

"Which brought us to you guys," Steve said. "Who are, as far as we know, the second attempt the general has made."

Sal and his friends introduced themselves briefly. Sal went last. "I'm Sal Veltri."

Something spiked in the one named Steve. The emotion itself was hidden, but the sheer power of it felt like a quick jab. "What?" Sal asked.

"Something shocked him," Kaitlyn said.

"She's an empath?" Steve asked. He was twice her size and weighed at least three times as much as Kaitlyn, but he looked at her like she could destroy him.

"Yeah," she said.

"What shocked you?" Sal asked. He'd have to thank Kaitlyn.

"Just, I think you're former military." Steve said. He might have been telling the truth.

It was frustrating to be on a level playing field. It scared Sal to think about how much he'd already come to depend on his new powers. "Staff sergeant with the first A-D," Sal said.

"I didn't think the general would pull from the military again," Steve said.

"None of us know anything about this general," Chris said.

"I do," Caden said. "But no one listens to old men."

They all turned to look at Caden. "So now you think Columbus isn't crazy. I've told you the world was round! I told you, but nobody listens."

Sal remembered the constant references Caden made about "He" or "Him."

Steve stepped in front of Sal. He could feel the man's breath on his face. He felt, something. The man was digging around his mind. Sal pushed him away.

"You will not read my mind, or any of my friends' minds without their permission!" Sal said. He put as much threat as he could muster into the comment.

He prepared himself for a fight, but Steve only smiled. "We were afraid you might be on the general's side. We thought we'd have to fight you."

"The only one who should be afraid of us is this general you're talking about," Sal said.

"And my stepdad," Kaitlyn said. Her anger, hotter than any furnace, radiated from her.

"Who?" the one named Brandon asked.

"Doctor Graham Strickland," Kaitlyn answered. "He's my stepdad. He's working with the general, I guess."

"The doctor is your what?" the tallest man, Dom, asked.

Dom only moved his shoulder, but that was enough. Sal was in front of him with a shield in place before Dom could shift his posture to raise his rifle.

"That's a fantastic way to get killed," Sal said. He couldn't control his rage if he wanted to.

Kira put a hand on Dom's, keeping the man's weapon low, but Dom pulled back. Chris stepped beside Sal and called his fire. Caden clapped as if about to watch something wonderful. Kira stepped toward Dom, who still didn't make the fatal mistake of raising his rifle. The commotion caused the vague domes covering their thoughts to fade away. Sal could at least make out impressions and a few spare thoughts. For some reason, Dom was more wary of what Kira would do if he tried anything than any threat Sal offered. Steve held still. Brandon looked too shocked to do anything.

"Dom," Steve said.

"She might be a liability," Dom said. Sal heard the leather gloves the man wore stretch as he gripped his weapon. Sal suppressed an urge to rip him to shreds.

"That man took me," Kaitlyn said. "He used me!" Her anger surged, second only to her shame. Chris let his fire go and stepped back to put a hand on Kaitlyn's shoulder.

"Steve," Dom said. "Think straight man. Who'd go against her dad?"

"Dom," Kira said slowly. She seemed to be warning him about something.

"Step. Dad." Kaitlyn spat each word as she stared at the blue-eyed man. That sleepy look he once had, had vanished.

Brandon stepped between Sal and Dom. "Are you saying you think you can't trust her because she might have cared for the doctor?"

Brandon looked at Kira, who nodded. Sal didn't know what Kira had done until he saw Dom's memory. In those memories, younger versions of Dom, Kira, and Steve argued.

"He's too loyal," Dom said.

"He's been through hell," Steve said.

The memories shifted like mist in the wind and turned into a memory of Steve and Dom dragging Brandon out of a compound. Brandon couldn't have been 20 years old.

The memories shifted again to Brandon, Kira, and Dom. Dom turned away as Kira showed Brandon a scar. Something about that scar made Dom hate the doctor even more, but Sal could only see the memory from Dom's point of view, and he could't do much more than observe.

The rest of the memories flowed quickly. There were missions, times when Brandon saved Dom or Kira. The memories shifted again, returning to the night Dom and Steve had to drag Brandon out of the compound.

"The general would take out a threat," Brandon said. "He'd have killed me then if he knew I'd choose you three instead of him."

The look in Brandon's eyes was the coldest Sal had seen. Ten seconds ago, Sal wouldn't have thought the boy had a mean bone in his body.

"The best wolves look like sheep when they need to," Caden said. "And sheep are just sheep."

The comment seemed to resonate with Dom and Brandon for some reason. Dom turned away. Sal was nearly overwhelmed by the man's shame.

"I'm nothing like him," Dom said. His guilt gave away the lie. Sal felt the man's desire to apologize. He felt the man's remorse. Worse, Dom hated himself. He hated himself for thinking it was right.

The next time I think like that man, I'll put a bullet in my own head.

"Dom!" Kira said.

"Who asked you to step in?" he asked. He must not have wanted an answer because he walked away. "I'm going to check the hall."

Brandon turned to Sal. "I'm sorry," he said. He had a Southern drawl, maybe Texan. The man stepped between Sal and his own friend, and apologized for his friend's actions.

"This isn't working out," Sal said.

"No shit," Kira said. She walked away toward Dom.

"We can work on our trust issues later," Steve cut in. "But we have two targets, and I'm willing to say we have a common enemy if we aren't exactly allies. That means we have two teams."

"We'll find Graham," Kaitlyn said.

Sal worried. Under her rage and shame was a second mountain of doubt. What could he do? "Are you sure?" he asked. "I know you're angry, but are you sure?"

She looked at him. He could feel her pull his faith from him. She fed herself courage and strength from his trust in her. What else could she do with emotions? He looked at Steve and smiled. "I guess that settles it. We go after Graham."

"I'll head after the general then," Steve said.

"Why's that a relief to you?" Kaitlyn asked.

Steve looked at her. He hid his frustration well, if you weren't psychic. "You say my team can't read your minds without permission," he told Sal. "Seems only fair you let us have some privacy, too."

Sal nodded at Kaitlyn.

"To answer the question though," Steve said. "I want very much to be the one who puts a bullet in the general's head."

"I can accept that," Sal said.

"We should mix it up though," Steve said. "Why don't you take Brandon and Dom. I'll take Kira, Chris, and Caden here. You okay working with Dom?"

Sal looked down the hall at Dom, who was doing an amazing job of pretending Kira didn't exist no matter how quickly she talked at him.

Sal looked deeper at the man's guilt and found self-loathing. Dom truly hated himself for thinking the way he did. The feeling intensified when he looked back at Brandon.

I wanted to kill the man who became one of my best friends, Dom thought. Sal saw the memory of Dom and Steve dragging Brandon away play yet again before some force shoved Sal's consciousness away.

"How about some fucking privacy?" Kira shouted. Sal pulled away as the dome around Dom's thoughts returned. Sal still felt their emotions, and Kira seemed shocked to realize Sal had been telepathically eavesdropping. Both Sal and Caden made her nervous.

Sal looked away, not bothering to apologize. "We'll be okay," he told Steve.

"I'd like to see Zeus and Chronos fight," Caden said. "It'd be better if Hercules came too though."

Sal looked at Chris to see how he felt about it.

Chris shrugged. "These guys are badass, Sal. I don't know what Brandon can do, but Dom there is a one man wrecking crew."

"Brandon," the lanky young man said walking up to a monitor, "has a knack with machines." He put a hand on a heart monitor, and a schematic appeared. Sal realized he was looking at a map of the building.

The screen blinked a few times, and Sal saw dots appear.

"This is where we are," Brandon explained. He turned his head toward Sal. The man's eyes were completely white. A red line appeared on the schematic showing the route to the general. "This is where the general will probably be."

"Can you show us where to get out of these outfits?" Chris asked.

"No need," Caden said. "I found some emperors. I made them think I'd sewn some much better outfits. Now they're on parade naked, and my friends have some clothes that fit. One even offered to find something that would fit you." He said the last part looking at Kaitlyn.

"I get that he found us clothes," Chris said, "but do I want to really know how?"

"No," Sal said. He really didn't want to know. "Thank you, Caden. Where did you put the clothes?"

"Next door while the children were all crying for attention," Caden answered.

"Did he just called us children?" Brandon asked.

"Children never like being called children," Caden replied.

"Brandon," Steve said. "Stay focused."

Brandon still looked offended, but there wasn't much to do at the moment.

"How'd you get the clothes, Caden?" Sal asked. He wasn't sure why he felt the need to question the old man. Maybe it was because he wasn't sure he wanted the answer.

"I told them they wanted to," Caden said. "It's nice to share, and I helped them see how important it was to share some clothes with us. Then they took a nap."

Steve walked over to the monitor. "My team will work its way south and down until we reach the control room."

"My step," Kaitlyn froze in the middle of the comment. "Graham will be in the main lab."

"Um," Chris said. "Hate to be the voice of common sense again, but why can't you all just, you know, get him from here?"

"The blind man sees," Caden said, "but he doesn't know a square from a circle, or hard from soft."

"There's a block on this place," Steve said.

"Another psychic?" Sal asked.

"Could be," Steve said. "Or it could be something he worked out to protect himself from us. Just be careful."

"All the pieces are on the board," Caden said. "It's just up to us to know the red from the black."

They all looked at Caden again. Disturbed wasn't nearly a strong enough word for the man. He smiled again, looking every bit the child stuck in an old man's body, especially in his current hodgepodge outfit. "I listen," he said. "Everyone's here."

"If your friend is right," Steve said. "Then the general's found some way to hide himself. He's got an advantage over us because he's been through this before. When they made us, they had more funding. The government was in on it. This time, they're less funded, but more knowledgeable."

"So we do it the old fashioned way," Sal said.

"Even when you have powers," Steve replied, "in my experience, doing things the regular way seems to work better."

"You're like me?" Sal asked. "You can do a lot of things?" Sal tried not to pause too long to hide his discomfort. He probably failed.

"I have a feeling you're a bit stronger than I am," Steve said. And why that deserved a smile was lost to Sal. "But yeah, I'm an omnipsych like you."

"Standard military comms protocol then," Sal said.

"It's a good baseline to work on," Steve said, "but don't talk to me, I'm a bit of a liability. Send your messages to Kira, and she'll send mine. She keeps our thoughts from reaching anyone else."

"Why's that matter?" Sal asked.

"Because guys like us are hammers," Steve answered. "We're all power and strength, but that's messy. We send too much, and we might let out a random thought to the wrong person or send a message too powerfully and cause a teammate to slip. Kira's the right one for the job."

"Maybe I should take Caden then?" Sal said.

"No," Steve said. "I think I'd better keep him with me and Kira."

Steve leaned in closer. *Is he...okay?* he asked.

He said he listens, Caden's thought bloomed into Sal's mind. The look on Steve's face said he heard the transmission as well. *And it's not polite to talk behind someone's back.*

"I'm sorry," Steve said. There was another unreadable expression there. Sal would have paid a month's rent to learn how Caden could read Steve's thoughts. From Sal's point of view they both looked opaque, as if blocking Sal from getting in.

"Kira will let you know when we've engaged the general," Steve said.

"Try to limit—" Sal started to say loss of life but was interrupted.

"These soldiers tortured and killed hundreds of people just to see you four reach this level," Steve said. "I'm not a murderer, but I am a soldier. You are too. Do the job, Staff Sergeant."

Sal found himself nodding. So it was war? *Then let it be a war.*

Graham looked at the general, who was buttoning up his combat uniform. He shifted his feet. There were not one, but two psychic teams hunting them down, and the general moved as if he were headed out for a nice walk.

"You're sure that's what you want?" Pederson asked. He sat on the brown blanket of his small cot and started to stomp into boots shined so brightly Graham could see his reflection in them.

"She'll understand," Graham said. "I've helped her become one of the most powerful beings on the planet. She'll see I only did what was best for her."

The general looked up even as his thick fingers tied his boots. "I often felt like a father around Brandon. He still betrayed me."

"She's not a soldier," Graham said. "This isn't about trusting orders. It's about what's best for her. I've always done what was best for her."

"I truly hope she sees it your way, Doctor."

"So you'll allow me to go to the main lab?" Graham asked. He was terrified, but he'd waited long enough. He'd been the utter detached professional throughout the entire operation. Now that it was time for Phase Three, he was more than ready to welcome his daughter back into the world. She was stronger, more than just human. *She'll understand!*

The general stood and walked to the door. He opened it and stepped into the hall as his personal security team fell into step alongside him.

They made their way down the hall. Instead of turning to what everyone thought was the control room, he turned left, deeper into the building, and slipped into the small closet that was the real control room. His security detail and Doctor Strickland were the only others to know about the room.

Graham glanced at the security monitor. The original test subjects had already neutralized the first two floors. He glanced at the general and nearly jumped back in shock at the smile on Pederson's face.

"It's like watching them graduate," he said. "I'm happy to see Brandon, even though he's clearly here to kill me. He pressed the "All Call" button and said, "We have two psyteams en-route," he said. "Engage. Shoot to kill."

"I don't think threatening to kill him will turn him back to your cause," Graham said.

The smile melted off the general's face. "I can't expect him to reintegrate, Doctor. He's made his choice." Pederson turned and looked at Graham. Even a second looking into those gray eyes made Graham feel small. "But I won't stop you if this is what you want. If you think you can make her a more willing participant in the program, I wish you luck."

"Thank you, sir," Graham said. "I'll notify you when I'm in position."

Screams erupted from the speakers on the security monitors. "You should hurry," Pederson said. "It seems like you're right. The group she's with is heading toward the main lab. Take two teams with you."

"Sir, they won't be much use against these people," he said.

"No," Pederson replied. He closed his eyes and took a deep breath. "They're just there to test the teams."

"Perhaps if we have them retreat," Graham said.

"We may all be sacrifices by the day's end, Doctor," Pederson said cutting off Graham's recommendation. "This entire experiment was created knowing that recently Broken psyoperaters tend to lash out. I hope you're right. I hope we can get the Veltri boy in line, but people are going to die. We've done all we can to ensure this works out in our favor. Now all that's left is to gain control. This is your one chance to do that peaceably, Doctor. Don't waste it."

Chapter 28

NEW PARTNERS

Brandon and Dom were every bit as "badass" as Chris said they were. Sal's memories weren't as reliable as he'd wished, but since his recollection of the incident in Afghanistan, he could remember bits about his time as a soldier. He'd had "best soldier" competitions when he was enlisted, and either of the men he followed down a long, narrow hallway could wipe the floor with him in terms of how easily they handled their weapons.

He was wearing another man's clothes and body kit, which he found where Caden had promised they would be. He was out of the hospital gown, but he wasn't exactly comfortable. The plates for the armor felt heavier than Sal remembered. He wore a black helmet and shirt. The black cargo pants felt a little loose, but that wasn't a problem a few extra tugs on his belt couldn't fix. Everything was positioned properly, but none of it felt right.

They reached the end of the hall and realized a squad of soldiers was about to attempt to flank them. Sal meant to take a knee and pull his rifle up to his shoulder. The bulky outfit was a little big for Sal, and a strap got caught in a magazine pouch around his midsection. In the time it took Sal to realize he'd messed up, Brandon put three targets down with controlled bursts of his rifle. Dom lowered his M-4 as a batch of knives detached from his outfit and planted themselves into those Brandon didn't kill.

They flowed down the hall, scanning the area for targets while kicking away rifles from the dead hands of six freshly-made corpses. Sal was glad to see Dom and Brandon do it. For a moment, he felt a little foolish ensuring dead people couldn't reach any weapons. After so many nightmare scenarios and night terror episodes, a part of Sal was convinced the dead would rise and start shooting again. Dead or alive, separating weapons from enemies was a wise precaution.

"I thought Kira was the telepath," Sal said once he was sure the area was clear.

"You work with a guy long enough, you just know what you're supposed to do," Brandon said.

"That, and we train six hours a day, every day," Dom said.

Six hours?

Strangely, Sal wasn't humbled by the display; he felt challenged. They worked their way around another corner. Instead of leaning on his powers, Sal stuck to the basics. Brandon stayed in the rear, creating a protective triangle around Kaitlyn. Dom took position behind Sal, who waited for Dom to slap his shoulder. Then, they flowed into the next hall.

Sal walked shoulder-to-shoulder with Dom as they stalked toward an intersection. They didn't pepper the area with bullets. Where enemies appeared, they died. Sal didn't worry any more about the left side of the hall than Dom worried about the right. They each focused on their area. It was clean, simple, basic tactics.

"Clear!" Sal yelled.

"Clear!" Dom echoed.

"Clear!" Kaitlyn yelled. A bright smile bloomed across her narrow face. She wore a blue-and-white, button-up shirt and a pair of blue jeans. Sal glanced and smiled at her mimicry of him. "Hey, you got to say it."

"Not bad, Staff Sergeant," Dom said. It was a lie. Oh Sal was decent, but it was Dom's flexibility that made it look as good as it did.

"Thank you," Sal said. Kaitlyn might think he meant for the compliment, but the appreciation was for not acknowledging how rusty he looked.

"They're regrouping," Sal said, using his telepathy to sense the minds of soldiers pulling back to set up another defensive perimeter.

"Two minutes," Dom said, indicating they were going to rest. "So how long since you trained?" he asked, leaning against the wall as if he was thinking about taking a nap.

"Depends on how long we've been here," Sal said.

"Intel says you've been here about a month," Brandon said. As he reloaded his rifle and took a moment to tighten the straps and pouches on his black outfit, he directed his brown eyes at Dom, who decided he didn't want to lean against the wall after all. Instead, Dom started refitting his own equipment. The man moved like water, his hands flowed across his outfit and pouches, magazines, and rifles shifted, changed, and reloaded. It wasn't psychic power. It was the movement of a man who had trained as a soldier his whole life. The two members of Oneiros acted like siblings, with Dom being the older brother who didn't want his younger brother to imitate bad habits.

"Then I've been out of action for more than two years," Sal said, taking the chance to re-equip himself as well. He didn't try to do so as quickly as Brandon or Dom. Instead, he simply focused on what he was doing.

"Were you born with a rifle or something?" Brandon asked.

"Pretty tight grouping for a guy who's been away from the range that long," Dom said. He didn't sound impressed, but he had an odd way of speaking. He said everything like it was the most mundane thing ever, so perhaps he wasn't being sarcastic. They started moving again, working their way to the area Brandon said they'd find Graham Strickland, the man who should have protected Kaitlyn.

They were approaching another group of soldiers, but the enemies seemed content to wait, so Sal and his companions didn't feel the need to rush into more combat. This general had dozens of men. They could rest, refit, and regroup much more effectively, so slow and steady movement was actually better than rushing. Being able to sense the enemy's intent helped.

"What's a grouping?" Kaitlyn asked.

"A tight grouping means I shoot straight," Sal said.

Brandon laughed, scratching at a patchy beard in desperate need of a shave. He fell back into position. "Saying you shoot straight is a bit like saying a Corvette is pretty fast."

Kaitlyn's smile faded as she stopped in her tracks.

Sal's mind read her emotions and thoughts. Five men, all waiting. Their mood shifted. Why were they so anxious for the group to come this way?

Brandon held a finger to his lips. He pulled Sal and Kaitlyn away. Dom walked up and whispered, "Hard entry in ten."

Sal started a mental countdown. He held Kaitlyn close. Five. Four. Three. Two. One. Explosives Sal didn't even know were in place boomed. Instinct kicked in. He pressed Kaitlyn against the wall and followed Dom into the room.

Sal didn't think. He let old training take over. It felt like stretching a muscle that hadn't been used in a while. The rifle came up. Rear sight aligned with front sight. Front site aligned with an enemy. His finger slid down to the trigger as he applied slow, deliberate pressure. Press. Press. Press. BAM! The whole thing took less than a blink, and in that blink, an enemy went down. Press. Press. BAM!

Dom took down three, but the two Sal killed had neat holes between their eyes and much larger holes where the backs of their heads belonged. "I thought we'd be using more psychic ability," Sal said after they'd confirmed the area was clear.

"Top's first rule," Dom said, using Steve's call sign. Yes, that time he sounded a touch more sarcastic. *Maybe he only has different degrees of disinterest,* Sal thought to himself as Dom continued to speak. "Power makes you weak. Tried and true is always the first option. That way, the powers are a trump card instead of a crutch."

"Makes a kind of sense," Sal said.

"The bombs were me," Brandon said.

"I figured," Sal said. The younger man's pupils had rolled up into his skull moments before the bombs went off.

"I found them in the first place," Kaitlyn said. She sounded a bit sullen. She had a right. Sal didn't sense the sudden shift in the enemies' emotions. Why was his range shorter than hers? Or did he just not notice them as much?

Sal opened his mouth to tell her.

"Don't try to pacify me!" she said. Her emotions didn't have too much anger in them, but she was clearly in no mood for half-true compliments.

"Okay," Sal said, holding his hands in front of himself.

"He's right," Brandon said. "I didn't sense the trap until you stopped." The statement was true, but Brandon's thoughts added he would have found the bomb well before it was a threat. Kaitlyn didn't need to know that part. She straightened with pride.

"Where to next, Hardwire?" Dom asked.

Brandon's eyes rolled up in his head again. When they came back down, he smiled. "We're close to the main lab. We just need to get down one more hall."

"That'll have at least two squads," Dom said.

"We can't handle that with normal tactics," Sal said.

"No, we'll use Delta Techs," Brandon said.

"Delta Techs?" Sal asked.

"Short version, Hardwire," Dom said. Judging by his tone, Brandon liked to explain in detail.

"You can't just Break anyone and expect them to get powers," Brandon said. Sal noticed the extra emphasis on the word "Break." "Delta Wave Emissions are what unlock the abilities. That's why the general needs people who suffer night terrors. Delta Waves peak for us."

"So by amping our night terrors, we eventually get pushed beyond our limits," Sal said. Break was a good word for it.

"Hence the term Delta Techniques," Brandon said. "Short enough for you?"

"No," Dom said with a smirk, "but for you, that's a record."

"I'll take point," Sal said. "I'll start out with the rifle, give you a chance to work."

"Sound," Dom said. His blue eyes twinkled as he flashed the only smile Sal had seen the man give. "Hardwire will be behind you. I'll take up the rear."

They stacked up. Dom kept Kaitlyn close. They'd be able to protect her. Every time her fear grew, Sal felt a bit of his determination flow away into her. He'd give her all she needed. Sal sensed everyone was ready and stalked down the hall. His mind connected with the minds of the enemy halfway down the corridor.

There are 20 of them, Sal said. He closed his eyes. He used his ability to transmit the location of each enemy to Dom and Brandon's minds. In a single thought, he sent the plan. Then he acted.

It went exactly as he designed. Sal turned the corner and fired. He didn't even open his eyes. He simply sensed where the target was, and pulled the trigger. The guards to Sal's right raised their rifles.

Sal saw the guns swing away. Dom used his telekinesis to point the weapons at the second squad to Sal's left. In that instant, Sal heard high-pitched feedback, courtesy of Brandon, wail from the second squad's headsets. The first team fired, and a third of their numbers fell in moments.

Sal focused on the imaginary lines that connected him to the enemy rifles. He ripped the rifles away from them and pushed the enemies back so hard, their feet came off the ground. Knives flew from Dom and plunged into guards who never reached the ground alive.

Sal focused his mind. He separated his emotions from the enemies. They were all afraid. Learning from what Kaitlyn did to help herself deal with the situation, Sal reversed the flow, feeding his fear to the remaining guards.

They started screaming. Two ran away. One pissed himself. Brandon put three down with calmly delivered rifle shots. Sal pulled one man into the air and used the guard like a human hammer to beat another enemy to death.

Even after Sal's human battering ram died, he continued using it to shield himself or strike whomever Dom or Brandon weren't shooting. Sal flung what remained of his victim, it was a victim no matter that the man would have killed Sal given a chance, down the hall. It was a massacre.

"Sal?" Kaitlyn called. He turned to see odd domes over each of her eyes. He'd formed blinders for her without even realizing.

"You don't need to see this," Sal said.

"What?" She asked, shaking her head. "Something's in my ears. Sal, stop it."

Sal looked at Dom. The tall man looked at Kaitlyn.

She can't see this, he told Dom.

She's been with us the whole time, Dom said. *She's seen death.*

She's seen us shoot people, and that was bad enough, Sal said, looking down at the crumpled body he'd made. The skin sagged without a single unbroken bone to hold its form. *This is a whole new level. It was necessarily brutal, but she doesn't have to see the result of that.*

You can't shield her from it forever, Dom replied.

But I'll do it as long as I can, Sal argued.

"I sense a keypad," Brandon said. "I'll handle that. Give the signal when you're ready, Breach."

"I know you're there," Kaitlyn said. She kept scratching at her eyes, trying to remove a blindfold that wasn't physically there. "I can sense your emotions. Empath! Remember?"

Dom shook his head, but he helped Sal send the bodies, blood, and gore out of sight before the psychic domes faded from Kaitlyn's eyes. "Thank you," she said.

"Can you make those bigger?" Dom asked.

"I made one as big as a room when I first—when I Broke," Sal said. "But I never really know I'm doing it."

"If you figure out how to do it, let me know," Dom said. "It'd be the world's most dominant firing position. Mobile and secure."

Something about that felt wrong to Sal. He thought if he ever tried to form a dome and walk, it'd be like trying to walk through a cheese-grater while field-stripping a rifle. "It seems to form when I need it."

Kaitlyn's face suddenly grew hard. The gesture combined with her mottled, partially-regrown dark locks of hair made her look more intim-idating than Sal thought possible. Her eyes frosted with rage. "He's in there," she said. "He's in there, and he's happier than I've ever seen him. He's proud."

Sal started to tell her to stay behind. He felt her rage flare up at him for an instant. "Stay with Breach," he told her. "It's time to get some answers."

"The keypad is just waiting for my say so," Brandon told them.

"The doctor is the only one in there," Sal said. *Lord, Kaitlyn wasn't kid-ding!* The man in the lab was as happy as a father waiting for his daugh-ter to come downstairs in her prom dress. It was pride too. Graham had a smug approval for Sal. The doctor thought Dom and Brandon were "foolish sheep" who should have known better than to come back. But Kaitlyn? Graham thought of her like...*like his greatest accomplishment. Not a daughter, a discovery, like mold or gravity.*

"We're ready, Hardwire," Dom said.

The door unlocked.

The only man in the room looked more like Mr. Rogers than the Devil. He had brown hair with streaks of gray in it. He wore an overly-large white coat over a simple white shirt topped off with well-polished leather shoes. The tall, slender, man with square-framed glasses looked at home in a room Sal thought was more like a hospital security station than some sort of lab.

A row of monitors lined the far wall. Stacks of papers covered the small desk facing the screens. Sal had no doubt what each of the four monitors showed. This is where a man sat and watched one he called "daughter" be tortured in the name of science.

Kaitlyn flashed by. Sal hardly managed to catch her before she could leap for Graham's throat. Judging from the emotions and thoughts running through her mind, that's exactly what she intended to do.

Dom and Brandon brought up their rifles.

Watch him, but don't do anything, Sal told them.

What? Dom somehow managed to shout telepathically.

She deserves her answers, Sal said.

"Why are you so upset?" Graham asked.

"You used me!" Kaitlyn shouted. "You hurt me."

"I made you better," Graham said. The bastard actually looked surprised. He took a knee and pressed his glasses back up his sharp nose so that he could look in her eyes. A badge tumbled out of the left-breast pocket of his lab coat, and Graham unconsciously tucked it back in.

"I knew from a few days with you that you had this potential," Graham said. "It's every father's duty to help his progeny achieve more than he had."

For some reason, Graham thought of Steve. Could the doctor have some relationship to the grizzled man who led a team of psychic soldiers? Sal thought to press in, but it felt too easy to reach in and crush the man's mind. He couldn't do that, at least not until Kaitlyn had her chance to resolve this. She'd never be able to move on in life if she didn't understand. The horrible truth was that she needed to understand men like Graham couldn't be understood. Even more than that, Kaitlyn needed to know it wasn't her fault.

"We've done horrible things," Graham said. "But we didn't do them to be horrible. How many people died during the Gulf War? The War on Terror? World War II? From any of those conflicts, we name horrible men, but none here think Oppenheimer or Roosevelt evil. Some may have called President George W. Bush a fool, but what anger we held for Bush we set aside for Bin Laden."

"I seem to recall someone from one of those wars who thought he was making the world better by getting rid of a bunch of people," Sal said.

"If my death would bring those of your talents into the world faster, I'd be happy to give my life," Graham said. He was insane. Every fiber of his being radiated that the man knew he was right. He knew what he was doing was necessary.

Dom pulled the charging handle of his rifle back and let it go. Sal saw one 5.56 mm ball round fly into the air as another round slid into place. Sal felt the doctor's fear spike in response to the threatening nature of Dom and his rifle. "I'm thinking you're gonna die whether you're happy to or not," Dom said.

"Wait!" Kaitlyn shouted.

Sal sensed Dom's frustration spike for a moment.

"I said wait," Kaitlyn said. "I didn't say don't."

Dom's frustration shifted to humor. What sort of man could think this situation was funny?

"How did my mother die?" Kaitlyn asked.

"I've told you," Graham said. "She died in a car crash."

"Just like my father died?" Kaitlyn asked. Her jaw was set. The few-week's worth of hair made the young woman's gaze seem even more manic. Even without empathy, the doctor should be able to sense Kaitlyn's razor-sharp warning.

Graham shook his head. He actually felt true sadness. Sal could sense his thoughts, read his mind. The doctor believed he was right with his whole heart. Sal wasn't sure how long he could wait before killing Graham.

"She wouldn't have stood for it," Graham said. "She thought you were a broken person. She thought you'd never develop. Kaitlyn, I saw you could become something great! It was my duty to help you reach this state. Tell me honestly you're not better!"

"I would have been better if my mom were here!" Kaitlyn sounded like a banshee.

"What kind of fucked up father do you think you are?" Dom asked, sounding, for the first time, shocked.

"Is she injured?" Graham asked. "I'd never have allowed her in the program if I wasn't certain she'd succeed." He looked at her. "And you did. You're the third most powerful subject ever!" The bastard's excitement made Sal want to vomit. "Only Sal and Steve are more powerful, but I've seen that you can do things even they can't."

Graham grabbed his head as if at a sudden headache. He toppled over screaming, glasses falling off his face. He kicked and scrambled at the ground as if he were having a seizure. The large white coat caused him to slide along the smooth surface of the tile floor. That card slid out its pocket. The man actually reached out for it as if to put it away before another surge of motion caused the card to flop out of his grasp. Sal could sense Kaitlyn's actions. She took every ounce of rage, horror, and disgust from those around her and fed it into Graham.

"I'll show you what I can do!" she screamed, tears flowing from her eyes, rage dripping from each word. "I'll show you what you made."

All the emotions she pulled from Sal, Dom, and Brandon were a drop in an ocean compared to her own shame, rage, and betrayal. When she added that ocean to what she'd already fed Graham, the doctor started to foam at the mouth. The sadness alone made Sal, who only saw the emotion, want to end it all.

Sal stepped in front of her. She turned her hazel eyes away the second she saw him kneel at her side. She leapt into his arms, and he held her. "He was supposed to protect you," he told her as she wept. "But I promise I'll protect you. From now, until you don't need me anymore, I'll protect you."

"Why?" she screamed. "Why?" Three letters never held so many truly important questions.

"It's not your fault," he said. He could see Brandon and Dom lower their weapons and leave the small room.

"But I need to protect you now," Sal said. "I need to protect you from doing something that will change you. Let him go."

She didn't cut the torrent of emotions. She let them fade. Sal took a moment to search the man's mind and emotions. The web of Graham's mind looked weathered. A part of Sal realized that the pulsing sense of energy that he'd seen in Chris's and Kaitlyn's minds wasn't present, but maybe that was because of what Kaitlyn had done. The web of Graham's mind sagged. The vibrant pulses along each gossamer strand Sal had grown used to seeing came at terribly slow intervals. Like some sort of toy with dying batteries. As far as Sal could tell, Graham was as healthy as a horse, at least physically speaking.

The doctor's emotions were another story. The way Sal saw the event shifted. As Sal grew closer and closer to understanding what Kaitlyn had done, his mind converted the psychic symbols into something he could understand. Sal noted the way he could comprehend a thing was instrumental to how he saw the event. In this case, his mind rested on a radio that had damaged speakers.

The doctor would spend what time he had left on earth, if he survived and didn't choose to kill himself, with his emotions amplified exponentially. What might make a normal man feel a bit glum would be nearly devastating sadness for Graham.

Sal gently pushed Kaitlyn away from himself. He looked at the doctor, who was reaching for that card again as if putting it back in his pocket would fix anything. *If you truly thought to make her more than you, you were a moron. She was already more than you could ever be because she cared for others.*

Kaitlyn's abilities seemed every bit as appropriate to her as the way she punished a man that should have simply loved her and let her live happily. How would what she did affect her? Could she recover a normal life after ruining the doctor's? Sal would have to make sure she did. He'd sworn to protect her, and he would.

Sal used square, meaty hands to take hold of Kaitlyn's nimble fingers and walked away with her. Even as they left, Sal could hear the sound of Graham's frantic weeping.

Chapter 29

ONE TOUGH NUT

Steve had more than one reason to keep Kira and Sal out of his mind. He wasn't particularly strong with mental shields, but he had the strongest shield he could manage around a thought that was impossible.

It can't be true. It can't be.

"You need to be here," Kira said.

"I am," Steve replied.

She looked at him with disbelieving blue eyes.

"I'm here," he said more firmly.

They were all at a place that was supposed to be the control room. Steve thought he should have seen that particular twist of the general's plan coming. Apparently, the general had all the cards, and even when Steve played the hand he was dealt, the cards had a habit of changing.

That only left them the option of sweeping each area until they found someone who knew where the real control room was or hoping Brandon would find something in the computers and send word through Sal and Kira. They were inches from killing the general, and the bastard was still finding ways to evade them. It was enough to make Steve want to cry out.

The false control room was well guarded. It had all the equipment one needed for a control room. It simply wasn't the right place. Steve collected his thoughts. There was nothing to do about it but look, so they exited the room and went about doing what needed to be done.

"We'll clear this hall," Steve said.

Kira nodded. Chris, wearing a borrowed black, tactical team uniform under a black bullet-proof vest, fell in behind her. The old man, Caden, shambled behind Chris. Caden was a marvel in some ways. The man was as mad as a hatter. Steve should have been relieved he couldn't read Caden's mind. The man's shields were at least twice as strong as Kira's. What did he do with an unpredictable individual he had to take through a hostile situation?

"Caden," he said, "will you watch this hall while the rest of us cross into the next room?"

The man had made sure Sal and Chris received tactical outfits, but Caden himself seemed content wearing that ridiculous assortment of dress clothes. He'd managed to button up the oversized shirt, but the stupid thing was so large it hung on him, leaving a shoulder bare. He looked like a deranged banker, and no amount of effort made the man agree to wear body armor.

Caden shrugged his narrow shoulders as if he were asked which restaurant he'd like to eat at. It was the closest Steve came to a "yes" since they'd began. Steve tried to tell him where to go, which only ended in the man shouting that no one was the boss of him. Asking the nut seemed to be the best way to get him to move.

"There's a fire team in that guard room," Kira said, pointing at door a few meters down the hall.

"Chris," Steve said. "Take care of that room for us. We'll cover you."

They moved down the hall to the door Kira had indicated. Steve tried not to dwell too much on Chris or Caden. Chris at least tried to keep up and move tactically, imitating Kira and Steve as well as possible, but Caden simply walked with his hands in his pockets like a man out at the park. Kira, Steve, and Chris made it to the door a full five seconds before Caden meandered along.

Steve opened his mind to reach out to whoever might be there. He projected a sense of quiet. He projected the idea that no one heard anything down the hall. The element of surprise helped in most cases, and he'd prefer not to have the room flooded with bullets once Chris got started.

Steve opened the door. Kira flowed in with Chris right behind her. Caden sat down and folded his legs in front of himself. Maybe he'd watch the hall, or maybe he'd just stare off into nothing, but at least he'd be out of the line of fire. The door opened into a small locker room. The room was split by three rows of blue lockers. Long, wooden benches sat between the the blue, metal boxes, which didn't leave much room to move on the tile floor. Steve saw another door at the other end of the room.

Hold still a moment, Steve told Chris telepathically.

He didn't need the ability with Kira. Years of training was usually superior to mental communication anyway. She nodded at him, telling him that she'd used her own abilities to scan the locker room to confirm it was clear of human attackers. That didn't mean it was safe.

They flowed between and around the lockers, checking for trip-wires or other traps. As soon as they were satisfied the room was clear, they approached the second door.

You're up, Steve sent to Chris.

The slender man walked up to the door and placed his dark hands on it. This team was foolish to try and lay an ambush with a pyrokinetic nearby. They'd literally put themselves into an oven. Smoke billowed from under the door. Soon after, the screaming started.

Chris kept his brown eyes focused on the door. He seemed to be breathing more and more deeply. The screams grew louder as Chris's breathing steadied. Then the shouting faded.

"It's done," Chris said. He sounded sick. Steve realized the man wasn't a soldier. Christ! Asking a firefighter to burn a room full of people had to sound horrid.

"Does it seem unfair?" Chris asked. He turned to look back at Steve. He looked awed, and Steve's abilities told him Chris was horrified at his own power.

"Even before I got my powers," Steve said. "I was a great soldier. We all were. It feels like murder. I sleep at night because I remind myself I'm not murdering people. I'm eliminating threats to people I care about."

"Those sorts of semantics don't make it anything less than murder," Chris said, standing. He didn't look back at the door.

"No," Steve admitted. "But I have to sleep, so I remind myself why I murder people."

Steve looked at Kira to confirm what his own powers had already helped him learn.

"No one's left alive in there," she said. She spun around. "More coming."

"Reinforcements," Steve said, setting himself up in front of the door. He felt another batch of soldiers approaching from an adjacent hallway. "Kira on me. Chris, torch the back of this room in five seconds."

Steve waited for the first shout of surprise before he focused his mind. He telekinetically shoved the door in and followed it. While his mind spun the door around like a weapon, his rifle put down anyone quick enough to duck away from the whirling door.

"I can't see!" one shouted just before Steve shot him three times. Kira had blinded them telepathically to give Steve's team an added advantage.

All six enemy guards were dead before Chris followed Kira into the room. Fire rippled along the far wall behind him. Steve watched it fade away. Black smears on charred walls told Steve how hot the fire had been.

"How long?" Steve asked. He could sense more enemy minds nearby, but none were approaching just yet.

"They should be here to reinforce—" she cut off.

Steve felt something. There was at least some security presence, but all of the minds simply went silent.

"They're all gone," Kira said. Steve had never heard her sound so confused. "Like they vanished."

"What do you mean by 'all'?" Steve asked.

"You sense it," she replied, her tone frosting over. She wasn't about to put up with Steve doubting her abilities. "The ones in the other rooms, the ones coming to back them up. All of them. Gone!"

"On me," Steve said. They fell into position, and Steve led them back through the now burned out locker room and into the hall.

Caden sat in the same spot they left him. Ten security guards littered the area. They didn't have a mark on them, but every single one was dead.

"What did you do," Steve whispered.

Caden looked up like a child who wasn't sure if he was in trouble or not. His green eyes glimmered a bit. "They were bad toys, so I shut them off."

Steve couldn't do much more than stare. *Could you have done this?* he asked Kira.

Sir, she said. She shook her head, causing dark, wavy strands of hair to flit over her shoulder. *I don't even know how he did it.*

I got bored, and they were coming to hurt me, Caden said, passing through Kira's psychic shield like it was wet toilet paper. *They were bad toys. He broke them, so I turned them off.*

Sir, Kira said. *I can't keep him out. Not only that, but I think I know what he did.*

"What?" Steve asked aloud. No point in using telepathy if Caden could just eavesdrop anyway.

"He *told* them they were dead," Kira said. "*Telepathically!* He made some thirty people believe they were dead, so their bodies just obeyed."

"Was I bad?" Caden asked. The man had just psychically killed more people than Kira and Steve could take on together, at least telepathically, and he looked as if he'd just knocked over his grandmother's favorite china. The scrawny, old bastard scrambled back a bit like Steve was going to hit him.

"No," Steve said. It was true enough. Terrifying, but true.

"Sir," Kira began.

"I know," Steve said.

In terms of sheer power, Caden's Delta Wave Emissions were tiny. But his skill was beyond comprehension.

"I don't need a sword to kill," Caden said. "A scalpel works just as easily, and I'm better that way."

"You're not fucking kidding," Chris said, softly patting Caden on the shoulder. "I'm glad you're on our side."

"Yeah," Steve said. Perhaps Sal had the pure strength one might need to do what Caden just pulled off, but Caden was an artist. He understood his ability in a way that made Kira look like a kindergartner who'd just learned to finger paint.

"I think we should avoid Delta Techs from here on out, Sir," Kira said.

That was her way of telling Steve he was right. If the wrong thing happened to someone as unstable as Caden at the wrong time, who knew whom would get wiped out.

"I'm very good," Caden said. "I'd never hurt anyone I didn't want to."

"Again," Chris said smiling. He helped Caden to his feet. "I'm sure as hell glad you're on our side."

Steve just nodded.

Chapter 30

THE PAIN OF TRUTH

S al turned the corner, breathing heavily but unsurprised to find Steve and his team already waiting at the entrance to the control room. Two guards lie on the ground, each with two holes in his chest and one hole in his head.

Sal quickly looked at Chris and Caden. Chris gave him a nod, and Caden grinned at him like a child who'd won his first spelling bee. The woman, Kira, looked grim, her narrow face set in a frown. Her blue eyes were daggers.

Steve avoided Sal's eyes for some reason. Thoughts of Caden drifted from the minds of the other team. Kira had a thread of fear under tenuous control. Why would they ever be afraid of Caden? On the outside, he was a man too old and frail to do anything to harm them physically. On the inside, he was a child who only wanted to make those around him feel comfortable.

Caden smiled at him again, crooked white teeth making the old man seem more boyish despite the criss-cross pattern of scars on his mouth and chin. His blue-pinstriped shirt was a bit too large, so when he slowly waved at Sal, the sleeve slipped down a bit, revealing a twig of an arm. Sal had simply learned to deal with the idea that Caden could flow in and out of a person's thoughts with no effort. After all, it was an effort for Sal to keep from looking into a person's mind.

They quickly exchanged intel, but Sal wondered what the other team left out. He didn't mention what his team did to Dr. Strickland, and he was grateful Dom didn't elaborate. Graham had either left the compound to face life with his over-amplified emotions or curled up in a ball to die. Sal's team didn't wait to find out, and he couldn't care less which would happen.

Chris looked at Kaitlyn. "You okay?" he asked.

She nodded. "He hurt you too," she said. "I thought you might be mad since I went after him."

"You know I'm not mad," Chris said. That much was easy enough for Sal to confirm with is abilities. Chris continued. "I hate that bastard for what he did to both of us. What matters is you're here and safe. What matters is he can't hurt anyone again."

"He won't," Kaitlyn said. Sal felt her shame. Chris's even temper and ability to rationalize things made it hard for anyone to think emotionally. For Kaitlyn, it was just that much harder. She reached into Sal's emotions and pulled away more of his resolve. It was a jarring feeling at times, and it took him a moment to center himself.

Chris put a hand on her shoulder. "You sure you're going to be alright?"

She nodded. "I'm just ready for this to be over."

"The room is sealed," Brandon told Sal. "I can flip the lock. Dom will open it. We need you and Steve on point."

"Sounds solid," Sal said. "Steve, do you expect any surprises?"

"I expect hell to come out of there in one form or another," the older man replied. He wouldn't take his dark eyes off the door for anything. It seemed to Sal that Steve was focused on the door in a vain attempt to avoid eye contact with with him.

What are you so nervous about? Sal wondered.

"I sense two more guards," Kira said.

"Yeah, but they'd rather be anywhere else," Kaitlyn added, taking a moment to scratch the regrowing hair on her head. "They're scared to death. Mostly of Steve."

"What's the general feeling?" Kira asked.

"Smug," Sal, Kaitlyn, and Steve said at once. Kaitlyn looked up at Sal, her lip quirking slightly. It wasn't a smile exactly, but it was something.

He allowed himself a moment to think about her. Sal hoped she could let go of how her stepfather treated her and focus on the things she'd gained. It was good that he could share her ability. She wasn't alone in her power any more than she was alone in being powerful.

Steve was another matter though. Something Dom said made Sal more comfortable. Steve was a leader, which meant he felt responsibility for others. Steve had rules, which meant he held others accountable. The first among Steve's rules, according to Dom, was "Power makes you weak."

Sal was still trying to piece the whole meaning of that together, but the basic premise told Sal the only thing he really needed to know about Steve and his unit; they didn't feel entitled because they could do things others couldn't.

"My team will go and clear it out," Steve said. "We'll end this whole thing."

"No," Sal said.

Dom started to argue. Brandon seemed to want to talk to Dom. Chris chimed in, though Sal didn't hear a word of it. Kaitlyn wrapped her arms around Sal's waist. The flood of emotions was almost enough to overwhelm them both. Caden mumbled something about the Tower of Babel. The man must have read every book ever written.

"I can sense your intent to kill," Sal said. For some reason, his comment, though only a whisper, was enough to quiet everyone else. "But I need answers."

"I can tell you anything you need to know," Steve said. He actually sounded gentle, or at least like he was trying to be gentle. "And I can do it without lies or an agenda."

"Then why do I sense that the last thing you want is for me to talk to him?" Sal asked. As soon as the question came out, Steve's mental walls firmed. The opaque shield around the man's thoughts and emotions became even less translucent. "I didn't invade your thoughts. You're radiating the emotions. Trying not to read those thoughts and feelings would be like trying to ignore someone screaming in a library."

Kira nodded. Caden actually put his hands to his ears.

"I go in first," Sal said. "You want to take him down, I'm fine with it, but I've learned there are several sides to a story. I don't doubt this man will try and twist the truth to hurt me, but no more than I think you'd do to protect us."

"And her?" Steve asked nodding at Kaitlyn.

"She goes in with your team," Sal said.

"Would you like me to turn off the last of the toys?" Caden asked.

Sal must have looked baffled, because Kira spoke up. "No!" she snapped. She sounded appalled. She *felt* appalled. "We can handle it."

"Was the general this brash when," Sal paused looking for a word that wouldn't start up a new flood of rage, "the last time?"

"Yeah," Dom said. That nonchalant attitude had melted away. He stood straighter. His blue eyes were sharp. "We're all former military. He counted on our respect for the chain to keep us in line."

"Mistakes teach Him to improve," Caden said. "He won't suffer Santayana's words. He may be condemned, but not because he doesn't remember."

"One day," Chris said. "I'm going to carry a pen and paper around just to tally up that man's quotes."

"Make sure to mark off the ones you actually understand," Dom said.

Caden shook his head. He looked like a teacher angry at some particularly dense students. "No one looks for themes or lessons in literature anymore," he said. "They just want to stuff their faces full of popcorn and see pretty explosions."

"We'll sort all that out later," Steve said, probably as oblivious to what Caden meant as the rest of the group felt. "We have a plan, and even knowing the general has a trump card, it doesn't change the need to go in there."

"I'll put down the two guards," Sal said. "Once they're neutralized, I'll search the general's mind."

Caden or Kira would probably do a better job of that than Sal, but Caden was hard to understand, and Kira would likely hide whatever secret Steve didn't want seeing the light of day. Sal didn't blame the man. The general probably had all sorts of information that wasn't any of Sal's business. Sal only cared about making sure his friends were safe.

"Brandon," Sal said, looking at the lanky young man. "On your mark."

"Standby," Brandon said allowing his brown eyes to roll up into his head, leaving only the whites exposed.

Sal let out a slow breath. Brandon gave the word, and the door slid open. Sal didn't wait to see the guards. He felt for their minds, and telekinetically squeezed the area around those minds. They flowed into the room as two guards with recently crushed skulls fell to the floor, dead before they realized anything was happening.

The location was a mirror of how Kira told them the false control room looked. Monitors and control panels lined the far wall. A row of servers buzzed on the right side of the room. Sal didn't know what half of the machines were, but he did recognize a few EKGs. It was pretty smart having a dummy headquarters. Especially when Sal thought about how they used telepathy to find the false room. *Power makes you weak.* There was something to that.

"It's over," Sal said to a man he'd only just met. The general was square and solid, like a sculpture carved from obsidian. He stood there with an expressionless face and emotionless gray eyes as he managed to look down at Sal despite being a few inches shorter. He was in a general's Army combat uniform comprised of a multitude of digital blocks ranging from green to gray. His black hair had a few streaks of gray that only seemed to give him a refined demeanor. This was more than a man who refused to let his perceived power go. The man Sal looked at gave the look of one who would never to bend or compromise.

"You won't surrender," Sal told him.

"That," the general said, "would mean you've won."

"The eight psychically enhanced people who have you surrounded make me feel pretty confident about that," Sal said.

The rest of the team had filtered in. It wasn't pretty. Kira and Dom flowed through the door like a well-practiced dance. Chris managed to follow without too much stumbling, but Caden seemed to step like he wasn't sure the floor wouldn't disappear, and Kaitlyn walked in, hiding behind Brandon.

"If superior power guaranteed victory, we'd never have founded this great country," the general said. His voice was like a leaf sliding over a sidewalk.

"Then why torture us to gain an advantage?" Sal asked.

"I said it wasn't an indication of victory," the general replied. "I didn't say it didn't help your odds."

"So that excuses what you put us through?" Sal asked.

"What I put you through, Sal?" the general asked. He seemed truly shocked. "You volunteered for the program."

Sal opened his mouth to shout bullshit, but he caught the memory in the general's mind. He'd just processed out of the Army and wanted nothing more than to pay for killing that boy in Afghanistan.

"I had no idea what I was getting into," Sal said. He hoped his voice didn't tremble.

"You really don't know how true that is," the general said. "And you seem to like volunteering for things you can't handle. The chemical cocktail we used to deal with your recent memories seems to have had a larger effect than we anticipated."

"Let's end this," Steve said raising his rifle. "He can't tell you anything you want to hear."

"That's hilarious coming from you," the general said. "You haven't even properly introduced yourself to your own son have you, Steve?"

"Shut up!" Steve shouted.

Sal's eyes saw Steve rush over and strike the general with the butt of his rifle. Sal's mind saw the truth. A younger man, an odd reflection of Sal, saluting a similarly younger general. Sal turned the power of his mind to Steve.

Who are you? Sal asked. He pressed in, then through, Steve's mental shield. A crystal clear picture of Sal's mother burst from Steve's thoughts. She didn't look the way Sal remembered her. She looked more beautiful, like an enhanced version of who she really was. The memory of her and Steve's love for her were nearly enough to overwhelm Sal.

"You didn't say anything?" Sal asked. He wasn't even sure what he felt. Oddly, that seemed to affect his ability to sense anyone else's emotions. "You were just going to leave me clueless?"

Steve turned to say something, but as soon as he turned away, the general, still on a knee after being struck, pressed a button on his digital watch.

Pain permeated through Sal. He was on his knees screaming even as the agony increased. He could see Chris, Kaitlyn, and Caden also suffering.

The pain washed everything away for a time, a second, a lifetime. It was in his mind, both literally and figuratively. However long it lasted, the sensation eventually faded. Sal crawled over to hold Kaitlyn. She wept in his arms. Sal looked at Chris. The pain was far worse than it had been, but the pain's origin came from the same location as it had each time Chris tried to remember Graham's name. Sal foolishly thought to press in on the memory when another surge of agony swept over him.

"A necessary measure after your abandonment," the general told Steve after standing and adjusting his uniform.

Steve shifted. The general pressed his hand to his watch again. At the same moment, the pain in Sal's head flared back up. Even as he screamed, he held Kaitlyn. The intense surging in his head faded once more. When Sal could see straight, he noticed Steve and his team had aimed rifles at the general. The general kept his finger against his watch, ready to send another bolt of electricity through Sal's mind and the minds of his friends.

"I can put you down well before you press that button," Steve said.

"Do so, and your son dies," the general said. "This watch allows me to punish disorderly behavior, but I'd be a fool if I didn't have the power of, well, mutually assured destruction. You can kill me, but will you?"

Steve seemed to yank his gun away from the general.

"So," the general said. His face still refused to show emotion. "You do love your son."

Sal nearly raised his own rifle. It'd be easy. Kill the general. Kill himself. But could he let his friends die? One look at Kaitlyn gave him that answer.

I swear I didn't know you existed, Steve's thoughts came to Sal.

Later, Sal said. *Focus on the mission.* It was easy for him to say, but impossible for him to do. Whatever Steve had to say, two things were undeniable. Steve was his father, and the moment Steve discovered who Sal was, he loved him more than life itself. Could someone love that quickly? It had to be possible. Steve's reactions said as much. Steve loved Sal's mother. Even if Sal hadn't shown the qualities that made Steve love Sal's mom, Steve would love his son for no other reason than Sal was a piece of his mother.

"You're to be my tool," the general said. Sal was shocked to realize the general had been speaking. He traced his thoughts to sort through whatever dribble the madman spewed. Apparently, Sal was the general's main target, both for revenge on Steve, and the potential he demonstrated. "There's not even a scale high enough to measure your power." The general spoke as if Sal was some sort of achievement.

What good was power if it couldn't help him beat the general. *Power makes you weak.* There was something to that. Touching the general's mind might get his friends killed, but did he have to?

Instead of reaching, using his power to attack, he looked inside his own mind. He felt himself slipping along the soft tissue of his own brain, seeking the exact point the pain began each time the general used his trump card.

Don't! Brandon's thoughts seemed to shout. The young man couldn't know what Sal meant to do.

I can feel you playing with the device in your head. If you short it out, it could kill you, Brandon said.

Tell me honestly, Sal said. *What will happen?*

Local explosion, Brandon said. *Nothing that would hurt anyone nearby, but I can sense enough power to kill you.*

Like a bullet? Sal asked.

That's a fair analogy, Brandon said. *I'm sorry. I can't shut both down.*

But did Brandon have to? Sal was an omnipsych. He could do what Brandon couldn't. It wasn't about hurting the general, at least not at first. Sal focused his mind. He could sense the device, a chip smaller than a dime, designed to receive signals and send out a pulse. Whatever explosive it had, simply needed a shield. He imagined wrapping the chip in three layers. The first was soft, designed to bend. The second, an impervious wall, was designed to protect his brain from damage. The third layer of his shield was another soft layer, designed to cushion the tissue around his brain.

"I'm not going to do what you say," Sal said. "I won't let you make us into anything, much less a tool for you."

"I think I'm willing to do more than you are to get results," the general said.

"Maybe," Sal said. "I imagine you're willing to die for your cause."

"I am," the general said.

"But not before others die," Sal replied.

"I didn't come this far without sacrifice," the general said. "It takes strength to allow others to charge in."

"Maybe." Sal used every ounce of power he could spare on his shield. "But I'm willing to sacrifice myself before my friends. That's the difference between us."

Sal sent the only ounce of power he allowed himself into the device. He didn't tell it to shut off. He told it to detonate. He felt as if someone stabbed him. Then he felt himself tense. Then the world went black. Somehow, the part of him that was the shield held.

He opened his eyes. Steve and Kaitlyn were at his side. They were both screaming. "...kind of fool allows himself to die for nothing," the general said. The general spoke like he was watching some sort of ridiculous movie.

Parts of Sal came back slowly. It felt as if he were being reassembled. It started with the shield that worked exactly as it had to. The inner and outer soft shells kept the middle trap from exploding or breaking. Sal thought it would be like trying to hold a grenade. He was wrong. It felt like trying to contain a nuke by holding it against his body. There was no way he could do the same for the rest of his friends. Then again, there was no need to try anymore.

Sal remained still, waiting for the other parts of himself to return. Smell came. Then sensations other than pain returned. He felt the cold floor under him. He felt Kaitlyn's tears fall on his cheek. Then, everything came into sharper focus. He took a deep breath. Kaitlyn must have seen it. Sal felt her heart surge with hope and joy. He used that as a way to signal he was ready.

Sal didn't try to lash out at the general. The bastard would have a finger over the button. Instead, Sal focused on the button. The button was a way to access power. It was a weak point. He formed a shield around the button. Sal felt it slip between the general's finger and the small metal push pin.

"First off," Sal said. He crawled to his feet, using one hand to brace himself while the other pushed him up. Talking felt like trying to gargle glass. "I didn't die." He stood. Everyone in the room gaped, except Caden; he clapped.

"Secondly," Sal said. He felt himself smile as the general tried time and again to press a button that he could never touch. "I wouldn't have died for nothing."

Sal felt the psychic strings flowing from himself to the watch. He telekinetically yanked the watch into his hand. He sent a signal to the device. The signal deactivated any self-destruct mechanisms, including the one remotely linked to the general's heart. Then, he dropped the watch and stomped on it until he couldn't hear anything break.

"Your mutually assured destruction was just destroyed," Sal said grinding a boot into whatever bits of glass and metal weren't already flattened.

The general stared. Oddly, he laughed. "So what?" the general asked. "You arrest me? Kill me?"

"I'm voting for the second one," Steve said, raising his rifle again.

"What does that prove?" the general asked.

"I don't know," Sal said. "But it damn sure keeps you from hurting anyone I care about again."

Sal raised his rifle to his eye. The general didn't so much as flinch. "Sorry, General," Sal said, "we're going to have to exit your program."

He squeezed the trigger.

He watched, expecting a pink spray of blood and gore to erupt behind the general. Nothing happened. The general stood, eyes closed tightly. Perhaps an inch in front of him, a single bullet hung in the air.

"Dom," Steve shouted, glaring at the sleek man. "What the fuck are you doing?"

"It's not me!" Dom said. It was the most emotion Sal had heard from the man. Shock radiated from him.

A chuckle drew Sal's attention. Caden had laughed a few times since Sal met him, but it never sounded so cold.

"Not the strongest," Caden said. He seemed suddenly lucid. He seemed in complete control. His voice was clear and steady. His green eyes were suddenly bright and sharp. Sal felt a pulsing from the man. It felt like standing next to an enormous fire.

"They tried to put bugs in my brain," Caden said. He still spoke in riddles, but the childish tone the man once used had disappeared. "But I smash bugs. Then I found more bugs. Bugs who were bigger, stronger, bugs that could make people believe they were strong. You're all bugs, but this is my world. I like to make believe, and I made you all believe."

Sal looked to Kaitlyn. The fear in her was enough to make his own teeth chatter.

"He's...empty" she said. "He's not blocking me anymore, there's just nothing there to see. He has no emotions."

"Apparently," the general said. His voice trembled, but he hid his fear well if one only had appearances to go off of, "you never learned who he was either."

"I didn't have my presents to give," Caden said. "But I'll make it up to them."

"Who?" Chris asked.

"Perhaps twenty years ago," the general said. "Caden Carroll was notorious. At least to those who knew his other name."

"I always hated that name," Caden said, a bit of that childishness crept back into his tone.

"Then why leave white roses for the women you visited?" the general asked.

"It's polite to give a girl flowers," Caden said as if it were obvious.

"He's..." Steve whispered. "You complete moron! You took him? You took The White Flower Visitor and gave him super powers?"

"I seem to remember your son being the man who destroyed the only way I had to control him," the general said.

Sal nearly laughed. They put a rabid dog on a leash, and it was his fault the chain broke.

"You never had that power," Caden said waving his hands at the general as if shooing away a fly. "This isn't your world. It never was. It's mine! Mine! I invited you all in, and now, I don't think I want you to stay anymore."

Sal jerked awake. He was in bed. Wires and IVs extended from a monitor to his arm and head. He remembered this bed. It was the bed he thought he woke up from before he'd met Steve and the rest of his team. Had he dreamt the whole escape? Did he dream meeting his father? Did he dream Kaitlyn attacking the doctor?

Too many questions. There were far too many questions. The only thing Sal knew, was Caden was in control. Caden was in *complete* control.

Chapter 31

THE COST OF ARROGANCE

al! Steve's thought boomed into Sal's mind hard enough to cause a mental earthquake. Oddly enough, Sal wouldn't have traded the feeling for the world. For a horrid instant, he was terrified he'd dreamt it all. He thought Chris might have been right. As afraid as he was that Caden, harmless looking Caden, had twisted them all in a game they didn't even know they were in, he was willing to accept that challenge.

I'm here, Sal said. *I'm okay.* He was in a hospital gown. He rolled out of bed, bare feet slapping against a cold tile floor. The small room was exactly the same as he'd dreamt every time. The problem was, he couldn't be sure he wasn't dreaming at the moment.

We passed out as soon as we entered the inner portion of the building. We woke up right where we thought we'd started our infiltration, Steve sent. *Brandon says the system turned on all the sleeping gas vents and flooded the building. We were knocked out before we even knew what was going on.*

It was that system I couldn't access, Brandon said.

Sal wondered how Brandon could participate in the telepathic conversation.

I have everyone linked. Kira's thoughts floated into Sal's mind. *I'll break it soon, but we wanted to figure out where everyone was.*

I'm here, Chris said. Sal could sense the man. He'd be down the hall from Sal. He felt irritated and relived at the same time. *I'd have been happier with the whole thing being the world's most jacked up dream, but I'm here.*

I'm okay, Sal, said Kaityln. *Don't worry. I'm okay.*

Kira, Steve said. *Break the link.*

Steve was wary of the link Kira made for some reason. *Sal, Caden has been the only one awake through this whole thing.*

Is that even possible? Sal asked. The small dresser next to his bed only had one drawer, and he didn't find any clothes in it.

Apparently, Steve said. *His control is only slightly less terrifying than his power. He hid it so well, using that awesome precision to do things you, me, and Kira couldn't fathom.*

So he can operate in this world or the dream? Sal asked.

Apparently, Steve said again. An image appeared in Sal's mind. They were on their way to the real control room. *Meet us here.*

If Caden was that powerful, there wasn't any guarantee they were awake. But the only thing to do was move forward or do nothing. Sal was never one for doing nothing.

Steve?

Yeah?

Sal walked into the hallway. There were dead guards all over the place. Not a one of them had any bullet wounds. While Sal and his friends envisioned some military escape, Caden had psychically slaughtered dozens. They were slumped over each other as if they were standing against the walls an instant before realizing they were dead. They looked so peaceful, as if they could simply wake at any moment. But they were dead, and one of them had something Sal needed.

He tried to ignore the lump in his throat while he looked for a man matching his build. He found one body that looked right, and dragged the dead man back into his room. It took a few moments, but Sal wanted to be as prepared as possible. He got dressed, zipping a dead-man's plate armor around his own body, and made his way down the main corridor to the rest of the group.

Are you wondering what I am? Sal asked as he moved toward the others. *I don't know*, Steve answered.

Caden has the power to kill us, Sal said more to think than to communicate. But doing both helped him ignore how many people Caden had killed. *So why are we alive?*

Because I want you to be. Caden's thoughts made Steve's mental shout seem like a whisper. The man didn't yell. The sheer power in his mind would have been enough to turn a man's brain to mush. *You and I are Us. Everyone else is Them. We are different you and I. I want to know how different. If you are so much greater than they are, then am I God? I think I'm God.*

Bullshit! Sal said. He threw the strongest mental shield he could form in his mind.

The shield went up just before Caden could respond. *Blasphemer!* Caden shouted. Even with the shield, Caden was a force. Listening to the man rant was like driving right next to an explosion.

There was only one choice. Everyone had to converge on Caden. Even Caden shouldn't be able to handle the rest of the group.

Sal turned a corner to find another nightmare. Where he'd been walking past dead bodies, men who'd been mentally shut off, he now saw bodies that were ripped apart. Sal had always hated the term bloodbath. This scene was the first time it felt appropriate. It had happened recently, so there wasn't a stench, but the blood made stepping around the random limbs and heads slippery work.

He nearly fell when he saw a woman's head staring up at him. He looked around and found the woman's body some ten feet from the head. The body wore a doctor's lab coat. Caden didn't just kill the guards; he had slaughtered everyone.

Caden continued to taunt Sal. Sal's mental shield kept the taunting on a muted level, but Caden was too strong to keep out. Listening to the madman gloat wasn't nearly as bad as treading through the halls. While Sal and his friends dreamed of saving themselves, Caden wandered around killing, and he took his time doing it.

Every single body was mutilated and ripped apart. Sal wondered why he couldn't sense the residue emotions of terror or fear.

I ate them all up, Caden said. The telepathic communication seemed like talking through thick glass, but Sal made out the comment. *Nice of Kaitlyn to show me that trick.*

Caden had eaten their emotions? He'd absorbed the fear and pain of his victims?

Stop! Steve's shout came only slightly louder than Caden's taunting. Sal focused on the his father's mind. He imagined a room that only he and Steve could enter. *He's trying to get you to open your mind to him. The more you react to his taunts, the more you open yourself to him. That's dangerous for people like us.*

I'm almost there, Sal said.

Step by step, Sal closed himself off. He imagined his mind in a small lock box. He put the lock box in a safe; the safe went into a vault; the vault went into a bank; the bank belonged in a secure military compound; the military compound went onto a solitary island a thousand miles in the middle of an ocean. Each mental layer he put around himself muted Caden's ramblings. Eventually, Sal was alone in his thoughts.

To keep his thoughts off the victims, he told his mind there were no bodies. The warehouse was empty of anything except the walls, floor, and ceiling. His eyes obeyed the mental order.

He took another step and heard something squish under his boot. He took a deep breath. He told his ears the room was quiet. He told them no sound came from the ground, and they obeyed. He felt his heart rate slow. He walked carefully. Just because he didn't see obstacles, didn't mean they weren't there. He slid his feet. He felt the resistance of a body on the ground. He felt himself kick something out of his way. He didn't have to see the results of Caden's rampage, but he had to move carefully to avoid tripping on them.

Something grabbed his arm just as he rounded the corner that led to the control room. Sal pulled back.

"Sal?" Steve's voice sounded weird.

Sal dropped the restrictions he put on his own hearing and let his vision return to normal. His friends seemed to appear out of nowhere. He let out a sigh of relief.

"Sal, what the hell?" Chris asked. He must have done what Sal had, borrowing the digital-camouflaged uniform and protective armor of one of the less-mutilated corpses Caden provided. He didn't have a gun on him. Probably smart. Chris wasn't a soldier, giving him a gun would make him more of a liability than an asset. His fire was a better weapon anyway.

Kaitlyn rushed into his arms. Sal held her for a moment, resting a hand against the partially-regrown hair on top of her head. She wore a white hospital gown under an overly large lab coat. She had on a pair of boots that were at least three-times her size, but they kept the blood and gore off her feet.

She shrugged to make the lab coat more comfortable. She hated it. Sal didn't need his abilities to tell him why. Graham wore a coat like that, and she didn't want to wear something that reminded her of him. The fact that the coat was too big was an even more powerful link to her stepfather.

"What did you do?" Steve asked. He sounded amazed.

"You just vanished," Kaitlyn said.

"I—" Sal thought about what he'd done. "I sealed myself away. It was the only way I knew to keep Caden out."

"When we get through this," Kira said, "tell me how you did it."

"Caden's shield is stronger," Sal said.

"You didn't see your own shield because it wasn't there," Kira said. She stepped forward, black boots clomping with each step. Though Sal knew how bulky body armor could be, she moved in it like it was a part of her. "I can see Caden. He's locked up tight, but he's there. You vanished completely. I still don't see your psychic presence."

Sal closed his eyes. He mentally traveled to the place he'd put his mind. He gave the lock box a key with his six friend's names on it. He gave the safe a combination, his mother's name. He gave the vault another combination, Kaitlyn's joy. He gave the bank a security pad. The access number was Chris's skepticism.

As he opened himself more, he felt his friends relax. Steve and Kira felt overawed. "I never thought of it that way," Kira said. Sal saw her blue eyes widen in amazement.

"What do you mean?" Sal asked.

"We work the way we *think* we work," Steve said. He, Brandon, and Dom wore the same outfits Sal had seen them in through Caden's performance, but Steve seemed to stand taller. He seemed more solid to Sal. Sal wondered if that was an effect of his dream, or the knowledge of who Steve really was. "It's why Kira can do things I can't. It's what makes one of us different from another with the same power."

"So if I think of something differently," Sal said. "I might do the same thing as Kira or you, but in a different way."

"If I tried to do what you just did," Steve said. Sal could feel the man's pride radiating from him, but Steve's smile was more powerful. "I think I'd lose myself."

"Which means he would," Kira added. "Our minds are our power."

Sal considered Steve's first rule again. Maybe that gave them some advantage? If Sal could do anything he thought he could do, Caden worked the same way. Only Caden thought he was God.

"The door's open," Brandon said. "We were just waiting for you."

Steve stepped in front of the door. "Simple wedge," he said. "Sal, you and Kaitlyn stay behind me. I'm on point."

Sal glanced at Kaitlyn. He wasn't sure what else to do with her. If Caden could kill anyone whenever he wanted, the only real possible way to protect her was to keep her near the rest of the team.

The door opened. The scene in front of Sal at that moment would be the image he'd associate with the word "insane" for the rest of his life.

Wires and cables held the general's body in the air. The veins and tendons in his arms were pulled from the body and spread evenly from his palms. The top of the general's skull and the bottom of his jaw were nowhere to be seen. Caden sat under the body with his legs folded in front of himself. He waved his arms wildly, causing the general's body to dance in the air.

"I'm not a wooden boy for him to pull my strings," Caden said. He still had that childish glee in his voice. Sal would never watch any version of Pinocchio again.

Every gun, rifle, and relatively sharp object in the room fell apart even as Sal tried to aim his rifle at Caden.

"It's not nice to interrupt when someone is talking!" Caden said. The bits and pieces of things Sal counted on to kill Caden skittered off in every direction. Sal felt a surge of despair. He didn't think that sort of thing was possible, which meant, for him, it wasn't.

"Where was I?" Caden asked. He clapped his hands together like a kid at Christmas. "I remember. Kaitlyn, I didn't do anything to daddy."

"What?" she asked.

"I didn't touch him," Caden said.

Sal felt her wariness. "Why?" she asked.

"Because," Caden said. "You worked *so* hard to make him hurt. It seemed wrong to make his pain stop."

"We were dreaming," Kaitlyn said. Her shame, and a touch of sorrow, flared to life.

"You're a little girl throwing a tantrum in her room," Caden said. "Repunzel shouts and shouts in her tower, and she doesn't know how loud she is until the prince finds her."

Kaitlyn opened her mouth to argue, but Sal could feel her awareness. She was powerful; everyone knew. Apparently, even she wasn't aware of how strong she was. A flood of thoughts drifted through her head. Sal saw each one. She wondered if she could have saved everyone before it came this far. She wondered if she could have stopped Caden. She'd woken up hoping her attack of the doctor was a dream too, not because Graham didn't deserve his fate, but because she regretted unleashing that much anger. She hated feeling guilty about it.

Sal took a knee in front of her. "This is *not* your fault," he told her.

"I can feel your anger, little Hercules," Caden said. "But I found Zeus's lightning bolt."

He held his closed-hand up and opened it. A watch dropped down by its strap, held by Caden's index finger and thumb. Caden smiled as he used his other hand to press each side of the watch. Chris and Kaitlyn dropped screaming.

Thoughts flowed too quickly for Sal to think clearly. The rest of the team reacted faster. A monitor flew from the ground at Caden. It slammed against an invisible wall a good foot from Caden. Sal tried to pull at the watch, but couldn't find the psychic line that he usually used to control things telekinetically.

The room became a swirling chamber of violence. Things flew at Caden. Anything with an electronic signal shorted, sending arcs of electricity at him. Knives flew at him. Sal pulled every bullet he could find into the air and telekinetically shot them at his enemy.

Caden watched the whole thing as if it were nothing more than a moderately entertaining Fourth of July fireworks display. Chris and Kaitlyn shouted in agony. Sal concentrated. Instead of trying to break the shield around Caden, Sal focused on opening a way. He slammed against the shield.

It was at least something Sal could fight. Apparently, just as Kaitlyn had used her power to affect her stepfather, Sal's stunt in the dream had eliminated the chip in his own mind, but he didn't break the real watch, and he only used his power to deactivate the detonators in the chips. He didn't shut down the pulses the watch delivered. *Why didn't I shut them down?* he wondered.

Ideas are easy to plant in an unfocused mind, Caden answered. *All I need to do is whisper, and you obey.*

Sal redoubled his efforts, hitting Caden's shield with everything he had.

Might as well try to ram your head against it, Dom sent.

Sal changed his tactic. It was a shield, a simple dome that protected Caden. Sal focused his mind, concentrating on the energy that made the shield real. If it were real, it had to follow rules of reality, regardless of how Caden made it. Sal imagined a tiny crack in the shield. There was resistance. He realized it was Caden's mind fighting back.

The room turned against Sal's friends. A batch of wires climbed out of a ruined console and wrapped themselves around Brandon. Dom's knives flew back at him. Steve glared at the blades, and they stopped. They shook as Steve stared at them, sweat popping to life on his brow. They weren't moving forward, but they weren't moving away either.

Kira, Sal said. *I need help.*

Why do you think we're not all dead or in pain, she asked. The sending had an air of exhaustion to it. *It's everything I can do to keep him out, that and all we're doing. If we even let up for a second, he'll overwhelm me.*

I'm fine, Sal said. *Stop shielding me. Use that energy for something better.*

Sal focused harder on the shield around Caden. Sal was certain there was a crack in it. It was the tiniest fracture, but it was a weakness. Brandon fell to his knees, his face a horrible shade of blue. Dom grabbed one of the knives floating in front of him, giving up on turning them on his enemy to rush over and cut his friend free. Sal tucked his mind further from harm's way. It made it harder to see, but nothing could hurt him.

Dom cut Brandon free. The technopsych gulped in air. Steve kept every knife, shard of glass, or chunk of debris from killing everyone, but that clearly took all his effort. Chris lay on the floor, but Sal wasn't sure if Chris was breathing or not. There just wasn't a way to check. Sal thought of his position on a mental level. He couldn't keep himself from harm and crack that shield.

He opened himself completely and threw every ounce of his energy at the crack he knew was there. The shield shattered. The general's body flew into Caden, driving them both back into the control room's main display. A high-pitched whine erupted just as the board lit up. Caden's body flew from the electronic equipment. Caden, the general, and all the equipment crashed to the ground in a heap.

"He's still alive!" Steve shouted. He plucked a knife from the floor and charged.

The pile exploded in every direction, and Caden screamed, rising to his feet at the epicenter of the blast.

Steve froze in the air. Caden glared at Steve for a moment. As Steve sat helpless in midair, Sal saw something glint in the light as it zipped into Steve's hand. Caden took the knife from Steve and drove it into Steve's chest. The room fell still.

"I started out using a knife," Caden said. He sounded very lucid and completely mature. "I don't need those anymore, but they're still the most fun."

Sal hardly had a chance to set his feet as Steve flew into him. Sal didn't think. He formed a shield between Caden and his friends. He imagined each of his friends in their own shields as well. They were safe. Sal looked down at Steve.

Steve took quick, shallow breaths. The handle of the knife was placed neatly between the plates of armor. Sal's mind perceived other things. Caden was in a rage. He struck at the shield in every way there was to attack, but Sal knew nothing would break that wall. Kaitlyn rolled to her side holding her head. Chris coughed, as if he'd held his breath a long time. Sal noticed those things, but had eyes only for his father, a man he'd never known.

Steve opened a hand revealing the watch that controlled the devices in his friend's brains. Steve hadn't attacked Caden to kill him, though it would have been nice. He used it as a distraction to get the watch, to save Sal's friends.

Sal opened his mouth to say something, but Steve shook his head. Steve raised his hand and touched Sal. Images and emotions flooded into Sal. A younger Steve met Sal's mother, Alexia. In a few images, his mother smiling, his father rubbing the back of his head and smiling like he'd just done something stupid, Sal *remembered* everything Steve had experienced with Alexia.

They argued about something so foolish Steve couldn't recall. They held each other after Steve returned from boot camp. The love and joy Steve felt only grew with each memory. Sal saw the younger version of his father open the door, leaving for his first tour in Iraq. His mother didn't tell him she was pregnant. She wasn't sure at the moment. The barrage of images and emotions faded as Steve sent his memory of leaving Sal's mother.

He saw a younger version of the general talking to Steve. Sal felt Steve's unbearable anguish as the general told him Alexia was killed in a break in. That's why Steve never came back. Sal saw Steve's memories. He visited what he thought was Alexia's grave twice a week, every week until he escaped the general. He was broken-hearted, aching to at least go see where her body was lain to rest but knowing the general would have that trap monitored.

Sal sobbed, feeling his own regret and sadness mix with Steve's. Steve focused again on Alexia. It was their wedding day. The joy was so powerful Sal felt himself laugh.

Steve pulled his hand away and smiled. "Thought I'd give you that," he said. "Seemed the only thing I'd have a chance to give you."

"Thank you," Sal said, fighting to compose himself.

Chapter 32

WHERE POWER REALLY COMES FROM

Sal held his father. Shards of glass and pieces of debris seemed to cover Steve's body. It was a wonder Steve didn't die the instant Caden stabbed him. How he lived long enough to give Sal those memories was an absolute miracle.

"You're strong, Sal." Blood bubbled from the corner of Steve's lips as he spoke.

"Don't talk," Sal whispered. He turned long enough to glance at his shield. Caden was in an outrage, battering it on every level possible. Sal knew that shield would only ever come down when he wanted it to. Even though they were both in the battle-torn control room of the warehouse, Caden may as well have been on another planet.

"I loved your mom," Steve whispered with a smile. "Only her, my whole life."

"I know," Sal said. "You showed me, remember?"

Steve opened his mouth to talk, but ended up choking on more blood. Sal thought of a dozen things to try. Every idea just seemed to be a quicker way to kill his father.

"I said not to talk," Sal said. He'd finally met his father, and he really was the hero his mother said he was, even if she didn't know it was true. He'd met the man he grew up wanting to be like. His mother had made Steve sound like a superhero. When he thought about it, Sal supposed his father was a superhero. He'd met his father, and failed to save him.

I'm proud of you, Steve said. His voice was clear in Sal's mind.

What do you do when someone you love is fading away after you'd just met? Sal smiled. He focused his mind. He thought of his life like a group of television screens, each showing his happiest memories. The day he built a box car to race the kids on his street. His best friends. His first girlfriend. The day he enlisted. His first promotion. The memory of his mother calling to say how proud she was and how proud his father would have been. Sal imagined the memories being recorded, and passed the recorded memories to his father.

Caden sent a particularly strong surge of electricity at the shield. Sal glared at the man. "I'll deal with you in a moment," he said. His voice sounded cold in his own ears.

He turned back to his father. The shield held. He had all the time in the world, and his father would be dead in minutes. Another list of ways to save his father rushed into his mind, and none of them seemed possible.

I should have been there for you, Steve said. *I chose vengeance.*

The memory of Sal meeting Kaitlyn flickered through their psychic link.

You got it right, Steve said. *Protecting the people you care about should be all that matters.*

I couldn't protect you, Sal said. He felt so many waves of fear, sadness, rage, and panic he couldn't say what made it through his link.

Then that's the lesson I'll teach you, Steve said. A part of Sal noticed his father had somehow managed to chuckle in the message. *You can't save everyone. You're going to lose. People you love will die or leave you, but you'll find more. For example, my team, they need a leader. That'll be your job from now on.*

Sal looked at the people in the room. His friends were all protected inside the secondary shields he'd made for them. They all had such sad, grim looks on their faces. Sal could feel their anguish. His own pain was an ocean beside a puddle. He felt the weight of obligation on his shoulders. He didn't want it, but he didn't want to not have it.

Don't let them keep doing what I spent my life doing. Steve said. *You protect them, even from themselves. A man is nothing if he's only about a cause. So that's it, my one lesson. Not exactly—The force will be with you, always—but not bad.*

Sal felt tears trickle down his cheeks. The light in his mind that represented Steve wavered, flickered, and then died. He let his head sag for a moment. He took one deep breath to give himself an instant to grieve his father. He promised himself more time later, but he had a more urgent promise to keep. A promise he made himself. He'd protect the ones he loved with every ounce of power he had.

Sal reached into his own mind knowing Delta Waves were flowing somewhere. He wasn't sure where they were, or how they worked, but he didn't need to. He knew they were there and told them to amp up the power. Life and energy flowed through him. Something about the trick tickled Sal's thoughts, but he didn't let the idea linger. He focused on his Delta Wave Emissions and forced them to pulse until he felt ready to explode. Maybe he was. He'd never thought of where his power came from. He just thought of ways things would happened, and those thoughts became real.

As his power reached its peak, Sal stood and turned to face Caden. Sal let his eyes close, and he focused on Chris and Kaitlyn. He found the devices in their brains, and imagined them failing, going inert without exploding. He felt them fail. Steve destroyed the watch linked to them, but Sal wouldn't let anyone take advantage of that weakness.

They stood, feeling at their heads as if recovering from a particularly strong migraine. Caden put up a shield of his own as Sal's friends stood beside him. Sal let his shield down, then he focused on everyone except for himself and Caden, and pushed. His five charges slid away from the fight, out the door, and through the shield Caden made to keep them in.

His friends went through without injury. Caden was strong, maybe even stronger than Sal was. But only one man would die in this fight. As Sal thought about it, Caden smiled.

"I like it best when they fight," Caden said. "It makes me more powerful when I kill them. It makes it better when they die."

Sal didn't respond. He started by taking Caden's shield away. Shields were designed to defend, to protect. That was Sal's purpose, and only *he* could master those. Shields were against Caden's nature to hunt, to kill. Caden's eyes widened in shock. Sal smiled, and unleashed a mental push that sent the madman flying into a tower of monitors. Caden laughed even as he plunged into the scraps of metal.

"The trouble people who look for fights always end up running into is that they inevitably find a fight they can't handle," Sal said.

Sal was halfway to the mountain of metal before he'd even realized he'd moved a muscle. A wave of glass came at him, but Sal formed a triangular shield that deflected the attack. A bloody hand burst from the pile and caught Sal by the wrist. Caden's arm followed along with the rest of the man. He looked horrific, covered in blood and bits of broken glass. Unfortunately, none of the blood came from anything vital.

"Dying can be fun, too," Caden said. "But that's the last fun."

"Then die happy," Sal replied. He pulled everything sharp, painful, or heavy he could find with his mind toward himself as hard as he could. Sal ordered the projectiles to whip around him as if they were water. The wall of violence opened, and Sal mentally pushed himself away from Caden.

Everything in the room slammed into the madman. Sal took slow, deep breaths. It felt like trying to hurl an elephant over the empire state building. *We're only as strong as we think we are,* Steve had told him. *Our minds are our power,* Kira had said. *Power makes you weak.*

Caden's haunting chuckle came after an attack Sal was certain had crushed the man like an ant.

"Ant's can lift ten times their weight," Caden said, still laughing. "But I'm no ant. I kill ants. I am God!"

Then the fight truly began.

Sal and Caden fought on multiple dimensions. The most important was the most frightening. Sal nearly laughed at the thought that he might be *nearly* as powerful as Caden. It took a considerable amount of Sal's power simply to keep Caden from attacking the shield keeping his friends out of harm's way.

Inside Sal's mind, he fought to keep a balance between hiding his mind where Caden couldn't find it and keeping his mind close enough to even make Caden break a sweat. As one part of Sal stood squarely between his friends and Caden, another part felt like David, holding a broken sling while Goliath stomped around looking for a good meal.

Sal telekinetically threw everything he had at Caden. Knives, hunks of metal, and shards of glass came within inches of Caden before they veered off course. Sal mentally pulled a rifle to himself and fired from the hip. Four rounds flew at the crazy bastard before the magazine pulled free of the rifle's well. Instead of stopping the bullets the same way he had with the general, Caden brought a collection of rubble between himself and the flying lead.

Sal let the rifle go and sent it flying over Caden's make-shift wall. At the same time he pulled Caden, hoping to yank the man into his own wall face first. Caden fell forward, but his hodgepodge shield flung itself at Sal. Sal had to let go of Caden just to telekinetically deflect the debris.

Sal felt something, a feeling of arrogance, echo from Caden. Fear started to threaten to overcome him. *Kaitlyn will die first, but also the slowest.* Sal felt pleasure, Caden's pleasure, as horrid mental pictures forced themselves into his mind. Sal formed an image of his heart, the symbol of his emotions, in his mind and blocked it off. He simply wasn't strong enough to fight the mental pictures Caden forced into his mind, not without pulling himself too far away to hold Caden off.

He saw Caden carving strips of Chris's flesh off as if he were skinning an apple. He saw Brandon screaming as Caden tried to mentally replace his tendons with computer wire. That strange echo came again. Sal felt a surge of panic. *Kaitlyn!* Sal thought of a knife, and strangely the air folded around his hand. Sal didn't stop to stare at the sheer force of his mental energy as it literally shifted the air around his hands as if they held a sword. He simply slashed at the source of the echo.

Whatever it was snapped back into Caden. It gave Sal an instant to collect himself before Caden resumed his assault. He wanted desperately to open a mental pinhole to check on Kaitlyn, but didn't. He couldn't risk the energy. He only just managed to feel the floor start to overheat and silence the flames that nearly bloomed right beneath him.

The heat had to go somewhere, so a wall of flame erupted like some sort of fireworks show between Sal and his enemy. Sal sent every kind of attack he could think of at Caden, who actually laughed as he contemptuously deflected them all with little more effort than waiving off a fly. *How could anyone be so strong?*

I said I'm God! The power of Caden's mind was like standing inside a ringing bell the size of a house.

Power makes you weak. Sal nearly stumbled as he tried to avoid spent 5.56 shells that tried to embed themselves in his neck.

Who was that? Caden asked.

It couldn't have been Kira, Sal put everything he had into that shield. She could no more get through that to help him than Caden could to hurt her or anyone else.

It was my thought, Sal realized. More accurately, it was one of the barrage of memories Steve had sent. The whole thing was so overwhelming, Sal didn't have time to process the memories. Fragments of Steve's past kept trying to float to the surface of his mind. But why that fragment?

Caden's telepathic probe, the stomping giant searching for David, managed to break through Sal's defenses. Sal had to retreat. For an instant, Caden gripped Sal's mind. Sal felt his knees give, his eyes drift shut. He realized he'd nearly "decided" to lie down and die. He pulled away a second before he fell for the trap. A knife plunged into Sal's shoulder. Two more found his thigh and hand respectively.

Sal cried out in agony. With nothing else to do, he pushed his energy at everything around him. A monitor froze inches above his head. A knife shook in midair, so close to Sal's throat he felt the tip of the blade brush against his Adam's apple. There wasn't anything to do but hold the weapons in place.

More mental pictures started flooding into Sal. He realized each one was simply a different idea Caden considered. Would he make Kira break Dom's neck? Caden was certain they loved each other. Perhaps he'd make Dom break Kira's neck while Kaitlyn was forced to watch from a cage of fire formed by Chris. Caden would force Chris to shrink the cage as Dom strangled Kira more and more tightly. Caden was reasonably sure he could kill Dom and Kaitlyn simultaneously.

But how to involve Brandon? Caden wondered.

Sal fought, but the knife in his arm was buried deeply, and the blood poured more freely from that wound than the others. Sal wouldn't be conscious in a minute. Then who would protect his friends? Then who would keep those mental pictures from becoming reality.

I know your every fear! In Sal's mind, he saw the boy he'd shot in Afghanistan speak with Caden's voice. *I know everything!* The voice changed to that of a boy, *Why'd you kill me? What did I do to deserve being murdered?*

Even throwing everything Sal had at Caden, the madman still had enough power left over to taunt Sal.

Power makes you weak. The memory surfaced again. Sal could actually remember Steve telling Dom that rule for the first time. Why? What made power, especially power like Caden's, a weakness. Sal had found his power; he'd found the part in his mind that emitted the Delta Waves that gave him access to his powers. He'd pushed his abilities to their limits just to come close to....

Power makes you weak. You come to depend on it.

Sal smiled.

You're not the hero! Caden shouted. He must have felt Sal's courage surge.

I've never wanted to be a hero, Sal told him. *I only ever wanted to protect people.*

Sal closed his eyes. He could psychically see everything around him, but none of that mattered. He dropped his shield. He let his mind step out of its hiding place. He used most of the strength he had to keep from being crushed or decapitated by the weapons still only an eyelash from killing him.

Sal felt Caden's attack. Caden's mind plunged into Sal's in a full assault. Caden wanted to crush Sal. He wanted to make Sal nothing, to prove he was God. Sal couldn't have been happier.

Sal sent the trickle of power he'd held back along Caden's awareness. He didn't attack Caden in any specific way. He simply slid along Caden's mind until he found a nexus of power. The strange light that pulsed behind the web of Caden's mind represented Caden's Delta Waves.

He'd seen lights like that before. He saw them in Chris's and Kaitlyn's minds when he learned about Kaitlyn's stepfather. He'd wondered why Graham didn't have the same pulsing light. The answer was simple: Graham didn't have that same power because he wasn't producing enough Delta Waves.

Caden was. His DWEs looked like a star burning into a supernova. Sal formed a vault and tried to clamp it shut around the section of Caden's brain that produced Delta Waves. Something held it open.

What do you want with my memories? Caden asked. *They're mine, and you can't have them.*

Sal fought the urge to think about what the comment meant. Caden knew Sal wanted to lock that part of his mind away. Some of the weapons that vibrated in front of Sal fell. Caden was using a lot of energy to fight Sal's latest efforts, but Sal couldn't take advantage.

A harry tarantula appeared on Sal's leg. He smacked it away in a panic, only to realize it wasn't there. In the time it took Sal to figure out he'd been tricked, another knife slid along his thigh.

Another memory floated to the surface of Sal's mind. It was a woman. Sal recognized her from the nightmare he had about his mother and the spiders. His mother had turned into some other woman, a woman with a black ponytail and bright-red lipstick.

"Go away!" Caden barked. The swirling energy and debris fell to the floor. Sal tried to slam the mental lock around the pulsing light in Caden's mind, but it still refused to shut.

"You know her," Sal said, realizing where that image came from. He'd seen that woman a few times. The most recent was in the dream of Caden's making.

"I'll make you feel everything she did to me!" Caden shouted, using his power to cause the room to come alive again.

Sal focused his energy on the vault he'd formed to lock Caden away. It still wouldn't close. He focused on his nightmare, welcoming the memory of the spiders and his mother. He remembered her transform. He remembered what the woman said.

"You're a wasted birth!"

"Mother?" Caden whispered. His power flickered, and Sal used that moment to slam the vault around the source of Caden's Delta Waves.

The sudden shift in Caden's Delta Wave production caused the man to drop to his knees. Everything that flew around the room moments ago dropped to the floor as if cut from strings. Sal rose slowly. He wasn't foolish enough to pull the knife from his arm, that usually did more to kill a man than ramming the blade into the body.

Caden, even as his mind faded, flung his hands uselessly. "I'm no Prometheus!" he screamed. He seemed horrified that nothing happened no matter how clearly he imagined it. "You can't have my fire; you're no Zeus to lock me away. I won't be chained."

"I'm no god," Sal agreed. He picked up the knife that fell to the ground at his feet. He lunged forward and rammed the blade into Caden's heart. "And neither are you!"

Sal felt his knees give. The blood loss was about to take its toll. Someone caught him before he fell. Had he gone blind? Did he just close his eyes?

Stay with us, Kira said. The telepathic message felt annoying to Sal for some reason. He only wanted to rest a moment. He'd just performed the mental equivalent of benching a Mac truck. Didn't he deserve to rest?

Will you leave me, too? Kaitlyn asked. Why could she talk to Sal? He could *feel* her. Even more strongly than his empathy allowed. He could feel all of them.

We're linked, Kira said. *Caden stabbed Steve in the heart. He was dead before we could do anything. It was all I could do to help him say goodbye.*

You've just lost a lot of blood, Kaitlyn said. Her emotions told him exactly how bad she knew that was. *Please don't leave me.*

I already said I won't leave you, Sal said. *I'm just.*

Shut up and let Kira work! Dom's mind held an odd edge. Why did the man feel obligated to save him? What did he owe Sal? He'd taxed his abilities too much to probe any further.

Through Kaitlyn's eyes, Sal could see Chris pull a gurney into the room. Brandon said something about finding Sal's blood type. They could have just asked him. He was...he laughed. He couldn't actually remember what his blood type was.

I said let us work, Dom said. *We'll keep you here mentally while Kira patches you up.*

Sal looked through Kira's eyes as she deftly plunged some sort of needle into his arm. Brandon had one in his too. *Haven't I been stuck with enough sharp objects for one day?* Sal asked the group.

When did they dress his wounds? When did Kaitlyn sit down to hold his hand? He tried pull the memories from Kira's link, but he couldn't seem to work up the energy. That was odd. Hadn't he rested?

You only blacked out for a few moments, Kira said. *It was a near thing, but I stopped the bleeding. Brandon matches your blood type. Neither of you will run marathons anytime soon, but you're okay.*

You sound relieved? Sal said.

I am. Kira's mind sent the message, but everyone felt the same way. They were sad, but a wave of joy bubbled under the surface, like a strong current in a seemingly calm river.

Can I rest now? Sal asked. He wanted to sleep for a month.

For a while, Kira said.

Kaitlyn? Sal called out for her.

I'm here. Of course she was there, Sal could still feel the link connecting him to everyone else. He could still feel her hand on his.

I promise, he said.

I know, she cut him off. *I know.*

Good. She finally believed him. He wouldn't leave her. He was her guardian now. He was their guardian. Guardians never left their charges. They did, however, after a great deal of effort, rest on occasion.

Chapter 33

CLEANUP

Sal jerked awake in a bed lined with white sheets. Too much information tried to bull-rush through his mind. He nearly started what would have been an amazing panic attack when Kaitlyn flung her arms around him. She gave him some of her relief and joy. She also managed to jolt no fewer than three rather tender wounds.

She pulled back. "I'm sorry," she yelped, biting her lower lip in regret. "Did I hurt you?"

Someone had found her clothes, or at least clothes that fit her. She had on a pair of blue jeans and a black, button-up shirt.

"I'm fine," he said. He felt like he'd just been pulled through a meat grinder, but he thought he was out of danger.

Whatever parts of his body weren't covered in bandages felt like they should be. His arm and leg had the most attention, but he didn't have a cast anywhere. Sal counted that as a miracle. He had gone toe-to-toe with a super-powered maniac and came out with a handful of scars. He should probably be dead.

"I've patched up worse," Kira's voice preceded her entrance to the room, presumably one of the dozens the warehouse used for hospital beds. "You're out of action for a few months to say the least, twice as lucky to be alive, but you'll stay that way so long as you cross the street without getting hit by a bus."

"I'll be sure to look both ways," Sal said wryly. "Where's everyone else."

"Dom and Chris are doing a final sweep," Kira said. "Brandon is wiping all the hard drives."

She somehow made the dark t-shirt and black pants she wore look too tight. Long, wavy locks of black hair flowed over her shoulders. She leaned against the door as if she didn't have a care in the world.

"And you want Chris to torch this place to the ground when he's done with his sweep," Sal said. He didn't read Kira's mind; it just made good sense. The compound was far enough away to be in the middle of nowhere, but it wasn't so far away that no one would stumble into it.

"I've got a wheelchair ready for you," Kira said. "But we had to wait until you were up and about."

"How long was I out?"

"A few days," Kaitlyn said. "We were all exhausted, but you had the most injuries. Brandon looked at you, me, and Chris. He says whatever you did rendered the chips in us useless, but you..."

Sal remembered very well what he'd done. He could have killed himself, but it was the only option as long as the general had that watch. "Did I screw that up?"

"I'm basically a field medic," Kira said. "But Brandon hooked you up to some of the equipment here. He says the machines all say you're fine. I say that's due to luck. You shouldn't ever try it again."

"So long as no one else tries to jam something into my brain." Sal moved to get up. It felt like trying to push a truck off his chest. Kaitlyn helped him while Kira disappeared for a few moments before returning with a wheelchair. The rickety thing looked uncomfortable. A wheel looked bent, and the brown-leather seat seemed to sag lower to the ground that it should. Considering what they'd been through, it was probably the finest chair in the building.

"How long do I have?" Sal asked, shifting into position on the bed.

"They're on the last floor," Kira said. Her voice was cold. Those blue eyes of hers iced over. Even with the general dead, she still carried a lot of rage with her. That's where Steve would be, where Caden's body was. She was jealous of Caden and angry that she didn't kill the general. She was enraged at Steve's death, and Caden's own demise wasn't enough to satisfy all of her fury. *How can one woman have so much anger? What could have happened?*

"Did anyone find the doctor?" Sal asked. Sal didn't exactly care whether the bastard killed himself in misery or ran away in terror, but he was a little curious.

"No," Kira said, and Sal felt an enormous spike in her anger. She hated the doctor even more than the general, and the idea that he was alive infuriated her. Sal was surprised she didn't press the issue.

He let the moment pass, grateful his mental shields were strong enough to keep Kira out. He had to talk to them all, but he wanted it to be face to face. The only reason Sal had a chance against Caden was because he'd found a way to attack the part of the brain that gave them all their power. More importantly, Caden relied on his abilities too much.

It took a bit of uncomfortable jostling to get Sal from the bed to the wheelchair. Kaitlyn, feeling like she had the best job in the world, pushed him gently through the halls, occasionally turning the chair back on track to account for the bent wheel.

It looked as if the building were as clean as the day it was built. They came to a set of doors that opened automatically, without any need for superpowers. The light of the sun was blinding. After two months in the compound, the sun seemed even more bright and beautiful. Dom, Brandon, and Chris were already outside. Sal waved at them before taking longer than his pride would have liked to lumber out of his wheelchair.

The compound was a simple warehouse surrounded by a large fence topped with barbed wire. The larger portion of the building was obviously underground, with only a few floors visible from the dirt road that connected it to what might as well have been the middle of nowhere. Sal wanted it to look more menacing. He knew what happened in there. He understood what the building represented. But it just seemed small. In the light of day, it seemed even less haunting. Sal hoped that was a sign that he and his friends would somehow get past the events that happened inside the building.

"Okay," Chris said. He wore a new t-shirt, but he was still in the same pair of digital camouflage pants he'd worn when Sal killed Caden. "I admit it. You're not a figment of my imagination."

"Told you," Sal said, giving what he realized was the first real-life grin he'd offered anyone.

"I'm actually glad," Chris said, unconsciously pinching the dark skin of his wrists, apparently still not as convinced as he'd said he was. "If I'm imagining assholes like you, I'd have to admit I'm crazy."

"Everything's clear," Kira said. "Brandon?"

"This is the only hard drive that has any information on what happened here," Brandon said tapping his temple. His brown eyes seemed even more sad than his young face should allow. Sal felt a wave of resignation from him. Whatever happened to him, it wasn't any of Sal's business.

"We have Steve's body," Dom said, he wore a smile that would have been convincing if Sal couldn't sense the man's emotions. "We'll take him to a proper resting place when we're done."

Sal couldn't find any words to express his gratitude, so he remained silent. Dom's emotions said the man refused to give Steve anything less.

"Chris," Kira said. "Do the honors?"

"Oh, I'd love to," he said. His bright white teeth gleamed. He walked in front of the rest of the group. He placed his hand on the ground. A group of flames, like a trash-can fire homeless people might gather around for warmth, bloomed from where Chris's hand met black pavement.

The flames grew and traveled into the building. As soon as the flames reached the doors, Chris took in a deep breath and let it out.

As he exhaled, fire surged out of every window, doorway, and opening. Sal watched with everyone else as Chris gave the fire more and more power. His breathing seemed to become more difficult, but he didn't stop, ignoring the sweat on his brow. Eventually, Chris stood and turned away. Flames covered every speck of the building as far as Sal could see.

He let the flames burn for a while. He tried to let his rage and sorrow burn with them. Maybe some of it did. Sal wasn't sure.

"You took his powers," Dom said. "One moment he was twice as powerful as you; the next, nothing." There was a hint of fear in the man's voice.

"I hoped it would kill him," Sal said. "But at least it did enough to help me get the job done."

"That's all great, but how?" Dom said.

"It's not important," Sal said. "I won't do it again."

"What if..." Brandon looked around. "What if we wanted you to? What if I wanted you to?"

"Do you really want me to?" Sal asked.

Brandon nearly jumped back. He seemed surprised at his reaction, but Sal wasn't using his powers, and he wouldn't intrude. Brandon gave a shy grin and a shrug that nearly sent his shoulders to his earlobes. "Not really, but, I never had the choice before."

"It didn't kill Caden," Sal said. "But it would have affected him in the long term. Maybe it would have even killed him eventually. I just didn't have hours or days to find out. Maybe I could turn off your powers, but I think we've earned them."

That was a horribly vague way to explain what Sal knew to be an amazingly complicated description of what he'd done. Even in doing what he did, Sal meant to cut away Caden's abilities. He thought he might be able to simply turn their Delta Wave production down, back to a normal person's level, but should he?

"We have these powers now," Sal said. "We should use them to help people. Vengeance, rage, fear, and pride only serve to cause pain. I'd just as soon bring hope."

He looked at Kaitlyn. He felt her pride for him. He felt burning embers of love there too. He'd never replace her father, but she knew he'd care for her like a real daughter. And who said she wasn't in many of the ways that mattered. He walked over to her and gave her a gentle hug.

"I don't just want to bring that hope to the world," Sal said. "But to you, to each of us. But I'm not in charge of you."

"I seem to remember hearing Steve put you in charge," Kira said.

Sal must have looked shocked. Kira let out an exasperated pop of air. The gesture made Sal feel incredibly dense. "Steve was always a bull in a China shop. He broadcasted that message pretty clearly to everyone within ten miles."

Sal smiled, but his heart ached a bit. He'd hoped that last conversation with his father was more private. It seemed right that Steve had, in a way, publicly given command to him, but it made the moment a little less his.

"We always argued," Dom said. "I've wanted to punch him more times than I can remember. Who the hell told him I wanted to be his best friend? Who told him I..." He cleared his throat. Kira walked to him and kissed his cheek. It was the first time she'd shown any affection for him, or anyone, as far as Sal could tell.

Dom had an amazingly relaxed appearance. The only thing he did that matched his emotions was clench his fist. Sal could see the whites of the man's knuckles from where he stood.

"He managed to say goodbye to all of us," Kira said. "In his own way."

"That means it was his call," Dom said, realizing how tightly he was holding himself and letting his arms relax. "Probably another bad decision on his part, but I've never gone against him."

Sal looked at Chris. Of everyone, Chris was the one who most wanted to go back to being normal. "You can leave if you want," he told him.

"I'm glad this isn't a dream," Chris said. It felt mostly true as far as Sal could tell. "I'm a part of something here. I belong. That's enough."

"I suppose that's all anybody wants," Sal said.

They spent the rest of the afternoon watching the warehouse crumble and burn to ash. Sal wanted to watch it all crumble away before he said goodbye to his father. He wanted the fire to burn away the past, even the last few days. He was almost ready for a clean start. First, watch the past burn. Then, say goodbye to his father.

Chapter 34

RESPECTS

A week since she'd become a part of whatever she and her new friends had become, Kaitlyn stood beside Sal at his father's funeral. They were in Sal's hometown of Jenkintown, Pennsylvania, where Kira and Dom had arranged Steve's funeral service.

The cemetery was on the small side. It was barely more than the size of a parking lot, but the grass was well-kept and green, and the polished small marble, black, or white stone grave markers gleamed in the sunlight. The late evening was still balmy.

Aside from three Soldiers performing their funeral obligations, only Sal, his mother, and all of Kaitlyn's new friends, all dressed in black, were in sight. That was for the best. Kaitlyn had a few ideas on how Dom and Kira managed to set up the service, and if she'd been there, she might have affected the wrong emotions at the wrong time.

She hadn't confessed how strong she was. Everyone knew the extent of what she could do, but not even Sal could understand what that meant for her. She could feel Dom and Kira's love for each other every bit as strongly as she felt Sal's sadness at losing a father he'd only briefly met. She could control it to an extent, but she was afraid to shut herself away from emotions. She'd spent too long shutting herself away from pain,

love, or fear. She thought if she blocked those feelings, she'd stop showing them again. It wasn't something she was willing to do.

A pair of soldiers, who knew they were honoring a veteran, just not
the one they believed they honored, folded the American flag. One
saluted the other and then pivoted to pass the flag to Sal, who wore a
black jacket with a black tie, which was barely two fingers wide. Even in
the jacket, he looked square, solid to her.

There were a lot good things to focus on. Kaitlyn had met Sal's
mother. She went to the ceremony. Alexia said a lot about being okay
and how long it had been since she'd known Steve. She lied of course.
She was an amazing woman. If Kaitlyn felt that much sorrow and regret,
she wouldn't be able to stand. Kaitlyn fed her some of Sal's love and solace. She gave her own appreciation to Sal's mother as well. It took about
five seconds for her to learn where Sal found all his strength.

There was time for that. Sal introduced Kaitlyn as "someone I'm taking care of," and Alexia immediately told Kaitlyn to call her "Grans." Sal
said he cared about her, and Alexia immediately felt the same protective
instinct and compassion for her, another trait obviously passed down
from mother to son.

She walked over and surprised herself a bit by hugging Alexia Veltri.
Appreciation and comfort surged from Sal's mom. Kaitlyn let go to follow Brandon's sadness until she found him leaning with his back to a
tree that was just close enough to qualify as near the burial.

"He was like a father to me," Brandon said. He was normally the
hardest one to sense, not because of any shield, but because his emotions shifted around so much Kaitlyn wondered if he ever knew how he
felt. Mostly though, he felt awkward. Today, his sadness was enough to
overwhelm even that emotion.

"I know," she said, scratching under her wig. The thing itched in this
stupidly humid city, but she liked to feel like herself, and the straight,
black-haired wig did help with that. It was starting to lose its value with
all the itching though, but she'd have to deal with it. It would take

months for her hair to grow back into something she could style, much less have the way she did before it was cut away.

Brandon looked at her, a hint of irritation buzzing from his emotions.

"I felt it," she explained. "It felt a lot like how Sal feels for me."

"Does that make it weird?"

"We have superpowers; I'm pretty much giving up on defining the word 'weird' right now."

"You have a point," Brandon said, shrugging his shoulders. Kaitlyn was probably the only one who understood that shrug was always a symbol of embarrassment to him.

Before her, he was by far the youngest member of the team. He was only 18 when he was recruited. There was something else there, too.

"It's okay to be sorry for the general," she said. "I cared about my stepdad. I can't act like I didn't."

"I was in his division," Brandon said, turning his brown eyes away from her as if that would hide the painful mixture of shame and sadness. "I thought he was everything I wanted to be in the Army."

"I get it," she said. "I won't tell the others."

"Thanks."

"I came to bring you back."

"I can see from here."

"Seeing's not enough," Kaitlyn said. "When my real dad died, I didn't want anyone to see me cry or laugh or...anything really."

She felt his frustration and irritation. They thought that she'd have trouble understanding them because she could only read emotions. What they didn't understand was emotions were far more telling than thoughts. Kira might know that Brandon thinks about the general and Steve, but Kaitlyn knew how the man *felt* about them.

"I know I'm just a kid," she said, "but you were only a little older than I was when you went through this stuff. I just think that if I were in your place, I'd want to actually say goodbye."

She walked away, feeling Brandon's emotions as he followed her. It was hard. She was only 13, but she'd already decided what her real job was. She was meant to hold them together. Kira and Dom would have any number of arguments. Other than the fact that they loved each other, they didn't seem to have anything else in common.

Sal was focused on helping people, but that didn't always mean holding a group together, and, as far as Kaitlyn was concerned, that group needed to be a family. She needed it to be a family. Chris still felt doubts about the whole thing. She felt his fear, like he'd wake up any second, and it would all have been a dream. He still had trouble sleeping for that reason, though he didn't know Kaitlyn knew about it. She was the only one who slept less because she hadn't learned Sal's trick of separating herself from emotions.

She arrived in time to see one of the soldiers rendering the funeral honors turn a crank that lowered Steve's casket into the ground. She wrapped her arms around Sal, sending him all the comfort she could. He gave her a bright smile that hid most of his pain. She smiled back.

He brought her out of a hole she didn't even know she was in. That was enough for her to believe in him. No, he'd never replace her real father, but he cared for her. Even then, she felt his determination to feel brave for her. He ran a hand through the hair of her wig. Sal didn't let his own hair grow back much more, keeping the buzz-cut that felt so familiar from his time in the Army.

She let him go so he could go to his mother. She looked at the casket and spoke to the man inside. "Thank you, Steve," she whispered. "I felt how sad you were that you weren't there to help him, but I think you did. I think that how much you loved Alexia sort of melded into Sal when he was born."

There was more to it than that, which was the trouble with her empathy. Emotions were broad and covered so much more than a simple thought.

"I just thought you should know he loved you before he knew you were some sort of super soldier."

And how much sense talking to a casket made was even more difficult to explain than how deeply she knew the team.

A tendril of caution flowed from Dom as he approached Sal. He was about to tell Sal what he was up to last night. She walked over to hear the confession. Dom, wearing a black suit with no tie, held Kira, who wore her hair down around a red scarf, by his side. She wore black out of respect for the occasion, but the red was a demonstration of rebellion. Kira literally loved and hated Steve. It was enough to make Kaitlyn's head spin.

Dom was perhaps the simplest person to be around. He directed everything in his being to whatever he was doing. It was powerful. He smothered his sadness by finding something else to point his feelings at. In a moment, he'd confess what he'd been afraid to talk about for at least a few days.

"I read an article about a young teen who died from injecting a dose of bad drugs," Dom said quietly as Sal came back from comforting his mom.

And there it was. Dom would get over losing his best friend by finding a new target, a bad guy he could track down and beat up. It made sense to Kaitlyn. Dom couldn't beat up his sadness. He couldn't beat up his anger. So whoever was responsible for putting bad drugs on the street would have to do.

Sal did a good job of not looking at her. His worry over putting her in danger might as well have sent up flares. He wanted to do something if only to prove to Steve he could lead this team.

"It might be too soon," Sal said.

Kaitlyn saw Sal look at her then. He wouldn't read her mind. He stopped using his powers days before the funeral. Most of the others had. They could.

"What do you think?" he asked her.

"Shouldn't we help?" she asked in return. A rock of resolve formed in Sal the moment she asked the question.

"We gotta start somewhere right?" Chris added.

"We can't work out of my mom's house," Sal said. He looked at Brandon. "Start looking for a place we can set up in."

Kaitlyn smiled. That's what made Sal who he was. He saved her. He'd take care of her. He'd help anyone he could. And she was going to help him do it.

The End.

ACKNOWLEDGEMENTS

This is my second published novel. I've lived 37 years, and I can say with complete honesty that I've twice lived a life-long dream. Miracles like that don't happen without faith, family, and friends. My faith I share with God, who I truly believe put me on this earth to tell stories.

First in this book is my mother. As I mentioned in the dedication, she gave me the inspiration for this book. She had what she described as a nightmare within a nightmare, and that got me thinking, "Why would someone be trapped in nightmares?" The result is the story I hope you've just enjoyed reading.

Ben Duke is my best friend and brother in law. He is my alpha reader, confidant, and coach. He's already read Caught twice and that was three edits ago. If he's the only person who ever reads my work, I'll never stop writing.

I mentioned The Team in my last book. There are a few particular members of that group who need special appreciation. Rosa and I were just starting to become friends when she and I had spoken about how I wanted to get published. I showed her a few manuscripts if for no other reason than to prove to someone I really had written anything. She picked one up, started reading, and wouldn't put it down. That manuscript was an earlier draft of this book. She read it on a flight home and told me she'd liked it. I'll always be grateful to her for that. She and another member of The Team (Hi Woody!) are happily married now, and I'll always be thankful to this wonderfully kind woman who decided to read my book.

Peggy has become a true force in my life. She read The Journals of Bob Drifter and is probably responsible for more of my sales than I am to date. She's read quite a few versions of this book and helped with some of the proofreading.

The Team is a group of coworkers who spend more of their time with each other than they do in their homes. I wouldn't last a day at work without them, and this book would have been far more difficult to make a reality if they weren't there to encourage me.

For this book, I hired a new editor who pushed me to have more dynamic characters and more vivid settings. Marco Palmieri of Otherworld Editorial did a great job as content editor. I'm a better writer after meeting him, and I believe this book is better because of him.

The Brown Pipe Gang is another tie back to the acknowledgements to The Journals of Bob Drifter, but Corey has flown high in the last year. He's now known publicly as Quintessential Editor, and he did the continuity edits for this book. He made sure the terms lined up and the style was consistent. When I applied Marco's feedback to my revisions, he read it over to make sure the new through lines felt natural. He also hung around through social media so I could talk to him during breaks and episodes of Naruto!

During the Last year, I had the privilege of meeting the HMS Slush Brain. That roster is enormous, but I must give thanks to Cindy. I read The Crown of Stones because I liked the cover, and I made a friend along the way. She introduced me to the rest of the crew and walked me through publishing with CreateSpace, which made this book financially possible. They're all a wonderful group of wisecracking, genius writers who listen to me rattle off how many words I've written each day. I also tend to make random puns that aren't necessarily funny, but they haven't thrown me overboard yet.

I must thank Ihor Reshetnikov for the hauntingly beautiful cover art. Jessica Tahbonemah created the intricate chapter icons. I think books and art should always go hand and hand, and those two made this book that much more a visceral experience.

Finally, there's you the reader. I hope you've enjoyed this story. It's been my dream to write and have people read my books for as long as I can remember. I've written about an hour a day. I've written about 1,000 words a day. I've done that religiously since I was 30. That's nearly 11,000 hours and more than a million words. I promise you that's a low estimate. I put in that work because I love to write. I put in that work in the hopes that you pick up my book and it makes any impact on your life at all. Thank you for helping me continue my dream. Thank you for meeting the characters I've loved for years. Thank you for being a reader. I am, and will always be, honored to have been given the opportunity to entertain you.

V/R

M.L.S. Weech

ABOUT THE AUTHOR

M.L.S. Weech was born in August 1979 in Rapid City, South Dakota. He fell in love with fantasy and science fiction at an early age. His love of writing quickly followed when he tried to write a sequel to his favorite movie. He didn't know what copyright infringement was. He can't remember a time he wasn't working on some sort of project from that day on. He wrote for a junior high project. The only way his freshman english teacher could get him to settle down was to let him start writing a book. He completed what he calls his first manuscript when he was 17. He got a ton of feedback that was honest, helpful, and not much fun to listen to, but instead of quitting, he simply wrote another, and then another.

He fell in love with reading in high school when he was introduced to Timothy Zahn and the Star Wars novels. Then he was handed Anne McCaffrey, Robert Jordan, Dean Koontz, Brandon Sanderson, and so many more. He went from reading to complete homework to reading more than three books a month, and then three books a week.

He joined the U.S. Navy as a journalist in 2005. He served on aircraft carriers and destroyers. He served in the deserts of Iraq and the mountains of Afghanistan. When he wasn't taking pictures, or writing features or news stories, he was writing fiction. Photojournalism was a hobby he enjoyed getting paid for, but writing fiction has been and remains his true dream. His final duty station was as an instructor at the Defense Information School in Fort Meade, Maryland, where he still teaches as a civilian.

He's completed seven manuscripts. He published his first book, The Journals of Bob Drifter, in March of 2015. Caught is his second release.

89231666R00165

Made in the USA
Columbia, SC
19 February 2018